W9-BQK-313

NO MERCY

"*No Mercy* grabs hold of you on page one and doesn't let go. Gilstrap's new series is terrific. It will leave you breathless. I can't wait to see what Jonathan Grave is up to next."

—Harlan Coben

"The release of a new John Gilstrap novel is always worth celebrating, because he's one of the finest thriller writers on the planet. *No Mercy* showcases his work at its finest—taut, action-packed, and impossible to put down!"

—Tess Gerritsen

"A great hero, a pulse-pounding story—and the launch of a really exciting series."

—Joseph Finder

"No other writer is better able to combine in a single novel both rocket-paced suspense and heartfelt looks at family and the human spirit. And what a pleasure to meet Jonathan Grave, a hero for our time . . . and for all time."

—Jeffery Deaver

AT ALL COSTS

"Riveting . . . combines a great plot and realistic, likeable characters with look-over-your-shoulder tension. A page-turner."

—Kansas City Star

"Gilstrap builds tension . . . until the last page, a hallmark of great thriller writers. I almost called the paramedics before I finished *At All Costs.*"

—Tulsa World

NATHAN'S RUN

"Gilstrap pushes every thriller button . . . A nail-biting denouement and strong characters."

—San Francisco Chronicle

"Gilstrap has a shot at being the next John Grisham . . . one of the best books of the year."

—Rocky Mountain News

"Emotionally charged . . . one of the year's best."

—Chicago Tribune

"Brilliantly calculated . . . With the skill of a veteran pulp master, Gilstrap weaves a yarn that demands to be read in one sitting."

—Publishers Weekly (starred review)

"Like a roller coaster, the story races along on well-oiled wheels to an undeniably pulse-pounding conclusion."

—Kirkus Reviews (starred review)

Also by John Gilstrap

FICTION

Scorpion Strike

Final Target

Nick of Time

Friendly Fire

Against All Enemies

End Game

High Treason

Damage Control

Threat Warning

Hostage Zero

Scott Free

Even Steven

At All Costs

Nathan's Run

NONFICTION

Six Minutes to Freedom (with Kurt Muse)

COLLABORATIONS

Watchlist: A Serial Thriller

JOHN GILSTRAP

NO MERCY

PINNACLE BOOKS
Kensington Publishing Corp.
www.kensingtonbooks.com

PINNACLE BOOKS are published by

Kensington Publishing Corp.
119 West 40th Street
New York, NY 10018

Copyright © 2009 John Gilstrap, Inc.

All rights reserved. No part of this book may be reproduced in any form or by any means without the prior written consent of the publisher, excepting brief quotes used in reviews.

If you purchased this book without a cover, you should be aware that this book is stolen property. It was reported as "unsold and destroyed" to the publisher, and neither the author nor the publisher has received any payment for this "stripped book."

All Kensington titles, imprints, and distributed lines are available at special quantity discounts for bulk purchases for sales promotions, premiums, fund-raising, educational, or institutional use. Special book excerpts or customized printings can also be created to fit specific needs. For details, write or phone the office of the Kensington sales manager: Kensington Publishing Corp., 119 West 40th Street, New York, NY 10018, attn: Sales Department; phone 1-800-221-2647.

This book is a work of fiction. Names, characters, businesses, organizations, places, events, and incidents either are the product of the author's imagination or are used fictitiously. Any resemblance to actual persons, living or dead, events, or locales is entirely coincidental.

PINNACLE BOOKS and the Pinnacle logo are Reg. U.S. Pat. & TM Off.

First printing: July 2009

10 9 8 7 6 5 4

ISBN-13: 978-0-7860-4501-3
ISBN-10: 0-7860-4501-9

Printed in the United States of America

Electronic edition: May 2015

ISBN-13: 978-0-7860-3723-0
ISBN-10: 0-7860-3723-7

AN APPRECIATION

by Jeffery Deaver

What's the one thing we don't have enough of nowadays?

Heroes.

In business, politics, education . . . I could go on and on.

That's why I, for one, was so drawn to John Gilstrap's character Jonathan Grave, the centerpiece of *No Mercy* and more to come.

Grave is a private investigator in job title only. He doesn't take pictures through cheating spouses' hotel rooms or deliver process. He slips into anonymity, grabs the latest high-tech armament, and goes where the police can't, or won't. At risk to himself, he takes on terrorists, kidnappers, and others who prey on the innocent, and, let's just say, doesn't hesitate to use all necessary force to rescue the innocent and save lives. Admittedly there's violence aplenty.

In this story of Grave's attempt to rescue a kidnapped reporter (his ex-wife's hubby, no less), we see self-sacrifice, tough decisions, and that determination to face down evil—the same attitudes that informed the beloved Westerns of my youth. *High Noon*, *A Fistful of Dollars*, *Shane.* (If only Alan Ladd had had a fully automatic MP5 . . . Take *that*, Jack Palance!)

Now, what's the other thing we don't see enough of? Tight (I mean, wound like a clock spring) plots in crime fiction. There are psychological crime novels that unravel the darkness of the human psyche; there are procedurals that are like clever jigsaw puzzles. I love them all. But when I sit down with a *thriller*, I want it to, well, thrill. Is that asking too much? We don't call them "ponderers" or "meanderers." Gilstrap understands this and moves the various plots forward with a bullwhip.

And, while I'm on the subject, okay, one final thing we don't see as much as I, at least, would like in crime novels: emotion. This has always been one of Gilstrap's strengths and, even in a superaccelerated novel like this, he manages to make us care, because Jonathan Grave does—about the victims, about his crew, and even about the villains he's forced to take out.

Like I said, a hero.

IN MEMORIAM

Ross Abdallah Alameddine
Christopher James "Jamie" Bishop
Brian Bluhm
Ryan Clark
Austin Cloyd
Jocelyne Couture-Nowak
Daniel Perez Cueva
Kevin Granata
Mathew Gregory Gwaltney
Caitlin Hammaren
Jeremy Herbstritt
Rachael Elizabeth Hill
Emily Jane Hilscher
Jarrett Lane
Matthew La Porte
Henry J. Lee
Liviu Librescu
G. V. Loganathan
Partahi Lumbantoruan
Lauren McCain
Daniel O'Neil
Juan Ortiz
Minal Panchal
Erin Peterson
Michael Pohle
Julia Pryde
Mary Karen Read
Reema Samaha
Waleed Mohammed Shaalan
Leslie Sherman
Maxine Turner
Nicole White

They are Virginia Tech.

APRIL 20

Chapter One

The fullness of the moon made it all more complicated. The intense silver glow cast shadows as defined as midday despite the thin veil of cloud cover. Dressed entirely in black, with only his eyes showing beneath his hood, Jonathan Grave moved like a shadow in the stillness. Crickets and tree frogs, nocturnal noisemakers by the thousands, gave him some cover, but not enough. There was never enough cover. He reminded himself that he was in Indiana soybean country facing a clueless adversary, but then he remembered the penalty for failing to respect one's adversary.

The Patrone brothers had been arguing for every one of the twenty minutes that Jonathan had been monitoring them. The bud in his left ear picked up every word, beamed to him from the tiny wireless transmitter he'd stuck to the lowest pane of the front window. From what he'd been able to determine from his hasty research in the past few hours, the Patrones were nobodies—just a pair of losers from West Virginia whose motives for this kidnapping adventure were unclear, and from Jonathan's perspective, irrelevant.

The stress of the kidnappers' ordeal had clearly

begun to take its toll. They'd counted on Thomas Hughes's parents coughing up the ransom quickly, and now they couldn't figure out what had gone wrong.

"I'm tired of being jerked off by that asshole," Lionel said. The older of the two, he was the hothead. "Old Stevie Hughes needs more proof, maybe we should just cut off a piece of Tommy and send it to his old man in an envelope."

Jonathan picked up his pace, kneeling in the dew-wet grass to un-sling his black rucksack and open the flap. With his night vision gear in place, the darkness burned like green daylight.

"You're not serious," said Little Brother Barry. His tone carried an unstated plea. He was the pacifist. Jonathan liked pacifists. They lived longer.

"Watch me."

Lionel continued to rant as Jonathan produced a coil of detonating cord from his pack and slid a K-Bar knife from its scabbard on his left shoulder. He measured out about an inch of cord, sliced it off the roll, and slid the knife back home. With a loop of black electrician's tape, he attached the det cord to the cable that brought electrical service to the house, then slid the initiator into place. Det cord was the best stuff in the world. A woeful bit of overkill in this case, but unquestionably effective.

"Chris said to wait," Barry said to his brother.

Jonathan pressed the transmit button in the center of his Kevlar vest and whispered, "Boss's name is Chris." It was the missing bit of data from three days of gathering intel.

A familiar voice crackled in his ear, "Copy that. Any sign of him yet?"

"I was going to ask you," Jonathan whispered. "I've only got two friends here." They knew from an eyewitness to Thomas Hughes's kidnapping that three hooded figures had carried the naked Ball State student out of his apartment in the middle of the night. Jonathan didn't like the fact that one member of the team remained unaccounted for.

The tone and pace of the kidnappers' argument told him that their frustration level had passed the tipping point into desperation. He moved faster.

"This whole thing is hopelessly messed up," Lionel said. "Maybe Chris got picked up by the cops."

"Maybe you're just paranoid," Barry soothed.

"This was supposed to be easy money. My ass."

Jonathan was at the back of the house now—the black side, as he thought of it—and it was time to prepare the doors for entry. The Patrones had stashed Thomas Hughes in the basement. In this part of the country, it was probably called a storm cellar. Or maybe a root cellar. Constructed entirely of stone, from the outside it could be accessed through two heavy wooden doors that sloped at a shallow angle from ground level. When the time came, those doors would be Jonathan's point of entry.

Pulling his cell phone from its pouch on his vest, Jonathan flipped open the cover and viewed the image transmitted by the spaghetti-size fiber optic camera he'd inserted between the doors. In the light cast by the single dim lightbulb inside, he had difficulty making out any real detail, but he saw what he needed. Their precious cargo hadn't moved in the last half hour. The fourth-year music major lay naked on the basement floor, his arms, legs, and mouth bound with duct tape.

"Hang on a little longer," Jonathan whispered. The kid had no idea that he was moments away from rescue. For all he knew, this was all he'd ever see again. Even after he was safe, there'd be no way to erase the trauma of these past four days. Whoever Thomas Hughes had been before the kidnapping would be forever changed. It would be years before he'd feel real joy again, and chances were, he'd never rediscover the trust he once felt toward others.

The speaker bud in his right ear—the one not occupied by the Patrones—crackled again. "Sit rep, please." Apparently two minutes had passed since they'd last spoken, and Jonathan's airborne partner, Brian Van de Meulebroeke—"Boxers"—wanted a situation report, per their standard operating procedure. They spoke on encrypted radio channels without worry of casual eavesdroppers.

"I'm preparing for breach now," Jonathan said.

Still using night vision, he removed three GPCs—general purpose charges—from his rucksack, one for each of the door hinges on the right-hand side, and a third for the heavy-duty padlock in the middle. Constructed of C4 explosive with a tail of det cord to ensure proper activation, GPCs were as malleable as modeling clay, infinitely reliable, and effective as hell. The phrase "shock and awe" would take on a whole new meaning when the blast waves were focused on a room as small as the cellar.

Lionel said, "Let's cut off the kid's balls."

Jonathan felt his stomach drop.

"*What*?" At least Barry was horrified. That was a good sign.

"You heard me. We'll cut off his balls and send them to his father for jerking us around."

"That's sick," Barry said.

"What's sick about it? He's gonna die anyway."

"Don't say that."

Jonathan pressed his transmit button again. "See our friend Chris yet? Looks like I'm going to have to pull the trigger on this thing."

In his ear: "Sorry, boss, I got nothing. Nearest headlight is two miles away and heading in the other direction."

"I copy," Jonathan said. *Just calm down in there.*

Lionel was explaining the way of the world to his little brother. "You seriously thought we were keeping him alive? Why would we do that?"

"Because they paid the ransom."

Lionel laughed. "That's why Grandma always loved you best. You were always the sweet naïve one."

With the breaching charges in place, timed to fire five hundred milliseconds apart, Jonathan took a few steps back from the doors and glanced again at the image on his phone. Thomas Hughes had shifted from his stomach onto his side, his knees still drawn up, just as they'd been in all the photos they'd sent. Jonathan scowled. If the kid hadn't had a chance to stretch in four days, he wasn't going to be much of a runner when the time came to move.

"Don't you get it, little brother?" Lionel went on. Jonathan could hear the sick smile. "Kidnapping gets you thrown in jail forever. Add murder and you get for ever plus a couple of years. It doesn't matter. I'm not taking the chance that Mr. Rich Kid is gonna testify against me. We get the money, we kill him, bury the body, and disappear."

"Nobody said anything about killing!" Barry protested.

"Because no one thought you were an idiot."

"So what's all this bullshit with the photos and everything been about?"

Lionel laughed long and hard. "Just what you said. Bullshit. The family was suspecting we were gonna kill him, so they kept insisting on a new, more recent picture. That meant we had to keep him alive until the money was in our hands. Get it?"

Jonathan winced. He himself had devised the ruse of demanding photographs—a proven tactic to buy time to figure out where Thomas was. He decided to move back around to the front of the house to see if he could get a peek through the windows and a better handle on their emotions.

"Hey, you know what?" Lionel said. His voice had dropped to a conspiratorial whisper. "We might be on our way to jail anyway. Maybe Chris went straight to the cops and told them everything. I bet they're outside right now." There were footsteps in Jonathan's ear, then ahead and to the left, the front door flew open and Lionel stepped out onto the front porch.

"Shit," Jonathan hissed. He was frozen in plain sight, but concealed by the house's moon shadow. If he didn't move, maybe he'd stay invisible. Certainly, this was not the time to duck for cover. His hand moved to raise his battle-slung M4 assault rifle to his shoulder. He had no desire to take his adversary here, but he wasn't going to get shot, either.

"Are you out here, assholes?" Lionel shouted. He held a pistol in his hand. "Why don't you come and get me?" He fired two shots into the night. To Jonathan's ear, they were .38s.

Barry's voice hissed in an urgent, whispered shout, "What the hell are you doing? The whole county will hear."

"What do I care?"

Jonathan could see them both now, out on the porch, and he wondered if Barry might become Lionel's first victim. Calculating the distance and correcting for the breeze, Jonathan slipped a gloved finger into the trigger guard and waited.

"I'm done with this shit," Lionel shouted. "I'm fucking done with it."

"We're almost home," Barry soothed. "We've come this far. We don't want to screw it up by—"

"Don't you get it? There's nothing left to screw up. We've been abandoned, little brother."

"You don't know that. Negotiations just aren't going as good as they were supposed to."

"You don't know *that*." Lionel was aching for a fight, and he'd take it however he could get it. The two brothers stood there, staring at each other. Finally, Lionel nodded. "Okay," he said.

Jonathan watched the tension drain from Barry's shoulders.

"You're right, Barry. It's just the negotiations." Lionel stepped back inside. Just from the length of his first stride, Jonathan knew that more was coming. "So, let's do something to speed them along." More footsteps.

Barry hurried after him. "What are you doing?" Panic had returned to his voice.

"What I should've done a long time ago," Lionel said.

"Shit. What are you doing with those?"

"Just what you think I am."

Jonathan cursed under his breath. His equipment didn't have the capability to monitor two images at once, and now he wished he'd opted to slip the camera into the top floor instead of the basement.

"We can't do that," Barry begged. "Not yet. We can't."

"Watch me," Lionel growled. "You just hold him down."

Jonathan dashed back to the cellar doors. This whole thing was coming unzipped. As the Patrone brothers moved away from the microphone, their conversation became muddled and difficult to understand. But he could see them both as they paraded down the interior stone steps. They looked remarkably like their driver's license photographs. He pressed his transmit button. "I think it's going hot," he whispered.

"Roger that, boss. I'll move in closer, but stay airborne till you advise."

Jonathan didn't bother to respond. Things were happening too fast now.

In the cellar, Lionel led the way, with Barry close behind. "We're not supposed to do anything till Chris comes back." He seemed to think that repeating the same sentiment could change the future.

"Fuck Chris," Lionel spat. "Spread his legs and hold him down."

Thomas Hughes bucked wildly on the floor, a futile effort to get away, to do *something*. Lionel fired a brutal kick into the boy's side, but Thomas only doubled the intensity of his struggle. In his hands, Lionel held a pair of long-handled pruning shears, the kind you use to cut through inch-thick tree limbs.

It was time.

Jonathan let the rifle fall against its sling, drew his .45, and pressed against the wall.

"Relax," Lionel said with a laugh. "This is only gonna hurt like a mother—"

Plugging his right ear to protect it from the concussion that was on its way, Jonathan punched a three-digit code into his cell and pressed Send.

Jonathan registered the explosions as four separate blasts, but inside it sounded like the end of the world. The first explosion severed the electrical service; the next three blew the right-hand door panel off its hinges. It fell inward, flat against the interior stairs, forming a kind of sliding board, which Jonathan utilized to skid into the room.

"Freeze!" he yelled. "Don't move or I'll kill you!" Victim and captors were blind in the darkness, but Jonathan could see every detail in the green hue that he'd come to think of as nighttime. The Colt 1911 was an old friend in his hand, the grip settling into his leather-palmed Nomex gloves. He never even glanced at his sights—there was no need. If he pulled the trigger the target would die. "Put your hands where I can see them!"

What happened next was as predictable as it was inevitable. Lionel was pissed, and he was scared, the deadliest of combinations. He flung the pruning shears to the side and drew his pistol from the waistband of his jeans. It was a little .380 automatic, and he fired toward the sound of Jonathan's voice. The bullet missed by more than a foot.

Jonathan's did not. He fired three times before the echo of Lionel's shot had faded, hitting the kidnapper twice in the heart and once in the forehead, dropping him like a rock. On the floor, Thomas Hughes reassumed his fetal position, trying to keep himself as small as possible.

Barry panicked in the darkness. "Lionel!" he yelled. He reached out with both hands, as if to parody a blind man.

"He's dead, Barry," Jonathan said. "And I'll kill you, too, unless you do what I say. Raise your hands and spread your fingers."

"You're lying," Barry said.

"Take two giant steps backward and raise your hands." Jonathan's tone was neither soft nor harsh. Matter-of-fact, it left no room for negotiation.

"Who are you?" Barry shouted. Panic rattled his voice.

"Hands, Barry. Don't make me shoot you."

Barry Patrone was clueless. Jonathan could tell from the befuddled look that he had lost his grip on what was real and what was not. The kidnapper's eyes darted to every compass point, his pupils glowing like monster-eyes in the infrared light.

Thomas hollered behind his gag.

"Thomas, be quiet. You're safe. This is almost over. Barry, I need to see those hands."

"Who are you?" Barry asked again. It was as if his brain was stuck, and couldn't progress until he got an answer. He was crying. He paced blindly, his brain lost in that corridor that separated panic from lunacy.

"I'm not waiting forever," Jonathan said. "If I shoot your knees, you'll hit the floor. Is that what you want? It's your call."

Barry shook his head frantically. He reflexively moved two paces to the left. No, he didn't want his knees to be shot. His sneakered foot bumped his brother's body, and he slipped in the gore, almost losing his balance. "What's that?" he whined. He stooped to his haunches and felt out into the darkness. "Oh, God. Is that Lionel?" His hands found his brother's shoulder. Then they found the gaping trench that had been gouged through his brain.

"On the floor, damn it!" Jonathan commanded.

Barry made an animal sound, part wail and part shriek. The sound reverberated off the walls. "You killed him!" he sobbed. "You killed him!"

Jonathan saw the hysteria in Barry's face.

"He left me no choice," Jonathan said, his tone more appropriate for a business decision than a shoot-out. "Don't make the same mistake."

Jonathan might as well have been speaking Swahili. Barry just stayed there, squatting on the floor, hugging his knees, making a keening sound. "You killed him. You killed him . . ." He said it over and over again.

Three feet away, Thomas tried to rise to his knees.

"Stay put, Thomas!" Jonathan commanded. The last thing he needed was to have his aim spoiled. "Just stay on the floor out of the way. You're not going to get hurt."

When Barry Patrone looked up, Jonathan saw that he'd made up his mind to be stupid. Uncannily, he looked straight at Jonathan when he said for the dozenth time, "You killed him."

"Don't be an idiot, Barry. You've got no cards here . . ."

Barry dropped to the floor and rolled to his left, on the concrete, drawing a snub-nose revolver from his pants pocket. The shoulder roll ended with Barry on one knee, aiming at the night. Jonathan took two baby steps to the side, knowing that right-handed shooters tended to pull to their left when they fired.

Barry fired, his bullet ricocheting off the concrete wall to Jonathan's right.

"Drop it now!" Jonathan roared. Barry didn't need to die, goddammit. Lionel had been the nut job, not him.

This time, Barry zoned in on Jonathan's voice and aimed dangerously close. It was done.

Jonathan's finger flinched by sheer instinct and his pistol bucked twice.

Barry made a barking sound as two .45 caliber slugs drilled his chest through a single hole, shredding his heart. He was dead before the second bullet hit.

"Damn it," Jonathan spat. How could a ransom be worth this? He dropped the magazine out of the grip of his pistol and replaced it with a fresh one from his belt, slipping the used one into the vacated pouch. He holstered his weapon with its hammer cocked, as always, and pressed the transmit button on his chest. "Room secure, two friends sleeping. Exfil in five."

Boxers replied, "I copy room secure. See you in five."

Thomas Hughes was screaming, but with the duct tape gag in place, nothing made sense. From the emphasis on the hard consonants, however, the smart money said that it was mostly obscenities. Jonathan approached the young man carefully, not wanting to get kicked, and even more, not wanting to leave any unnecessary footprints in the spreading pool of gore.

"Thomas, be quiet," he said. "You're safe. I'm here to take you home. They're both dead, and you're going to be just fine. Do you understand that? Nod if you do."

Thomas hesitated, and then he nodded. It was clearly a calculated move. The fear remained in his eyes, but how could he go wrong allowing the new attacker to think otherwise?

"I'm going to get us some light now," Jonathan explained. As he snapped his goggles out of the way, he reached behind his head into a side pocket of his rucksack and produced a glow stick. He cracked it and shook it to life. The room glowed green again, only now they could both see.

The fear in Thomas's eyes peaked when he saw Jonathan's masked face. The rescuer tried hard to make his eyes look friendly. "I'm going to cut you loose," Jonathan explained. "That means I have to use a knife. Don't freak out when you see it."

The eight-inch tempered steel blade of the K-Bar was honed to a razor's edge, and looked scary as hell. It was every bit as deadly as it was utilitarian, and Jonathan didn't relish the thought of the kid wriggling his way into a knife wound. He took care as he slipped the blade between the boy's ankles first, to free his feet, then his knees, and finally between his wrists.

"I'll let you get the tape on your mouth yourself," Jonathan said. He imagined that it was pretty much welded to the kid's skin by now.

Thomas Hughes seemed to have a hard time finding the margins of the tape. Jonathan left him to work it out himself, turning to the task of picking up his spent shell casings. All five had landed within feet of each other over in the corner nearest the splintered steps. He slipped the shells into a pouch pocket in his trousers.

Thomas found the handle for the tape on his mouth, and he peeled it away with a moan.

"Are you hurt?" Jonathan asked.

"They were gonna cut my balls off," Thomas said. He seemed at once terrified and amazed. "Are you a cop?" He whipped his head around trying to find the other party in the room. "Who were you just talking to?"

Jonathan ignored the questions. He found a roll of paper towels near a slop sink in the corner farthest from the blasted doors and pulled off a healthy length, wrapping them around his fist. Then he soaked the wad with water from the spigot and handed the dripping mess to Thomas.

The boy eyed him suspiciously. Jonathan nodded toward Thomas's befouled thighs and nether regions. "Thought you might like to clean yourself up."

Self-conscious, Thomas took the towels as Jonathan looked away to grant him some measure of dignity. Jonathan stooped to Lionel's body and sifted through his pockets. "When you're finished wiping down, I need you to strip this guy and get into his clothes as quickly as possible. There's one more of these assholes out there somewhere, and I don't want to be here when he comes back."

"No," Thomas said. "There's only these two."

"Nope, trust me. There's one more. Come *on* now, move." Finding only a wallet, Jonathan moved on to Barry's corpse, which yielded the same. He put both billfolds into a zippered pocket on the side of his ruck. Thomas still hadn't moved. "Come *on*, kid. Unless you want to go naked."

Thomas squatted and started fumbling with the laces on Lionel's boot.

"Hurry," Jonathan urged. "We've got zero time to dawdle."

"If you're not a cop, then who are you?"

Jonathan had had enough. "I'm going upstairs and look around. When I get back, I want you dressed, understand? Naked or dressed, we're out of here in three minutes."

He held the boy's gaze, then turned on his heel. "Two minutes and fifty seconds," he said.

CHAPTER TWO

The main floor smelled only slightly less awful than the cellar. The Patrone brothers had decided to keep the windows closed despite the warmth of the day, and with the one tiny air conditioner in the living room silenced when Jonathan cut the power, the odor had physical weight. The place reeked of sickness and old age, a legacy, Jonathan figured, of the grandmother who'd only recently passed the property on to the next generation. Every upholstered seat back and arm cushion sported a doily. Gingham and lace were the fabrics of choice for window coverings.

Jonathan used a fist-long Maglite to illuminate his search for any documents or notes that might reveal Thomas Hughes's identity. Sooner or later, the brothers' bodies would be found, and he didn't want to leave a trail.

The Formica-topped kitchen table was covered with coffee cups and soda cans and newspapers from Muncie, Bloomington, and Chicago. Jonathan guessed that their paranoia had driven the Patrones to check for a story that might have been leaked by the Hughes family. Stacked in the corner by the stove, he also found the copies of the *New York Times* they'd used as background in photos to prove that Thomas was still alive.

None of this was of any use to Jonathan.

What *was* of use, though, was the spiral notebook he found under the newspapers, in which one of the brothers had noted everything that had transpired over the past days. There were times and dates and talking points for their demands. The handwriting had a juvenile quality, as if the characters had been more drawn than jotted.

Jonathan stuffed it all into the big pocket of his rucksack. Even the newspapers, on the off chance that the kidnappers might have made notations in the margins.

Reasonably satisfied, he headed back to the basement.

Five minutes had passed, yet Thomas had made no progress. He was just as naked as before, but he'd moved from Lionel's body to Barry's. When the kid heard Jonathan's footsteps, he jumped like a child who'd been caught in the act of being naughty. "This one has less blood on him," Thomas said.

Jonathan sighed. "Good thinking," he said. As always, the victim proved to be the weakest link in the operation. "When was the last time you had anything to eat?" he asked. Thomas looked thin to the point of malnourishment.

"How long have I been here? I haven't had anything since they took me."

"You've had nothing to eat for four days?"

"A little water, but no food."

Not a surprise, but not at all what Jonathan wanted to hear. Hungry people moved slowly and tired easily. He reached into yet another pocket of his ruck and withdrew a package of Pop-Tarts. Cherry. "Have these," he said. "Enough carbs to keep you going for a while."

Thomas eyed the package, but didn't reach for it.

"They're not poison," Jonathan said. "If I wanted to hurt you, you'd be hurt." To emphasize the point, he tossed a glance to the bodies on the floor.

Thomas accepted the pastries and pulled open the wrapper. "Thanks."

While the boy ate, Jonathan went about the business of stripping Barry's corpse. He understood Thomas's hesitancy to handle death. Jonathan hated it, too, and this was hardly his first time.

"Is Tiffany okay?" Thomas asked. He seemed to need conversation.

"Who's Tiffany?"

"Tiffany Barnes. My girlfriend. I was with her when they came to get me. They hit her pretty hard."

With Barry's shoes removed, Jonathan moved north, to the waistband of his jeans. He unbuttoned, unzipped, and pulled. "I don't know. I haven't heard anything about a Tiffany Barnes."

"So you're not a cop."

The comment drew a look.

"If you were a cop, then you would have known about Tiffany."

Jonathan paused and rested his forearm on his knee. "Sometimes the police are not the best option," he said. "Once they're informed, you might as well fax an announcement to the press." As he pulled the trousers free, Barry's heels thumped against the concrete. He handed the pants to Thomas. "Here."

Hesitantly, he took them. "I don't want the shirt. It's bloody."

"You need to wear it."

"I won't." The point was not negotiable.

Jonathan sighed. "Fine. Put the pants on. And the shoes. I'll be right back." He stood.

"Where are you going?"

"Get dressed, Tom."

Jonathan took the steps two-at-a-time into the kitchen, again using his Maglite to lead the way, this time to the bedroom. There, he found a T-shirt on the floor. He snatched it up and headed back. In the thirty seconds he'd been gone, Thomas had pulled himself into Barry's pants. They were three sizes too big, but that was better than three sizes too small.

"Hey," Jonathan said, getting his attention. He tossed him the T-shirt. "No blood."

Thomas smelled the shirt and winced, then put it on anyway. "I'm ready," he said.

"What about the shoes?"

Thomas shook his head. "Way too big. I'm better off barefoot."

"Jesus, Thomas, will you please quit resisting me? Barefoot is not an option, and that will make sense to you in a while. I don't care what size they are. This is not a fashion show."

Finally he did as he was told. "What about them?" Thomas said, glancing at the Patrones.

"They're dead," Jonathan said. He started for the ravaged doors to the backyard.

"But we can't just—"

Jonathan grabbed the boy by his upper arm and pulled hard enough to let the kid know that he really had no vote in this. "Before you start feeling sorry for them, remember what they were planning to do to you."

Thomas pulled back. "Where are you taking me?"

"Home." His smile showed in his eyes, and the kid

relaxed. People didn't realize how beautiful a word "home" was until they'd been ripped away from it.

In his earpiece, Jonathan heard, "Abort, abort, abort. You got visitors."

"Shit. Tell me."

"What's wrong?" Thomas asked. "Tell you what?"

"Not you."

Boxers said, "You've got a vehicle approaching down the drive. Headlights are on, they're going normal speed. I don't think you've been made."

"That must be Chris, our third guy," Jonathan said into his radio. "Stay high and away. I don't want to spook him." To Thomas, he added, "You stay here. We've got one more to take care of."

"But I'm telling you there were only two," Thomas protested.

Jonathan made a growling sound. "Now I know why they taped your mouth shut. Stay put and keep low." He turned away and climbed back out onto the grass with fluid grace. No night vision this time; the headlights would blind him.

For nearly a minute, he saw nothing but darkness. Then, through the trees that surrounded these acres of farmland, he saw the first flash of light, and with it the whine of an out-of-tune engine and the groan of an equally out-of-tune suspension.

His plan was to wait here on the lawn outside the root cellar until he could tell whether Chris would get spooked by the darkness of the house and try to bolt. When the vehicle—it turned out to be a paneled van—stopped abruptly ten yards short of the driveway apron and extinguished its headlights, he had his answer.

He snapped the night vision goggles back over his eyes and pressed his transmit button. "We're made."

As if the driver had heard his words, the van pulled hard to the left. The engine raced as the driver tried a 180-degree turn to make a run for it. Jonathan couldn't let that happen. The last thing he needed was a bad guy on the loose. Operating by instinct, Jonathan brought the slung M4 rifle to his shoulder, aimed, and fired six quick rounds at the van's front left fender. The muzzle blast ripped like thunder through the humid night. He'd loaded every third round in this clip as armor-piercing, and he wanted to make sure to blast two holes in the engine block. He was rewarded with the infrared flash of two heat plumes as the vehicle stopped dead on the pavement.

With his rifle still up and ready, Jonathan moved toward the crippled vehicle.

His earpiece crackled, "I'm on infrared, and I've got visual on you and the vehicle. There's movement on the far side. He's out of the car, moving north toward the woods. He's using the vehicle to cover his retreat."

Jonathan didn't take time to acknowledge, but he liked knowing that Boxers was watching from the air. In his gut, he wanted to ignore the vehicle and chase the bad guy, but doctrine wouldn't allow it. There might be a second guy in the van, and he couldn't afford having someone sneak up behind him while he was trying to sneak up behind someone else.

The passenger side window—the one closest to him—was up and unbroken. Keeping the rifle tucked against his shoulder with his right hand, he used his left to pull his collapsible baton from its pouch on his web gear. He approached in a wide arc to come in from the rear. The back cargo doors of the van were closed, and their windows were intact.

"Careful there, cowboy," Boxers said in his ear. "There's only one of you."

Jonathan stooped low to the ground near the back doors, let his rifle fall against its sling, and lifted a tear gas grenade from the right side of his web gear. He pulled the pin, and with the safety handle squeezed, he rose, shattered the glass in the back door with one enormous punch from the baton, and tossed the grenade into the van. As the cloud of noxious gas bloomed, he moved forward and shattered the glass on the passenger door. He confirmed in a single glance that it was empty. The fleeing driver had come alone.

"Vehicle's clear. Where's my target?"

After a pause, the voice in his ear said, "Sorry boss, I was watching you. I lost him. Can't have gone far."

Terrific. "No exfil till we find him."

"Understood. Gauges say lots of time." Translation: he had enough fuel to hover for as long as it took.

Something popped inside the van, and Jonathan whirled on it, rifle at the ready. Heavy black smoke was pouring from the broken window in the back. He must have lobbed his CS grenade onto something combustible.

"Your van is burning, boss."

Jonathan started moving away from it, closer to the farmhouse, giving the vehicle a wide berth. You never knew what people carried in vehicles with them. He'd seen portable drug labs in Colombia—perfectly harmless looking trucks or vans—go high order because of the bizarre mixture of chemicals they needed to make the shit they sold. He snapped his NVGs out of the way again, turning the night from iridescent green back to shades of black, silver, and gray.

His earpiece popped again. "You got company coming in from behind you. Blind side. From the house."

Shit. Jonathan dropped to his knee and tried to become small as the fire grew behind him, creating an ever more perfect silhouette for a shooter. The NVGs came back down, and there was his target: Thomas Hughes. Goddamn kid. These were the times when he hated working alone with Boxers. If this had been a Unit operation, somebody would have been sitting on this kid's back keeping him from being stupid. "Get down!" Jonathan called.

Thomas froze in his tracks. "Don't shoot! It's me!"

"Get down!"

"It's me!" The kid was terrified.

Jonathan rushed him, closing the thirty yards that separated them in five seconds. He slung his arm across Thomas's chest, pivoted his hip, and flipped the precious cargo onto the wet grass. When he was down, he covered the kid with his own body. "I didn't ask who you were," Jonathan hissed. "I told you to get down. I swear to God, if you don't start listening, I'm gonna shoot you myself."

"I heard shooting," Thomas said, grunting against the weight on his back. "Then I saw the fire and I got scared."

"So you wandered *toward* the guns and the fire?"

Thomas wriggled to get rid of the weight. "Get off of me."

Jonathan unpinned him, and scanned the horizon again for Chris.

"I came out because I thought you might be hurt."

The comment drew a look. "Thanks, then," Jonathan said. "I need you to stay down because the driver of that van is no friend, and he's still out there."

They had to move away from the van. The light made them too good a target, and it rendered his night vision gear useless. Into his radio: "Do you see anything?"

"A big-ass hot fire, but not much . . . wait. I've got movement—"

Jonathan saw it, too, at exactly the same instant he heard the crack of a bullet passing disturbingly close to his head. A second bullet tore into the ground near his elbow.

Thomas yelled something that Jonathan didn't care to hear. He was busy. "Stay flat!" He nestled the M4 back into his shoulder.

The gunman kept shooting, his muzzle flashes providing all the visual input Jonathan needed. Twenty yards past the burning van, the posture said pistol shooter; the range and accuracy said good one. Jonathan squeezed his trigger, three quick rounds. He went for center-of-mass. He knew that his first shot found its mark because he saw the target stumble backward. He was pretty sure about the second shot, but the third was anybody's guess. When he thought he saw additional movement, he fired two more.

Then the silence returned, except for the sound of Thomas screaming. He had his hands over his ears, shouting for it to stop. It was the sound of raw terror.

"Hey!" Jonathan barked.

Thomas jumped, his arms up to ward off an attack.

"Are you hurt?"

"What's happening?" Thomas yelled.

"Are you *hurt*?"

The kid shook his head and stammered, "N-no. I d-don't think so."

"Then shut up. Stay down."

A kill wasn't a kill until it was confirmed. He pushed himself to his feet and headed for the tree line. Keeping low, he skirted the light-wash from the van and charged the spot where he'd seen the shooter fall. "Talk to me," he said to Boxers.

"Not much to tell. I saw the muzzle flashes, and I think I saw him fall, but nothing confirmable. I don't see any movement."

The movement part was all he needed. Jonathan knew that the target was hit hard. Speed now trumped surprise. Jonathan sprinted through the underbrush with the speed of the Olympic contender that he once was, his rifle at the ready. A heartbeat later, he had the gunman's sprawled, supine form in his sights. The wounds looked fatal, but the shooter was still breathing. "Don't move," Jonathan said, and he stepped closer.

What he saw next surprised the hell out of him.

Chapter Three

The shooter was a woman. She lay on her back among the weeds, her blood black in the moonlight, pumping from a wound somewhere beneath the hand she clutched to her abdomen. The other arm had been rendered useless by a second bullet, which had caught her high in the chest and transformed her shoulder into a blooming rose of gore. The copious flow from the belly wound and its location relative to other body landmarks told Jonathan that he'd pierced her liver. She'd be dead in minutes. The odd angle of her legs, and the stillness of them, told him that his bullet had clipped her spinal cord as well.

He told Boxers, "One more friend sleeping."

"Copy. Ready when you are."

"Begin your final. We'll be ready for exfil in five."

An expensive 9 mm Beretta lay on the ground next to her. He kicked the pistol beyond her reach. She wore low-rise, high-cut denim shorts that no father would approve of, and an Abercrombie T-shirt that probably cost a hundred dollars.

Carefully avoiding the rivulets of blood, he let his weapon fall against its sling and again lifted his night vision gear out of the way. He knelt near her shoulder, brushing luxurious auburn hair off her face. With no real thought, he folded her hand into his glove. She appeared no older than Thomas. With high cheekbones and thick lips, she could have been a model. The thought of killing someone so beautiful cramped his stomach. "Who are you?" Jonathan asked.

Her eyes showed only terror. "Help me," she said. "It hurts. I can't feel my legs."

"I know," Jonathan replied. "You've been shot. Are you Chris?" Until this moment, he hadn't considered the possibility that "Chris" might have been a Christina.

"I think I'm dying."

Jonathan nodded. Very softly, he said, "You are. It won't be long. Are you the last, or are there more of you out here?"

For a moment, it appeared as if she wanted to answer, but then her eyes grew hard.

"Answer me," Jonathan pressed. "I'll stay here with you till it's over."

Her pupils seemed unnaturally bright as they reflected the moon. "Fuck you," she said.

Jonathan smiled, squeezed her hand gently. He'd seen a lot of people die in his time, and he always admired the ones who accepted their fate with guts. Good guy or bad, heaven reserved places for those who showed courage to the end.

He continued to hold her hand as he fished his flashlight from his web gear and thumbed the switch. The white light hurt. He held the light in his teeth, and with his free hand he started patting her down. "Let me know if any of this hurts," he said.

"Who are *you*?" the girl moaned.

Blood soaked into the waistband of her jeans as Jonathan reached into the front pocket and found an

Indiana driver's license. "You're Christine Baker," Jonathan read aloud. In this light, it was hard to tell if the picture on the card looked anything like the woman on the ground. "Is that your real name?"

He neither expected nor got an answer. The other front pocket produced twenty-three dollars in cash. He returned it where he'd found it, and concentrated again on Christine's face. There was blood in her mouth now.

He hated the killing. He'd gotten way too good at it. The least he owed his victims was the dignity of looking them in the eye as they died. He longed for the old days when the people his bullets found weren't people at all; they were enemies who had to die so that the friendlies could live. He missed the simplicity of war.

As Christine's breathing became steadily more difficult, he fought the urge to look away. He stroked her hair. "It'll be over soon," he whispered.

She could no longer form words, but the hardness in her eyes had dissolved to fear.

After one great defiant gasp, Christine's chest rose and fell for the last time. Her eyes glazed and she was gone.

Something moved in the bushes behind him. Jonathan's hand found his rifle as he whirled on his knee, his finger in the trigger guard at half-pull.

"Jesus!" Thomas shouted, putting his hands in the air. "Don't shoot. It's me. It's me."

"*Goddammit*," Jonathan spat.

"I wanted to be sure you're okay."

Jesus, that had been close. Jonathan lowered his weapon and shook his head in disgust.

"Oh, my God," Thomas gasped, looking past Jonathan to the body on the ground. "What did you do?" He pushed past Jonathan and knelt on the other side of Christine. "My God, you shot Tiffany."

Jonathan's jaw dropped. "Your *girlfriend* Tiffany?"

Thomas reached out to touch her face, but Jonathan grabbed his hand to stop him. "Don't," he said. "You'll leave trace evidence."

"But you have to help her."

Jonathan shook his head. "It's too late," he said. "She's gone."

"You killed her?" His tone was equal parts anger and disbelief.

"She was trying to kill *you*."

Thomas shook his head and leaned away from the body. "No," he said. "That's not possible. We were in love."

"Tom . . ." In the background, he could hear Boxers approaching with the chopper.

"No! I know what you're thinking, and you're wrong. We *loved* each other. We were *making* love when they crashed in and took me. We've got to get her to a hospital."

"No, Tom. She's dead." He glanced over his shoulder and saw the blacked-out AgustaWestland chopper flaring to land. But for the light of the burning van, it would have looked like an ink stain against the night. "It's time to go."

Thomas was frozen; by fear, perhaps, or maybe by grief or rage. But he wasn't moving.

"Thomas!"

The college student looked like a lost little boy.

The radio broke squelch. "Ready to load."

Jonathan acknowledged the transmission with a tap on the transmit button and softened his tone. "She shot at us, Thomas, and now it's over." He saw the anger boiling. "We're done here, Tom. Let's get you home."

The kid was overwhelmed. Jonathan felt for him, but his patience was running out. Gunshots followed by fire and the sound of a helicopter were a surefire recipe for 9-1-1 calls, and he wanted to be nowhere around when the lights and sirens started. In ten seconds, Thomas was leaving, one way or another. Jonathan had carried unwilling—and therefore unconscious—precious cargo to safety more than a few times. Once more wouldn't bother him a bit.

Just about the time his clock had ticked to zero, Thomas stood. He said nothing as they ran in a crouch toward the chopper that would take them home. As they ran Jonathan pulled out his cell phone and scrolled down to the predetermined number that would tell the kid's father that his son was finally safe.

In Jonathan's world, there was a vendor for everything. All you needed was the right credentials and the right connections. The whisper-quiet AgustaWestland chopper with its infrared optics, missile detection, and countermeasures and super state-of-the-art avionics belonged to a man he knew through Boxers, and whose public name was, unlikely enough, Oscar Meyer. Oscar made the chopper available to anyone willing to pay the rental fee, but only after said party had posted the $6 million bond that would pay for the bird's replacement should something go wrong. You break it, you buy it, writ large.

Boxers favored the bird for reasons he'd never shared. Not a pilot himself (although trained for certain airborne emergencies), Jonathan rode in the back of the chopper after a PC exfiltration. You never left precious cargo alone. After what they'd been through—and in Central America, he'd seen kidnapping negotiations play out over years—very little about their world made sense to them anymore, and it wasn't unheard of for them to turn on their rescuers. The confusion of Stockholm syndrome was very real, and it was never a good idea to let crazed, paranoid former hostages run loose.

Even as he climbed aboard, Jonathan could feel that the chopper was light on its wheels, undulating slightly in the lowest possible hover. As soon as Thomas's butt was in the seat, but before Jonathan had a chance to strap him in, Boxers poured on the power, and they were airborne, pulling an easy two G's as the rotors bit into the night and lifted them away from the Patrone farm and the corpses it sheltered.

Instead of congratulating himself on a successful rescue, Jonathan berated himself for a sloppy operation. In his rush to get the hell out, he'd left behind shell casings from his M4. He'd left evidence, and as modern forensics technology became more and more advanced, even a tidbit of evidence could expose him.

Jonathan was also bothered by Thomas Hughes's sullenness. He'd just had his life delivered to him, yet here he was in the back of the chopper moping over the death of Christine Baker. Jonathan knew that he should just let it go—just let the kid be alone with his thoughts—but he couldn't help commenting.

"Hey, Thomas," he said, drawing the boy's attention. One huge difference, Jonathan noted between this sleek corporate helicopter and the choppers that had ferried him from place to place when he was with the Unit, was the ability to converse normally over the quiet hum of the engines. "Quit beating yourself up. You didn't do anything wrong. She was trying to kill you, and I'm the one who shot her."

It wasn't what Thomas wanted to hear.

"She didn't love you, Tom," Jonathan pressed. "Listen to me. She was part of the plot to put you in that cellar."

"Just be quiet, okay? You don't know what you're talking about."

Jonathan sighed. When would he learn to leave things like this alone? "Look. Nothing is what you thought it was. Let me guess. You met her in a bar, or a coffee shop, right? Some public place."

"Library," Thomas said.

"Like I said, public place. It seemed at first that she was interested in you, but then, just as you were getting up the guts to move over to her, she made an excuse to get away. Maybe you never even got to speak to her that first time."

The baffled look in Thomas's eyes told him that he was hitting close to home. It was the way these things worked. The CIA recruited agents with this script all the time. Seem too anxious and the prospect runs away. You had to make them want *you*.

Jonathan continued. "Then suddenly she seemed to be everywhere. You both notice it and think it's funny. You go out for a movie, out for laughs, but never anything really serious. She probably told you that she was saving herself for marriage."

"She said she had a boyfriend." Thomas's anger was transforming to bewilderment.

"Close. You finally make the big date, and when the moment comes for you to get laid, I'm guessing she proposed the place. Your place, not hers. She wanted you to be comfortable."

"How can you know this?"

"It's the way it always works. Finally, you got to your place, the clothes came off. You'd just gotten to the down and dirty when all hell broke loose, and you ended up tied up with duct tape in a basement." He let the words soak in.

Thomas's face sagged, the exhaustion aging him ten

years. "But she spoke my thoughts," he said. "I thought we were soul mates."

Jonathan hesitated before driving the last nail. Poor bastard thought he'd been in love. "Were they the same thoughts you'd posted on your Facebook page?"

The boy's jaw dropped. "How did you know?"

"The first thing I did when I got this gig was a Google search. I found your site in a few seconds, and twenty minutes later, I knew everything about you. Christine—*Tiffany*—probably did the same thing."

Thomas leaned back onto the leather seat. "But I don't get it. *Why*?"

"For the money."

"Not from us," Thomas scoffed. "We don't *have* any money. Dad works a thousand hours a week just to keep things going."

Jonathan scowled. They had to have money to afford his fee.

"Who are you, anyway?" Thomas asked. "I know you're the guy who saved my ass, but what's your name?"

"Don't worry about names," Jonathan said. "The less you know about that, the better off you'll be."

Everything about these last few days—they felt like weeks—had left Thomas feeling dizzy. There was the hunger of course—that Pop-Tart hadn't helped much—and the exhaustion and the fear, but mostly the world didn't make sense anymore.

As he thought about what had almost happened, as he remembered that crazed look in that guy's eyes as he prepared to cut his balls off, he wondered if the Pop-Tart might return. What had he ever done to provoke that kind of cruelty? And who the hell were these commandos with their guns? God bless them for what they did, but what could make them risk so much for him? He was nobody. This business about his folks being rich was crazy.

He felt disoriented. It was as if he'd awakened one morning, and the sky was brown and the grass was purple—like being in a world of talking dogs and barking cats. Some things in your life are supposed to be a certain way. Every day at noon there's a sun in the sky, and when you get out of bed, gravity is there to keep you from floating away. In that same vein, falling in love was supposed to be natural and good. When the moment came to finally get naked and make love, it was supposed to be a wonderful thing. Tiffany would have been his first. But then it turned to blood and violence.

They flew in complete darkness. The silver glow of the moon on the meaningless landmarks below was Thomas's only evidence that they were flying at all. It wasn't till his eyes adjusted fully that he noticed the pilot was wearing night vision goggles.

Their flight lasted less than half an hour. From what Thomas could tell, they landed in a dark field in the middle of nowhere. The rotors were still turning at nearly full speed when the commando at his side unclasped his seat belt and rose to an awkward, half-standing position. He took a half-step forward and said something in the pilot's ear, soliciting a nod and a thumbs-up, and then he turned to face Thomas.

"Okay, Tom, here's the deal. I want you to stay put with your belt fastened until I come back for you. We have a car waiting."

"Why can't I just come with you?"

"Because I want to make sure that this last step is truly secure. If anything is wrong, I'll tell the pilot, and he'll take off outta here like a rocket. That's why you stay in your seat with the belt on. You're almost home."

With that, he opened the side door, inviting in all the racket of the rotors, and stepped out into the night with his weapons. When the door closed again, the quiet—which wasn't really all that quiet—seemed oppressive.

Thomas couldn't take it anymore. "Excuse me," he said loudly, nearly a shout. "Mr. Pilot?"

The pilot turned, still only an ink stain against the night.

"What's happening?" Thomas asked.

"You haven't figured it out yet?" the pilot asked, his tone light with amusement.

"No. I haven't figured out anything. I'm totally lost."

The pilot laughed. "Like hell. You're as found as anybody could hope to be."

Jonathan had stashed the rental Explorer in the back forty of someone's rolling farmland nearly six hours ago. They'd chosen this location by studying aerial maps and determining that it offered privacy while still being reasonably accessible. It also offered a good chance to fly in and out unnoticed.

He approached the vehicle by the book—slowly and methodically, with night vision in place as if anticipating an ambush. Nobody ever died of caution. With the scene secure, he went about the business of transforming himself from Night Stalker to Regular Guy. He moved to the back of the vehicle and opened up the tailgate. No dome light came on because he had disabled it first thing. Two zippered duffel bags waited for him just where he'd left them, looking like two deflated balloons. His rifle and rucksack went in one, his vest, web gear, and night vision equipment in the other, along with his black coveralls, mask, and boots. The transformation was complete within three minutes.

Just like that, Jonathan could have been anyone—a rancher, maybe, on his way to town. A rancher with a .45 still strapped in a high-hip holster that was concealed by a denim jacket. When the duffels were full, he zipped them up, closed the gate, and headed back to the chopper. He opened the side door and announced, "Okay, we're all set. Let's go."

Thomas didn't move. He looked terrified.

Jonathan scowled. "What's wrong?"

"You took your mask off." Thomas's tone was heavy with dread.

Up front, Boxers laughed. "A man in a black mask might attract attention on the highway, don't you think?" he asked.

"But I don't think it's good for me to know what you look like."

Jonathan appreciated the honesty. "Relax, Thomas. I'm one of the good guys."

Chapter Four

The chopper ride in had been a hell of a lot smoother than the ride out in the Explorer. Jonathan had to shift the four-wheel drive to low gear to keep from digging trenches in the soft tilled ground. When they got to the paved road, he looked at the clock on the dash. It was nearly four in the morning.

"You need a name," Thomas said, out of nowhere. "I have to call you something."

Jonathan laughed. "If you're worried about seeing my face, why the hell would you want to know my name?"

"Because you saved my life? I've got to know who did it."

Jonathan liked that. "Tell you what. Call me Scorpion."

Thomas scowled. "*Scorpion*? Like the insect?"

"Yeah, like the insect. You know, strikes fast, looks scary."

"That's not a real name."

"It's as real as you're going to get."

"Okay. Scorpion, then. Can I ask you a question?"

"Ask what you want, but don't necessarily expect an answer."

"Somebody's going to find those bodies," Thomas said. "What happens then? What are the police going to think?"

Jonathan glanced over at his passenger's silhouette. "You tell me."

"Isn't going to look like murder?"

Jonathan nodded. "Like a triple homicide."

"And that doesn't worry you?"

"Not particularly." Jonathan realized how harsh he sounded. "Look, I work on the side of the angels, okay? I often find myself outside the law, but never really on the *wrong* side of it. If people look at bad guys' bodies and see homicide, that doesn't change reality. My conscience is clean."

"Then why not use your real name?"

"I said side of the angels, not realm of the idiots." He knew he was wasting his breath. He'd had a commanding officer once who'd preached the value of never speaking to victims after this kind of 0300 mission—personnel rescue. Nothing you say makes anything better, and everything you say confuses people more. Jonathan was beginning to wish that he'd paid better attention.

Thomas kept pushing. "The police aren't going to know about your angels. They're just going to look at the evidence and then they're going to know—"

"Nothing," Jonathan interrupted. "They're going to know nothing. Nothing about your kidnapping, nothing about the ransom. They won't have any clue that you were *this close*"—he separated his thumb and forefinger a fraction of an inch—"to being murdered. All they're going to know is that a few people were killed in a gun battle."

"So why not stick around to set the record straight? You're going to come out of this looking like a murderer. What happens when they come looking for you?"

Why was he having this conversation? "They're going to get frustrated as hell. They won't find a thing."

"But if they do."

"They won't."

"But *if they do*."

The Explorer bounced in a deep rut. "You think that the police are these efficient do-gooders that you see on television. You think that they can chase bad guys with impunity, crash doors, and save the good guys. Well, that's not always true, because ridiculous rules get in the way. If I had to jump through all the hoops that police and prosecutors do to assemble intelligence and put together a plan, you'd be dead now. And if they knew who I was, they'd put me in jail for saving you. Not because of the outcome, but because of the process. And this is ten times more about my business than you ever needed to know."

"What about trace evidence?"

Jonathan laughed. Everybody on the planet watched *CSI* these days. "Look, I know what I'm doing. There is no trace evidence. I am entirely untraceable."

"But I'm not. I'm way traceable."

Jonathan agreed. "To a certain extent, yes. That's why I didn't want you touching the girl. I didn't want you transferring fibers or fingerprints onto Chris . . . *Tiffany*." Hard to know which name the kid would find more comforting.

Even in the darkness, Jonathan could see Tom's displeasure. "We have to report this!"

"Not gonna happen. Not by me, anyway."

Thomas turned sideways in his seat, beginning a serious negotiation. "If we call the police right now, then they'll know it was all self-defense. If we *don't* call, then they're going to draw all these wrong conclusions, and I can end up in jail."

"Nobody's going to put you in jail, Tom. Don't be so melodramatic. We're not calling the police. Period."

Thomas wasn't done yet. "I don't think you understand, Scorpion. I don't think I can keep a secret like this. I'm going to have to tell somebody. Not even to call for help, necessarily, but just because it happened, and when I get together with my friends over a couple of beers, it's going to slip out."

Jonathan shrugged again. "Then it slips out. You can tell anyone anything you'd like. You didn't do anything wrong. You're a victim here, for God's sake. You have nothing to feel guilty about. Rejoice in your freedom and quit worrying."

Thomas started to speak, but then swallowed the words to reconsider. "So you're saying it's okay if I report this all to the police, but that you're not going to. If I do it's fine."

"As far as I'm concerned it's fine," Jonathan said, directing this conversation down the same path he'd steered it so many times in the past. "Once I drop you off, your life is yours to do with as you please. I don't care who you call or what you tell them."

Thomas grunted and turned back around in his seat to face forward. He seemed satisfied.

"Just understand that what you say may hurt the people who hired me. What I do, because of the nature of its outcome from time to time, might not reflect so well on them."

"How do you mean?" Thomas was back on edge.

"Well, you had a point before. There's a right way to

do certain things. How many times have you heard people warn others about the dangers of 'taking the law into their own hands'? Everybody thinks that the police are the best investigators—until one of their own is taken, and they hear that threat to kill if anyone calls the police. After that, the law-abiding citizen crap goes out the window. When it's your own, you want *action* not *process*. That's precisely how I got involved. It was more important to your parents to bring you home than it was to construct a court case against your kidnappers. They chose well, I think. But to get you home, I had to find you first, and to find you, I had to take shortcuts."

"What, did you like beat information out of people or something?"

Jonathan ignored the question. "Police want convictions, Thomas. More times than you'd like to think, saving good guys takes a backseat to convicting bad guys. When you go to them, you might skate because you were a victim, but they'll want the people who cheated them out of a court victory to pay with a different court case of their own. When they don't find me—and they won't—they'll come for the people who hired me."

It took Thomas a moment to connect the dots. "You mean my parents."

"A victory's a victory."

He got the point. "Jesus."

"It's a lot to take in all at once, isn't it?" Jonathan said. "If I were you, I'd look at it this way—it's better to be alive on the outer fringes of the law than dead and in full compliance. Keep your options open for a while."

Back in his days with the Unit, he scooped up the good guys, neutralized the bad guys, and let professionals handle the psychological crap. He never had to dwell on the humanity. In Jonathan's version of a perfect world, hostage rescue was all about the operation, not about the people involved. Bad guys were targets and their victims were packages. It was easier that way.

Thomas Hughes was only a boy. Sure, he was twenty-two years old—Jonathan had served with battle-hardened men who were younger than that—but Tom's worldview was still rooted in childhood. You could see it in the way his eyes glinted in the dark, and hear it in the stress of his voice. The kid needed to talk, but Jonathan didn't need the additional burden.

The next forty-five minutes passed in silence. From the rhythm of Thomas's breathing, Jonathan figured he'd fallen asleep.

They reached Hamilton, a town about thirty-five miles from Muncie. Following directions he'd memorized, Jonathan wound his way through the sleepy streets until he found the pharmacy on the corner of Bremmer Pike and Old Bridge Road. The sign out front advertised that the store was open twenty-four hours a day, but the empty parking lot indicated a business better suited to the regular workday.

"Hey," Jonathan said. "Wake up, we're here." When the kid didn't move, Jonathan tapped him on the shoulder.

Thomas jumped. "What? Where are we?"

"This is the end of the line," Jonathan said, smiling. Shifting his weight so he could get to his wallet, he fished out a fifty-dollar bill and handed it to the kid. "Hang around inside for a while. The Greyhound comes by at 6:23 on its run to Chicago. It'll hit Muncie around

7:15. The ticket's about fifteen bucks. From the Muncie bus station, pick up a cab to your house. If traffic is smooth, you'll be home in time for breakfast."

Thomas looked stunned. "That's it?"

Jonathan smiled more broadly. "You want more?"

"Aren't you coming with me?"

"Can't. It's not smart for us to be seen together. Don't worry, you're safe from here. Time to get on with the rest of your life."

Still, the kid didn't move. "I still don't know that I can keep all of this a secret," he said. His eyes looked sad.

Jonathan gave a half-shrug. "You can only do what you can do."

"What about you?" Thomas asked.

"I already told you. I'm untraceable."

That wasn't what he meant. "If I say something, are you going to come back and . . . Well, you know."

Jonathan allowed himself a tired sigh. "I'm not an assassin. Don't make life unnecessarily difficult, and you'll never see me again."

Thomas smiled nervously. "So I only worry if I see you knocking on my door?"

Jonathan chuckled. "Well put. Now get out."

Thomas still was not comfortable leaving the truck. He looked to his lap, searching for something to say.

"It's okay," Jonathan assured.

The kid nodded. He held out his hand for Jonathan to shake. "Thanks."

Jonathan smiled and shook. "You're welcome. Here's to never seeing each other again."

Thomas opened the door, and Jonathan watched as he walked toward the pharmacy's double glass doors. This was what he loved about his job. This was why he kept putting himself in harm's way: the look on the PCs' faces when they realized—really *realized* for the first time—that their nightmare was over. It was like being the Lone Freaking Ranger.

He watched until Thomas reached the door, then slipped the transmission back into Drive.

As he pulled away from the curb, Jonathan pressed a number on his speed dial.

CHAPTER FIVE

Venice Alexander never slept well on the nights when her boss was on a mission. (It's pronounced Ven-EE-chay, by the way. Everybody got it wrong the first time, but second mistakes were not suffered kindly.) She always tried, but until the phone rang with the all-clear, she never really rested. In a perverse way, she preferred the larger, more dangerous operations where she was needed to man the computer and the phones in the office over these so-call "milk-run" 0300 ops. Add to that the stress of managing the details of a dozen or so investigation cases by other associates in her charge, and even fake sleep was impossible tonight.

Pulling on a Karen Neuburger robe—Roman, her eleven-year-old son, called it "teddy bear material"—Venice rolled out of bed and pushed her feet into a pair of luxurious slippers. She knew for a fact that Mama had fried more chicken than she'd served at dinner, and a cold drumstick seemed exactly the right prescription to settle her down. That and a cup of hot water with lemon. Snagging her cell phone from the nightstand and dropping it into a big patch pocket, she headed for the hallway and the stairs beyond.

"You're up late," Mama said as Venice opened the kitchen door.

She jumped. "Jesus!"

"Watch your mouth," Mama scolded. The rotund black woman sat at the long oval table, in front of a plate that was nearly as loaded with chicken and green beans as the one she'd consumed at dinner.

Venice padded to the cabinet over the flatware drawer and pulled out a white Corelle plate for herself. She sat across from her mother. "I was hungry," she said, and she reached for the last leg on the serving platter.

Venice had no memories of her father, a policeman killed in the line of duty before she was born, and it was a source of pain that she'd never truly overcome. For as long as she could remember, she'd always dreamed about what her father might have sounded like and smelled like. The picture on Mama's dresser gave her a face, but she'd never know the voice that went with it. She regretted that she'd passed the fatherless legacy on to her own son, albeit with a huge difference. If Roman ever wanted to do the research to track his daddy down, he was welcome to. Last time Venice heard, Leroy was somewhere in Afghanistan.

Mama mourned every day for her beloved Charles. As she closed in on her sixty-eighth birthday, she talked a lot about her fear of dying lonely. Not likely, Venice told her. Not with Resurrection House in her life. Seated on two acres in the middle of Fisherman's Cove's business district and next door to St. Katherine's Catholic Church, the gleaming new boarding school was the most stunning building in town, having wrested the honor from Mama's sprawling Victorian mansion that shared the same property. Except for the courthouse and the hospital, which was not technically a part of Fisherman's Cove but rather of the unincorporated environs of Westmoreland County, Resurrection House had more square footage than any other structure.

Until five years ago, the mansion and the land that housed the school had been the boyhood home of Jonathan Grave. Upon inheriting the property from his still-living father as part of a court proceeding that no one fully understood, Jonathan decided that he didn't need any of it, and he signed the property over to St. Katherine's parish for a dollar. A change to the deed dictated that the property be used in perpetuity as a school for children of incarcerated parents. Mama Alexander would live in the mansion for the rest of her life, and she would hold the position of house counselor for as long as she wanted it. Jonathan covered all costs out of his own pocket.

A third condition was more a matter of paperwork than substance: Jonathan's involvement in the modification of the building and the endowment of seven teaching positions, plus his high-six-figure annual contribution to the care and maintenance of the place were never to be publicly disclosed. As far as anyone outside St. Kate's immediate family was to know, those expenses were covered only by the Family Defense Foundation, a nonprofit that Jonathan had formed through one of the many cutout identities he had established over the years.

"No word from Jonathan yet?" Mama intuited.

Venice avoided eye contact. "I've got a lot of things on my mind."

"I suppose he's on one of his *missions*?" Mama leaned on the last word in a way that made clear her disapproval.

"Mama, I don't want to talk about it, and you shouldn't either. Digger's safety depends on secrecy."

Mama didn't like it, but she didn't fight. "I hate it when you call him that. I don't need to know the details to know that you're worried. I see it in your face."

Venice sighed. "He's late reporting in."

"How late?"

Venice's veneer started to crack. "A couple of hours."

Nobody moved for a moment.

"He's been late before," Venice added.

"But tonight's different?"

Venice's cell phone chirped, and she thrust up a hand for silence. Only two people in the world called her on her cell, and one of them was upstairs in his bedroom. She got the phone open at the end of the second ring. "Digger?" She could hear the anxiety in her own voice, and knew that he would not approve.

"Good morning." It was Jonathan, all right, and she could tell that he was smiling. "Everything went fine."

Relief lasted for two seconds, and then anger swept in to replace it. "Why didn't you call?"

"Open line," he admonished, reminding her of long-standing security precautions. If people knew how much cell phone traffic was intercepted and monitored—roughly all of it—they'd be far more circumspect about what they said. "It got late. I didn't want to wake you."

"I can't sleep when you don't call. Neither can Mama."

Jonathan's voice got smaller. "Sorry. I didn't make final delivery until just now. We'll be on the road soon."

"Is Boxers with you?"

"Not yet. In about an hour. Pick me up around four-thirty this afternoon?"

"I'll be there," she said.

"You're the best, Ven. One more thing." She should have known he wouldn't close on a personal note. "Since you're up already, can you find me everything there is to know about a Christine Baker, a.k.a. Tiffany Barnes?"

Venice had to rummage quickly through a kitchen drawer to find a pen. She wrote the names on a napkin. "Where's she from?"

"Not sure, but she used to hang around Ball State University."

"Used to?"

"Open line, Ven."

That meant that no more details would be forthcoming, at least for a while. "I'll find what I can."

"See you soon." With that, he hung up.

Venice closed her phone. Now that she had work to do, all she wanted was to go to sleep.

Chapter Six

A cluster of bells over the door announced Thomas's arrival. Simms Pharmacy was a business pulled off the set of a 1950s movie, complete with the first soda fountain he'd ever seen, with green-cushioned swivel stools and a chrome-trimmed raised counter. Two dozen rows of tightly packed shelves displayed hair care products, candy, cold remedies, and sundries, while high shelves along the perimeter held hundreds of other trinkets, from kiddie pools to a display of bicycles that were at least three design years out of date.

Thomas's borrowed shoes clicked against the maple-colored hardwood floors as he strolled inside. He had an hour to kill, and he hoped to find a mindless magazine to erase the blood and the violence of the night, but the movie screen in his head kept replaying the image of Lionel Patrone with his huge shears, and the emptiness of Tiffany's face as she lay dead in the harsh glare of Scorpion's flashlight.

I should call home, he thought, but then he pushed it away. Scorpion said to wait for the bus. If his folks had wanted him to call home, that's what they would have put into the plan. Nothing that seemed obvious or easy at first glance was anymore. The only thing he knew for sure was that Scorpion had thought things through pretty well. It made no sense to start deviating from the plan at this point.

When a man stepped from behind one of the end cap displays to greet him, Thomas jumped enough to startle them both. The fear passed in an instant, and they both laughed.

The man wore the smock of a pharmacy employee, with a name tag that identified him as Al. At sixty or so, he looked too old to be working this late. "What can I do for you?"

"You scared the shit out of me." Thomas meant it as a simple statement, but it came out angry.

Al's face darkened. "I don't much like that language."

Thomas blushed. "Sorry," he said. "I'm here to wait for the bus to Chicago. Comes in about an hour, right?"

Just like that, all was forgiven. Al checked his watch. "An hour and ten if it's running on time. I think I'd count on something closer to an hour and a half. Want something to eat while you wait? Some ice cream?"

The mention of food brought Thomas's stomach back to life. "That would be great. Are you still serving food?"

Al smiled and started for the soda fountain, beckoning Thomas to follow him. "All night means all night, young man. I'd prefer not to fire up the grill, but if it can be microwaved or taken from the freezer, it's available." He stopped halfway there and turned to extend his hand. "Al Elvins," he said. "I'm the late-night manager. My brother owns the place."

"Thomas Hughes." He returned the handshake, and wondered if it had been a mistake to use his real name.

"You as hungry as you look?" Al asked, walking again.

"More tired than hungry, I think."

When they arrived at the soda fountain, Al lifted a section of the bar to step behind, and Thomas mounted one of the stools.

"That's it," Al said. "Make yourself comfortable."

The light was better up here, and in it, Thomas caught something odd in the clerk's expression. It was the way he looked at him and quickly looked away.

"You want a hot dog?"

"Can I have two, please? And a large Sprite."

"You can have as many as you like," Al said, again with a quick glance. He seemed to prefer concentrating on the task of opening the package of frankfurters. "You know," he said without eye contact, "there's a bathroom in the back of the store if you want to clean up a bit."

That sounded like a good idea. While his meal cooked in the microwave, Thomas walked to the men's room. One look in the mirror explained everything. He was filthy. The face in the mirror was years older than the one that he'd last seen. His hair was a matted, mottled mess, and the bags under his eyes reminded him of one of his sixty-year-old uncles. Stripping off his T-shirt so that he could *really* wash, he could actually count the bones in his chest through his skin.

He let the water run hot as he stuffed paper towels into the sink's drain to fill the basin, and added six pumps of liquid soap from the bulbous dispenser on the wall. With the water off again, he cupped his hands into the cloudy, bubbly mixture, leaned low to the sink, and buried his face in his hands.

That's when it hit him. Contact with something as

civilized as hot soapy water made him realize how fortunate he was to be alive. He understood that strangers had risked their lives to deliver him from an agonized death.

As his face pressed into his palms, and the water drained through his fingers, Thomas began to cry.

"Thought maybe you fell in," Al said cheerily when Thomas returned to the lunch counter. Then his face darkened again. "You okay, son?"

Thomas nodded, knowing that he looked like holy hell. "I'm fine."

Al looked like he wanted to press further, but he let it go. "You say so."

Thomas settled in for his dinner. The two hot dogs rested in paper sleeves on top of a single paper plate. It took him a minute to load them with ketchup and mustard, and then he devoured them in three bites apiece. He'd never tasted a better meal. Next came the Sprite, which he finished in one long chug. When he was done, he rested the glass back on the counter, suppressed a belch, and smiled sheepishly.

"Been a while since you've eaten, has it?"

Apparently he'd made quite a pig of himself. "I was pretty hungry."

Al considered his next question before he launched it. "Are you in some kind of trouble, son?"

Thomas tried to look surprised. "I don't think so."

"I don't believe you, all respect." Al's tone was anything but threatening. Thomas half-expected the guy to offer him a bed. "You look terrible, you nearly ate the plate, and you're hanging around a bus stop in the wee hours of the morning. To me, that spells runaway."

Thomas chuckled. "I'm twenty-two. I'm too old to be a runaway."

"Not if you're running away from something you done, you ain't. Now, you don't look like much of a criminal, but you do look like somebody who maybe needs to talk to a cop."

Thomas tried to force a smile, but Al had landed too close to the truth. A cop was exactly the person he needed. This secret was going to kill him. As exhaustion closed in, he didn't know if he had the strength to continue the charade.

"I'm really fine. I don't need to talk to anybody." He hoped that his tone sounded light enough. After what Scorpion had done for him, how could he betray the man so soon?

Al wasn't buying. "You sure? Nobody can hurt you here, you know. You want, I can hole you up in a back room for protection and we can just give the police a call."

"Honestly, I'm okay. Really. I'm just on my way home."

"Home from where?"

The question stopped Thomas dead. "Out of state," he said, conjuring a quick lie. "Kentucky."

Al smiled a little too broadly. "Where from? I love Kentucky."

Thomas felt fear rising in his throat. He said, "Louisville," because it was the only Kentucky town he could think of.

The druggist knew he was lying; Thomas could tell it from his narrowed eyes. But he let him off the hook. "I never did spend much time in *that* part of the state," he said.

They just looked at each other, saying nothing, until

Thomas pushed his paper plate off to the side and rested his head on the counter, using his folded arms as a pillow. Seconds later, the world disappeared.

"Hey, Tom, wake up."

It was as if the words were coming to him through galvanized pipe, garbled and hollow.

"Wake up, Tom." This time, the command came with a substantial poke in his arm, and the physical contact rushed all of the events back into focus. He jumped upright on his stool, ready to fight.

Al backpedaled from the threat. "Whoa, son. Your bus is here. Won't wait for long."

Thomas stared, understanding the words, but unable to respond to them through the fog of exhaustion.

"That means you gotta get going."

The bus. To Chicago. Now he remembered. "How long was I asleep?" He saw that the dishes had all been cleared.

"Over an hour. You were out cold."

Jesus. Fastest hour in history. He spun himself off the stool and found his feet again. "Thanks for waking me." He paused. "You didn't, you know . . . what we were talking about?"

"Call the police?" Al shook his head. "Naw. I'm still not convinced that I shouldn't have, but you're old enough to know when you're in trouble. I don't want to pry." As he finished that last sentence, the phone rang, prompting Al to look at his watch. "At this hour, it's got to be somebody's baby is sick." He stepped behind the counter again to answer it. "Travel safely."

"Thanks," Thomas said. "And *thanks*."

Al acknowledged with a friendly wave, but aimed his voice at the telephone. "Simms Pharmacy."

Thomas could see the silver and blue bus waiting at the curb on the other side of the store's front window. He felt naked as he walked to the door, as if he should be carrying something; if not luggage, then at least his school book bag.

"Hey, Tom!" Al called. He hadn't yet taken five steps.

Thomas turned.

"There's a Julie Hughes on the line. Says she's your mother. Don't have to take it if you don't want to."

Thomas couldn't think of a voice he'd love to hear more. "I'll definitely take it!" he said and he spun on his heel to head for the phone. Outside, the bus blatted his horn. "Can you ask him to wait for a minute?"

As the druggist handed over the phone, they changed places. "I can ask, but I don't know if he'll do it. They're pretty jealous of their schedules."

Thomas snatched the receiver to his ear. "Mom?"

"Thomas!" she exclaimed. "I was terrified I'd miss you."

"You nearly did. The bus is right outside."

"Don't get on it," she commanded. "No matter what you do, don't get on that bus. I'm coming to get you."

"How did you know I was here?" He lowered his voice. "Did Scorpion call you?"

"Did *who* call me?"

"Scor . . . Never mind."

"I knew you were going to be on a bus, and that the bus's destination was Chicago. I've been calling every single stop looking for you. Are you all right?"

"I'm fine." It's the answer he would have given even if he was missing a foot.

"Are you hurt?"

"A little bruised, but I'll be okay."

"Well, don't you go anywhere, you understand? I'm coming to get you."

That didn't make sense. "Why don't I just take the bus?"

"There's big trouble, Thomas. We're all in danger."

From across the store, Al yelled, "Tom, they're about to leave without you."

Thomas begged for time with a raised forefinger. He turned away from Al and lowered his voice. "What do you mean we're in danger? I'm free now. I've been rescued."

"I know," she said. He could hear her moving even faster now. "I can't talk about it. Not on the phone. I'll tell you when I get there. I'm on my way now. What will it be, about an hour?"

"I have no idea. Mom, I don't understand—"

"Tom! Five seconds and he's gone," called Al. His voice was heavy with stress.

Thomas ignored him. "I'm exhausted, Mom. I could just sleep on the bus, and when we get home—"

"No!" she whispered harshly. "That's just it. We can't go home. Not ever again. That's why I'm coming to get you."

"Jesus, Mom, what are you—"

"Don't talk to anyone. Don't do anything or go anywhere. I'll explain when I get there." With that, she hung up, leaving him staring at the phone. He held it in his hand, as if wondering whether it might come to life. As he rested it back on its cradle, he felt Al approaching from behind him.

"Well, they left. I tried to keep them around, but the driver said—" One look at Thomas, and his words froze in his throat. "Goodness gracious, are you okay?"

It was a good question. Thomas wished he had an answer.

Chapter Seven

For Sheriff Gail Bonneville, this was shaping up to be one hell of a day.

For as long as it had been on the map—one hundred fifty-three years, to be exact—the little burg of Samson, Indiana, had been able to boast to the world that no one had ever been murdered there. Suicides, yes, and the occasional hunting accident, but never had anyone willfully taken a life on Samson soil. And wouldn't you know it? The day they logged the very first one, it was a triple. Shortly after first light, a couple of boys hoping to catch some breakfast in the river had wandered up on the body of a young woman who'd bled a gallon into the weeds from a hole in her belly. The boys had freaked out, naturally, and lit up the phone lines. By the time Gail marked on the scene only twenty minutes after the first call, she wondered how the entire county had managed to get there before her.

Nothing pulls people away from the breakfast table, she supposed, quite like the buzz of murder. In addition to the corpse, there was also the hulk of a burned-out van.

Oliver Eddlestein, God bless him, the first arriving

deputy on the scene, had done his best to keep people away to preserve the crime scene, but it was hard to be tough on people when you knew you going to see them in church on Sunday. It wasn't that the crime scene had been trashed; it was just that Gail was a purist about such things, and she knew what antics defense attorneys could play when they sniffed even the slightest flaw in a murder investigation. A few extra footprints on the ground could go a long way toward establishing reasonable doubt.

Sheriff Bonneville had just gotten her bearings on the investigation in the field when word came that two more bodies had been found in the basement of the house. Tax records listed the place as belonging to Beatrice Patrone, deceased, and was presumably empty. Neighbors insisted, however, that two boys were living there now, and when no one answered the door, the investigating deputy got curious, and started looking around. That's when he found a spent shell casing against a pillar near the front door. It was clearly the wrong caliber for the wounds inflicted on the female victim. His curiosity piqued, he walked around to the back of the house, where he found the splintered storm doors and the severed electrical lines.

The deputy called it in on his radio, and then all hell broke loose.

The tiny world of Samson transformed into a crime scene. All vacations were canceled, off-duty deputies were called in, and now the state police were involved. Gail had heard rumors that the local FBI field office had begun to sniff around the case, looking for a jurisdictional back door.

The good news was that the Patrone house, in contrast to the yard and the area around the burned-out van, was a pristine crime scene. With the exception of

Jesse Collier, last night's shift supervisor, and the deputy who'd first stumbled onto the place, no one had been in or out. Even Gail was hanging back a ways until the state police crime scene guys could do their thing.

In such a small space, the violence and misery of a murder took on a physical presence. Spooky was probably the wrong word, but it was the only one that came to mind as Gail took in the results of what clearly had been a shoot-out.

"Any ideas, Sheriff?" Jesse asked. He flashed the gap-tooth grin that Gail never quite knew how to interpret.

"I've got a couple," she said.

"Let's start with why one of them is in his skivvies." Jesse had been an early competitor in the race for sheriff last November, but had taken a dive at the request of the Indiana Democratic Party, which was in a lather to install a female sheriff in this rural community. Gail Bonneville had an FBI pedigree and a doctorate in criminal justice to go along with her law degree. The party didn't want to run the risk of someone like Jesse walking away with the election simply because his was the more familiar face. Gail had always felt guilty about her engineered victory, and had never fully trusted Jesse as a result of it. He had plenty of motivation to torpedo her career.

Paranoia aside, however, she had no concrete reason to suspect him of anything but total loyalty. "I have no idea," she said, addressing the fact that one of the boys had clearly been stripped of his clothes. It was the way his underpants were skewed, and his socks were half-pulled from his feet. "But I think we've got ourselves a couple of dead kidnappers."

Jesse's eyebrows scaled his forehead. "Whoa, that's quite a leap out of the gate. How did you get there?"

Gail shrugged. It really wasn't all that much of a stretch, when you thought about it. She knelt closer to the floor. "Look at the duct tape," she said, pointing with her pen at the gray and white shreds on the concrete. "Doesn't that look like it was wrapped around somebody's wrists? And that one around the ankles?"

Jesse nodded. The tape was wrapped repeatedly around itself, yet cut cleanly through all layers. Looking carefully, she could see short, curly hairs still attached to the sticky side of the remnants. "Somebody rescued him. With all that hair, the victim certainly wasn't a girl."

"That's what I'm thinking."

Jesse made a sweeping gesture toward the corpses on the floor. "So one of these is the good guy and one is the bad guy? They shot it out between them, and neither made it out alive?"

Gail shook her head. "I don't think so. The angles are wrong. Look here." She shifted and pointed to the bodies. "They've both got weapons, but all the bullet strikes are over there." She pointed to the star-shaped divots in the stone near the shattered door. "I don't think they were shooting at each other. I think they were defending themselves from somebody else."

"Somebody *else*?"

She waited for him to connect the dots.

Jesse's eyes grew wide. "You think it was a third party?"

Gail smiled and nodded. "You've seen the doors, right?"

He gave her an exasperated look that said, "Duh."

"Well, have you looked carefully?"

"I see a lot of splintered wood. Looks like he used dynamite."

"Close. The FBI's Hostage Rescue Team uses entry

techniques like these." She stood and led Jesse to the collapsed panel of the door. "Look here." She pointed to the nearly perfect half-moons that had been gouged out of the spots on the frame where the hinges had once been mounted. "I'm guessing this is where he put his breaching charges. He waited until the bad guys were all gathered in the basement, and then he pushed his button."

Jesse gave a low whistle. "That must've made their ears ring."

Gail laughed. "Can you imagine? And that was the point, I think. Our guy blows the doors off, swoops in, and he's got all the elements of surprise."

Jesse nodded as he thought it through. "So, you think the shooter was a professional. Some kind of vigilante, maybe—someone who knew what he was doing."

"Strong possibility. That would explain the marksmanship, too. Look at that one." She pointed to Lionel's body. "Dead center in the heart, and one in the forehead. That one, too. Perfect shot to the heart." She gestured to Barry's corpse. "You don't get better shooting than that." Gail thought. "It must have been one hell of a shoot-out, though. These boys were throwing bullets everywhere."

The best part of investigative work, Gail thought—and the part that she missed most about the go-go life of the FBI—was the way a crime scene could tell a story. Whatever happened, happened in exactly *one* way, and the investigator's job was to sift through often-conflicting bits and pieces to construct the one true story. Blood spatters formed telltale patterns because of the laws of physics and biology; the same was true of bullet entry and exit wounds, and even ricochets. Barring interference from insects and marauding animals—and there certainly were no signs of any of that here—a murder scene was a frozen moment in time, remaining exactly as it existed at the instant when the last living person walked away. There was something awe inspiring about that.

Gail Bonneville felt a responsibility to the deceased to fully and accurately chronicle their last moments on earth. To her, catching the bad guys was never the point. That played a part, of course—she was as much a competitor and a fan of justice as anyone else—but it was the historical value of what she did that really stirred her juices.

"You just traveled off someplace," Jesse said, bringing her thoughts back to the present.

She blushed. "I do that sometimes." No one in Samson yet recognized what the Chicago Field Officc had once named the "Bonneville stare."

"So, are you going to talk to me, or what?" Jesse pressed.

She smiled. "Sorry. Okay, here's what I'm thinking so far." She led the way closer to the bodies. She started with Lionel. "Let's call this guy 'Vic One,'" she said.

"Now look at his pockets. They've been turned inside out, and then shoved back in. Whoever killed them rifled through his pockets. Why?"

"Looking for money?"

Gail shook her head. "I don't think so. If you've got the money to pull off an operation like this, you don't need pocket change from your victim."

"What, then?"

She shrugged. "Identification, maybe? I don't know. But the very fact that he took that kind of time tells me that our shooter was a pretty calm guy. Also look at the stains on the floor there." She pointed to a long, paramecium-shaped discoloration of the stone floor, just a few feet away from Vic One, in the middle of which sat one of the duct tape shreds. "Want to hazard a guess?"

He made a show of sniffing the air like a dog, and then grew serious. He whispered, "I smell dead people."

"Urine," she said, laughing at his Haley Joel Osment impersonation.

"Excuse me?"

"Don't you smell piss?"

"That's what I said. I smell dead people. Blood, piss, maybe a hint of shit."

"I think that's what the stain is."

Jesse scowled. "That means your kidnap victim was here for a while."

"And when you're hog-tied with duct tape, you do what you have to do where you have to do it." Her eyes got big. "It just dawned on me right now as I was standing here. I know why Vic Two doesn't have any pants on."

Jesse got it, too. "Because our *real* victim pissed all over his own. So, where are those?"

"Maybe he didn't have any."

Jesse's face read utter disgust. "They kept him naked?"

"Bingo."

"That's twisted." Jesse said the words as if they tasted bad. After a beat, he added, "But I think you've hit on something." There was a hint of paternal pride without patronizing. "What else you got?"

Gail started to speak, then stopped herself. She was scooting out pretty far on a limb here. If she guessed too much, and it all proved to be wrong, that'd be a lot of crow to eat.

What the hell. "Okay, one more," she said. "Count the shell casings."

Jesse played the beam of his flashlight across the floor. "One," he said. "Looks like a .380."

"Exactly. And look here." She walked an odd, weaving course, avoiding all the obvious physical evidence as she made her way to the revolver near Vic Two. She slipped her pen through the trigger guard and lifted it, illuminating it with the beam from her own light. "A .38 special," she said. She peered down the business end, into the chamber openings in the cylinder. "One shot fired." She pivoted and shined her light on the back wall again. "One plus one equals the two holes we have in the wall."

Jesse shrugged. "Okay . . ." He was waiting for the rest.

"Where are the other casings? The ones from the killer?"

"Maybe he used a revolver, too."

Gail shook her head dismissively. "I doubt it. Triple-taps are hard to do with a revolver. No, he had an automatic, and it was a big one. That head wound over there had to be at least a .44, probably a .45. So, where are the shooter's casings?"

Jesse's expression said that this was a no-brainer. "He picked them up?"

"Yes. He picked them up. Who but a professional would think to do that? And why would he pick up only his own?"

Jesse crossed his arms and smiled. He didn't have an answer, but he wasn't going to give his boss the satisfaction of saying so.

"I think it's because he wanted us to figure it out. I think he wanted there to be enough evidence on the scene so that we would know that this was not a random homicide."

The scowl returned to Jesse's brow. "Are you thinking someone staged this?"

"No," Gail said, but then she retreated. "Actually, I hadn't thought of that." It was possible, she supposed, but it had been her experience that killers—like everyone else in life—followed the simplest path, not the most difficult one. "But I don't think so. I think this is the work of someone hired to do a job, and maybe the job went the wrong way and got messy. By leaving the tape and the bodies and the casings, I think maybe he's trying to show us that at least he killed for the right reasons."

"Hoping that we'll back off, maybe."

"Or at least not press as hard."

Jesse regarded Gail. "He bet wrong, didn't he?"

She smiled. "Oh, yeah. This isn't the Old West. You want justice done, you call the police. Or, if you pull something like this, with these results, then you still call the police and own up to it. Let a jury decide who's the good guy and who's the bad."

CHAPTER EIGHT

Jonathan dropped the Explorer off at a self-storage place on the outskirts of Muncie and locked the door. Within a few hours, the owner of a body shop that specialized in under-the-table repairs would enter the storage bay and examine the vehicle for any bullet holes or other damage that might need repairing. Finding none, he would return it to the rental car lot at the Indianapolis Airport. No one would know anything of the events in which the vehicle had participated.

Leaving the storage yard, Jonathan walked down the street to a no-tell motel and took a cab to Indianapolis Airport. Of the day's long ordeal, Jonathan's fifteen minutes on airport property were his most nerve-racking. The pundits on the news who complained that American airports remained soft targets for terrorists needed to get their heads out of their asses. The place swarmed with police and dogs and electronic surveillance gimmickry, and there he was, walking around like a living training toy. Step a little too close to the wrong dog and he'd have some major explaining to do. Even though he never entered the main terminal, the proximity of this much security made him nervous as hell.

He headed straight for the cabstand. The hack who picked him up was an Arab, Jonathan's first lucky break of the day. Ever since 9-11, most Middle Eastern ex-pats went out of their way to avoid contact with anybody, and many of them were particularly uninterested in cooperating with police. If some lucky flatfoot was able to connect the dots as far as the airport, the trail would likely stop dead, because no one would step forward to tell anybody anything.

God granted good fortune to those who were perpetually careful.

He paid cash for his ride to a Sheraton in Indianapolis, and cash again for a second cab ride to the bus station. From there, it was a long bus trip to Evanston, where he caught yet another cab to O'Hare International Airport. He told that driver to drop him at the long-term parking area on Bessie Coleman Drive. When the cab was out of sight, it was then time to walk across the street to begin the final leg of the journey.

The executive air terminal at O'Hare was a lot like executive air terminals everywhere, much more sparsely appointed than the uninitiated would expect. There were no concessions to speak of, unless you counted the self-service coffee station, which at present was serving a product more suitable to a fountain pen than a coffee cup. People with their own planes don't need a concession stand.

Besides, Boxers was already waiting for him. At six-five, 290 pounds, Boxers was a solid mass of beef. To the casual eye, he might even have looked fat, but this was a man who could bench-press two Jonathan Graves and drink a beer at the same time. He was also the only human being Jonathan had ever known who had been hit with a .50 caliber round and lived to recover. His barely noticeable limp was testimony to the six inches of titanium rod that made up for his missing femur. In addition to being huge, tough, and endlessly loyal, he could also fly anything that had wings or rotors, and he could land them in places that would turn others into a greasy fireball.

Boxers and Digger Grave went way, way back.

The big pilot took the two duffels without asking. "You're late." He started walking toward the exit.

"I didn't realize you had better places to be," Jonathan quipped.

Boxers led the way across the departure lounge and out onto the tarmac, where a slick, beautiful Gulfstream jet awaited. The plane was registered to Perseus Foods, whose president, Richard Lydell, had utilized Jonathan's services a while back after his thirty-year-old daughter had been kidnapped by guerrillas while on a Presbyterian mission to Costa Rica. Jonathan had agreed to lead a four-member rescue team in return for a fee that included ten years' on-call access to the corporation's private jet. It'd turned out to be one hell of a mission. Two weeks of planning had culminated in a seven-second firefight that relieved the world of eleven terrorists, while returning eight missionaries to their Christian works. Jonathan's blood pressure still spiked when he recalled how one of the wire services had quoted "reliable sources" with "positive evidence" that the rescue had been the work of the Navy's Seal Team Six. Jonathan never minded his anonymity, but he hated it when the Navy got credit for Army training.

Within ten minutes, they were rolling, and twenty minutes after that they were in the air. By the time they climbed through ten thousand feet, Boxers tired of silence. "Drop-off go okay?"

"The kid's nervous," Jonathan said.

"The guilt thing?"

"Some of that, but mostly he's worried that he can't keep a secret."

"What did you tell him?"

"The usual—that I'm a lot less vulnerable to prosecution than his folks would be. I don't know how convinced he was."

Boxers shook his head in mild amusement. "Do you think any of them really keep the secret of their rescue?"

Jonathan shrugged. "I'm sure a few of them do. I'd bet real money that they all do for a while—long enough that they start confusing what little details they knew in the first place. It all works out in the end."

"Well, congratulations, boss. Another life saved." Boxers turned to smile at Jonathan, but didn't like the expression he saw. "You okay?"

"Hmm? Oh, I'm fine."

"You look troubled."

Jonathan considered his words before speaking. "I guess maybe I am." He shifted in the seat so he could look at the pilot. "Something the kid said. In fact, he said it more than once. His family has no money, they live in the burbs, just average people. How the hell did they afford my fee?" The minimum Jonathan charged for 0300 missions was $250,000, payable in advance. With expenses and additional odds and ends, this one came to damn near half a million.

"Never know about people," Boxers countered. "You read about zillionaires living in cardboard shacks surrounded by cats. Nobody'd ever dream that they had money. Could be something like that."

"I suppose," Jonathan said, but he wasn't convinced.

"Besides, somebody's kid gets picked up, the family's gonna dig deep to come up with money they didn't even know they had."

Jonathan conceded the point with a nod. “And what do you make of the girl in the woods with the gun?”

“I think she should’ve dropped it instead of shooting it.”

Jonathan smiled. Leave it to Boxers to get straight to the heart of an issue. After a minute or two of silence, Jonathan lifted himself out of the copilot’s seat and headed for the back of the plane. “It’s time for me to catch a little shut-eye, if that’s okay with you.”

Boxers smiled. “Computer says you got an hour and forty-two minutes.”

Chapter Nine

It was nearly five in the afternoon when Jonathan finally stepped through the double doors into the Signature Aviation Terminal at Washington Dulles International Airport. Boxers had work to do to close out the Gulfstream, and would drive himself home in his Nissan pickup. Jonathan had a ride waiting for him.

Venice stood in the lobby, arms folded and wound up tighter than a watch spring. When they finally made eye contact, it looked as if she'd just taken her first breath of the day. He saw tears in her eyes. Venice was a famous crier.

"Welcome home," she said. "I was worried."

Jonathan allowed himself to be hugged. "Like I always say, do what you do best."

Venice understood that he'd just said thank you. "Want me to help with a bag?"

"Nah, I got them. Did you bring the monstrosity?"

"Her name is Glow Bird," Venice said, fishing through her purse for her keys, "And I got a terrific parking place."

By any man's yardstick, Venice Alexander was hot. Her skin was the color of milk chocolate, and there were days when her smile could put the sun out of business. Jonathan could tell from her clothing that she was proud of her recent weight loss. They both knew that the pounds would come back—the same twenty came and went on a three-year cycle—but for now, it was nice to see her strutting a little.

"Tell me what you found out about Christine Baker," Jonathan prodded as they approached the door that would take them to the parking lot.

"Who is she?"

He hated it when people answered questions with questions. "She's my big surprise for the night. We knew about the Patrone brothers and a third party. She was the third party."

The door opened onto a beautiful spring day. The perfect blue sky made even the parking lot look vibrant. "Well, it's not exactly a unique name," Venice cautioned, "and the picture you sent was not of the best quality."

"You're hedging."

"I'm explaining that there aren't definitive data. But from what I could pull together, she was a committed cause-worker. Lots of symbolic arrests at various protests—mostly antiwar and antibusiness. Always anti, by the way."

Jonathan chuckled. "Protesting others' decisions is always easier than making one of your own." Up ahead, the Monstrosity awaited them: the world's only blaze-orange Mazda Miata.

"Well, there's no violence in her background," Venice continued. "None that I could find, anyway. Although it seems that she belongs to a group that the FBI has been watching. Something called the Green

Brigade, a radical save-the-whales outfit. Lots of tree-hugging, but no confirmed violence."

The curious phrasing caught Jonathan's attention. "*Confirmed* violence?"

"Wherever zealots gather, there's always the potential for violence. That's what's got the FBI sitting up and taking notice. There's some suspicion that they burned down a ski lodge under construction a few years ago, but no solid proof." She opened the trunk of her ugly-ass car and invited Jonathan to load his bags into it.

"You couldn't have brought the Hummer?"

"I hate that big thing. Talk about monstrosities. You're free to take a cab if you'd like." She walked toward the driver's side.

Jonathan had to laugh. He always said he liked independent thinkers, and in Venice, he got that with plenty to spare. He filled the trunk with one duffel, and had to thread the other one into the space the Mazda people had the guts to call a backseat. He'd worn shirts that were bigger than the front seat.

He'd just stuffed the second bag in when a familiar voice called from across the parking lot, "Jon!"

A quick look across the lines of cars confirmed that he recognized the voice. He shot an annoyed glare at Venice.

"Oh yeah," she said in a tone more suitable to seeing a pustule than a person. "Ellen called. She needs help from you. But I swear to God, Digger, is you fall for another of her—"

Jonathan shut her down and turned to meet his ex-wife halfway as she navigated the last three rows of cars. He extended his arms for a hug. She allowed herself to be enfolded. "What a wonderful surprise," he said, his voice dripping irony. "You're finally coming back to me."

"Oh, Jon, I'm so frightened."

He broke the embrace and eased her away to arm's length. "Of what?"

She scowled and glared past his shoulder at Venice. "She didn't tell you?"

He followed her gaze. "Who? Venice? Tell me what?"

"I've been trying nonstop to reach you since yesterday."

Taking the mention of her name as an invitation to join, Venice stepped up.

"Is that true?" Jonathan asked. "Has Ellen been trying to reach me?"

Venice planted her fists on her hips. "Don't takc that tone. You've been on the ground for all of five minutes."

He turned back to Ellen. "What is it, then?"

From the corner of his eye he saw Venice assume body language that said, "Wait till you hear this."

"Tibor's missing," Ellen said.

Jonathan smiled. "And you wanted to deliver the wonderful news in person. How thoughtful."

Venice sniggered, earning a withering glare from the ex.

"Must she stay?" Ellen snapped.

"I already told her," Venice explained, "that we don't drop everything to search for someone who's been missing for only a day."

Jonathan looked to Ellen for confirmation.

Her shoulders sagged and her eyes pleaded. "Please, Jon. There are extenuating circumstances."

Tibor Rothman was a certified prick, dedicated to making Jonathan's life as difficult as possible. It wasn't enough that he stole away the woman he still loved; now he insisted on prolonged legal battles to wring even more money out of him. Jonathan wouldn't give Tibor Rothman the sweat off his balls if he was dying of thirst.

But Ellen was looking at him with those enormous brown eyes. "Maybe you could drive me home," he suggested. "We could talk in the car."

Venice protested, "Dig, you can't—"

He raised a hand for silence and softened his tone. "Ven, thanks a million for driving out to meet me. Would you mind awfully driving the bags back to the house for me? Just leave them inside the door."

You bet your behind she minded, and Digger darn well knew it. But this was not the place to air all that. "Sure," she snapped. Venice turned on her heel and stormed back to Glow Bird.

Jonathan took care to stay out of the way as she backed out of the space and roared toward the exit with as much speed as the Miata's lawn mower engine could muster.

"She doesn't like me much, does she?" Ellen observed.

"Thinks you're the devil incarnate," Jonathan said. Venice had witnessed the divorce wars firsthand, and made no bones about which side she was on.

They walked to Ellen's new S-Class Mercedes. Black, with black interior. Jonathan assumed that Tibor had picked the colors to reflect his cheery outlook on the world.

"Did your mission go well?" Ellen asked as she backed out of her space and headed onto the drive that would lead them to the Dulles Toll Road.

Jonathan reared back. "Excuse me?"

"Your mission," Ellen repeated. "Isn't that what you call them?"

"Ellen, we've *never* talked about my work."

The only ear he could see from the passenger seat turned red. "I didn't mean to pry," she said.

He let it go. Jonathan's secrets had always been difficult for Ellen. Even when he'd been doing the bidding of Uncle Sam, it had bothered her that she could not share with her friends what he did for a living. They told people back then that he was regular Army, but he'd always sensed that the ordinariness of the cover story embarrassed her. After he separated from the service and started plying his trade in the civilian world, the need for secrecy doubled in no small part because of the widening fissure in their marriage.

"I worried about you, you know," Ellen said softly as they turned onto Fairfax County Parkway—a shortcut to southbound I-95. At this time of day, anything that reduced the time on the interstate was a terrific strategy.

"I know you did," Jonathan said. The direction of the conversation was making him feel uneasy.

"I still do, actually. I never fully understood any of it, but the randomly occurring scars and bandages were pretty good hints."

"Can we talk about something else, please? I thought this was about Tibor."

She fell silent for several miles of stop-and-go, moving from one light to another. Jonathan figured she'd get to what she needed to say in her own time. "I just don't think that you ever comprehended the level of worry," she said. "You could have shared with me. I wouldn't have sold you out to the Russians."

Jonathan suppressed a chuckle. "The Russian problem was a little before my time."

"The Bosnians, then. Or Al Qaeda. You know what I mean."

"I do know what you mean. And the Defense Investigative Service and the FBI would both disagree with you."

Another mile passed in silence. "I just wanted you to know," Ellen said.

The darkness of her tone startled him, as if her words masked a good-bye. "Are you all right?"

Her voice cracked. "I'm just really, really scared."

"About Tibor?"

"I should have heard from him by now," she said. She sniffed to regain control of her voice. "He always calls when he goes away."

"Has it really been less than twenty-four hours?"

She looked at the clock on the dash. "Not anymore. Almost thirty."

Jonathan knew he needed to be careful here. His hatred of Tibor was stratospheric, but he didn't want that to cloud the sensibility of what he was about to say. "Isn't it a little silly to push the panic button when he's only been out of your sight for a day?"

"He's been out of my sight for three days," she corrected. "Almost four." She turned her head to address Jonathan directly. "He's religious about calling in. He does it every single day. Except yesterday. And today."

Jonathan shifted his gaze to watch the road for her. "Is there reason to suspect foul play?"

"You know what he does for a living. He reports stories that anger people."

"What he does is hardly reporting," Jonathan scoffed. "Ruining people's lives isn't the stuff of Pulitzers."

"I know you don't like him—"

"Imagine that."

"But he's a good man."

"He's a thief and a liar."

Ellen started to argue, then settled herself. "Is that what you need me to say to get you to help me?" she begged. "Okay, he's a thief and a liar and a very bad man. And I love him."

The words cut deeper than he'd expected.

"I know that's not what you want to hear, Jon. And I don't want to hurt you. But I'm desperate."

"Still, we're talking about so little time. Where has he been?"

"Covering a story. I don't know what kind, or what the topic is. I never do. Apparently I'm only attracted to men who insist on shielding their lives from me."

Jonathan smiled at the irony. "Here's the thing, Ellen," he began, silently praying that he sounded earnest and reasonable. "Adults have the right to take time off for themselves. As long as they pay their bills and they don't abandon their children, they're free to take protracted vacations without telling anyone. Seventy-two hours is thought to be the minimum time that an adult be gone before anyone even begins to take an interest."

"But this isn't a vacation."

"It's a job. A story."

She shook her head vehemently. "Not this time. It's more than that. He's been . . . stressed."

He pointed up ahead. "You see those brake lights, right?"

Rather than slowing, she chose to swerve around the backup in the right-hand turn lane, and maybe even sped up a little to make the light.

"Are you worried that he had a heart attack or wrecked his car or something?"

She gave him a fearful look.

"If that's the case, then he's sure to turn up. He'll check into a hospital, or somebody will find him." That last part slipped out before he could stop it. Ellen never had been one for bluntness. "Look, I don't mean to sound crass, but there's a very practical element to finding a missing person. If your real concern is about his health, somebody's going to put the wheels in motion to find you." He cocked his head to look at her profile. "But that's not really your concern, is it?"

Her posture straightened. "What are you implying?"

"I'm implying the obvious," Jonathan said. "Fidelity isn't exactly his long suit. Your relationship is living testament to his willingness to break up a marriage."

She made that puffing sound that always used to spin him up. "He did not break up our marriage, Jon. *You* broke up our marriage by never being married."

"Hey, at least I was always faithful."

She coughed out a laugh. "To the Unit, not to me."

He felt color rising in his cheeks. "I never screwed around on the side. I never would do that."

Ellen glared at him again. "Fidelity isn't just about sex. It's about emotional commitment."

Jonathan let it go. He'd taken full responsibility for their breakup a long time ago, and it had long been a source of great shame. There was no sense in scraping the scab off the barely healed wound. "My point remains," he said. "Ninety percent of the time those adult missing persons turn out to be Exhibit One in a divorce."

Ellen softened, too. "Tibor's not like that. Not anymore. He wouldn't just walk out on me like that."

Saint Tibor. "So what's left?" Jonathan asked. "If he's not cheating on you and you're not worried about him lying dead in a ditch, what *are* you worried about?"

Her race to make the next light failed, and she stood on the brakes to get the Mercedes stopped at the line. "He's been different lately. Just in the last week or so. Anxious, I guess."

"Good anxious or scared anxious?"

"A little of both. He's been consumed by this story.

When I asked him what it was about, all he'd say was that it was big, and that I'd be proud of him when he was done. Then, when he left, he just disappeared. He called me from the office to chat as he walked to the post office to mail something, and another call came in. I got tired of sitting on hold so I hung up. Next time I heard from him he said he was out of town, but he didn't want to tell me where. He called a second night just to tell me that everything was fine, but I sort of knew from his voice that it wasn't. And then I didn't hear from him again."

Jonathan agreed that the circumstances were strange. "But there's just been so little time. Even if he's in imminent danger, we don't even know where to look."

"But you could find that out, couldn't you?"

"You're talking a lot of resources, Ellen. If it turns out to be a dead end—"

"If I was the one missing, would you be able to do something?" Ellen used the question with the skill of a surgeon using a laser, cutting straight to his soul.

"I'll see what I can do," he said.

Chapter Ten

The basement murders and the yard murder were officially two crime scenes, at least for the time being, and now that the State Police technicians had arrived, Gail Bonneville tried her best to stay out of everyone's way. Preferring fresh air, she decided to hang out near the spot where the girl had fallen.

Staying quiet and passive was not her long suit, however. Over to her right, she saw a technician whipping up a batch of plaster. She yelled to him just as he was tipping the pitcher to take a mold of what appeared to be a wheel print out in the grass, about fifty feet from the burned van.

The technician, a youngster who had a certain computer-geekiness about him, responded angrily. "What!"

"Have you photographed that print yet?"

"Of course."

"From a high angle or a low angle?"

"Both," he said.

Gail gave him a hard look, judging his sincerity, and then nodded. "Go ahead then." It had been a trick question, and he'd given the right answer. Gail couldn't count the number of latent fingerprints, footprints, and tire prints she'd seen ruined over the years when the transfer process went awry. Without the backup of good photographs, they'd be left with nothing.

Besides, the Indiana State Police loved to snatch command of major incidents away from local authorities, and Gail knew that if she didn't continually piss on the fire hydrants, the territorial lines could easily become blurred. Her thirteen years with the Bureau had taught her volumes about snatching command.

The charred van, they'd found, was registered to Lionel Patrone, whose DMV record had confirmed that he was one of the corpses in the basement. Another DMV search had found brother Barry. The inside of the van reeked of chemical lachrymator—tear gas—and one of the techs easily found the source, a CS canister that had apparently been tossed in through a broken window in the back door.

Beyond that, the charred vehicle produced little else but rolls of duct tape, singed junk food wrappers, and the twisted, melted remains of a five-gallon gas can. The crime scene techs would continue to search, but the fire damage was so complete that Gail doubted they'd find much of substance. Their best bet for usable clues, she thought, lay with the van's engine block, which had mostly escaped damage from the fire. She wouldn't know for sure until the ballistic analyses were completed, but it looked as if the shooter had thought to load armor-piercing ammo. At least two of those bullets had done their work to kill the van.

Unlike the bodies in the house, Christine Baker appeared to have been killed with a rifle. Her belly wound was through-and-through. They were still scouring the woods looking for the source—indicating something high-velocity, which was entirely consistent with the

5.56 millimeter shell casings they'd found in the yard. The second wound—probably non-fatal in and of itself if it had received prompt medical attention—had made a hell of a mess of the girl's shoulder. All of it was consistent with Gail's theory that the shooter was a professional. Young Christine Baker, however, was not.

Gail sat on a deadfall out of the way and opened the newest of the black-and-white speckled composition notebooks for which she was famous among her colleagues. Identical in every way to the notebooks she'd carried with her through elementary school, they were her favorite means by which to document cases. If you shopped carefully, you could buy them for less than a buck at Staples or Office Depot, and they were nearly indestructible. She liked the way the pages were securely stitched into the cardboard binding. Even more, she liked the way the wide-ruled paper accommodated her loopy and admittedly girlish handwriting.

Every case, no matter how small, got its own notebook, into which went every name, phone number, thought, and intuition. Some cases filled four, five, six volumes—her record was seventeen, and that case had never closed—while others filled only a few pages. Over the years, she'd accumulated dozens of them. She fantasized about writing her memoirs one day, and when the inspiration finally hit, she'd be ready. She even liked to assign titillating labels to her cases, imagining that sometime in the future they would become chapter titles. The most provocative of all would become the title of the book.

She'd already labeled this case "The Samson Mercenary." There was danger in drawing early conclusions, but she was certain she'd nailed this one. The large-caliber entry wounds in the young men's bodies, without corresponding exit wounds, only served to buttress her assumptions. When amateurs used big-bore weapons, they often grooved on the blasting of huge wounds through-and-through, while professionals like Seal Team Six and her alma mater, the FBI's HRT—Hostage Rescue Team—intentionally modified ammunition in such a way that every bullet stopped in its intended target without passing through to harm others. How else could you hope to shoot it out in the confined spaces of an aircraft fuselage and not end up with a bloodbath on your hands?

It was unusually warm for April, easily eighty degrees. She found herself wishing that the killings had occurred closer to the river, if only to have a place to dangle her feet in the water. Wiping sweat from her forehead with a swipe of her forearm, Gail reviewed what she'd already written on this case. The first few pages of every notebook were always reserved for the listing of raw evidence. In the nearly five hours that they'd been working the case, they'd covered a lot of ground.

The evidence all pointed to the work of a hostage rescue specialist. Rare was the time when those people fired only one round, particularly after an explosive entry—the very moment when the bad guys were most unbalanced. The idea was to use enormous, stunning violence in the shortest possible time; seconds, in most cases. The first two shots always went to the center-of-mass—the belly or chest, for the greatest stopping power—and a third shot went to the head as insurance against the possibility of body armor. In HRT and throughout the door-crashing community they called it a triple-tap.

"Hey Boss," said a familiar voice from behind.

Gail looked up to see Jesse Collier approaching, his face pulled back in the wide smile that she was finally beginning to trust. "What are you thinking about?" He nodded to her notebook.

Gail glanced at her notes, then self-consciously closed the book. She didn't like people seeing her raw notes. "I'm trying to decide if our boy was very careful or very foolish."

Jesse cocked his head in what Gail had come to call his puppy-dog face. "I don't follow."

"What do you know about .45s?" she asked.

Jesse smiled. "I sense a Sheriff Gail Bonneville history lesson on the way. Okay, I'll bite. I know that they blow big holes in people, and that the military moved away from them because they're not very accurate."

Gail blushed. "Actually, accuracy was not the problem. Recoil was the problem. Most soldiers could get the first round where they wanted it, but couldn't recover from the kick well enough to place a decent second shot. The military switched to the 9 millimeter because it was user friendly, and because they wanted all NATO rounds to be interchangeable."

She saw equal parts confusion and boredom in Jesse's face.

Gail went on, "In the right hands, the .45 was a hell of a weapon. *Is* a hell of a weapon."

"There was the magazine size, too," Jesse said quickly, almost competitively. "The standard .45 only holds seven rounds."

"Eight, with one in the chamber," Gail corrected. She couldn't help herself. "And that fact is the one that confuses me. Why would our shooter come into a closed environment with so little ammo and triple-tap his bad guys?"

"To kill them?" Jesse guessed.

"How did he know that there weren't four or five people in here?"

Jesse shrugged. "He obviously had another weapon. A rifle. That's what he used to kill the girl. Two-two-three caliber, right?"

Gail still thought of that round as a five-five-six millimeter, but it was all the same. "So how come he didn't use the rifle in the basement? Why the pistol?"

"He must have known," Jesse said.

"Exactly. Which means he'd been watching the place. He knew what he was getting into before he came in."

Another shrug from Jesse. None of this was anything he hadn't already thought of. "Okay, so he was watching. We found the remnants of a fiber optic camera, remember?"

Gail nodded. "But what did he see? Let's talk about the shears we found on the cellar floor. What do you suppose that was all about?" She had her own theory, but this was the way she liked to work out the details. If someone else could draw the same conclusion, then chances were better that the conclusion itself was on target.

"I know you don't believe in coincidences," Jesse said, "so I won't even bother to suggest that maybe they were a means to, you know, shear things. Branches, maybe."

Gail smiled.

"You're thinking that the dead guys were about to cut off a part of the good guy."

Gail nodded. "Exactly. And our shooter knew that."

"Because he'd been watching. We went over that."

"Watching from the outside, no less. We know that because he blew the doors to get in, and yes, the fiber optics tell us that he was doing some high-tech snooping beforehand. What does that tell you about our hero's level of sophistication?"

Jesse caught up with the direction of her logic. "He's no street punk."

"It tells us that he's a professional."

"I thought we already decided that, too."

"We suspected it. Now, I'm trying to talk myself into believing that I'm right."

"So, what's with the girl?"

She paused. The body in the woods was the most perplexing element of her theory. "I don't know," she said.

"Want to hear my thoughts?"

Gail folded her arms across her chest, inadvertently emphasizing her cleavage.

"I think she was what our shooter was waiting for," Jesse said.

Gail didn't understand.

Jesse squatted to bring himself to Gail's eye level. He seemed excited to have the floor, and his excitement made her feel even less threatened by his presence. "The shooter had been watching, waiting. It took a while to put his charges in place. If he wanted just to crash in and take them, he could have done that anytime he wanted to. Especially if he's as good at what he does as you seem to think he is. The evidence in the house shows that the Patrone brothers were all over the place, upstairs and downstairs. Why didn't the shooter take them there, when there was no chance of a stray shot hitting the kidnap victim?"

Gail cringed at his loud use of the phrase, "kidnap victim." "Let's keep that part of the theory to ourselves for now, okay?" she said, checking over her shoulder to see if anyone might be listening. "That's the kind of thing that the press loves to jump on, and if we turn out to be wrong, that would be a hard one to cover."

Jesse nodded. "Yeah, okay, but it's the theory that makes the most sense to me, and it's been bothering me all day. Why would he wait till the worst possible moment to make his entry?"

A scenario started to form in Gail's mind. "That's where the shears come in. They forced his hand by threatening the victim."

"No, before that. I think shearing the victim is why he didn't wait any longer. The question I'm asking is why did he wait as long as he did?"

Gail's eyes traveled to the spot where the girl's corpse had lain. "He was waiting for her."

Jesse clapped his hands together. "Bingo. Which meant that she was part of the plot in the first place."

Gail let that simmer.

Jesse nearly vibrated with excitement. "Clearly he did his homework, and clearly he had good intel. He watched and waited so long because he was waiting for Christine. When the shears came out, the wait had to end. Bang-bang, time to go. I'm figuring that just happened to be when Miss Christine Baker pulled up in her van. Really, really bad timing on her part."

Gail weighed his words and nodded. She liked the theory.

Jesse continued, "Judging from the tire tracks in the driveway, I'm guessing that she pulled up on all of this and got spooked. She panicked and spun her wheels trying to drive away, and our shooter had to stop her. That explains the bullets in the engine. Then she tried to shoot back."

"Problem was, she wasn't very good."

"Not as good as our guy, anyway." Jesse let a beat pass. "I've got to tell you, I'm finding it harder and harder to think bad things about this guy."

Gail scowled. "Don't go there, Jesse, please. This isn't Tombstone, Arizona, and it isn't 1870. People are dead, and it all looks premeditated. That makes it homicide, and last time I checked, juries are the ones who get to determine guilt or innocence. Our job is to find this guy, and to give him a chance to tell his story."

Jesse looked uncomfortable. "You think he should have called us—called the police—before taking on a job like this." His eyes narrowed and he dropped his voice. "If he had, do you really think we could have done this good?"

Gail's eyes grew hot as she tried to determine her deputy's intentions. Her memory still ached with the images from Waco, where she'd been an HRT shooter, and it had been an issue in the early days of their campaign against each other.

"What we need to do," she said, changing the subject completely, "is find out more about these victims. If our theory is right, our best shot is to find out who he was trying to rescue. To get there, we need to find out what links Christine Baker and the Patrone brothers to whoever they tied up in the basement with duct tape. Once we find a link, we've got a case."

Chapter Eleven

Jonathan was thankful that Ellen didn't want to stick around after she dropped him off at home. Every moment he spent with her was an exercise in agony; not because of the divorce, per se, but for the loss of the life he believed they could have had together.

After he'd agreed to help, he'd spent a solid half hour on the phone with Venice, coaxing and cajoling her into doing some preliminary research into the Tibor thing. It was awkward talking in front of Ellen—a fact that Venice understood and capitalized on by making comments to which he couldn't respond—but in the end she gave in. The remainder of the drive was spent convincing Ellen that the information would likely take hours to obtain and that she probably would not hear back from them until tomorrow morning. Like it or not, it was the best they could do.

And now, finally, he was home.

Fisherman's Cove was a peaceful place, a town where people probably could—but rarely did, he would imagine—keep their doors unlocked. The main industry in town was still commercial fishing, along with the businesses that supported fishermen and their suppliers.

Because the main business district still thrived, people had money to spend, and that kept shops and restaurants profitable. The nearest big box stores were ten miles away, too far for everyday shopping needs.

With over two miles of waterfront on a wide part of the Potomac, and with four major commercial marinas, Fisherman's Cove had only recently become a weekend tourist attraction for families wanting to ditch the hassles of Washington and Richmond without incurring the hassles of the major beaches. It's funny, Jonathan thought, how you never think of your hometown being the subject of postcards until people come from somewhere else to take the pictures.

Having rid himself of the childhood estate that was now Resurrection House, Jonathan moved to a place in the business district, just one block up from the river. The house, located on First Street, had been Fisherman's Cove's first firehouse, back in the days when horses pulled the pumpers and hose wagons. As a child, when the building was still an active four bay fire station, Jonathan had fallen in love with the structure's brick design and fifteen-foot ceilings.

Some of Jonathan's fondest memories were tied to his years as unofficial firehouse mascot. As a skinny ten-year-old, Jonathan learned to tie a rescue knot that would allow him to be safely lifted out of a burning basement. When the guys got their hands on a scrap car, young Jonathan would sometimes play the role of the trapped kid who had to be lashed to a backboard. By the time he'd turned twelve, he'd been secured to every conceivable rescue device at least a dozen times. In return for being the mascot, he got to shine (and use) the brass fire pole and wash the apparatus.

Those firemen from his youth—Hack Dean, Big Dave Millan, Fi-Fi Pfeiffer, and the rest—kept him from following too closely in the footsteps of his father. They treated him like a valued member of the team, even as they wouldn't put up with any of his shit. They taught him to play poker, but they expected him to play with his own money and they never threw the game to let him win. Every pot he pulled off the kitchen table was earned fair and square.

In a weird twist of fate, at the very time when he was signing the papers to transfer ownership of his childhood home to Resurrection House, the Cove town commissioners had decided to relocate the firehouse to more modern digs closer to the interstate. Jonathan bought the old station without negotiation. The third floor served as the offices for Security Solutions, and the rest of the 12,000-square-foot building was his home. It cost a fortune to air-condition and heat, but he couldn't imagine living anywhere else.

As Ellen drove off, Jonathan heard running feet closing in on him. You'd think he'd have learned by now. The seventy-five-pound Labrador retriever took him out at the knees. Jonathan saw her only as a black blur as she closed the last five yards, and as she knocked him to the concrete apron of the firehouse, he found himself thankful that this wasn't one of her frequent crotch shots. Jonathan went down hard, laughing all the way as JoeDog bounced around him as if on springs, yelping and whining as she pummeled his face and neck with her cold nose and enormous tongue.

"Hello, Joe," he said, doing a rope-a-dope until she settled down a bit.

At the sound of Jonathan's voice, the five-year-old puppy took off on her victory lap, tearing off at a dead run to the end of the block, then turning on a dime to sprint back at him, breaking off from another collision at the last instant to bolt past him to the other end of the block, where she turned again and repeated the maneuver. It was a dog thing, he figured—like licking your own ass or turning in circles before lying down.

He'd never sought the company of a dog, and he'd never officially adopted her, but she'd appeared in his life one night, whining outside his door on one of those rainy nights that Disney producers love—the kind where you can't turn an animal away. She was maybe eight weeks old, and after she fell asleep on his sofa that first night, she'd claimed it as her own. She spent time at Doug Kramer's place, too. As police chief, Doug called her his K-9 Unit.

As the beast ran her circuit, Jonathan unlocked the personnel door he'd installed in the middle of one of the old overhead doors. Stepping inside, he nearly tripped over the bags Venice had dumped in the foyer. One duffel carried firearms and explosives, the other clothing, body armor, and initiators. The wall of cool air embraced him as he stepped inside. With it came the smell of fresh paint. He'd been remodeling this old place for years, and he wasn't sure it would ever be done. He wasn't sure that he *wanted* it to be done. Hammers, spackle, and power tools were among his favorite toys.

He hefted the bags and humped them through the expansive living room, then through the hallway that led past his dark-paneled library on the right and the dining room on the left. In the very back, he walked through the utility room, and on through the steel door that led to the thirty-foot tower that had once been used to hang folded fifty-foot sections of fire hose to allow them to dry. A door in the far corner of the hose tower led down to the cellar. Years ago, it had been the only part of the place that young Jonathan Gravenow had found too scary to enter.

Now, of course, he had Joe to protect him. She was

right there as he opened the door, and pounded down ahead of him the instant it was open. Joe liked doors, and she liked going first. Again he figured it was a dog thing.

Made of stone and sporting only a six-foot ceiling, the cellar spanned an area that was fifteen by twenty feet. Without looking, Jonathan found the light switch with his shoulder and brought life to the overly bright fluorescent ceiling fixture. Despite his frequent toils in the shadows, he didn't relish living with them in his own home.

He U-turned to the left at the base of the stairs and carried the bags to the far wall, where he dropped them near a long-unused 300-gallon heating-oil tank. He pushed the tank out of the way to expose a heavy wooden door that was painted to look like the surrounding bricks. Behind the tank, the random patchwork of stones wasn't quite as random as it might appear. Without a thought, he found the stone he needed and he dislodged it to reveal an electronic keypad. Jonathan carefully punched in a memorized fifteen-character random cipher. He took his time. He'd designed the system to allow only three consecutive tries, after which it would lock down forever. It was outrageous overkill—more suitable to a Swiss bank vault than a weapons locker—but Jonathan did love his toys.

Besides, there was a second way into the vault that virtually no one knew about. It was equally protected—with the same code, in fact—but the chance of such a monumental screw-up occurring twice was statistically implausible.

With the code entered, he pressed the red button at the bottom of the keypad and heard the hydraulic locks pull away from their housings on the other side. The heavy door floated in silently, revealing his tunnel. It was the one place where Joe wouldn't go. As soon as she heard him moving the stones, she headed back upstairs to shed on the sofa.

The tunnel ran exactly fifty-six yards from this point in his basement, under his parking lot to its termination at the near wall of the basement of St. Katherine's Catholic Church. Jonathan had commissioned the construction years ago from a contractor who owed him the kind of favor that only people in Jonathan's line of work seemed to amass. To protect against mold and critters, he'd finished the interior walls with tiles, the shape and color of which were reminiscent of New York subway stations. About halfway down the hall on the right, a 25-by-25-foot vault served as his weapons locker; its door was built of reinforced steel and resembled the door of a bank vault—the purpose for which it was designed. For this, there was a six-number combination. As he pulled the door open, it nearly blocked the passageway.

Steel cabinets designed for fire protection lined the inside of the vault. With all the concrete and steel, it was difficult to imagine a scenario in which a fire might start in the tunnel, but if it did, he didn't want his stock of high explosives cooking off. Not only would that require an explanation that he didn't relish, but it could also open up a crater big enough to swallow a neighbor or two.

Jonathan liked it down here. He enjoyed the solitude. Much as a gifted artist enjoys the aroma of his paint or clay, he relished the unique aroma of gun oil and pyrotechnics. The first order of business was to clean his weapons. Both had been fired, and that meant both had to be stripped and oiled. Since the weapons had killed people, he would also have to retool the receivers and the rifling before he used them again.

He had just pulled himself up onto the stool in front of the waist-high worktable that dominated the center of the vault when he heard footsteps and whistling in the tunnel. He knew it was Dom. Father Dominic D'Angelo frequently visited Jonathan when he returned from missions, and when he did, he always whistled as he strolled down the tunnel from its secondary access in St. Kate's. Jonathan figured it had something to do with never wanting to startle a man surrounded by firearms.

"I hear you, Dom. I won't shoot you."

"How reassuring," said the voice from nearby. Dom appeared in the doorway smiling and carrying a six-pack of Coors. Tall and trim and sporting a helmet of black hair, Dom had no doubt triggered more than his share of very un-Catholic fantasies among his female parishioners. "I bring hydration. Today I offer up brain cells as a sacrifice for my flock." He dangled the six-pack like a bunch of grapes, offering the cans to be plucked.

Jonathan laughed. "God must be very proud." He reached across the table and pulled one of the beers from the plastic ring. "Where were these sacrifices when I was a teenager? I'd have grown up way more devout."

"We try not to divulge the inner secrets until the flock is old enough to appreciate them." Dom helped himself to the stool opposite Jonathan's and his tone turned serious. "Venice called me. Lots of shooting, I hear. You had us worried, Dig."

"I had me a little worried, too," Jonathan said. Donning a pair of latex gloves, he pulled the magazine out of his M4 and cleared the breech in preparation to strip the weapon. Thanks to previous arrangements, his fingerprints were nowhere on file, but it never hurt to be cautious.

"Can we talk about it?" Dom asked.

Jonathan tossed off a shrug. “Sure.”

“Go ahead then.”

A look. “What?”

“What happened?”

Jonathan scowled. “I made my entry, and the bad guys drew down on me. I had no choice.”

Dom smiled. “I would never think otherwise.” Jonathan Grave and Dominic D’Angelo first met on the day they both moved into Tyler-A, the structurally questionable freshman dormitory on the campus of the College of William and Mary in Virginia. Both shy in their own way, they’d bonded instantly, and became inseparable, shadowing each other all the way through college and into Army OCS, at which point Dom finally listened to the voice that had been calling him to the priesthood while Jonathan pursued his own talents.

Jonathan laid the M4 on the table and made his first real eye contact with the priest. “There was a girl, Dom. Another youngster. I don’t get it. She came up at the last minute. I disabled her van, but she started throwing lead at me.”

Dom took a pull on his beer. “Self defense, right?”

“Absolutely. But that’s not the part that bothers me. These folks were total amateurs. They all had IDs on them, they were hotheads. I got the package home safely, but I’m not convinced that we got the top dog on this one.”

“Maybe you just need to declare victory and drink your beer,” Dom ventured.

Jonathan downed half of his Coors and wiped his mouth with his forearm. “There’s a lot that’s odd about this mission,” he said, leaning forward onto his elbows.

“Do tell. I’m told I’m a pretty good listener.”

Jonathan gathered his thoughts. “The client, a guy named Stephenson Hughes, contacted me the usual way, through one of the blind e-mail addresses. He tells me that his kid is missing and that the kidnappers are talking about a huge ransom. It took forever to track leads down to a farm in Indiana, where I found the kid."

"You reunited him with his family?"

Jonathan lifted one shoulder. "I got him to where he needed to be."

Dom looked confused. "Then it's a happy ending. What's the problem?"

"I guess it's the dichotomy of it all. On one hand, it feels very professional, yet on the other it seems Mickey Mouse and amateur."

Dom raised his can. "I'll drink to the amateurs."

Jonathan smiled, but there was no humor in it. "Another thing. According to the kid I rescued, there was no way that anyone in his family could have afforded to pay my fee."

The priest shrugged. "Kids don't know anything about their parents' finances."

Jonathan shrugged back. "I suppose."

Silence followed as they approached the path they'd trod together so many times over the years.

"Okay," Dom said, finally. "Let's hear it. In total, how many fewer souls will walk the earth tomorrow than walked it today?"

Jonathan took his time answering. Killing always hurt, but today it seemed especially wasteful. "Too many," he said.

Dom's cocked head, waiting.

"Three," Jonathan said. "The girl suffered."

Dom nodded some more. Their relationship had evolved past platitudes and rationalizations a long time ago. That Digger detested every shot he fired and that he only killed for the right reasons did nothing to ease the burden that two more mothers had forever lost their children at his hand. It was the curse of the warrior that good works brought misery.

Dom downed the rest of his beer and stood abruptly. “Consider it done.”

It was time for the final act to every one of Jonathan’s missions. Standing to gain better access to the front pocket of his trousers, Dom withdrew the tiny leather pouch that contained a square patch of purple satin. He shook it and the fabric fell away to form a stole. Dom kissed it and draped it over his neck. Then he carried his stool to Jonathan’s side of the worktable and bowed his head while Digger crossed himself.

Jonathan said, “Bless me, Father, for I have sinned . . .”

Chapter Twelve

In this part of southern Indiana, the scenery never changed. On either side of the interstate, rolling farmlands extended to the horizon. Rather than heading back to the office, where she would have to deal with the press, curious staffers, and the endless administrivia that defined the job of a sheriff in a small community, Gail Bonneville chose instead to go home.

In Samson, "home" meant the house of her dreams, complete with seven gables and a deep porch that wrapped the front and two sides. The backyard featured the overgrown remains of what had once been a magnificent garden. With a little imagination, she could still see within the out-of-control boxwoods the shadowy remains of a sculptured pig, turtle, and donkey. Or maybe a goat. A farm animal of some sort.

Fixing up the gardens and restoring them to their previous grandeur was high on the list of things that Gail was going to take care of once she got a little extra cash. Fixing the gardens, in fact, was trumped only by her goal of buying furniture for the living room, dining room, library, parlor, and three spare bedrooms.

Gail lived in the Petrie house, named for the family who'd built it in 1915. In the early 1990s, Natalie Petrie, the ancient family scion, had started listening more intently to television evangelists than she did to the pleas of her own children. By the time the children could convince a court to intervene, they had seen their inheritance plummet from something close to $10 million to something more along the lines of a dollar ninety-five.

It was literally the house of Gail's dreams, à la Natalie Wood in *Miracle on 34th Street*. She offered the family's asking price, and within days, the deed was done. Now, eight months later, workers still labored on to bring the plumbing and electrical services into the twentieth century, never mind the twenty-first.

Gail's purchase of the Petrie house was a source of great scuttlebutt. How could a single woman on a public servant's salary afford to pay $550,000 for a house, and then go on to fund extensive repairs and renovations? Her political enemies had their theories, of course, fueled by ugly rumors, but few people actually believed that she was selling drugs out of the basement, or had accepted hush money to protect those who did.

She protected the reality as nobody's business. Her father had spun an independent accounting firm into a fairly successful investment practice, and when he passed away, he'd left her with enough of a nest egg that she could afford her love of law enforcement without suffering the financial hardship that most cops endured. She could afford to tell the Bureau where they could stick their good-old-boy network. She'd never been a boy, never would be, and never even rode a bicycle as a child. She was done with working three times as hard as her penis-carrying colleagues just to get some modicum of recognition, and she was doubly done with the small-minded resentment that accompanied the recognition when it finally came.

After her father succumbed to the cancer that had been eating him for over a decade, she'd left the Bureau with extreme prejudice, not caring if she ever saw a badge again. After a while, though, when you're good at it, busting bad guys becomes a part of your DNA. She'd heard about the desire of the local Democratic Party to find themselves a good female candidate for sheriff in Samson, and the rest, as they say, was . . . well, you know.

The ten-block-square section that defined downtown Samson looked like something off a movie set for Depression-era urban living. Its main streets sported storefronts and taxpayer construction that looked at first glimpse to be the American dream—all the infrastructure for a midsize city combined with the feel of a small town. She liked the people here more than she didn't like them, but a reality of law enforcement in a small community is that you could never allow yourself to get but so close. Every citizen was her boss, and one day, any one of them could end up on the business end of her nightstick. When the borders were as close as they were in Samson, and the line between accepting help and accepting graft was so fine, it helped to keep people at arms' length.

Gail was just entering her driveway when her cell phone rang. "Sheriff Bonneville."

"Afternoon, Sheriff," said a very cheerful and very southern voice. "This is Max Mentor with the state crime lab. How you doin'?"

Gail smiled. She'd worked with Max a couple of times since her election and always found the experience to be pleasant. "I'll be better when you guys can give me some hard data."

Max laughed. "Then I'm about to make your day. You ready to copy?"

Gail opened her notebook to a new page, balanced it on the center console, and clicked her pen. "Couldn't be readier."

"Okay, I got info on ground impressions you sent in. Footprints first, because they're going to be the least help to you. The boot prints are a standard Vibram sole that you can find on any one of dozens of different brands of shoes. Boots, most likely, the sort that you could find in a recreational equipment outfitter."

"Or at a tactical supply store?"

The pause told her that Max hadn't considered that. "You mean, gun nut stores? Where you can buy bulletproof vests for hunting? Yeah, I suppose you could buy them there. So, now you're thinking this guy is a cop?"

"Nah, I'm just thinking out loud. What else do you have?"

"Okay, let's talk about the tire prints. Somethin' weird about those, you know? We only got prints. No tracks. It's like it just appeared there. The tread's unusual, too—not typical of any car or truck in the database."

Gail felt an excited flutter in her chest. "Are you thinking helicopter?"

"Bingo. Given the wheelbase and the depth of the depressions relative to the weather conditions, we're looking at something pretty big."

"Help me with 'big,' Max. We talking Vietnam-era Huey?"

"Oh, God, no. Not that big. Probaby something more like the slick Aerospatial units they've got out there now.

Besides, Hueys had skids, not tires. I've got a buddy of mine who's a plane fanatic going through his databases to see if he can cross-reference the measurements with a particular model. I'll tell you he's not very optimistic. But no harm in trying."

Gail entered the data into her notebook. "You got stuff on the bullets now?"

"Yep, and you were right about the slugs in the wall down in that basement. Both of our boys contributed to those. Letter A came from the .38 revolver. B came from the .380." He was referring to the evidence diagram they'd prepared. "Oh, and as you might have guessed, the shell on the front porch bears the same receiver marks as the .380."

She wrote some more. "Anything on the slugs that killed them?"

"Not yet," Max said. "Somebody's gotta carve 'em out before I can look at 'em. The autopsies ain't finished. Three bodies in one day. It'd take a while to carve that many turkeys on Thanksgiving."

Okay, that was more colorful than she liked. "Anything else?"

"You betcha. We confirmed that the piss and shit are both human, but that's about as far as we've gotten. We were able to pick up a few latents off the floor, but nothing usable. Where we do have readable prints of something, they look like gloves. Your killer was good, Sheriff. If I were a bettin' man, I'd say that he wiped the place down before he left."

Gail teased, "Why, Max, if you didn't work for our side, I'd swear that I hear admiration in your voice."

"Hey, I admire anybody who's good at what they do. I found fibers around the pockets on one of the basement boys that matches fibers we took off Christine Baker's pockets. It's a Nomex/Kevlar mix. There's another tactical team connection for you. The prints I was telling you about make me think they had leather palms—also consistent with ballistic gloves. If you find the gloves, they should have enough blood on them to match the owner to the scene."

Gail laughed in spite of herself. "I'm guessing that our boy's smarter than that. What else have you got?"

"Just like a woman. Ain't never enough to have what I give you, you always want more."

"Size matters, Max, what can I say?"

"Well, I got bad news on the explosive residue. Looks like C4 and standard-issue det cord. PETN. Nothing exotic. With fifty bucks and a wink, you can buy it from your local hardware store."

Gail recorded his words verbatim. "And the detonators?"

"Your boy knows how to make them go away. I'm guessing that he used some sort of remote mechanism—I found a hair-size bit of wire that might have been an antenna—but there again, a twelve-year-old who knows what he's doing can put the circuitry together at RadioShack."

The phone went silent as she wrote some more. "Is that all of it?"

"For now. I'll get back to you when I know something about the killer's bullets."

"Now I'll give you a prediction," Gail said. "Five to one, you won't find anything useful on the slugs."

"Sounds like somebody's working on a theory."

"Theories make me feel alive, Max."

She hung up the phone, and right away the wheels of her imagination started to whir. She no longer harbored any doubt at all that her shooter was a consummate professional. He wasn't one of the goombah thugs that the Italian mobs used to use for hits, and he certainly wasn't the friend of a friend who just happened to be a gun nut. This guy had been able to get in and out of Samson with surgical precision, with his mission accomplished and his targets dead. She was equally convinced that his mission was a righteous one—to rescue somebody from the clutches of those who lay dead at the Patrone farmhouse.

Opening her phone again, she punched in a speed dial number and waited for Jesse Collier to pick up.

"Hello, Sheriff," he answered

"Hi, Jesse. I have a mission for you. I just found out from the lab that our hypothesis about the shooter coming by helicopter is right. I need you to find the chopper for me."

"Do we know where it is?"

"Of course not. If I knew where it was, I'd find it myself and hog all the glory." She hoped that her smile showed in her voice. "But I'm thinking that it might not be impossible. First of all, let's assume that our shooter is an out-of-towner."

"I'd sure like to think he's not a neighbor."

"Helicopters only have but so much range on them, so he must have rented the one he used from an airport that's reasonably close by."

"You want me to call the airports?"

"Exactly. But I want you to think it all the way through with me. The chopper was bigger than the standard news chopper, according to Max Mentor. So that's one data point. The next one is the timing. How many overnight rentals can there be on the records?"

"Not many, I can't imagine," Jesse said. "I'd think most of the rentals are for long periods of time. Months and years, not days. Rich folks got enough money to spend on a full-time pilot, but they don't want to deal with all the ownership crap."

"So, that's good, right? It should be easy to trace."

"It'll be as easy as it is. Sounds like a long shot to me, tell you the truth. How do we know he doesn't have his own, or that he doesn't just borrow it from a friend? If I need a tractor for an afternoon, I don't rent one, I borrow my neighbor's."

There was that fluttery feeling again. Something in Jesse's words caught Gail's imagination. "Suppose he borrowed a whole airplane?" She paused as she field-tested the thought. "If our shooter is from out of town, then it only makes sense that he flew in, right?"

Jesse wasn't buying. "Or he could have driven or taken a train."

"But if he flew, he wouldn't fly commercial," she pressed.

"Not with all the armaments and shit, no. Christ, one dog get a whiff of that and it would be all over for him. All the more reason to drive."

Gail felt strongly about this. "I don't think he would. An operation like this, he'd want to put as much mileage behind him as he could, as fast as he could. Don't you think?"

"I think it's a leap, but it's worth exploring," Jesse said. "I'll call every airport within a hundred miles. See what turns up."

APRIL 21

Chapter Thirteen

Jonathan Grave considered himself fortunate that he did not dream. Lord knew he'd seen enough to earn a lifetime of nightmares, but so far they'd kept their distance. He figured it had something to do with the years of sleeping on command. When you're in the boonies, waiting for hours or days for a go order, you learn to make a few minutes of sleep in the rain feel like a full night at the Waldorf.

Dom had his own theory on the dreams, as Dom had his own theory on every aspect of Jonathan's life: normal people woke up to escape their nightmares; for Jonathan it was the other way around—he sought sleep to avoid the reality of his days.

Tonight, the telephone sounded ultra-amplified, and he knew before he moved that bad news was on the way. Come to think of it, he couldn't remember a time when a phone call had brought good news. Add the fact that it was the middle of the night, and the sense of dread trebled. As he swung his head to look at the clock, the ghosts of last night's eighth and ninth beers haunted him with bed-spins. The LED readout burned

9:10 into his retinas. Okay, forget the part about being the middle of the night.

He snatched the phone off its cradle. "This had better be one hell of an emergency," he grumbled.

It was Venice. "Digger, I'm sorry. I know how hard repentance is on your liver, but I had to call you. The police are looking for you."

Wrong about the middle of the night, but dead-nuts right about the bad news. "What did I do?" He forced himself to sound even grumpier to cover for the knot that just formed in his gut. As much as he talked bravely to Thomas Hughes about being invisible, he did harbor a special fear of crossing swords with the law.

"You didn't do anything," Venice said. "It's Ellen. They're at her house, and something bad has happened there."

As if someone had thrown a switch, Jonathan came completely awake and his head was clear. "What happened to her?"

"I don't know. They wouldn't tell me. They called the office looking for you and I told them that I'd be in touch the instant I hung up with them. I have a number for you to call."

Jonathan swung his feet to the floor and stood. "You do it," he said. "Call them and tell them that I'm on my way. Without traffic I can be at Ellen's house in an hour." He didn't wait for her to confirm before he dropped the receiver back onto its cradle.

The Rothman home—Ellen's home—sat on five acres atop a hill in Vienna, Virginia, a tribute to Tibor Rothman's ego. Serviced by a 300-foot driveway, the 5,000-square-foot colonial was so perfectly proportioned that from the road it looked a fraction of its actual size. It wasn't until you approached up that long driveway that you saw the grandeur of the place. Every time he saw it, Jonathan couldn't help but admire the three acres of front lawn—the very lawn that was now packed with all manner of police vehicles, most of them parked in the grass. Closest to the garage, parked on the pavement, was a large van labeled CRIME SCENE UNIT in the distinctive red, white, and blue lettering of the Fairfax County Police Department.

Of the half dozen or so officers milling about, all of them reacted defensively as Jonathan piloted his BMW M6 up the lawn to park near their vehicles. Watching their hands twitch near their sidearms, Jonathan realized that during his days in Iraq, he'd have guiltlessly shot anyone who tried a similar stunt at one of his roadblocks.

"I'm Jonathan Grave," he explained to the approaching uniforms as he stepped onto the grass. "I was asked to report here by an Officer Weatherby. Ellen Grave is my ex wife."

It seemed to be what the cops wanted to hear. "*Detective* Weatherby is inside," one of them said. "I'll get him for you." The cop started walking.

Jonathan followed.

The cop stopped short, clearly annoyed. "Wait here, sir. I'll bring the detective out to you."

"She was my *wife*, Officer. I have a right."

The cop pointed emphatically at the ground. "Here," he said.

For the first time, it occurred to Jonathan that he might need a lawyer, that he was very possibly being considered as a suspect in whatever had happened.

A barrel of a man with a huge head and a fleshy face appeared at the front door. He scowled as he listened to the uniformed officer, and he followed the man's pointing finger to make eye contact with Jonathan. The detective nodded curtly, and walked down the stairs to the front yard. As he closed to within a few feet, he extended his hand. "I'm Detective Weatherby," he said. There was a humorless intensity about the man that reminded Jonathan of a thousand other pricks he'd met over the years who confused professional intimidation with the need to be an asshole.

Jonathan shook the cop's hand and wasn't the least surprised to find that he was of the bone-crushing school of hospitality. "Jonathan Grave. What's going on here?"

"Are you the husband?"

"Ex. Is Ellen all right?"

"When did you see her last?"

Jonathan felt his blood pressure rising. "Look, Detective, I swear to God I'll answer any and all questions you may have, but I want to know if she's hurt."

Weatherby stewed, and then nodded. "Yes, sir, I'm afraid she is. It appears that someone broke into the house and hurt her very badly."

Jonathan's anger transformed to fear. "*How* badly?"

"I'm not a doctor. I don't know how to answer that."

"She's alive."

"Yes."

"And expected to remain that way?"

Weatherby averted his eyes.

Jonathan's world spun. "Jesus, what happened to her?"

The detective answered carefully. "She was beaten up pretty bad. The house has been torn apart."

"What, like she stumbled in on a burglar and he panicked?"

"Actually, no, sir, it was nothing like that at all. To

my eye, it appears as though she was targeted specifically, and that the people who did so were looking for something they thought she had."

Jonathan let the pieces drop. "You're saying she was tortured?"

Weatherby studied Jonathan's face. "Yes, sir, that's exactly what I'm saying. Now, I don't have any more details, okay? That's all I know. You'll have to get the rest from the hospital."

Jonathan turned back toward his car. "Which hospital?"

"Whoa!" Weatherby commanded. "Not yet. I need to ask you some questions."

"Am I a suspect?"

"Of course you are. You're the ex-husband. Next to the current husband, you're number one on the list. By the way, where is Mr. Rothman?"

At one level, Jonathan admired the cop's candor. Mostly, though, it annoyed him. "It's not my turn to watch him."

"I gather from your tone that you don't like him much?"

Jonathan snorted. "Understatement of the decade. I can't stand the son of a bitch. A quick hike to the courthouse will show you why."

Weatherby waited for it.

"For the past five years, we've been locked in a lawsuit over money I inherited, yet he somehow feels he has a right to own."

Weatherby scowled. "So there really is bad blood between you all."

"Run into a lot of friendly divorces, Detective? Of course there's bad blood. But I assure you there's no homicidal blood."

Weatherby regarded his prey with slit eyes, then gestured toward the front door with a toss of his head. "Come on inside."

On a different day, the first thing a visitor to the Rothman home would have noticed was the splendor of the hardwood floors and the intricacy of the moldings and wainscoting. It was a home designed to dazzle visitors, and it rarely failed in its mission.

Today, though, the intricate architectural details were invisible against the savage dismemberment of the place. Inside the front door to the left, every book had been pulled from the shelves of Tibor's library, his pride-and-joy collection of first editions of French and English literature. Pages were torn from the bindings and the cushions of the dark leather furniture had been slashed, with feathers and stuffing erupting from massive wounds. The same level of damage pervaded everywhere. It was as if someone had turned the house upside down and shaken it.

Weatherby led the way as if he owned the place, marching Jonathan down the main hall into the kitchen and then a hard right into the dining room, where the police had established a makeshift command post. The detective pointed to an upholstered hardback chair. "Take a load off," he said.

Jonathan continued to stand, not so much on principle as a need to keep examining the house. "Where did you find Ellen?"

"Upstairs. In the bedroom."

"I want to see."

"I don't think you do."

The gravity of Weatherby's tone made a connection. "Jesus, Detective, what did they do to her?"

The cop took a long, loud breath through his nose. "Start with the worst you can imagine, and that would be only the beginning. Twenty-three years on the force, Mr. Grave, and this is the worst I've seen. Sorry to put it to you that way, but I'm shocked that she survived."

Jonathan's mind whirled out of control. The worst he could imagine was pretty goddamn awful. His brain conjured images of Rwandan women with their breasts sliced off, and of Croatian women raped by bayonets. Surely, Weatherby assessed "the worst" on a different scale than that. "Was she raped?"

Weatherby answered with his eyes the instant he looked away. "Savagely. Repeatedly, I would guess. And there was some torture, though I'd rather not go into the details. She was also stabbed."

Now it was time to sit. Jonathan helped himself to the offered chair. "Who would do something like that?"

"That's why we called for you."

"For Christ's sake, Detective, you couldn't possibly think I had somthing to do with that."

Weatherby let his guard drop an inch. "As I mentioned outside, I sort of have to, but in my gut, no, I don't believe you did. Can you account for your whereabouts last night?"

"I was downing beers with a buddy. A priest, in fact. Father Dominic D'Angelo, pastor of the St. Katherine's parish in Fisherman's Cove." Responding to the cop's confusion, he added, "It's a community down in the Northern Neck."

Weatherby made a note. Clearly, Dom should expect a call soon. Jonathan gave him the phone number from memory.

"What do you do for a living, sir?" Weatherby asked.

"I'm a private investigator. I run a company called

Security Solutions. I don't have a card with me, but we're in the book. Our office is in my home."

Another note. "I don't know many PIs who have enough money that someone with a house like this would want to hijack it in the courts." Translation: Jonathan's story had holes.

"I was born well," Jonathan said.

Weatherby scowled.

"My mother was quite wealthy, and when she died, my father's name went on the accounts."

"And what was the source of her money?"

This couldn't possibly have anything to do with the detective's investigation, but to refuse to answer would have just made things more difficult. "Her father was in the scrap business. My father worked for him, and inherited the business when the old man died."

Weatherby smiled. "The scrap business? Like Sanford and Son, the junk dealers on television way back?"

Everyone always made the same connection in their minds, and they were always wrong. "My parents' name was Gravenow. My father was Simon Gravenow."

Now he had Weatherby's attention. "*The* Simon Gravenow?"

Jonathan nodded. His father had been a fixture on the dark side of Washington politics for years—the subject of more grand jury and independent counsel investigations than anyone on the planet.

"And he got his money in the junk business?"

"Scrap, not junk," Jonathan said. "There's a difference." And that, he didn't add, was only the legitimate cover for the way his father had really made his living.

"So if he's your dad, why do you have a different last name?"

"He's not my *dad*, Detective, he's my *father*. There's a difference there, too."

"I don't understand."

Jonathan shrugged. "We're not here to talk about my childhood. You said that Ellen was tortured. . . .

"That makes no sense. It's impossible for me to believe that she could cross paths with people who are capable of that."

"Maybe she wasn't the real target," Weatherby offered. "What do you know about Tibor Rothman?"

"Beyond the fact that he's an asshole, not much." Could this explain Ellen's fears that Tibor was missing?

"We've contacted his newspaper," Weatherby went on, "but no onc has heard from him for a while. Any ideas where he might have gone?"

"As you might have deduced, we don't keep in close contact. He certainly doesn't clear his travel schedule with me."

"So you know he's been traveling?"

Jonathan suppressed a smile. Cops were the same everywhere; so constantly on the lookout for that *Columbo* a-ha moment that they loved to pounce on innocent phrases. "I didn't say that, Detective. You told me that he hadn't been in the office, and I connected the dots. That's all. You're thinking that he might have held the bit of information that the torturers were looking for?"

"The thought crossed my mind. It also crossed my mind that maybe Mrs. Rothman was trying to track him down when she called you yesterday." Weatherby had sprung that last part as a trap, and it nearly worked. Jonathan hadn't seen it coming, but he was experienced at this particular form of poker.

"Actually, she didn't call *me*, she called my office and spoke with one of my managers. At the time of the call, he hadn't been missing for more than twenty-four hours, and, frankly, I didn't much care if he was missing or not. I told Venice, the manager, to do a quick credit card trace to see what she could turn up."

"And?"

Jonathan shrugged. "I don't know. I woke up to the call to come here, so we haven't discussed any of it this morning." Jonathan was in the business of parsing information, and he determined that this much was easily traceable and therefore safe to relay. If he was less than forthcoming, Weatherby would know it within hours if not minutes. The rest of it—his ride home with Ellen—was nobody's business.

"Does Mr. Rothman have any enemies that you know of?"

Jonathan scowled. "You know what he does for a living."

"I know he's a writer."

"But you don't know what he writes?"

Weatherby shook his head. "I'm pretty much a sports page guy."

"Well, you won't find Tibor Rothman articles there. He's a syndicated columnist. A muckraker. A career killer. He'd call himself an 'investigative reporter,' but that's just code for legitimized gossipmonger. He says whatever he wants, then hides behind the First Amendment when he gets the details wrong. If you could line up every person with a reason to harm Tibor, I imagine it would take you three weeks to get through the interviews."

"Is he political?"

"Aren't they all? They wake up every morning and proclaim themselves to be the smartest guys in the room. If you disagree, you get hammered in their column."

Weatherby's eyes narrowed, and Jonathan caught the subtext.

"Oh, relax, Detective. I freely admit to motive and means. And probably opportunity, too, if you stretch far enough. What I don't have is the desire. If you want me to speak frankly to you, then you need to suspend your suspicion for a while. Otherwise, I'll call for a lawyer, and give you nothing. Which will it be?"

Weatherby took his time answering. "You can speak freely," he said.

Jonathan studied the man's face. Weatherby could be lying through his ass, and none of it would matter. The cops were going to check out everything he said anyway. As long as he stayed as near the truth as he could afford, he'd be okay. And the more cooperative he was, the sooner he'd get the hell out of here and on to the hospital to be with Ellen. "Thank you," he said.

"Let me ask you one other thing, Mr. Grave. Is it at all likely that the person who ransacked the house was in fact looking for *you?*"

The question shocked him. "I don't see how."

Weatherby recrossed his legs. "Well, you're in the window-peeping business, right? Private detective? Isn't that what 'security' really means in Security Solutions?"

That was a gratuitous shot. "My clients include insurance companies and Fortune 500 firms who need to gather intelligence data for one reason or another. I've never thought of it as window-peeping. Do you think of yourself as a child-shooter?" His own gratuitous jab recalled a recent incident in which an off-duty county cop shot and killed a kid who was trying to drive away from a pancake house after stealing a couple of bucks. The rising color in Weatherby's face told him he'd scored.

Jonathan stood. "You know what, Weatherby? We're done here. I'm going to the hospital to see Ellen." The detective grabbed his arm to stop him. Under any other circumstance, Jonathan would have broken his jaw.

"Wait a second," Weatherby said. "I'm sorry. I shouldn't have characterized your business that way. I don't know why I did."

Jonathan pulled his arm away. "Bullshit doesn't become you, Detective. You characterized my business that way because you wanted to get a rise out of me. Now you're apologizing to see how fast I recover. Apparently you think you're the only one who reads basic psychology texts. I've been working hard to play things straight with you while you're playing cop games with me. I've never had much of a bullshit tolerance, and you've soaked me to saturation in just a few minutes."

It was a sore point with private investigators everywhere. Cops never showed a fraction of the respect many of them were owed. While there were ample ambulance-chasing incompetents out there, far more PIs were perfectly professional, and Jonathan could point to a dozen cases in which associates in his firm had found evidence that the police had either missed, never thought to investigate, or merely got wrong. The root of the animosity, Jonathan was convinced, lay in the fact that a county cop in the middle of his career was lucky to pull in a fraction of the salary at which associates in Security Solutions began their careers.

Weatherby stood be to at eye level. "Duly noted. But you didn't answer my question."

"The question being whether the bad guys might have actually been after me? I suppose it's possible. Every legal case has a loser, and losers are never happy."

"I'll need a list of your clients," Weatherby said. The

lack of eye contact telegraphed that he knew that he was asking the impossible.

"Not gonna happen."

Eye contact returned, and it was not pleasant.

"Client confidentiality," Jonathan explained, as if the detective didn't already know. "And before you waste a lot of time arguing, just imagine me not budging and possessing the resources to take my case all the way to the Supreme Court. Anything else?"

Weatherby examined his notes, then looked up with a squint that foretold something unpleasant. "Do the Rothmans have any children?"

Jonathan nodded. "Ellen did, by her first marriage. I was her second. A boy. His name was Kyle. He'd have been around twelve by now."

"He's no longer alive, I take it." People are never comfortable using the word "dead" when it comes to children.

"He drowned on a camping trip about five years ago."

Weatherby made a note. "A family trip?"

Just the mention of the event tightened his stomach even more. "No, a Scout trip. They were canoeing and tipped over. Kyle got caught in a hydraulic and they couldn't get him out in time. It was awful." He didn't bother to mention that he himself was on deployment at the time and unable to lend any support.

Weatherby took longer than necessary to jot his note. Respect for the dead, maybe. "What's the nature of your legal battle with Mr. Rothman?" he asked when he was done.

Jonathan sighed. He didn't welcome this deep a probe into his private life. "It's complicated," he said.

Weatherby gave a commiserating nod. "Legal battles usually are."

What the hell. "It's about my inheritance—sort of. As you probably know, I am not yet an orphan. Simon Gravenow is still a guest of Uncle Sam. When he saw that it was all going to hell, and that he was going to prison, he transferred most of his holdings into my name—not because he wanted me to have them, but to keep them out of the government's hands."

Weatherby cocked an eyebrow. "How much?"

"A lot."

"Seven figures?"

"Nine figures. A *whole* lot. Ellen and I were married at the time, and while Virginia is not a community property state, Tibor wishes it was . . ." He let Weatherby connect the dots for himself.

The cop looked confused. "So it's your wife who's suing you?"

Jonathan shook his head. "No, that's all Tibor. He smells money like a shark smells blood. He's rich enough to keep the battle going, and I'm rich enough to keep him outside the gates. Meanwhile, the lawyers are thrilled."

Weatherby said nothing as he jotted a paragraph, then looked up. "Is there any other family that I should know about?" he asked.

"Tibor has family in upstate New York, I think," Jonathan said. "A sister. I don't know why I know that, but I'm pretty sure. Never met them. Can I go now?"

Weatherby regarded him, unblinking. "Can I ask you what your intentions are?"

Another surprising question. "What do you mean?"

"I'm getting a vibe that you're thinking about taking justice into your own hands."

Jonathan had to award a point to the cop's column on that one. It was a sucker punch that landed perfectly. "If you're asking me if I'm likely to pursue my own investigation, then my answer is that it's none of your business." He started walking away, retreating through the ravaged living room toward the front door.

"If you interfere, I'll arrest you," Weatherby called after him.

Jonathan tossed off a wave without looking. "Thanks for the warning," he said. If he was first to touch the people who hurt Ellen, no one would ever find what was left of their bodies.

Somehow, the flock of cars outside had grown even larger. From the front stoop, Jonathan thought someone might have boxed him in with a nondescript Chevrolet. As he walked closer, though, he realized that the other driver had in fact left enough space, thus eliminating the need for Jonathan to break out the Chevy's windows and flatten its tires.

He had just opened the door to climb into his BMW when someone called his name from behind. He turned to see a rail-thin disheveled man in his late thirties climbing out of the Chevy. He knew just from his appearance that the guy was a reporter. Jonathan waited for him to approach. "Do I know you?" he asked.

"So you *are* Mr. Grave? Jonathan Grave?"

"You'd be wise to get to the point. This isn't a day to be on my bad side."

The man stopped just out of range. "I'm Will Joyce with the *Washington Post*. I'm wondering if I could ask you a few questions."

"You a friend of Tibor's?"

"A colleague, if not a friend." Funny how Tibor Rothman inspired that kind of noncommitment from people who knew him.

"How do you know me?" Jonathan asked.

"You used to be married to Ellen, right?"

Jonathan smiled. "You first. How do you know me?"

Joyce looked at his feet, clearly conflicted. Then he made up his mind. "Okay, fine," he said. "Tibor mentioned you."

"In what context?"

Joyce weighed his words. "Let's just say you weren't his favorite person."

"Why does this concern you?"

"That doesn't concern me. What does concern me is that I should have heard from him by now, and I haven't. Now I come by his house and I see all of this. Is he dead in there or something?"

"No, but my ex-wife was assaulted. Tibor is nowhere to be found, apparently."

Joyce's face registered shock. "You're not suggesting he had something to do with it."

Jonathan shrugged. He cocked his head. "Why should you have heard from him?"

"He was working on a story. Apparently something pretty scary." He hesitated. "Something about you, in fact."

"What about me?"

Joyce shook his head. "I saw him pulling up some research on you a few days ago."

Oh, Christ, Jonathan thought. There was no way that could be good.

"Breaking news to me, Mr. Joyce," Jonathan said.

"So you don't know anything about what happened in there?" He nodded to the house.

"I'm not the police. Ask them your questions. I'm off to visit Ellen in the hospital." He had no idea why he felt compelled to share that detail, and he was angry at himself for doing so.

Joyce reached into his front pocket and pulled out a stack of business cards. He gave one to Jonathan. "If you ever need to speak to me . . ."

"I won't," Jonathan said.

"But in case you do." He let the card hover in the air until Jonathan had no choice but to snatch it away and stuff it in his shirt pocket without looking. Jonathan was halfway into his seat when Joyce added, "I hope she's okay, Mr. Grave."

Jonathan closed the door.

CHAPTER FOURTEEN

If there was such a thing as the perfect place to sustain critical injuries, Fairfax County, Virginia, was it, thanks in no small part to the Inova Fairfax Hospital system. The sprawling namesake for the system—Fairfax Hospital itself—was the jewel in the crown. Located on Gallows Road, just a chip-shot from the Beltway, the hospital attracted the best in every medical discipline, from neurology to cardiology, and the miraculous save rate in their Level-One trauma center rivaled that of any medical facility in the world.

Jonathan Grave knew all of this, but as he sat outside the trauma department, just another face among dozens of terrified relatives desperate to squeeze some trace of good news out of a night that had brought mostly bad, the record of past miracles meant little. The *present*—today, now, this moment—gleamed brilliant and awful while the future loomed in shades of gray and black. It didn't help that most of the doctors looked like they might have still been in college, and all seemed more comfortable speaking Urdu than English.

Dom had joined him, alerted by Venice after Jonathan had called her from his car. After three hours, the surgical team was still working on Ellen, and no one could find time to speak with the ex-husband.

"How are you doing?" Dom asked, his voice scarcely a whisper.

Jonathan answered with a look. He didn't trust his voice, and he sure as hell didn't trust the hot blood that was pumping through his veins. The beasts who did this were going to pay. Dearly. He was going to hunt them down and kill them, and when he was done, he was going to defile the bodies, set them ablaze, and piss on their ashes.

"Get rid of the thoughts, Dig," Dom whispered, his eyes boring through Jonathan. "You're not an assassin. You're not a vigilante. You've said it a thousand times." He kept his voice at a level that made him unintelligible to anyone more than a few inches from his lips.

Jonathan met his gaze.

"I know what you're thinking. What the clenched jaw doesn't give away, the burning eyes do."

Jonathan considered saying nothing, but in the end, didn't have the willpower. "They *tortured* her, Dom."

"Yes, they did."

"I can't ignore that."

"You can't change it, either."

Jonathan snorted. "I sure as hell can avenge it."

"That's the anger talking."

"I've done some of my best work when I was angry."

"Bullshit."

Jonathan reared back, bitterly amused. "What the hell do you know about my work?"

"Enough to know that you're a pro and that like all pros you know that decisions made in the heat of emotion are never the right ones."

Jonathan leaned back in the barely upholstered chair

and rubbed his eyes with his palms. "What say we save this for another time?"

"Excuse me, Mr. Graves?"

Jonathan's head whipped around to see a doctor approaching. The guy was younger than Jonathan's shoes. He wore the requisite green scrub suit, and he moved with a gait that could best be described as cautious. Jonathan stood, and Dom stayed close.

"Grave," Jonathan corrected. "Are you Ellen's doctor?"

"Doctor Malstrom," the kid said. His eyes shifted to the priest.

"This is my friend and priest," Jonathan said.

Dom clarified, "Father Dominic D'Angelo."

"Pleased to meet both of you. Please, have a seat." Malstrom gestured back to the butt-abusing chairs, and pulled one around so he could sit backward, with his forearms crossed against the back of the seat. It was not the posture of a man delivering good news.

"Is she alive?" Jonathan asked.

"Yes, she is," Malstrom said, but his expression did not lighten. "But she's very, very seriously injured. We have her in intensive care, and to be perfectly honest, I just don't know what to tell you about her odds for survival. A lot depends on her physical strength, and on whether we were able to stop all the bleeding. We think we got it, but with all the body systems that are involved, it's just too difficult to say."

As Jonathan absorbed the words, he could feel his anger boiling. "Can I ask you to start from the beginning, Doc? Give me the list of her injuries."

Malstrom's eyes darted toward Dom as he searched for the words. "Well, you know she was raped, right?"

Jonathan nodded. "The police told me that."

"Okay. Well, there's a lot of tissue damage. A lot of bleeding."

Dom reached out to grip Digger's arm.

Jonathan could feel the heat in his face. Weatherby's version of the worst that could happen might very well be similar to his own. He'd said torture, after all, and these were the methods of a monster. "What else?" he asked. Even as the words passed his lips, he knew that he really didn't want to know.

"Broken bones in her fingers and toes. Broken tibias in both legs. Bruised liver and kidneys. Broken ribs. There's really quite a lot wrong, sir."

"Any head trauma?"

Malstrom broke eye contact as he nodded. "Yes, sir. One really solid strike to the head."

"Jesus Christ," Jonathan breathed, and then he shot a quick apologetic glance to Dom. "This is inconceivable to me."

Malstrom said nothing. What was there to say?

"So, what's next?"

The doctor launched a soliloquy about treatment strategies and possible surgeries. He talked about Ellen being "in the woods" for a long time, by way of explaining that it could easily be weeks before she would be "out of the woods." Throughout the speech, Jonathan's head was in a different place entirely. What the hell had Tibor Rothman done to bring this kind of evil into his home?

Finding Tibor was the key to everything. Suddenly he wanted the doctor to be done so that Jonathan could call Venice and discover what she'd found in her search. As if on cue, Jonathan's cell phone rang. It was Venice. Malstrom seemed offended that Jonathan took the call.

"Hey, Digger, how is she?"

"Bad," he said. "We're just now finding out the extent of it."

"Well, as soon as you can get out of there, I need you in the office."

"What's going on?" He didn't like the panicky edge to her voice.

"Not on the phone."

"Can't you at least tell me what it's about?"

Venice made that growling sound. She told him what she'd learned. Not all of it, just enough to whet his appetite.

Jonathan clapped the phone closed and stood. "Doctor, I have to go."

Malstrom looked as if he'd been slapped. "Excuse me?"

Dom stood with Digger, but he looked confused. "Yeah, excuse me?"

"I have to get to my office. An emergency situation has arisen and I have to attend to it."

"Now?" Dom asked, stunned at the rudeness.

"Right this second." He offered his hand to the doctor. "Doctor Malstrom, I'm sorry for being so abrupt, but I really have no choice. Thank you for taking care of Ellen. I owe you." He nodded to Dom. "You, too, Dom. I'll talk to you soon."

But Dom hurried after him. "Digger," he hissed at a stage whisper, "where the hell are you going?" It was a struggle keeping up with Jonathan's rapid pace.

"I told you."

"You said there was an emergency. Since when do you have emergencies in the office?"

Jonathan still didn't slow. "Since Venice found Tibor. He's dead."

Chapter Fifteen

Security Solutions occupied the entire third floor of the old firehouse. At first glance, the inside of the place looked like any other modern office, with its rabbit warren of cubicles where the seventeen investigators in Jonathan's employ—"associates," according to their business cards—toiled for eight to ten hours a day, supported by their assistants, who, to Jonathan's eye, were the hardest working group in the whole company. Senior associates got bigger cubicles that were closer to the windows, while junior associates and assistants made do with smaller spaces awash in fluorescent light. Jonathan Grave was the wrong guy to bitch to about rank having its privileges.

He wasn't remotely apologetic about the opulence of the executive suite. Given the cumulative years in which he'd labored in swamps and deserts, he'd come to enjoy nice amenities, and since he owned the company, he outfitted it the way it needed to be outfitted. At the end of the day, that translated roughly to giving Venice just about anything that Venice said she needed.

Jonathan let Dom enter first into the high-tech swirl of the executive office suite. In here, everything was state of the art, from the software and the computers to run it, to the phone system and the copy machines. From this office, thanks to Venice's genius, they could track down virtually anyone who had ever touched a computer keyboard, and once found, they could examine every crease and coil of their lives, digging into details that civilians would never dream were visible. It frustrated Jonathan at times that he himself didn't understand how three-quarters of this stuff worked. His expertise lay in manipulating people; he left electronic manipulation to others.

This executive corner of the office housed only three people: himself, Venice, and Boxers (when he was in the office). Each had identical 400-square-foot offices, decorated to their own personal tastes. While Jonathan's ran toward gentlemen's club, Venice was chrome and glass all the way. Everything in her office was trim and sleek and impossibly well organized.

She turned as she heard the footsteps approaching, and stood when she saw the men in the doorway. Walking around her desk, she spread her arms with a hug for Jonathan. "I'm so sorry about Ellen."

He accepted the hug, but returned it only with one arm. Touchy-feely was nowhere in his DNA. "Thank you," he said.

As they separated, Venice asked, "What do they say about her? Is she going to be okay?"

"They don't know," Jonathan said. He told her about his discussion with the doctor. "All we can do now," he concluded, "is find the bastards who hurt her."

Venice's expression darkened as she exchanged glances with Dom. "We're not about revenge, Dig."

Jonathan let it go. "What do you have on Tibor?"

"No, no," she said, shaking her head. "We're not just

brushing past that point. I'm not being a part of some plot to go out and take vigilante justice."

Jonathan shot a look to Dom. "What, did you coach her?" He turned back to Venice. "Tibor," he prompted.

Venice hesitated, as if deciding whether she was ready to move on, and then stepped to her side of the desk. As the others followed, she shooed them back to the front. "Have a seat, both of you," she said.

Jonathan steeled himself. Clearly, she'd planned a show, and she was not going to be hurried. He waited for Dom to choose the black leather sling-back of his choice, then helped himself to the other one.

"You told me to find him," Venice began. "I decided to start with his credit cards. He used his Visa two nights ago to check into a Rodeway Inn on the outskirts of Cincinnati."

Jonathan arched an eyebrow. He'd pegged Tibor Rothman as more of a Ritz-Carlton guy. "You called the hotel?"

She looked insulted that he would even ask. "Of course. According to the clerk, the car is there, but Tibor is not in his room. He never checked out, so as far as the kid at the desk is concerned, he's still a guest. But I don't think so. He would have called Ellen. So I dug deeper. I went into ICIS and did a real-time search for that whole area—Ohio, Kentucky, Indiana, even Illinois."

He recognized the acronym for the Interstate Crime Information Service, a post–9/11 invention that allowed police agencies to cross-reference ongoing investigations to identify trends and to recognize and disrupt criminal activities. Before ICIS (pronounced EYE-sis) was established, the only way to match one crime with another was to wait for the official reports of the investigations to be completed, and for charges to be filed. Nowadays, police agencies shared details of open, unsolved cases, and supercomputers could be goaded into making comparisons based on modus operandi and categories of evidence. The bugs hadn't all been worked out, but it was shaping up to be an invaluable tool for police agencies that knew the secret of its existence. To protect against the prying eyes of casual Internet gazers and hackers, the information was heavily encrypted.

Venice had found a way to pop in and out of the database at will.

She continued, "I had a definite time frame to work with, so I wasn't all that concerned about the size of the search population." Venice spoke quickly, the rhythm of her speech displaying her enthusiasm. Jonathan nodded, feigning comprehension and waiting for her to get back to sentences that he could understand.

"A body was found last night in a Dumpster in Sparta, outside Columbus."

"That's like a hundred miles away."

Venice raised one eyebrow. "Exactly. And according to the information in the database, it was a midfifties male who showed signs of torture."

"What kind of torture?"

Venice tried to sound cool, but there was no getting around the pride she felt at her own sleuthing skills. "I called the Sparta PD and asked that very question. Normally, the state police would handle a case like that, but I figured that I'd have better luck with a smaller bureaucracy. I got hold of a Sergeant Semen, who told me—"

Jonathan held up his hand as his mind rocketed back to junior high school. "Sergeant *Semen*?"

"Can we be grown-ups, please?"

"I'm just thinking that with a name like that, he must be one tough son of a bitch."

"Forced throughout his life into fighting people like you. Somebody drilled through his kneecaps."

All the humor evaporated. It was an unspeakable horror. The Irish Republican Army had for years earned a reputation for brutality by blasting the kneecaps of their enemies with bullets—an agonizing and permanent means of crippling those who had crossed them—but at least that damage was done in the space of a heartbeat. To subject flesh and bone to the slow, relentless tearing of a drill bit said that the killers were true animals. Jonathan noted that this was the second time today that he'd used the word "animal" to describe a perpetrator of violence. If the body from Venice's research truly was that of Tibor Rothman, then there no longer was any doubt that Ellen's attackers had been looking for information. Still, something was missing. The Tibor Rothman he knew couldn't possibly endure the attentions of a torturer. "How do you know you have the right guy?"

Venice looked at her notes. "Blue eyes, graying brown hair. And the tips of the ring finger and pinky on his left hand are missing, the result of an old injury."

Jonathan drew a noisy breath at the last revelation. Tibor had made much over the years of his childhood fireworks accident. It had to be him. "Do the police know who they have?"

Denise shook her head. "And they don't know that I know. Sergeant . . . The sergeant talked to me because he thought I was a reporter."

Jonathan's eyes narrowed. That was a terrible cover story. Cops hated reporters more than they hated arsonists.

She caved. "Okay, he talked to me because he was beguiled."

"Oh?"

Venice smiled. "It took two calls. The first time, he cut me off, told me to contact the public information office. Obviously, I wasn't going to do that. So I went to the Web, and sure enough, Sergeant Horace Semen has a Web site. It took maybe three minutes to do the research. I called him back and did a little begging, telling him how hot he was."

Jonathan recoiled at the thought. "He gave you information because you complimented his Web site?"

"No, you idiot. I didn't tell him about the Web site. The Web site just showed me what he looked like. From there, I could blow sunshine about how he helped me during an auto accident, and couldn't he please just do me this one little bitty favor."

Now he got it. "You used your phone sex voice."

She blushed and the eyebrow rose again. "We have a date next Saturday."

Jonathan laughed. "In Sparta, Ohio."

Venice beamed. "Well, Columbus. While we were talking, I pulled up bookstores there. Found one called the Book Loft of German Village. We're going to meet there at seven on Saturday. But there's more. Tibor sent us some mail." She held up a square blue piece of plastic, smaller than a postage stamp. "This arrived today. It's a memory chip," she explained. "The modern equivalent of film."

Jonathan and Dom leaned forward in unison for a closer look.

"It's loaded with an Mpeg," Venice went on. "A movie. I haven't had a chance to look at it yet."

"So we're in time for the premiere."

She pivoted her screen so they could all have a clear view, and she clicked her mouse.

Jonathan and Dom pulled their chairs closer.

Dom asked, "Did the file name give you a clue what we're about to see?"

"There *was* no file name. I just plugged it into my H-drive and had to figure it out from there. Have I mentioned that Digger doesn't pay me enough?"

The twenty-one-inch flat panel screen blinked and everyone leaned closer to see what was about to happen. Somewhere in the middle of the flickering brown, there was a picture, but it was all shades and shadows. "Can you play with the image?" Jonathan asked.

"You don't want me playing with it now," Venice told him. "We're looking at the original. I can copy it and play with it, but I doubt I can do much. This was shot at night. I can't create light where there wasn't any in the first place."

Jonathan squinted and leaned in.

"Looks like an empty room," Dom said, articulating Jonathan's thoughts. The image was difficult to decipher. Poorly lit, and perhaps in black-and-white, the video appeared to have been shot indoors, but there were no obvious clues to the venue.

"Concealed camera, do you think?" Jonathan asked.

"I think so," Venice said. "The roundness of the aperture and the graininess of the image give it away."

"You mean like in a pair of fake glasses?" Dom asked.

Jonathan answered, "It could be in glasses, in a briefcase, in a wristwatch, or just about anything."

"Is there sound?" Dom asked.

Venice checked the volume knob on her monitor. "I've got it up all the way."

"Any predictions what—"

Jonathan's question was cut off by the sound of a door opening on the video, and of movement in the room. A male voice said, "They're here."

"That's Tibor!" Jonathan exclaimed. "I recognize the voice."

The image on the screen danced as the camera moved. "Glad you could make it," another voice said from the computer's speakers. "Who's this? I told you to come alone."

Then a third man's voice: "This is Tibor Rothman, a columnist with the *Washington Post*. He's here to make sure you get all the publicity you need. Where's Thomas?"

"You were supposed to come alone."

"You were supposed to have my son."

A pause. "All in good time," said the newcomer. The camera moved to look at the person who was arriving, but the angle was wrong. All they could see was the man's chest. He wore a sport coat and an open-collar shirt. A second man appeared next to him, dressed similarly, but wearing a tie. From the way that he held himself, and the way that he stood so closely to the other man, Jonathan wondered if he was perhaps a bodyguard. Jonathan assumed that it was the visitor with the open collar who said, "Thank you for being so cooperative, Mr. Hughes. And welcome, Mr. Rothman. I'm a great admirer of your work."

"Stop!" Jonathan commanded, and Venice moved the cursor to the pause button. She and Dom both looked startled. "He called the other guy Mr. Hughes."

Venice and Dom both scowled, and said in unison, "So?"

"My mission was for Thomas Hughes. 'Where's Thomas' followed by a 'thank you, Mr. Hughes' means that they were tied to the mission. This is all locked together somehow."

Venice looked horrified. This was a terrible development at multiple levels. First of all, no one was supposed to know the true nature of the work Jonathan did as Scorpion—especially not Tibor Rothman, the tattletale of Washington, DC. The wrong kind of attention would not only put the most lucrative division of Security Solutions out of business, but it could land its president in jail.

If Jonathan was right—if Tibor was somehow linked to the mission—then someone had done some serious lying to make it happen. Jonathan would never take on an 0300 mission for someone who wished him harm the way Tibor Rothman did. He remembered the reporter in Ellen's yard telling him about the article Tibor was writing.

"Could it be a coincidence?" Dom asked. "Is it possible that they didn't know that 'Scorpion' was really you?"

"There are no coincidences," Venice answered on her boss's behalf. It was, of course possible—there were only a handful of firms in the world that performed freelance hostage rescue—but the closeness of the ties in this case were too weird to be mere happenstance.

"Go ahead and start it up again," Jonathan said, nodding at the screen.

The camera dipped in a way that made Jonathan assume that Tibor had nodded to the compliment. When the angle rose again, he seemed to remember that faces were important, and they got their first glimpse of the newly arriving party. The guy in the open shirt had a professorial air to him. Rail thin and with a graying beard and shoulder-length hair, he struck Jonathan as the type to lead an antigovernment protest on a college campus. The guy next to him—in the tie—looked vaguely familiar. Squatty and thick, he had the physique of a reformed weight lifter. He also had a vicious scar across his right eye.

"Stop it again," Jonathan said.

This time, Venice didn't move. "Yes, I'll go back and blow up the pictures and run them through the recognition programs," she said.

Okay, that was creepy. She had actually read his mind.

The professor type said, "You brought the items you promised?"

"We did," said Stephenson Hughes, Thomas Hughes's father. "But you don't get any of it before I see my son."

"That's not how it works," the professor said. "You have no say in these proceedings."

"I do as long as we're at this stalemate."

"Mr. Conger, please," said Tibor. "Be reasonable. He's done everything you asked."

Jonathan said, "Venice?"

She nodded emphatically. "Got it. Conger. I'll see what I can find."

Conger said, "That's not true. Our agreement was, you provide the evidence, and then I provide the kid."

"Then he'd have no bargaining power," Tibor said. "When this story is written, sir, I don't think you want to come off sounding like a common kidnapper. You don't want to sound like a thug. You want to sound like a businessman who had no choices left. It's impossible to have it both ways."

"But a deal's a deal," Conger said.

"Your side of the bargain is an inanimate object," Stephenson Hughes said. "My side is a human life. My son. They don't equate."

"Your side of the bargain, as you say," corrected Conger, "is actually *thousands* of lives, Mr. Hughes."

The chirping of a cell phone made Jonathan reach for his pocket until he realized that the sound was coming from Venice's speakers.

"Don't answer that," Conger said.

The picture shifted as the camera caught Hughes reaching for his pocket.

"I said don't answer it."

"I'm just seeing who it is," Hughes said. After a pause, he added, "Thank God. We're good."

All hell broke loose as the picture went wild and the speakers projected the sound of skidding and falling furniture.

"Put your hands up," said Stephenson Hughes. "Don't move a muscle if you don't want to get killed."

The image on the screen settled down enough to show both the professor and his sidekick looking startled as hell, their hands in the air.

"Have you lost your mind?" Conger demanded.

"Your kid is dead," said the man with the scar, his first words. "You'll never see him again."

"Too late," Tibor said. Jonathan recognized the smugness of his tone as one he'd heard countless times himself. "That phone call confirmed that the boy is safe and sound. You've lost this one, Conger."

"And we've got it all on tape," Stephenson added.

"Steve, hush," Tibor growled.

"What're you going to do, shoot us?" asked Scarface. Hearing the voice, Jonathan grew more convinced that he'd seen this guy before.

"No, we're going to see that you're arrested," Stephenson said. "Now, I want you both to put your guns on the table there. And do it slowly."

At first, neither of them moved. Then, with a resigned nod from Scarface, they both produced pistols from under their sport coats and laid them on the table. Scarface made a show of using only two fingers.

"Now step away," Stephenson said. They did, their hands back up in the air.

The picture moved again as Tibor approached the table and stepped back. The frame didn't show any weapons at all now—not on the table, and not anywhere else. If Tibor had them in his hands, then he was holding them out of the frame.

"Don't move," Stephenson repeated. "We're going to leave now, and if I even see your shadow, I'm going to kill you. Do you understand?"

"We understand," said Scarface.

Jonathan scowled. The banter was all wrong. Scarface—the muscle—was being way too accommodating. "Oh, Christ," Jonathan said aloud. "They've got backup pieces."

The picture whipped as Tibor turned his head. They got their first peek at Stephenson Hughes, who held a revolver at arm's length in a two-handed grip that made Jonathan think that he'd had firearms training. The picture continued to move. They watched a door open, and the light got really bad. They were outside now, in the middle of the night, and the camera saw nothing.

"I'll see if I can't fiddle with the image later," Venice said without prompting.

"Let's get out of here," Tibor said, his voice heavy with fear.

The speakers on Venice's monitor projected the sound of movement and heavy breathing as the screen continued to reveal nothing but differing shades of darkness. Then they heard a door open, and the screen was overwhelmed with more light than the automatic iris could handle, only to go black again when the door closed. The engine started.

"This is where it gets ugly," Jonathan predicted. The others didn't seem to understand, and he didn't bother to explain.

Another blast of light as the passenger side door opened. In the frame of the video, they could just see Stephenson Hughes's hand as he pulled himself in by leveraging against the dashboard. "Go, go, go!" Stephenson yelled.

The engine roared, and then things started breaking inside the cockpit of the car. The crashes and flashes were accompanied by the distinctive staccato pops of gunfire.

"They're shooting at us!"

"Fuck! Close the—"

The screen went blank, and the speakers fell silent. There was nothing.

"What did you do?" Jonathan snapped at Venice.

"I didn't do anything," she snapped back, matching his tone.

"Where did the movie go?"

"That's it," she said. "That's the end of the file."

"Just like that? Just poof?"

"Looks like. That's everything on the chip."

Dom turned to Jonathan. "You think he got shot?"

Jonathan punted to Venice. "Any gunshot wounds on the corpse in Ohio?"

She shook her head. "Well, only one, but it was the kill shot at short range. They still had to torture him first."

The thought gave Jonathan a chill. "He probably didn't turn the recorder off on purpose. It wouldn't make sense to turn it off right then. There was too much left of interest to record."

"Why would Tibor be there in the first place?" Dom wondered aloud.

"One of a million really good questions that we need to answer," Jonathan replied. "Maybe he knew this Hughes guy."

"Or maybe he was covering the story," Venice offered.

"Any or all of the above."

"Clearly, he wanted a record of it all," Dom said.

Jonathan agreed. "But why?"

"To write a story," Venice said again. "It makes sense to me that he wedged himself into whatever was happening so that he could write a story. Don't reporters always record their meetings?"

Jonathan shrugged. He had no idea what reporters did.

Venice said, "The way to find out for sure is to call his editor at the *Post*. Under the circumstances, they could sift through his notes and such and come up with what happened."

Jonathan shook his head. "Let the cops do that. We've got our own evidence to work on."

Venice's eyes widened. "So you're not sharing this with the police either?"

"Of course not. If Tibor had wanted them involved, he would have sent the chip to them. I can't disrespect his final wishes like that."

Dom winced. "The man is dead, Dig. Don't desecrate that."

Jonathan conceded. "I apologize. But we're still not sharing with the police." A new thought stirred in his head. "How did the chip come to us, Ven?"

She shrugged. "In an envelope."

"Just like a regular letter?"

"Yep. In fact, there was a letter with it. It was just another salvo in y'all's lawsuit."

"Do you still have it?"

Venice pulled the envelope out a larger evidence envelope and handed it over.

Jonathan saw that his address was laser-printed on the front. "How about that? Running for his life, he took time to type an envelope."

Dom scowled. "I don't think so."

"Neither do I."

"He must have had it filled out already," Venice said. "Why would he do that?"

"Maybe he was expecting things to go wrong," Dom offered.

Jonathan didn't think they had it. "Let me see the letter that was with it." Venice handed it to him. She was right; it was just another letter like all the others in the ongoing lawsuit, clarifying one of the finer points of discovery. These things were supposed to go through the lawyers, but Tibor was always on the lookout for ways to keep his fees low.

"You know what?" Jonathan thought aloud. "Ellen told me on the ride home that Tibor had been on his way to the post office when he got sidetracked onto his mystery trip. I think he didn't intend to mail this chip to me at all. I think he wanted to get rid of it, didn't have any time, and just happened to have this letter in his pocket, probably already stamped. If he'd lived, maybe he would have tried to get it back unopened or something."

Venice's eyes got big. "That's it. The killers knew there was a tape—'Steve' told them as much. If the killers couldn't find it when they found him, and if Tibor didn't give it up to them, they might have assumed he'd mailed it." She looked sadly to Jonathan.

"They'd assume he mailed it home," he said, completing her thought. "They'd assume Ellen had it." He glanced at the postmark. "The dates work."

"So that's the reason for the beating," Dom said, connecting the dots. "The torture. For both of them."

Air escaped from Jonathan's lungs in a rush. "They did all of that to her, and she never had a chance of giving them what they were looking for. Bastards." He rose from his chair and paced. Everyone understood that he was trying to tame his temper, and until he was done, no one dared to say anything. As the raw anger drained from his face, a different kind of concern took its place. "Let's lay this out for a second," he said. "Thomas Hughes, son of Stephenson Hughes, a mid-level executive somewhere—Venice, we need to find out where he worked and what he did. Let's find out who he had the potential of pissing off this badly. Thomas is kidnapped mid-coitus by Lionel and Barry Patrone, with the full cooperation of Thomas's girlfriend, who doesn't mind luring him into a little action before the actual action begins.

"The kidnapping itself is part of a larger plot to extort something from Stephenson—something that is not money, because the Hugheses don't have much of that. The perpetrator of the kidnapping is someone named Conger, whose connection to the Hughes family is a total mystery at this point. Sound right so far?"

Dom and Venice nodded in unison.

Jonathan continued, "So, Stephenson Hughes involves Tibor Rothman, who, with or without knowing who I am, pays me to snatch the Hughes kid, even as he—Tibor—and Hughes are making the payoff. Then things go wrong—"

Venice's hand shot up, as if asking a question, silencing him. "Things didn't go wrong until after you called. We all agree that the phone call in the video came from you, right?"

Jonathan nodded. "Right. Then somehow my phone call screwed things up."

Dom took his turn. "You didn't screw anything up. You just came through later than they were expecting. You told me that you were running late on the mission timetable. Maybe when they hadn't heard from you, Hughes had no choice but to go through with whatever ransom demand this Conger guy was making. When you finally did come through and made your call, you freed them to get the hell out of there."

Venice became even more animated. "They even planned for it. They knew exactly what they were going to do when the phone call came."

Jonathan agreed, grateful that the pieces were beginning to fit. "They had to be there. If the 0300 mission hadn't worked out, it was their only play to keep Thomas alive."

"So what happened?" Dom asked. "At the end, with all the shooting?"

"Well, clearly they got away," Jonathan said. "At least until Tibor got himself killed. Ven, I need some fast research from you."

"I know, I know, I've got the notes."

"There's more. Look around for reports of shot-up vehicles. It sounded like a friggin' war out there at the end. There have to be some holes in Tibor's vehicle."

"What does he drive?"

"I don't know, look it up. A sedan of some sort. Something overpriced."

Venice made a note.

"What about Stephenson Hughes?" Dom asked. "What do we think happened to him?"

Jonathan shrugged. He looked to Venice.

"Got it. Hospitals and police records looking for

gunshot wounds." She looked up from her scribblings to make sure she had Jonathan's attention. "Anything else? If not, then I've got something."

The raised eyebrow told her to go on.

"Back to ICIS reports," she said. "There's a lot of activity in Indiana, with the sheriff of Samson—the little town you visited—turning the world upside down looking for whoever shot the three people at the farmhouse."

Jonathan dismissed the concern with a flick of his hand. "We were careful. What little they have should point them directly to what went down. They might figure out the what and the why, but they'll have no shot at the who."

"That's ego talking," Venice cautioned. "There's a new sheriff in town—and I mean that literally. She's former FBI. She's got connections, and she's not a bit hesitant about cashing in on them."

Jonathan pinched the bridge of his nose to squeeze out the encroaching headache. Venice was right. The FBI connection concerned him. He turned to Dom. "Can you reach out to Wolverine?"

"She's going to get tired of us."

"Don't be silly," Jonathan said with a smirk. "We make her job easier."

Dom snorted a laugh. "Oh, yeah. By giving her more to do. I'll see if she can meet with me Monday."

The friend they referred to was about as high in the law enforcement stratosphere as one could get—a woman who got more done with a phone call than any congressman could accomplish in three months of hearings. She and her agency had used Security Solutions in the past to perform a few missions that would make Congress choke on its own pork if they ever found out.

"Thank you."

"As sinners go, you're pretty demanding."

Venice's cell phone rang, a loud, annoying version of a pop song that Jonathan vaguely recognized from the radio. Her face grew excited as she checked the caller ID. "It's my friend from Sparta," she smirked.

Jonathan's eyebrows scaled his forehead. "Sergeant Smegma?"

She rolled her eyes again and flipped the phone open before the second verse could play. "Sergeant Semen? This is Veronica Harper." It was her standard alias. "In fact, I'm here with my boss, so I'm going to put you on speakerphone."

Jonathan could hear the surprise in the deputy's voice when he spoke. Clearly he'd been expecting something more intimate than a speakerphone. "I, uh, have some information on another killing that I thought you might find interesting."

"Outstanding. Thank you."

The deputy hesitated. "Who are you with again?"

"My name is Leon." Recalling the ruse she had used, he added, "I'm Ms. Harper's editor. Everything you say will be held in the strictest confidence."

"No names, right?" Semen clearly wished he had never made this call.

"Absolutely no names," Jonathan promised.

"Really, there's nothing to worry about," Venice reassured. "As my editor, he has to know everything about what I write anyway."

Semen hesitated.

"Honestly, Sergeant, you can trust us."

The cop caved. "There's been another body found. This one was in Kentucky, just over the Ohio border. It was decapitated and its hands and feet are missing. Chunks of flesh, too."

Venice said, "Yuck."

"We figure whoever killed him didn't want the body to be identified."

"That means the head and the extremities are not with the body?" Jonathan asked.

"No, sir, they aren't."

"What makes you think that this murder is connected to the one in your area?"

"The violence of it. We're a small town, surrounded by small towns. Same with the town where this other body was found. It looked like somebody tried to conceal it, but they didn't do a very good job. In both their case and ours, the perpetrators seemed to be in a hurry."

While the deputy spoke, Jonathan rummaged for a pen and a scrap of paper. He jotted a note for Venice. Her look told him there was no way she could ask the question, to which he responded with a look of his own that made the question a requisite for continued employment.

"Do you have a photograph of the body?" Venice asked. She knew exactly how the question would be perceived, and she was exactly right.

"What the hell do you need a photograph for?"

"It would be really helpful if you'd e-mail it to me."

"What kind of paper prints pictures like that?"

It seemed like a lost cause, but Jonathan thought he'd take a shot at saving it. "Stories like this often trigger inquiries from the public. If we had a photo on file—"

"You guys aren't with a paper at all, are you?" Semen said.

Venice backpedaled. "What do you mean?"

"Goddamnit," he spat—at himself, Jonathan imagined. "How could I be this stupid?"

Jonathan decided to punt. "We're private investigators," he said. "Williams and Thomas, LLC, out of Springfield, Virginia. Look us up and you'll see us in the yellow pages. This is all part of a case we're working on." The firm was real, one of the many cutouts that Jonathan used to cover his tracks.

"What kind of case?"

"I can't tell you that. Client confidentiality."

"Well fuck you. Both of you." Apparently, next week's bookstore date was off.

"Don't hang up!" Venice said. "Please. I really needed that information you gave me, and I didn't think you'd talk to me if I told you the truth."

"So you lied."

"Yes. And I feel terrible about it."

"Do you know what this could do to my career? Did you ever think of that?"

Jonathan was getting fed up. "Hey, Sergeant. If your career was all that important to you, you'd have kept your mouth shut. Since you were willing to share when you thought you were going to get laid, you don't exactly have the high ground."

"Hey, asshole, I don't know who the hell you think you are—"

"I'll tell you exactly who I am. I'm the guy who has your balls in my fist. I didn't want this to get ugly, but you're in no position to bargain. We want to see photographs of the body—and any other information you might have, for that matter. Cooperate and nobody ever knows that you and Veronica spoke. Refuse, and I guaran-damn-tee you that everybody from the *New York Times* on down will know that Sergeant Horace Semen is willing to sell out for a roll in the hay."

In the silence that followed Jonathan could hear the wheels turning in the cop's head, even as he could feel

Venice's glare burning a hole through to his spinal cord. In the end, Semen went peacefully. "What's your e-mail address?"

Jonathan gave him the address, an untraceable one that would cease to exist within hours after the information was received.

"You'll have it in five minutes," the deputy grumped. "But before we hang up, I want you to know that I probably would have helped you even without the lie."

"Thank you, Deputy," Venice said. "That's good to—"

The click of the dead line clipped her last words. She killed the speakerphone and glared at Jonathan. "You didn't have to be such a jerk," she said.

It took twenty minutes for the e-mail to arrive from Deputy Semen, no doubt a bit of petulance from a pissed-off cop. Jonathan was surprised that the guy hadn't fought back a little harder. He was, after all, the one who had the information they wanted, and any impropriety they laid on his doorstep would implicate them, too. Had the positions been reversed, Jonathan would have recognized the bluff.

The photos of the body came as attachments to an e-mail, a total of five of them. Venice hung close to Jonathan's shoulder as he clicked on the first image, but as soon as it materialized, she looked away and busied herself with straightening a stack of papers on her desk. Even Jonathan had trouble looking at it for more than a few seconds.

Jonathan had seen far more horrifying sights than this on battlefields, and while he'd never gotten used to it, dismemberment was oddly natural to the environment of warfare. The same images, though, in the context of home soil, triggered revulsion and anger. When soldiers killed soldiers, the underlying nobility of the conflict dulled the edges of the horror. That such defilement could be an end unto itself, as it clearly was in these awful photographs from Kentucky, left him feeling empty and sick.

Jonathan thought about poor Thomas Hughes, and the additional emotional damage that his father's fate would heap upon him. He didn't like feeling such empathy for a case that was supposed to have been locked away in his cerebral filing cabinet by now. It made viewing Stephenson Hughes's vivisected corpse even more difficult.

It wasn't clear from the photographs whether they had been taken before or after the corpse was moved from where it was found. Two crushed Budweiser cans were clearly visible, plus a sprinkling of broken glass, the shape and the colors of the shards suggesting yet more retired beer containers. Beneath the body, bottles and cans and twisted tufts of grass grew like leafy cancers from a flat gray bed of gravel. It was one hell of a way to treat a human being.

Deputy Semen's description of the corpse didn't touch the reality of what the photographs showed. It was true enough that the hands had been removed, but so had the elbows and a good portion of the upper arms. Dried blood in wild spray patterns decorated the naked chest, which showed the lack of muscle tone that was typical of forty-something desk dwellers. The head was likewise missing, severed by a hacking cut just below the jawline. If Jonathan's estimates were correct, the larynx had been left behind. Stephenson Hughes had been transformed into a slab of pale flesh that gleamed like a beached fish.

"Jesus, Digger, do you have to put those on *my* computer? I feel like I need to wash it now."

"They tortured him, too," Jonathan said.

Venice reapproached the screen cautiously, as if afraid that the power of the images might hurt her. "How do you know?"

He pointed with a crooked forefinger—testament to the limitations of field-splinting broken bones in the middle of a Latin American firefight. "Look at all the blood spray here around the amputations," he explained. "You don't get that after the heart has stopped. That means they cut off his arms while he was still alive." When he saw the scowl on Venice's face, he drove the point home. "Dead people don't bleed."

He browsed through the rest of the photos. Each of the five displayed a different angle on the horror, and with each click of the mouse, the grisliness of it grew.

As Venice acclimated to the gore, she leaned in closer to the screen. "What's that?" she asked, pointing.

Jonathan had been wondering the same thing. A patch of flesh, roughly the shape of a triangle and the size of a hand, had been excised from the victim's chest above the left nipple. The wound was an ugly purple thing with none of the telltale signs that it had been inflicted during life. In fact, had the wound been viewed out of context, it might have looked like an example of modern art—the kind that Jonathan never understood, but seemed to be all the rage among the MOMA set. Swarming flies capped it all off with a disturbingly surreal quality.

"Are we looking at a serial killer?" Venice asked. "A collector?"

"Don't think so. This looks like the work of a professional to me. Collectors take body parts as trophies. Professionals take them to prevent identification."

Venice didn't press for more details, probably because she didn't want to know the source of Digger's knowledge.

He continued, "I think that missing skin used to be a tattoo. The killer didn't want the tat pointing the way to the corpse's identity."

"Did Stephenson Hughes have a tattoo?"

Jonathan shook his head. "I don't know. Apparently." Looking at these photographs, at the brutal violence that they represented, he couldn't help but think of the unspeakable agony that Ellen must have suffered as these animals came at her and bludgeoned her for information that she never knew. He heard her screams in his head.

He said, "Rattle Boxers' cage and bring him back to work. We've got stuff to do."

Chapter Sixteen

Of the four civil aviation companies at the Indianapolis Airport that rented helicopters, it turned out that all four had choppers out during the critical period from April 19 to 21. Of those four, three sported a lateral wheelbase in the range of seven feet, the nominal separation between the tire prints in the grass, and the fourth was a Bell Jet Ranger that didn't have tires at all, but rather took off and landed on skids.

After seven hours of drive time and investigation, Gail Bonneville's case hadn't progressed at all. The number of suppositions and intuitive guesses were compounding, and without something definitive, some bit of hard evidence that they were even on the right track, she would soon have to regroup and start over from scratch.

"I think you're right," Gail said to Jesse as they walked from the civil aviation terminal toward Gail's official unmarked vehicle. "They borrowed instead of renting."

"Or they could own their own," Jesse offered. "But, I know, we're stipulating that they're from too far out of town for that. I want to show you something." They reached the vehicle and he used the hood as an impromptu desk. From his briefcase, he produced a black imitation-leather portfolio from which papers sprouted in all directions. As he searched for the one he wanted, he explained, "When we first got here, you remember I asked for the civil aviation arrival and departure records?"

Gail nodded.

"Well, here they are." He produced a laser-printed sheet filled with numbers. "We're actually looking for two flights. One executive jet and one helicopter. And yes, I'm assuming jet because, if they're doing this kind of work, they ain't doing it from a Piper Cub. I asked the aviation guys to separate fixed-wing arrivals and departures from helicopter arrivals and departures. Where we can find close enough matches, we've got a decent shot at landing on the right flight."

"Assuming they used this airport," Gail said.

Jesse looked up, annoyed. "You can't keep changing assumptions on me, Sheriff. Either we're pursuing this line, or we're not."

She pulled back. "We are."

"Okay, then." He went back to his printouts. Gail watched his eyes dart from the fixed-wing page to the rotary-wing page. From the level of concentration, she determined that he was probably one hell of a Sudoku player.

It took him all of three minutes. When he was done, he'd left check marks on three pairs of flights, and then, on second review, he scratched two of them off. "Here it is," he said, handing her the sheet.

Gail looked at it, scowled. "I have no idea what you're showing me," she said in total candor.

He took the pages and positioned himself so it would be easiest for Gail to follow along. "Look here," he said, pointing. "See this Gulfstream G150 on the chart? That's a really nice plane, by the way. We're talking serious coin. Tail number N244JT."

"I see it," she said, surprised that he'd actually waited for an answer.

"Okay, look at its touchdown time. Nineteen thirty-two hours on April 19. That's seven thirty-two."

"Is it really?"

He looked up. "Oh. Of course you knew that. I was just . . . Never mind. Anyway, look at this." He shifted to the other paper. "This chopper here—tail number N47302—lifted off fifty-five minutes later. I don't know what kind of aircraft it is, but we can find out by tracking down the tail number."

Gail was still confused. "I don't understand. All I see is pure coincidence."

"That's because I'm not done yet. Fast-forward a few hours, and look here. At zero six twenty hours, a helicopter with tail number N47302 lands at the west end of the field, and then, twenty minutes later, the same Gulfstream, tail number N244JT, takes off with a flight plan filed to Chicago. The chopper sits there at the airport until noon—12:12—and then it takes off again, no flight plan filed."

"Why no flight plan?" Gail asked.

"Not required if you're flying VFR—visual flight rules. That is, no instruments." He said it as if it made perfect sense, and Gail pretended that it did. "Anyway, we don't know from this list where the chopper ended up, but we do know that the Gulfstream hung around at O'Hare for a few hours before it took off again and eventually ended up in Washington, at Dulles International Airport." He waited a few seconds for Gail to complete the circuit on her own, then added, "When we find out who owns these aircraft, we should have the answers we need."

Gail had to agree. "Are these answers we should be able to get over the phone?"

"I don't see why not."

"Then let's get started back home."

The helicopter's tail number turned out to be a complete fabrication. There was not now, nor had there ever been, a chopper in the United States registered with the tail number N47302. Without a registration and without a flight plan the aircraft was invisible. They inquired via the telephone whether the radar record could be resurrected to show where they traveled, but the answer, much to Gail's and Jesse's surprise, was negative. A helicopter without a flight plan could literally fly under the radar and disappear into the vast American airspace.

The Gulfstream jet, however, was traceable. It was registered to Perseus Foods Corporation, headquartered in Rockville, Maryland. Gail started making phone calls. Thus far, she'd had no luck whatsoever getting through to anyone at the corporate headquarters who could answer any questions.

Back at the office, after an hour in the car on the way back to Samson, Gail completed her third call into the bowels of Perseus Foods, and found herself not a single step closer to an answer. After someone named Lakisha had promised to "ask around" to see who might know something, Gail could feel her blood pressure rising. She hung up the phone aggressively enough to bring Jesse's head up from the pile of reports that had flooded into the office while they were at the airport. With the blinds closed to protect them from the eyes of the media outside, the atmosphere inside the office was positively funereal.

"I hate people sometimes," she said in reply to Jesse's quizzical expression. "No one knows anything, and the Maryland State Police isn't anxious to push people's buttons for us. They don't think we have enough to justify the dedication of manpower."

Jesse didn't seem surprised. "Want me to grab a flight out there and talk to someone? It's easy to stonewall when all you have to do is press a hold button. It gets a little more complicated when you have to look people in the eye."

Gail stood and stretched. "It might come to that."

Jesse turned to a page in his pile of reports. "I have an interesting lead here," he said. "Day before yesterday, outside of Muncie, a pharmacist called the local cops to report what he thought might be a runaway. The report here says he was a kid, a teenager or maybe very early twenties, and he was filthy and clearly distraught. He waited there a long time for the bus to Chicago."

Gail cocked her head. "How is that a lead for us?"

Jesse sensed disapproval and his shoulders slumped a little. "The timing works. As far as I'm concerned, wherever the stars align, there's a potential lead. On the morning of the attack, there's a kid waiting for a bus to the same place where our Gulf Stream headed. All things considered, it's a pretty close match."

The sheriff didn't get it. "If they were going to Chicago, why not just fly him to Chicago? What's the bus thing all about?"

Jesse gave that some thought. "I can't say for sure, but a bus doesn't go right to a location, does it? Maybe he intended to get off somewhere in between."

Gail looked at her deputy. For the first time since she'd taken office, she saw why this man was so popular among the troops. His mind was suited perfectly for this line of work. "Do we have a name?" she asked.

Jesse nodded, and quickly scanned the page. "We've got two, actually. We've got a name for the pharmacist, and we've got a name for the kid."

Gail's jaw dropped.

Jesse chuckled. "Yeah, that sort of surprised me, too. Apparently the kid gave his name as Hughes, either Thomas or Tony, the pharmacist wasn't sure. His name is Al Elvins. I've got a number."

They called it, and learned little more than what was in the report in terms of fact, but they learned a great deal more in terms of emotion. It turned out that Al Elvins was quite concerned about this kid who had shown up in the wee hours of the morning. More than just exhausted, the kid had that deer-in-the-headlights, terrified look that Mr. Elvins said he hadn't seen since he was a kid in uniform back in 'Nam.

"At first, I wasn't going to call it in to anybody because the kid looked old enough to be on his own and he begged me not to. Then, the more I thought about it, the more I realized that calling the police was the right thing to do. Be honest with you, though. Nobody seemed particularly moved when I did call it in. I'm surprised to be hearing back from anybody. I'm glad somebody cares."

Gail soothed, "Sometimes, things turn out to be bigger than they seem at first glance. I'm glad we had a chance to talk." She checked her notes one more time to see if she was missing anything, and then, with a start, she realized that she was missing something huge. "One last thing, Mr. Elvins. What time did this Hughes fellow leave on the bus?"

He dropped a beat. "Didn't I tell you that?" he asked. "He never did get on the bus. A lady called just as the bus was arriving—said she was his mother—and talked him out of getting on the bus at all. About an hour later, she came by and picked him up herself."

Both Jesse and Gail sat bolt upright at that news. "In a car?" Jesse asked into the speaker phone.

Elvins laughed. "As opposed to a horse? Yes, she was in a car."

"Did you—"

"It was a yellow Oldsmobile Cutlass Supreme. I'm gonna guess vintage 1980. I dated a girl when I was in college who drove one very much like it."

Gail wrote it all down. This was huge. "Did you get a license plate number?"

"Didn't think of it," Elvins said sheepishly.

"Not a problem," Gail assured. "Is this the number the mother called you on?"

"The only one we have," Elvins said. She could tell from the sound of his voice that he was happy to be able to help. "Can I ask you what's going on? Does this have something to do with that shooting down your way?"

"We're thinking it might," she said. Jesse was already on the other phone tracing the calls. "I can't thank you enough, Mr. Elvins." After some final pleasantries, she hung up.

Gail was about to check up on the Oldsmobile when her phone rang. She pressed the speaker phone button. "Sheriff Bonneville."

"Is this Sheriff *Gail* Bonneville?" said a male voice she didn't recognize. There was sternness to the tone that made her uneasy.

"It is," she said.

"Hold for Governor Swensen, please."

Boy, did *that* bring Jesse's head up. Three years into his first term in the State House, Indiana Governor Peter Swensen's name was already on people's lips as a future Democratic nominee for president of the United States. A notorious fan of tax-and-spend financial strategies, he was also tough on crime, and widely touted as a police officer's best friend. During the six seconds of silence while she was waiting to be connected, Gail found herself cataloging and prioritizing the details of the shooting investigation so far.

"Sheriff Bonneville?" This time, the voice on the phone was as familiar as a sound bite on the evening news.

"Yes, sir, Governor. I have to say, it's quite an honor—"

"What the hell are you doing stirring up trouble in Maryland?" Gone was the velvety smoothness of Peter Swensen's public face. In its place was blunt, cold efficiency.

"Excuse me?" Governor or no governor, Gail donned her battle armor.

"I just got a call from Governor Baskin of Maryland, who'd just gotten an earful from three state senators that you were harassing Richard Lydell, president of Perseus Foods, about how he uses his private airplane. What the hell is going on?"

"To be honest, sir, I don't know how I can be harassing someone when I haven't even been able to talk to him."

"Perseus is one of the biggest companies in the country, Sheriff Bonneville. Did you know that?"

"I certainly knew they were large, but I don't see why—"

"And not to put too fine a point on it, Mr. Lydell himself is a huge help to the Democratic Party. My party. Yours, too, if I'm not mistaken."

Gail felt her face getting hot. "It is my party, sir, but as sheriff, I can't consider—"

"Do you have evidence that Mr. Lydell has done something wrong, Sheriff Bonneville?"

"We certainly have suspicions, Governor. If they could answer just a few questions—"

"I believe I used the word 'evidence,' Sheriff. Not suspicion. There's a difference. Do you have evidence to justify a search warrant, for example?"

Gail recoiled. "What, from Perseus? No. Not yet, anyway."

"Then maybe you should stop stirring up a shit storm a thousand goddamn miles away until you do."

"How can I get evidence if—"

"Do you know who Colin Barksdale is?"

"He's the state attorney general. Of course I kow who he is." Across the room, Jesse rolled his eyes.

"Good. 'Cause here's the deal. I'm going to ask Colin to call his counterpart in Maryland and tell them officially to ignore whatever shit you're trying to pull with them."

"With all due respect, Governor, that's obstruction of justice."

"With all due respect, Sheriff, go fuck yourself. When you've got something better than a suspicion, we'll talk again. But for the time being, as the governor of the State of Indiana, I'm telling you to leave the residents of the State of Maryland alone. If you choose not to, you might just find yourself on the wrong end of your own investigation by Mr. Barksdale. Could I make myself any clearer?"

Gail locked her jaw. Only a career-long respect for official protocol kept her from hanging up on the bastard. "No, sir, you have made yourself perfectly clear."

"See to it," Swensen said, and then he hung up.

Gail and Jesse both stared at the phone until the circuit broke and the dial tone turned to a squeal. She turned it off.

"Well, that wasn't the warm and fuzzy guy we see on television," Jesse quipped. "Want to kill a political career? I'll back you up all the way."

Gail smiled. "It wouldn't work. One politician to another, that's often the way conversations go."

Jesse leaned back in his seat and crossed his legs. "You're not going to stop pushing, are you?"

"I don't have to," she said. "We already have our answer." She made sure that she had Jesse's full attention. "Anybody who goes to that much trouble to avoid talking to the police, even before he knows what we're looking for, is definitely guilty of something."

"And anybody that rich can certainly afford the services of an independent hostage rescue contractor," Jesse agreed. "We can't prove anything, of course."

Gail shrugged it off. "We're too early in the process to worry about proof. Right now, let's just celebrate our first real break. Now we have to find out what Thomas or Tony Hughes has in common with Richard Lydell of Perseus Foods."

Chapter Seventeen

Richard Lydell was apoplectic, his voice betraying a level of rage that Jonathan hadn't heard since his days in the Unit, and that diatribe had involved a mud bog and a colonel's Corvette. "Scorpion, do you understand the peril you've put me in? Do you understand how I am not cut out for this kind of pressure?"

Jonathan adjusted the earpiece of his Bluetooth telephone receiver and strolled a circle around the interior of his office. Sometimes, people just needed to vent, and by staying out of their way, you made it easier on everyone. "I'll say it again, Mr. Lydell, you don't have anything to worry about. Frankly, I wish you hadn't decided to stonewall them. Sometimes, protection of one's constitutional rights is a very small step away from an admission of guilt." He winced as soon as he heard the G-word pass his lips.

"What the hell have I got to feel guilty for?" Lydell boomed. Then, before Jonathan could answer, the CEO of Perseus Foods took care of it himself. "The answer is nothing! Under any reasonable circumstance, the answer should be that I'm guilty of nothing. But now that you took my airplane to do whatever terrible thing you did—and I figure it had to have something to do with the triple murder in Indiana that's all over the news—you've made me an accessory. My God, man, do you have any idea how much danger you've put me in?"

Jonathan stood with his back to his Italian mahogany desk, staring out the window at the swarm of boats clogging the river. "Mr. Lydell, whatever danger you are or are not in is now a permanent part of your life. I do everything I can to mask my movements, and you were well aware of the nature of my business when we negotiated my fee."

"I didn't know that you'd be killing people in the United States. I had assumed that your . . . *business* took you mainly abroad."

Outside of his office, in the reception area of the executive suite, Jonathan heard a door slam open, and a voice bellow, "This had better be goddamn good!" Boxers had responded to Venice's summons. It was going to be a long day.

"Look," Jonathan said into the phone. "I don't know what you want from me. I never made any promises to you regarding the nature of my business, and I don't remember a lot of caveats from you when that business involved bringing your daughter home. You do what you think you have to do, but I assure you that your blood pressure should be a far greater concern right now than being linked to my activities."

His office door erupted open, and Boxers' frame filled it. He looked like hammered shit. Clearly, he hadn't bothered to glance in a mirror before he'd driven in from his house in DC. The quaintness of Fisherman's Cove was wasted on Boxers, whose primary yardstick for neighborhood quality measured the quantity of alcohol served within staggering distance of his front door. The big man had obviously planned a big entrance, but when he saw that his boss was on the phone, he muted himself. He wandered to the bar, found the twenty-four-year-old Lagavulin, and poured himself thirty dollars' worth.

Jonathan continued, "I won't share the details of my precautions, but I can tell you this—the nature of our agreement has not changed. Please try to have a nice day."

Lydell was just about to open a new round of negotiation when Jonathan pushed the disconnect button.

"The hell was that about?" Boxers rumbled as he fell into the leather sofa near the fireplace.

Jonathan wandered his way and helped himself to the wooden William and Mary rocking chair. The slatted back was somchow casicr on his twice-broken vertebrae than the really soft stuff. "Richard Lydell is whining again. The cops in Indiana are better than we gave them credit for."

Boxers scowled. "We in trouble?"

Jonathan shook his head. "Nah. The locals in Samson put the right pieces together and figured out that we flew in from out of town. They traced some records at the airport to Perseus, and when they called, Lydell refused to talk with them."

Boxers looked concerned. "That's like wearing an 'I'm guilty' sweatshirt."

Jonathan chuckled. "Lydell's connected. He got the politcos involved. That investigation won't go anywhere."

Boxers took a hit of the scotch and winced. "I wish you wouldn't talk directly to people like that. It's a security breach. You're gonna get yourself in trouble one day."

"What, the phone call? Christ, the Scorpion calls are

routed through so many switches, nobody could ever know where it's coming from."

It had been a bone of contention between the two of them for some time. Boxers had long believed that Jonathan took too many security shortcuts, arguing that the little things add up over time. Jonathan's side of the argument was all about personal contact. Without it, he felt, a mission was never whole. You had to make some kind of contact with every client, or else you risked getting set up. Jonathan respected his own ability to judge people by their voices.

Boxers let the point drop. "Sorry to hear about the ex, Dig. How's she doing?"

"Not well, but so far, no change. They're just hoping that they'll be able to pull her through it." He modulated his voice to filter out all emotion.

"Been to see her?"

"I've tried, but they won't let me into ICU. I'm not family."

"Ven told me that Fuckface is dead, too. Real shame about that." Like Venice, Boxers had witnessed the Divorce Wars.

Jonathan wasn't in the mood for that kind of bantering. He stood. "Come with me to the War Room," he said. "I've got something you need to see."

Boxers stood, shifting his drink to his left hand so he could use his right to push himself up from the seat. "I saw the Angry One in there cuing something up for the screen. Is that it?"

Jonathan never did understand why Boxers and Venice hadn't found a way to get along, but he'd decided years ago to stay out of it. He led the way to the War Room—a paneled conference area with every conceivable electronic gadget lining the walls and ceiling, plus more embedded in the teak conference table. When they entered and Jonathan pushed the door closed, Boxers helped himself to a seat close to the LCD video panel at the head of the room and placed his scotch on the table.

"Use a coaster," Venice commanded, and she slid one across to him.

He glared and placed the leather disk between the sweaty glass and the table.

Jonathan gestured for Venice to begin. "We got this in the mail this morning," he explained. "We think that this was going down at the exact moment when we were executing the 0300 mission in Indiana."

Using an LCD command console, Venice touched the appropriate buttons to make the lights dim and the screen resolve into the video that Jonathan had already watched a dozen times. Once again, Stephenson Hughes and Tibor Rothman addressed the strangers, and once again, the impending deal fell apart and the soundtrack erupted into shooting. After the final frame froze, the screen faded to blue, and the lights came up again in the conference room.

Jonathan looked to Boxers. "Initial thoughts?"

The big man was sitting much taller in his seat now, and he'd pushed his scotch off to the side. His was the body language of a man fully engaged. "I've got a lot of initial thoughts," he said. "The first one is I think it's no wonder that those bozos got themselves killed. The second one is who the hell mailed you the tape?"

"It's a chip," Venice answered. She caught him up on the conclusions they'd drawn about how the mailing led to Ellen's torture.

"Jesus," Boxers grumbled. "So now we go and kill the sons of bitches, right, Dig?"

Jonathan waved Venice off before she had a chance

to make her vigilante speech. “We’re not killing anyone,” he said. “Not unless they try to kill us first. We don’t even know who’d be on the list.”

“Sure we do,” Boxers said.

Jonathan cocked his head. A distant memory stirred.

“Didn’t you recognize that guy with the scar? Didn’t he look really, really familiar to you? There was a guy at Bragg, a Ranger, I think, about eight, ten years ago. Went on a black op over in the Balkans and got way carried away with his interrogation techniques.”

The proverbial bell rang more clearly. “He killed a family, right? Some local chieftain or something.”

Boxers nodded enthusiastically. “Exactly. But he also raped the daughters and mutilated the son. Shit that was way over the top. Anyway, I remember when that was first breaking, they published a picture of the guy. He had a scar just like the guy on the tape.”

Yes, he did. Jonathan remembered it now. “I thought he was court-martialed and sent off to pull hard time.”

Boxers shot him a look, and Jonathan knew right away what he meant. Crimes committed in a war zone rarely brought the penalties that were delivered in the World. Ten years would have been more than enough time for someone to pay his price and get cycled out.

“What the hell was his name?” Boxers asked himself. “It was different. Foreign. I remember making fun of it at the time. It would be like someone being named Osama today. Was it Russian, maybe?”

There went the bell again. Jonathan’s mind raced. Russian sounded right to him. It was something simple, of that he was sure. Not Vladimir. “Ivan?” he asked.

Boxers snapped his fingers. “Bingo. I don’t remember the last name, but I’ll bet ten bucks that Ivan is right.”

“Patrick!” Jonathan announced, pulling the name out

of nowhere. "Ivan Patrick. Now I remember the news stories. Real sicko. Likes his torture. I think you're right."

Venice raised her hand, as if posing a question in school. "Wait a second," she said. "Is your testosterone world really *that* small? I mean, what are the chances? I know you don't believe in coincidences, but my heavens."

"I don't think it's outlandish," Jonathan said. "Clearly, this guy was hired muscle, and the population of ex-Army types who would go to the dark side is refreshingly small. When Rangers go bad like this one did, it's big news in the Community. The kick in the ass is that the very personality traits that make him bad news for the military also allow him to name his price in the World."

Boxers asked, "So what was Fuckface delivering as ransom?"

Jonathan arched his eyebrows. "That's the million-dollar question, isn't it? Whatever it is—was—it's worth hiring a real badass for protection." He looked to Venice. "What was the scraggly looking one's name again?"

"Conger," she answered without hesitation and without consulting a note. "Care to hear what I was able to dig up on him?"

Jonathan's eyes widened. "You know something already?"

She gave her coyest smile. "I did a little poking around on the Internet. I searched the combination Conger and Hughes, and I didn't get anything usable. Then I tried Conger and Stephenson Hughes and didn't do any better."

For the second time in a day, Jonathan settled into his chair for the long version. He folded his arms, crossed his legs, and committed himself to hearing her out.

She continued, "Then I tried just Stephenson Hughes, and I didn't get much of anything there, either. It wasn't until I threw Indiana into the mix that I got my first break. Stephenson Hughes and Indiana gave me his place of employment. He works for a place called Carlyle Industries."

"That's a defense contractor," Jonathan said, instantly recognizing the name. He didn't mention that Carlyle made far more money off the black projects that no one ever heard about than they did off the high-profile stuff they ran on their television commercials.

"Exactly," Venice agreed. "So then I searched for Conger and Carlyle Industries, and guess what I got?"

"To the point, I hope," Boxers said.

She glared, then turned her attention solely to Jonathan. "I got hits. Not many, but quality." She paused to open the manila file on the table in front of her and page through to the notes she wanted. "Here it is. Fabian Conger. Born in Ypsilanti, Michigan. Thirty-five years old, a graduate of Florida State University with a degree in sociology. Seems he's been at war with Carlyle Industries for about a hundred years. He claims that Carlyle manufactures chemical and biological weapons in violation not only of U.S. law but also of the Chemical Weapons Convention, which specifically forbids those kinds of weapons."

Jonathan avoided eye contact with Boxers, who he was certain was doing the same thing. Created to eliminate chemical weapons throughout the world, the Chemical Weapons Convention was overseen in the United States by the State and Commerce departments, which together moved heaven and earth to manage the destruction of thousands of tons of the stuff. When they were done, all known stores of chemical weapons were obliterated.

That left only the growing stores of covertly produced new stuff that made the old stuff look like getting a bad cold.

"Where did he make these claims?" Jonathan asked.

"Apparently to every newspaper in the country. Nobody wrote a story about it, as far as I can tell, but I found mentions of him on various blogs and discussion boards frequented by reporters. He called them all, yet all of them blew him off."

"Was Tibor one of them?" Jonathan asked.

She shook her head. "I can't tell. Tibor was famous enough to turn up over a million hits when I searched for him. I can say, though, that a search for Tibor's name and Conger's name turned up nothing."

Boxers asked, "But *because* he's so famous, isn't it fair to assume that they knew each other? Or at least corresponded?"

Jonathan shook his head. "They might have corresponded, but they certainly had never met. We see that in the video. Conger didn't know who he was."

Venice turned to a transcript she'd made. "As for the weapons," she said, "what was that line from the video?" She riffled through the sheets. "Here. When they were talking about whether Hughes brought the 'itcms' and he holds off, wanting to see his son—Thomas, is it?"

Jonathan nodded.

"Right, he wanted to see his son Thomas. Hughes says, 'Your side of the bargain is an inanimate object, my side is a human life. My son. They don't equate.' To which Conger replies, 'Your side of the bargain, as you say, is actually *thousands* of lives, Mr. Hughes.'" She looked up to see if they had drawn the same conclusions. "It makes sense," she said.

Jonathan leaned forward and pulled at his lower lip. "If Conger had a bug up his ass about his assumption that Carlyle Industries was manufacturing chemical weapons, the thing he'd want most in life would be to have a sample to show people."

"But nobody would ever step forward to do that," Boxers said, taking up the line of logic.

"*Could* anyone step forward?" Venice asked. "Does Carlyle actually make chemical weapons?"

Jonathan stepped in. "If it was true, Ven, it wouldn't be something we'd be free to discuss. All that matters is Conger thinks it's true. What better way to get the proof he's looking for than to kidnap the child of one of the workers? What was Stephenson Hughes's job there, anyway?"

Again, Venice answered from memory. "His job title is senior contract administrator. A paper-pusher. He earns just over a hundred thousand a year, and his wife doesn't work."

Jonathan scowled. "Why would they kidnap *his* kid? Why wouldn't they go after some senior executive? Or at least someone with direct access to the project?"

Boxers scoffed, "As if your job title ever reflected what you do for a living. Or mine, for that matter. For all we know, he could have been the grand imperial poobah of special weapons."

"And he certainly implied that he had what Conger was looking for," Venice said. "Even if he never handed it over."

"That was probably his contingency plan," Jonathan agreed. "Like we said before, handing the stuff over was the only hedge he had to keep Thomas alive."

"They'd have killed him anyway," Boxers grumbled.

Jonathan shrugged. "Of course they would. But what choice did his dad have? It's why kidnapping works so well as a bargaining tool."

"Let's get back to Fabian Conger," Venice said, returning to her notes. "He's a member of a group called the Green Brigade. Sound familiar?"

Jonathan cocked his head. "It does. Why?"

She so loved having the upper hand in these things. "Remember the name you had me research? Christine Baker?"

Jonathan pounded the table. "The girl in the woods! Is it the same Green Brigade?"

"There's only one that I could find. It's a wacko environmental preservation outfit that is known for doing just about anything to make a point."

"Stuff like what?" Boxers asked.

"They burned down a ski lodge under construction a few years ago, and they've been known to drive steel spikes into trees they want to preserve so that lumberjacks are killed instead of owls. That sort of thing."

Jonathan scowled. "Any kidnapping and murder on their rap sheet?"

"Ever seen what happens to the lumberjack whose saw hits a spike?" Boxers grumped.

"I meant that in the more immediate, premeditated sense."

"I know what you meant," Venice said. "I've seen nothing in the record about murder plots, per se. But the leader of the Green Brigade—they like to call themselves the Green Bees—is a guy named Andrew Hawkins, and he lives in Frederick, Maryland. Maybe you want to talk to him."

Jonathan exchanged looks with Boxers. "I think you're right," Jonathan said.

"And Stephenson Hughes, too," Boxers added.

"He's dead," Jonathan said.

Venice's mouth gaped. "He is?"

"Of course. He's that other body. The one we have pictures of." Seeing Boxers' quizzical expression, he caught him up on the missing details.

When he'd heard it all, Boxers asked, "So, how do you know it's Hughes?"

"Who else could it be?"

Venice looked at him like he'd grown an extra nose. "Aren't you the very person who lectures constantly about drawing conclusions too early?"

"It fits that pattern. The torture, the brutal death."

"But the mutilation of the body is entirely different," Boxers cautioned.

"The mutilation of the body was to prevent identification," Jonathan argued. "Who's left? That film showed two good guys and two bad guys, and so far we've got two bodies. I'm going to edge out on a limb and say that neither Tibor nor Stephenson Hughes the paper-pusher are up to the task of beheading people they've killed in self-defense."

"What Venice's saying," Boxers interjected, "is that this could be bigger than the people in the video. For all we know, there might have been two dozen other people out there."

"And they were all bad guys! Why mutilate each other?" Jonathan changed the subject. "So what else do you know about these people?"

Venice looked wounded. "It's only been a few hours," she said.

APRIL 22

CHAPTER EIGHTEEN

Jonathan opened his eyes at 05:58 with the sensation of lying on a bed of ax handles. JoeDog had joined him during the night, and she was attempting to push his kidneys out through his navel while pretending to stretch. "Don't forget to make up the bed," he grumbled as he rolled out and put his feet on the floor. It was time for him to be up anyway.

Boxers was supposed to show up at seven for their trip to visit Andrew Hawkins of the Green Bees. Jesus, what a stupid name for a terrorist group. Scratch that. *Activist* group. Sometimes it was hard to tell the difference.

He walked to the window and took a peek toward the east, where a gorgeous pink glow on the horizon foretold a clear morning. Beyond the rooftops of the buildings across the street, he could see the last of the commercial shrimpers on their way out for the diminishing daily haul. He envied them their freedom.

Stretching again and scratching, he turned away from paradise and padded across the creaky hardwood floors to the bathroom. His route took him through his massive teak-paneled closet, past the sauna on the right and the steam room on the left. When he crossed the threshold into the bathroom, he touched the master light switch on the wall. Vanity lights, shower lights, and a wall-mounted twenty-seven-inch flat panel television all jumped to life.

Jonathan liked his showers hot. Not tepid, not luke-anything. Hot. He'd spent too many years shivering through dribbling cold-water freeze fests. Now he was a civilian, he was rich, and he had enough water pressure to strip the red off a brick wall. After fifteen minutes, he was awake, refreshed, and ready to meet whatever the day had in store.

As he pushed on the steamed-over glass door to get out, it opened only three inches, then hit a hard stop. "Dammit, Joe," he said, instantly diagnosing the problem. "Move." She didn't move until he yelled at her a second time, and then it was only to go as far as the foot of the marble sink that was Jonathan's next destination.

His sink. One of two. His and hers.

As crazy as it was, he'd always held out a wild, ridiculous thread of hope that Ellen would one day realize the mistake she had made by leaving him and hooking up with Tibor Rothman. In his wildest imaginings, he'd allowed himself to believe that there was room in the adult world for the kind of do-over that you negotiated as a kid. He'd made mistakes, and he'd learned from them, so it only seemed right that he should get a second chance. As many times as he'd sacrificed for others, you'd think that God could arrange that little bit for him.

He faced himself in the mirror. A pockmarked disk of scar tissue on the right side of his abdomen was a souvenir from the first Gulf War, and the six-inch monster scar just to the left of his navel marked the path that Army doctors had used to pull the bullet out along with his spleen and a chunk of his liver. The zippers on his left shoulder and knee were keepsakes from Panama. Then there were the uncountable two-and-three stitchings all over his body that were the marks of a modern warrior.

The U.S. Army had invested millions of dollars to make him the stalwart defender of freedom that he had become, and for the investment, they'd received the kind of man who consistently returned to duty weeks before his official recovery period was over. Given the time and the tools, no mission was beyond the capabilities of former First Sergeant Jonathan Grave.

Jonathan's gut wound from the Gulf had triggered one of the dreaded visits from the Unit chaplain. Seeing himself in the mirror, he realized what a nightmare it must have been for Ellen every time she saw him with his shirt off. It wasn't that the wounds were disfiguring; it was the fact that he'd already been lucky so many times, with mere centimeters making the difference between recovery and death. Anticipation of loss had displaced the anticipation of love. No woman—no *person*—could be expected to hold up under that.

Getting her back had always been a long shot, but it had been a dream for him. And now Ellen lay clinging to life in Fairfax Hospital. Tortured. Beaten. And they still wouldn't permit a visit.

The telephone rang, a deep thrumming noise that made the floor vibrate under his feet. He'd specifically designed the ring to have a tactile element so that he'd be able to hear it ring in the shower. Broken from his pity party, he said in a strong voice, "Command. Answer."

The voice recognition software muted the television and activated the speakerphone. "Grave," he said.

"Mr. Grave, this is Detective Weatherby with the Fairfax County Police," a familiar voice said. "I'm afraid I have some bad news."

Jonathan's heart jumped. "Is it Ellen?" He'd tried twice to get in to see her, but the Cossacks at the nurses' station wouldn't let him. Family only, they'd said, and ex-husbands didn't qualify.

"No, sir, it's not," the detective said. "Sorry to startle you. It's her husband, Tibor Rothman. He's been found dead in Ohio."

"Damn shame," Jonathan said. He didn't even try to hide his loathing.

"I just thought you should know."

Jonathan turned on the water at the sink and let it run hot. "Thanks for the update, Detective. Is there anything else?"

A brief pause. "Your alibis all checked out for the time of your wife's attack," he said. "You should know that I'm going to run them again for Rothman's murder."

"I'd expect no less," Jonathan said.

It was just after ten when Boxers piloted Jonathan's Hummer H2 from the interstate onto Market Street in the heart of old town Frederick, Maryland. The town itself was much more alive than he had expected. The picture he'd drawn in his mind had not anticipated the charm of the place, with its 150-year old homes and storefronts. He'd been ignorant of the city-sponsored gentrification projects. At an hour when Fisherman's Cove felt abandoned by the commuters who'd fled to the city, downtown Frederick teemed with businesspeople.

"I kinda like this town," Boxers mused aloud.

"Too big," Jonathan said. As the chief cheerleader for Fisherman's Cove, he would have felt treasonous acknowledging the charm of another community.

"There's the bar up there," Boxers said, pointing ahead and to the left. "It's a little early to catch him, don't you think?" Venice had been able to divine that Andrew Hawkins earned money to be an environmental zealot by working as a first-shift bartender at the Market Street Grille, an upscale dive that appeared from the outside to be more geared to the burgeoning yuppie population than the blue-collar crowd for which the bar was originally built.

"His Web site says they open at ten thirty," Jonathan said. "Gives him time to clean the spit out of last night's beer glasses."

"Ah, now there's an image I need," Boxers grumped.

At this hour, it was a cinch finding a parking place, even for a beast as huge as the Hummer.

"We just gonna knock on the door?" Boxers asked.

Jonathan opened his door and started to climb out. "Rules never change," he said. "Exhaust the simple solutions before you try the exotic ones."

As it turned out, they didn't even have to knock. The door was unlocked. A *ping* announced their arrival, but the hostess station was empty. In fact, at first glance, the whole room was empty.

Dark in both lighting and décor, the place was obviously more bar than grille, with considerable homage paid to the ambience of an Irish pub. The bar itself, on the left-hand side of the deep rectangular room, easily stretched twenty feet into the darkness. Along the back wall, a raised platform, a couple of music stands, and some dormant amplifiers were evidence of a recent live band performance. Four-legged wooden tables crowded the place in the front and along the right-hand side.

"We're not open yet!" a male voice called from the kitchen behind the bar.

Jonathan put a finger over his lips to signal Boxers to remain quiet. "Stay near the door here," he whispered, and then walked farther into the bar. He intentionally moved a chair just to make some noise.

"I said we're closed!" This time the voice shimmered with annoyance, and a few seconds later, its owner appeared in the kitchen doorway. "We don't open for another half hour."

Andrew Hawkins looked exactly like the picture that Venice had been able to pull down from the Internet. Although shorter than Jonathan had expected, at say five-eight, Hawkins wore his long hair in a ponytail, and sported a mountain-man beard. Jonathan pegged him as midforties, and figured the gnarly nose evidenced a close familiarity with the product he served. Whatever friendly demeanor existed for his customers was nowhere to be found for his early morning gate-crashers.

"Good morning, Mr. Hawkins," Jonathan said in a tone that was equal parts cheer and menace.

Hawkins's tired, pale blue eyes narrowed as he tried to make a connection. "Do we know each other?" He tensed as he caught sight of Boxers' towering hulk blocking his exit out the front door.

"In a manner of speaking," Jonathan said. "We've got the Green Brigade in common."

"Don't know what you're talking about," Hawkins replied a little too quickly. "Now I'll be happy to serve you in a half hour." He turned on his heel and disappeared back into the kitchen.

"He's bolting," Jonathan said, but Boxers was already out the front door, on the way around back. Jonathan took the more direct route. He planted his hands on the polished mahogany of the bar and vaulted his feet over, scattering glassware and a sealed plastic container of olives, cherries, and lemon wedges onto the webbed rubber matting on the floor. Ahead, from the other side of the wall, he heard the sound of running feet and clattering pans. That meant Hawkins was not lying in wait just on the other side of the door, which in turn meant that Jonathan could crash through the door with abandon.

Half as wide as the bar and grille, the kitchen was a place that no customer should ever see. Jonathan recorded it as a blur of greasy walls and food-spattered floors as he watched the back door to the alley close. Three seconds later, he hit the door at full speed, slamming the crash bar and launching the door open with enough force to rip it free of the automatic-closer hardware. A glance to his left showed Boxers turning the corner doing his best to run, and a glance to the right showed Andrew Hawkins sprinting for all he was worth, but already slowing.

Jonathan tore after him. After ten strides, he'd cut Hawkins's lead in half. "If you make me catch you, I'll make it hurt!" he yelled to the little man. "I just want to talk!" Behind him, he could hear Boxers lumbering to catch up.

Hawkins at first sped up his stride, and then gave up, drawing to a trot and then a walk as he raised his hands in surrender.

Jonathan fought the urge to tackle him anyway, and instead opted to keep his distance. Without looking at Boxers, he made a sideward waving motion to indicate that he should likewise show restraint.

Stopped now, with his hands still raised, Hawkins turned to face them both. He looked both frightened and embarrassed. "Running's not as easy as it used to be," he said, sheepishly.

Jonathan kept his voice calm. "Put your hands down. We're not cops, and we're not your enemies. We only want to talk."

Hawkins lowered his hands. His expression was pure suspicion. "You mentioned that. What are we going to talk about?"

"The Green Bees."

"I don't—"

"And please skip the denials. We're in an alley, for God's sake, because you made like a track star last time I mentioned the Green Brigade."

Hawkins shifted his eyes between Jonathan and Boxers, and as he did, he seemed to find resolve. "Maybe I don't run so good, but I'll tell you right now that I don't scare easy. If you've got blackmail on your mind, I got nothin' worth extorting."

"We're not here to extort anything, Mr. Hawkins. Can I call you Andy?"

Hawkins scowled. "Not even my mother calls me Andy. Andrew's fine. And what's your name again?"

"Leon," Jonathan lied.

"That's no more your name than mine is Mona," Hawkins said.

Jonathan neither confirmed nor denied. "You're the leader of the Green Brigade. Yes?"

Hawkins watched as Boxers worked his way around to block his only escape route. He sighed. "Look, the true answer is no, but I know if I tell you that, you're gonna beat the shit outta me."

"What makes you think that?"

"If you didn't want me to think that, you wouldn't have brought Lurch here to block the sun."

Jonathan smiled in spite of himself. Back in the Unit, a few people had tried to make the name Lurch stick for Boxers, but the big man didn't like it. *Really* didn't like it. "He's back there because you looked twitchy as hell inside, and because you ran. Think of him more as a roadblock than a menace. All we want is the truth."

Hawkins shrugged. "I used to be the commander of what used to be the Green Brigade. But it doesn't exist anymore. At least not as I knew it."

Jonathan cocked his head.

Hawkins patted his shirt and then his pants pockets before he stopped himself. "You gonna shoot me if I get a cigarette?"

"If the cigarette doesn't have a trigger, you'll be fine." As Jonathan spoke, a gentle press with his right elbow reconfirmed the presence of the .45 on his hip.

Hawkins told his story as he slid a Marlboro between his lips and lit it with a flourish from his Zippo. "When I joined the Green Bees, it stood for something. We were an environmentalist group. We talked trash, smoked a little weed, organized protests, and circulated petitions."

"What were your causes?"

"A lot of animal rights stuff. Habitat preservation, clean air legislation, that sort of thing. You know it's shameful how we treat the defenseless creatures of this planet." He caught Jonathan's telltale glance toward his clothing. "Yeah, okay, I know. The leather belt and shoes argument. I eat meat, too, but it's different. You don't want the whole stump speech, but let me tell you, the day will come when cynics like you will be damned sorry that you turned people like me into punch lines. Thing is, by the time you realize it, my environment's gonna be as fucked up as yours, and there'll be no escape."

Jonathan said nothing while Hawkins went on.

"There was a time when the Green Bees meant

something good. And unlike some of the other *famous* environmental groups"—he did finger-quotes—"what we did was based on *real* science. We were a good cause."

"You keep speaking in the past tense," Jonathan observed.

"Well, yeah. Because about five years ago, it all started going to shit. We got this hardcore militia-loving element flooding in, and it got scary. Suddenly, we weren't talking about saving stuff as much as were talking about burning stuff down. That's not what I was about. In the end, I had no choice but to get the hell out. So whatever you think they did, good luck with nailing them, 'cause I got nothin' to do with them."

"What about Fabian Conger?" Jonathan asked. "Where did he fit in?"

Hawkins's face lit up. "You know Fabian?"

"Let's agree that I'm the one asking questions." It sounded like a threat but he didn't mean it that way.

Hawkins took a long pull on his Marlboro. If Jonathan read the body language correctly, he was witnessing a crisis of conscience. That meant Conger was a friend. People generally don't mind ratting out enemies. It also meant that he had to be careful not to take too much of what he was about to learn at face value.

"I liked Fabe," Hawkins said. He crushed the spent butt under his shoe and fished another out of the pack. "When he first came aboard the Green Bees, he was a true believer, a real hard driver, you know? Ask him to do anything and it was done." He chuckled as a private joke bloomed in his mind. "You ever see that Gary Larson cartoon where the kid is trying to get into the School of the Gifted, and he's pushing for all he's worth on the door that's marked 'Pull'?"

Jonathan smiled. It was one of his favorites, in fact.

That one and the one with the deer with a three-ring target as a birthmark on his chest.

"Well, that was Fabe. The guy knew more shit about stuff you never needed to know, but he just didn't have any damn common sense. In a classroom, you'd think he was brilliant, but on the street, you'd think he was an idiot. You know the kind of guy I'm talking about?"

"I meet them every day," Jonathan said. He was beginning to like Andrew Hawkins; trust him, even.

"If you know the type, then you know they can be talked into anything if the sales pitch is right. So when this new guy came on board—an Army-type who was all about environmentalism through world domination—Fabe was all over it. I mean Jesus Christ, they started talking about killing people to save the oceans. It was crazy."

Army type. A bell rang in Jonathan's head. "What was this new guy's name?"

Hawkins shook his head. "That one, you'll have to get for yourself. No way I'm gonna cross him."

Jonathan snorted a laugh. "What, you think I'm going to rat you out?"

"I don't give a shit what you do. I'm just sayin' you ain't gettin' that info from me. He's a sick fuck, that one."

"So, you're talking about Ivan Patrick," Boxers said from close behind.

Hawkins scowled. "If you already know this stuff, why are you busting my balls?"

Boxers scoffed, "If we were busting your balls, you'd be bow-legged." Diplomacy had never been the big man's long suit.

Jonathan stepped in. "There's stuff we know we know, and stuff we think we know. We're counting on you to help us figure out which is which."

Hawkins closed his eyes and took a deep breath. He really didn't want to do this. "That's his name," he said, drooping his head and rubbing the back of his neck. "But nobody calls him that. He goes by Palmer now. No last name—or maybe no first name, who knows?—just Palmer. The guy's charismatic as hell, the way Hitler had charisma. He says the wildest shit about anything, and people eat it up."

"What kind of shit?" Boxers asked.

"Crazy shit. He's got this one speech about how Paul Revere and the Boston Tea Party guys were the first terrorists and that patriotism and terrorism are all in the eye of the beholder. It makes sense when you first hear it, you know? I mean, if you were a Nazi in France in dubya-dubya two, you're not gonna see the French Resistance as freedom fighters, you're gonna see them as terrorists, right?"

Jonathan had walked that line of reasoning a thousand times, as had every military warrior. "So, I gather that it *didn't* make sense to you?"

"Sure it made sense to me. At first, anyway. But when you start spiking trees and burning buildings in the middle of the night, you've sorta crossed a line."

"So you did those things?" Boxers asked.

"I'm not confirming or denying on that. But let's say that the Green Bees did it. Better yet, the group I used to know as the Green Bees did it. Palmer did away with 'Green Bees,' by the way. He'd only tolerate 'the Brigade' or the 'Green Brigade.' Anything else, and there'd be trouble."

"What kind of trouble?" Jonathan wanted to know.

Hawkins shrugged. "Palmer was all about discipline. Pushups and running and shit. All kinds of boot camp crap. And people did it! It was the wildest fucking thing. I mean some people quit, but most of them didn't. I think Palmer's style of leadership was what a lot of them—people like Fabe, for example—were looking for. And once he named himself commandant, we started getting all kinds of Palmer clones joining the outfit, people who wanted to spend more time blowing shit up than influencing policy."

"And that's when you knew it was time to get out?" Jonathan prompted.

Hawkins dropped the current cigarette to the ground and fished for a third. The guy was a living chimney. "We're bein' honest here, right? No bullshit?"

Jonathan shrugged. Hawkins seemed happy to be shedding himself of baggage.

"I wish I could say it was. I'm tellin' you, this guy Palmer was good. So what if some fat cat developers lost their property if it was in the name of a good cause? They had insurance, right? They had more money than they knew what to with, so they could weather the storm. That kind of logic resonates if you want it to. And keeping it real, I gotta say I wanted it to."

Boxers moved around from behind Hawkins to take a less threatening position where he could be seen. "What changed your mind?"

Hawkins thought before answering. "Too much concentration on weapons. They couldn't get enough of them. Rifles, shotguns, machine guns, pistols, grenades. If it fired a projectile or threw shrapnel, they wanted it."

Jonathan exchanged glances with Boxers. This was all beginning to make sense. "What did they say they wanted it for?"

"You look like you was in the military once," Hawkins observed. "I was, too, a million years ago, and he wanted them for all the reasons every outfit wants weapons. Offense and defense."

"Defense against some raid to take your guns away?" Boxers asked.

"Exactly. Palmer was obsessed with Waco and Ruby Ridge. He talked about it all the time. That was what our fascist government did to freedom fighters. Those were his words, not mine. You had to be prepared for the assault."

"That's a lot of violent talk for an environmentalist group."

Hawkins laughed. "Ya think? Only we stopped being an enviro group ages ago. Palmer turned us into a revolutionary group. And like I said, guys like Fabian Conger ate it up. It's like Fabe finally had something to do that he considered important, and he was by God going to see the revolution through."

Boxers shook his head, as if rattling his brain would make the pieces fit. "What was the revolution against?"

"Well, that's the thing!" Hawkins said, raising his voice for the first time. "You'd think someone would ask the question, but they never got around to it. We were going to *take it to the government*, and we were going to *change the way things worked in Washington*, but that was as far as the plan went. There was no enemy that I could think of. I mean, there are plenty of enemies if you think hard enough—everybody from the judges to the congress to the president—but you don't change that stuff with violence, you change it with good ideas that spread from person to person. *That's* what he had wrong when he compared Paul Revere to the terrorists. Their violence was in support of a definable idea, with a real goal—freedom from tyranny. The violence during the Revolution wasn't the endgame, it was a last resort. For Palmer, the violence and the speeches were all there was. And the people who followed him gnawed on his ideas like dogs with a bone, and they played soldier up in the hills."

"Which hills?" Jonathan asked.

"We got some property west of Charleston. Way west. Don't ask me who owns it, because I don't have a clue. We've always had it. It's like a little frontier town. In the old days, it never even had a name—we just called it the retreat—but Palmer took to calling it Brigadeville, and the name stuck. Last time I saw any of those pricks was a year and a half ago. I just knew they was trouble, and I wanted none of it no more."

"How would I find it if I wanted to?" Boxers asked.

Hawkins scowled. "Trust me, you don't want to. Palmer takes his security very seriously. I'm talking armed patrols, triple rolls of razor wire, the whole nine yards. I'm tellin' you, these people are seriously armed."

Boxers' mouth twisted into the kind of smile that projected only coldness. "Pretend that I'm crazy and wanted to go there anyway."

Hawkins shot a nervous look to Jonathan. "Well, I guess you'd start driving west out of Charleston, near Kermit. It's not like the roads are marked out there, you know? Given Palmer's paranoia, that wouldn't have made any sense. You'd just have to know the land marks."

Boxers wanted more.

"Honest, guys, that's all there is. It's not a place you want to go if you're not invited."

"Was there any trouble when you decided to quit?" Jonathan asked.

Hawkins laughed. "You don't quit the Brigade. You're a brigadier for life." His voice was heavy with disdain.

"Are those his words?"

"Those are everybody's words," Hawkins said. "It's even on the tattoo." Jonathan's shocked expression made Hawkins laugh. "That's some shit, ain't it?" He patted his left breast, over his heart. "Right here. To be a full member of the tribe, you had to get this ugly-ass coat of arms lookin' thing tattooed on your chest. Red, white, and blue, with 'brigadier for life' across the bottom. I mean, the thing is fuckin' huge."

Jonathan and Boxers shared a look. Unless Stephenson Hughes had a matching tattoo, it looked like Jonathan was wrong about him being the mutilated corpse from Sergeant Semen's jurisdiction. "Let's talk more about Fabian Conger," Jonathan said. "I get the impression that you two were friends."

"There were no friends in the Brigade. Only fellow brigadiers. But given that, I guess Fabe and I were about as close to friends as you can get. I haven't heard from him since the last time I was at the retreat."

"How did he and Ivan—Palmer—get along?"

Hawkins shook his head. "You're not getting it. You're assuming some kind of social motivation, and I'm telling you there was none of that. There used to be, back when I was in the leadership, but not after. There was the mission, and there was nothing else. No one 'got along' as you think of it. People followed orders and they drilled and they listened. Every now and then, they'd actually launch a mission, but more often than not, it was all about *preparing* for some unnamed apocalypse. If you haven't been there, I know it sounds stupid. Hell, it *was* stupid, but I'm telling you that's the way it was. As for Fabe and Palmer, I think the best way to put it is Fabe was an acolyte. A disciple. Palmer thought about saying 'jump' and Fabe was already out of his chair."

Jonathan turned what he'd learned over in his head,

weighing what they knew coming in against what Hawkins was feeding them. It was time to go from the general to the specific. "Does the name Carlyle Industries mean anything to you?"

Hawkins jumped like he'd been zapped with electricity. He whipped his head around to see if anyone was listening. "Holy shit," he hissed. "Who told you about Carlyle Industries?"

Jonathan said nothing, made no move. His face remained pleasantly impassive.

Hawkins raised is hands in surrender and turned to walk back inside. "You guys are hell-bent on getting me killed. I'm outta here."

Boxers blocked his way, and Hawkins looked as if he might cry. "Come on, guys," he whined. "Please don't do this to me. People are gonna know where you got this shit, and they're gonna come after me. As it is, the Brigade is paranoid that I don't come around anymore. All I've got going for me is their trust that I won't screw them."

"Quit panicking, Andrew," Jonathan said.

"You don't know these assholes. Panic is all I got."

"Think about what you're saying," Jonathan coached, his voice the essence of calm. "They can't know that you told us about Carlyle because you *didn't* tell us about Carlyle. The first time the name came up is when we mentioned it to you."

Hawkins's expression turned to an odd mix of surprise and disgust. "Facts don't matter with these people. *Appearances* matter. They watch me, you know. Not all the time, not every day, but enough. I see them hanging around. They find out about this meeting and they're going to make two and two equal six just because it suits them."

"You got nothin' to lose, then," Boxers growled.

"They been watchin' us, they're gonna blame you for what we already told you. You might as well go ahead and give us the rest."

Hawkins let Boxers' words sink in, and then he burst out with a laugh. "Jesus, you guys are good. Answer this for me. Why shouldn't I just walk away?"

"You tell me," Jonathan said. "You're the one who's still here."

Hawkins shot a look to Boxers. "I got a grizzly bear blocking my way."

Boxers met Jonathan's glance for an instant, then stepped aside. "I'm not blocking anything."

Hawkins sniffed the air for some kind of trap. He hesitantly took a step forward, paused again, and then without a word reentered the restaurant through the back door.

Boxers turned to Jonathan with his palms upturned. "What the hell was that?"

Jonathan sighed. "I was playing his bluff. Except maybe he wasn't bluffing." They waited a whole minute—Jonathan clocked it on his watch—and then started walking toward the mouth of the alley. "I thought maybe he would have an attack of conscience," he confided.

They were only fifty feet from the street when they heard the restaurant door open again. They turned together to see Andrew Hawkins in the middle of the alley, his hands thrust into his pockets. "I'm an idiot for doing this!" he called.

Chapter Nineteen

At the Archives–Navy Memorial Metro stop, Venice rode the escalator to street level and looked around to get her bearings. Like so many residents of northern Virginia, she rarely traveled into the District. Given its beauty and its attractions, you'd think it would be a regular thing. On this crystal clear day, she paused to allow her eyes to adjust to the bright light, and then crossed Pennsylvania Avenue to begin her short walk to the National Archives.

One of the great unsung American treasures, the Archives of the United States was a researcher's dream. Between its cavernous reading rooms and those of the Library of Congress down the street, there was nothing that could not be traced to ground if you knew how to massage computer databases. Want to see the rifle Lee Harvey Oswald used to kill John F. Kennedy? It's at the Archives. So are the thousands of other pieces of evidence—paper and hard—that define the hunt for truth in that crime of the century. The Declaration of Independence is there for the world to view, as are original copies of the U.S. Constitution, the Bill of Rights, the

Federalist Papers, and the personal correspondence of every political appointee in the history of the republic.

More important than those touristy documents, Venice marveled at the catalogs of public and private documents that had been collected over the years. In the Archives, if you hit the right keys on the computer, or if you filled out the right slip of paper and handed it to a clerk, you could find out the name, rank, and unit number of every soldier who ever served in the U.S. military, going back to the French and Indian War, even before there *was* a United States to defend.

On this day, Venice's trip into town was geared toward a single name.

After passing through the security station and verifying that she had no weapons, food, drink, or sources of fire, she walked the well-known route to the research room. There, she waited her turn for a computer, and when it finally arrived, she produced her driver's license and her research card and was allowed to begin.

She was looking for everything there was to know about the man known as Ivan Patrick. Settled into her carrel, she started typing. She began with the Army databases to find out what Ivan Patrick's crimes had been. Since that was all a matter of public record, she easily navigated her way to what she was looking for. The openness of American society was a little crazy when you thought about it—the sheer volume of information that was available to anyone with the notion and ability to look for it. In fact, the very reason that Delta Force—Digger's old outfit, officially the First Special Forces Operational Detachment Delta—did not exist on the books was to keep the names of its members out of the public record. If the Unit were official, then the names would be available to anyone who wanted to file a Freedom of Information Act request. Thus was born one of the nation's worst-kept secrets.

Everything Jonathan and Boxers remembered about Ivan Patrick turned out to be true. He'd raped a Serbian girl in 1997, made her family watch, and then killed them all. The original sentence had been eighty-five years at hard labor, but under the terms of military court-martial, that meant that he was eligible for—and in fact received—a parole after serving only eight years. Since then, he'd been more or less invisible, having retreated from the public record.

Frustrated by the lack of more contemporary information on Ivan, Venice shifted gears and looked into the dealings of Carlyle Industries. Formed in 1982 by two entrepreneurs named Rocko Bunting and Dean Philips, Carlyle was the number-six defense contractor in the country, sporting revenues in excess of $6 billion per year. Employing four thousand people all over the world, the company was into a wide spectrum of defense materiel, everything from bombs to propulsion systems to unmanned aerial vehicles. In the years since 9-11, the company's revenues had tripled.

She read up on Bunting and Philips, hoping to find a link to illegal activities, but when she came up with blanks, she decided to tour the entire executive staff. Everybody looked on paper just as they were supposed to look when they worked for a company like Carlyle. advanced degrees, international recognition in their areas of specialty, plain vanilla and boring. Her trip was proving to be a complete waste of time.

She dug deeper.

Stephenson Hughes, according to the company's directory, was a senior contract administrator for government and special projects. The title piqued her interest. "Special Projects" sounded a lot like the kinds of weapons programs that Fabian Conger had been screaming about in the news. She copied what information she could find about him and pasted it into an e-mail and sent it to herself.

She read through dozens of other names, all of the Carlyle employees who were tied into the program office. None of them seemed particularly sinister, or even particularly interesting.

After an hour or so, she cruised the administrative levels of the company. There, she found one particularly interesting character named Charlie Warren, the corporate director of security. With a background in the military police, followed by time in the Boston Police Department, he'd been with Carlyle's security group since 1996, and was promoted to director in 2004. His official photo made him look more like a banker than a cop. With slicked-back hair and unnaturally white teeth, he looked at the camera in a way that made him look like he was going to buy it a beer.

This was the kind of research that Venice could do for hours and never even look at the clock. She immersed herself in Carlyle Industries. Their Government Products Division made guidance packages for missile systems and armored plates for Bradley Fighting Vehicles. Their Government Services Division made computer programs for project management tracking and fire protection systems for military installations throughout the world. Meanwhile, their Defense Systems Division was in charge of unnamed specialized munitions for delivery by "multiple interservice weapons platforms." Clear as paint. Nowhere in the annual report was there a mention of chemical or biological warfare agents.

She turned to the page that displayed the salaries of the key employees—$8 million a year for Bunting and

Rooney, down to $320,000 for Charlie Warren, in all cases before benefits and bonuses. Further down the page, she found the list of key suppliers and contractors, and on that list she saw the name that made her heart jump.

Last year, Carlyle Industries paid $527,468.27 to Ivan Patrick Enterprises for "unspecified security services" performed for the Special Projects Division.

"Good Lord," she whispered aloud. Her heart racing and her brain screaming at her to shut down the search and contact Jonathan right away, she paused.

What is the Special Projects Division? she asked herself. She navigated backward on the file to reread the entire description of the company, but there was not a word to be found.

"Hmm," she mumbled. Research became a thousand times more interesting when you had specific questions to answer.

She dug deeper and hit bedrock. The Carlyle files were all heavily encrypted. Venice smiled. This was going to be fun.

Walking into the lobby of the Frederick Palace Hotel was like passing through a portal to the past. Small by the standards of modern hotels, the Frederick Palace's soaring lobby and dark hardwoods gave a sense of charming warmth that even further endeared this little burg to Jonathan. At Andrew Hawkins's request, they chose a conversation group in a corner of the lobby farthest from the front doors, across from the empty lobby bar.

Back in the alley, he'd confessed that the reason he'd told so much so far, and the reason why he would answer the rest of Jonathan's questions was, as he put it, disgustingly mundane: by cooperating, there was a good chance that lives could be saved. Besides, he was sick of carrying these secrets around. He had no idea who the man calling himself Leon really was, but Hawkins sensed that he was on the opposite side of Palmer, and for the time being, that was enough.

Once seated, they dropped their voices to barely a whisper. "You know that Carlyle Industries is a weapons manufacturer," Hawkins said, easing back into the topic. When he got nods, he pressed on. "And you know that these are not just everyday weapons, right?"

"I've heard rumors," Jonathan said.

Hawkins seemed to understand the hedging and he acknowledged it with a nod. "Yeah, well I've heard rumors, too, and I happen to know that they're true. They're manufacturing biological weapons over there. We're talking the kinds of weapons that kill people thousands at a time—millions and millions over time. They've got some germ shit called GVX that is engineered to be incurable, because it constantly mutates as it passes from one person to another. Nobody can develop a vaccine, because by the time the vaccine is made, the germ is a whole new disease."

Jonathan kept a poker face. He'd heard of such weapons being researched, but he had no way of knowing if one had ever been produced. Privately, he'd always dismissed them as useless—a foolish venture that would be strategically counterproductive. "What's the point of a weaponized virus?" he asked. "What's the point of launching something on the bad guys that is ultimately going to kill the good guys, too?"

Hawkins scowled and made a huffing noise. "Hey, I'm just telling you what I know. I'm not sayin' I understand the strategy."

"You know this because Fabian Conger told you?" Jonathan asked.

Bingo. Hawkins settled himself. "Fabian's not a nut-case, okay? He's overly exuberant, and he's easily swayed, but he's a smart, smart man. He did the research. It's all out there. He looked at the revenues of the company, and he looked at their production, and he looked into the backgrounds of the corporate officers, and he worked with contacts he has in the government, and all this adds up. And I'll tell you something else that should make you shit your pants."

They waited for it.

"Carlyle's selling stuff to the enemy."

Jonathan cocked his head. "Which enemy?"

"Our enemies. The Arabs. The terrorists. I'm not talking about legitimate contracts. I'm talking about illegal shit that's under the table."

"Why would they do that?" Jonathan asked.

"Why do you think? If the enemy ever stopped shooting at us, Carlyle would start losing money. The longer the shooting keeps going, the fatter they get."

Jonathan wasn't buying. Neither was Boxers.

Hawkins caught their silent exchange. "Look, you don't have to believe none of this that I'm telling you, but you're fools if you don't. Nobody *wants* to believe any of this, but on September 10, 2001, nobody wanted to believe that there were thousands of terrorists out there who wanted us all dead. Wanting and not wanting don't mean dick."

Jonathan decided to try his diplomatic hat. He didn't want to push Hawkins away, but Jesus. "That's a huge accusation against a big company with a lot to lose if word leaked out. A little evidence would make this easier to swallow."

Hawkins's expression said, *duh*. "Well, that's the thing, isn't it? That was Fabe's obsession when I last saw him. He was pulling every string he could find to get somebody to pay attention to him, but it always ended up right where you said: 'Where's the evidence?' It's one thing to find evidence on paper, but it's something else when you try to get your hands on some of this stuff. Apparently, it's locked up tighter than a nun's . . . well, it's locked up tight."

You could always kidnap an executive's kid, Jonathan thought. But that was a card he didn't want to show. "How was he going to show that they were selling weapons to the enemy?" he asked.

Hawkins shrugged. "I don't know how he was going to do any of this stuff. But if you prove that these weapons exist illegally and make it public, how difficult can it be to prove the rest? Once the news media get ahold of one really bad thing, they'll be happy to keep going till they find every bad thing they can. The hard part is that first step—getting people to pay any attention at all."

Boxers asked, "Do you think he was capable of violence to get what he wanted?"

Something clicked in Hawkins. "That's what all this is about, isn't it? Fabe went and hurt somebody, and you're trying to find out why."

Jonathan jumped in to control the spin. "We don't know that Fabian Conger did anything wrong. There's been some violence, yes, and his name floated onto our radar screen, but we don't know anything for sure yet."

"Fabe isn't violent. I mean he could be talked into stuff, but I never saw a violent streak in him. Never."

"What about Ivan Patrick?" Boxers asked. "Palmer."

"Well, now there all bets are off. You tell me he rapes bunny rabbits and field dresses babies and I won't call you a liar."

CHAPTER TWENTY

The BlackBerry that the security guards had found and ignored in Venice's purse wasn't really a BlackBerry at all, at least not in the sense that anyone else would think of it. Every other unit that resembled hers could transmit and receive e-mail, make telephone calls, and perform all the functions of a personal digital assistant. She had one like that as well; it sat in the center console of her car back in the parking lot of the Franconia-Springfield Metro Station in Virginia. This unit in her purse was a portable disk drive packed with encryption-cracking software, and the tubular handles of the purse itself concealed the USB cable that would allow her to hook up to the computer in her carrel. That process took some finesse not to draw attention, but when she was done, it looked to the casual observer as if she'd merely placed her purse on the table next to the computer tower.

It took twenty-five minutes for the software to do its thing. Once into the system, she posed as the system administrator to break into Carlyle's internal e-mail. Her theory went like this: Given the nature of Ivan Patrick's background, his most likely service to Carlyle would be either executive protection or corporate espionage work, and in either case, his contact would likely be the corporate director of security. So, she found her way into Charlie Warren's account and did a global search for "Ivan Patrick."

It's not often you hit a homer on your first swing, but it sure feels good when you do. These guys were regular pen pals.

From: Ivan Patrick
Sent: April 5 10:29 AM
To: Charles S. Warren
Subject: Your Problem

Chuck,

Rock star is going to make his move on your information soon. I have a plan to make it all go away. Let's talk soonest.

Ivan

Make his move on your information was the phrase that snatched her attention. Information was what people tortured other people to receive. *Rock star* confused her for a second, and then she remembered Conger's first name: Fabian. Just like the rock star.

The e-mail string continued:

From: Charles S. Warren
Sent: April 5 11:14 AM
To: Ivan Patrick
Subject: RE: Your Problem

Ivan,

Rock star is not a threat. Whatever he says, no one will believe him. No further communication on the matter is necessary.

Charles S. Warren
Director of Corporate Security

Carlyle Industries, Inc.
15000 Carlyle Boulevard
Muncie, IN 47302
765-555-8515
765-555-0915 (Fax)

From: Ivan Patrick
Sent: April 5 11:17 AM
To: Charles S. Warren
Subject: RE: RE: Your Problem

Don't be an idiot. I would not be making this contact if I did not have solid information. His plan is a good one and it will take you down. Trust me. It's already in motion, and he's already causing leaks that you don't even know about yet. WE NEED TO TALK! I have a plan that will make all of your problems go away PERMANENTLY and seal those leaks. Rock star trusts me. Not trusting me will be your biggest mistake. Call the ball.

Ivan

But Charlie Warren didn't call anything for two days. When he did, there was a certain air of panic in the subtext:

From: Charles S. Warren
Sent: April 7 5:17 PM
To: Ivan Patrick
Subject: RE: RE: RE: Your Problem

Ivan,

I'm convinced. Meet me at usual location @ 2200 tonight. Do I need to visit the bank first?

Charles S. Warren
Director of Corporate Security
Carlyle Industries, Inc.
15000 Carlyle Boulevard
Muncie, IN 47302

765-555-8515
765-555-0915 (Fax)

From: Ivan Patrick
Sent: April 7 8:18 PM
To: Charles S. Warren
Subject: RE: RE: RE: RE: Your Problem

Negative. New fee structure. See you tonight.

Ivan

Venice stared at her screen, toggling between the different entries. She knew just from the tone and the logical links that she'd landed on a pivotal exchange between the two men. But what did it mean?

She highlighted the entire string and pasted it into an e-mail to herself; and none too soon. Five seconds later, the screen went blank as all data disappeared.

A thousand miles away, deep in the bowels of Carlyle Industries' corporate headquarters, computer technician Felix Harrison returned from an extended bathroom break to find an alert flashing on his terminal. Someone had hacked into secure corporate files. This was the second time in as many weeks. Unlike the first attempt, which was a clumsy one from inside the building, this one was both sophisticated and successful.

"Shit!" he spat. Heart racing, Felix slapped the panic button to take the entire system offline and stanch the flow of data. Christ Almighty, this was exactly the kind of stuff that pushed Mr. Warren over the edge—the kind of thing that ended careers in a heartbeat. Hands trembling, he started right into his forensic work.

It would only be a few minutes before Mr. Warren

responded to the identical alert he would have received on his pager. When he called, Felix's only chance of continued employment would lie in his ability to trace down the origin of the attempt.

It took him two minutes to trace the hit back to the National Archives in Washington, DC. His heart sank. Using public facilities like that made it virtually impossible to trace—

Wait a second. He smiled. This particular hacker had made a critical error. He'd sent himself an e-mail. Or herself. It was too early for that level of detail.

It took Mr. Warren over an hour to make his inevitable phone call. When he did, Felix was ready for him.

CHAPTER TWENTY-ONE

Lab technician Max Mentor was a genius. After learning from the druggist about Tony or Thomas Hughes, Gail had called her friend with the southern drawl and asked him to see what he could find out. Working backward from the name they already knew—or suspected—he bent a few rules and dipped into databases that were officially off limits, but unofficially a treasure trove. It turned out that twelve years ago there'd been a push in the Muncie elementary schools to have kids fingerprinted as part of Project Lost Child, one of those paranoia-based child identification programs, and a young Thomas Hughes had been part of it. Fingerprints don't change with age (they just get bigger), and the ones recorded by that little boy were an exact match to a couple that were found in the Patrones' basement.

Now, six hours later, Gail Bonneville offered a seat to Jesse on the other side of her desk.

"I have interesting info on the Hughes kid," he said. "He's just about finished with his senior year at Ball State, a music major, and he doesn't seem to have a lot of friends. Acquaintances everywhere—people all agree that he's a nice kid—but we never turned up any close friends. I did hear rumors of a hot-looking girlfriend, though, a pretty young thing with a great body and blond hair."

Gail cocked her head. That description sounded very familiar.

Jesses caught the suspicion in the air and smiled. "Yep, it's our very own Christine Baker, but under a different name. I pulled up her driver's license picture and got a positive ID from two of the acquaintances. As for the alias, I could only get agreement that it started with a T."

Gail raised her eyebrows. How interesting was that? "Nice work, Jesse."

He beamed. "But wait, there's more. Nobody's seen him for over a week. Nobody's seen her, either. The neighbors in the apartment building where Thomas lives say there was commotion there a little over a week ago—Monday or Tuesday, depending on which story you want to believe. It was late, people made noise, but no one peeked to see what was going on. I'm guessing that's when the snatching took place."

Gail liked it. She opened her speckled book and wrote. "This means that the late Christine Baker was playing him the whole time."

Jesse nodded. "I think it does, yes. I mean, she clearly wasn't a victim like the Hughes kid, just because of where she was when the shooting started."

The record on Christine Baker showed nothing in the way of serious illegal activity. Just a couple of symbolic arrests for protesting.

"I got one more interesting bit of information," Jesse went on. "The neighbors I spoke with told me that I wasn't the first one to be poking around about Thomas Hughes. A guy who never identified himself by name dropped hints that Thomas was upside down on some loans from bad guys, and that he—the guy asking the questions—was trying to protect him from harm. A couple of the people I talked to were creeped out by him and didn't say anything, and another couple told him essentially what they told me, about the commotion in the middle of the night, but nothing else."

"Did you get a description?"

Jesse went back to his notes. "I did, but I'm not sure it'll help a lot. White male, thirty-five to forty-five, five-ten, one-seventy, light brown hair closely trimmed. No facial hair, no scars that show. By that description, we've got about fifty million suspects. On the positive side, at least we have a motivation for the kidnapping."

Gail waited for it.

"The loan sharking thing. The kid owes enough money to the wrong people, they're gonna come looking for him."

Gail shook here head. It didn't sit right. "Does that really fit the profile we've built for Thomas Hughes? He's a good student, from a good home, with no criminal record. Not even a speeding ticket, for God's sake, and he's twenty-two! Everybody has a speeding ticket by the time they're twenty-two."

Jesse scowled. "I'm not sure I'm making the connection."

"People who use loan sharks are people in trouble. They owe a dealer, or they bet a lot of money at the track, or they need to cover up some other crime. Plain vanilla kids from Muncie don't need a loan shark. It just doesn't feel right to me."

Jesse became defensive. "Well, there's a first time for everything, Sheriff. Even crime. Or drugs, or gambling debts. Besides, the guy who was poking around said—"

"What he said is irrelevant, Jess. People can *say* anything." She saw the hurt expression, and then held up a preemptive hand. "I'm not attacking you, Jess. Or your theory. It's just that in my experience, people so rarely tell the truth to anybody, words stopped meaning a lot to me."

"I'm telling you that these people I interviewed were all straight-up. Besides, their descriptions of the guy and what he was looking for were so similar, I don't know how they could have colluded."

"I'm not talking about the people you talked to," Gail said. "I'm talking about the guy who talked to them. I'm thinking that that guy is our killer, doing recon work before he started pulling triggers. In his position, there'd be no reason to tell the truth."

The phone on her desk rang—her personal line—just as something came together in her head. "In fact," she continued, "now that I think about it, a guy who does freelance hostage rescue for a living would need to keep the fact of a kidnapping secret."

The phone rang for a third time, and she picked it up. "Sheriff Bonneville, hold on a second, please." She put the call on hold. To Jesse, she continued, "If word leaked out that someone had been nabbed, somebody would call the police, and then the contractor would lose control of his operation."

Jesse's defenses started to fall as he saw it, too. "And the real reason to use an independent contractor in the first place would be because the kidnappers warned not to involve the police."

Gail smiled and winked. "Bingo." She pushed the hold button again and brought the phone to her ear. "I'm sorry to keep you waiting. This is Sheriff Bonneville."

"Medina." The special agent in charge of the Chicago

Field Office announced his name as if it were an accusation, but the sound of his voice brought pleasant memories to Gail's mind. "You ready to have your world rocked?"

"I'm going to put you on speaker," Gail said as she pressed the button. "I'm here with Jesse Collier."

"Hey, Jess," Medina said. "This kid you're looking for, Thomas Hughes? Son of Stephenson and Julie Hughes?"

Gail glanced, and Jesse nodded. "That's him," she said.

"Well, when you find him, hold him, will you? His folks are murderers."

Gail startled visibly. "*What?*"

"Yep, how's that for a kick in the head? Looks like they murdered a woman, her two children, and their nanny in Muncie. Ugly scene, too. Early reports say torture."

"Oh, my God," she breathed. "What the hell is going on, Vince?"

"Soon as I know, you'll know. Just thought I'd share. It came up on ICIS if you want to track it. Gotta go."

With the line silent, she felt pale.

"Love to hear a hypothesis on this one, Boss," Jesse said.

Chapter Twenty-two

The security breach while surfing through the Carlyle site had shaken Venice. She'd wasted no time getting out of the Archives and back to the safety of Fisherman's Cove. Safely back in her office now, she held her breath as she logged into the Interstate Crime Information System for an update on the Indiana investigation. Her stomach fell. By far the most critical investigation in the country—the one that was garnering the most bulletins and alerts—was Jonathan's triple shooting in Samson, Indiana. Since the last time she'd signed in, authorities had figured out that the incident had involved a kidnapping, but it wasn't obvious whether they thought the shooter was a rescuer or a kidnapper.

Even more startling was the fact that Indiana investigators had tied the name Thomas Hughes to the location of the shootings. They had him identified as a twenty-two-year-old college student from Ball State University, and he was currently being sought as a "person of interest," which Venice knew from past experience was a label that spanned everything from potential witness to primary suspect. Whatever it meant in this case, it was not good news.

Thomas Hughes's name on the screen was highlighted as a hyperlink, which usually foretold involvement in a second or related criminal investigation. When Venice clicked it, she gasped and brought her hand to her mouth after reading only the first two sentences.

This was impossible.

With her hands trembling from the sudden shot of adrenaline, she logged out of ICIS and pulled up the link for a super-encrypted telephone site. She donned her headset as her fingers flew across the keyboard to pull up Jonathan's secure satellite phone.

The Hummer was a ridiculous waste of natural resources, Jonathan knew, but given the specific demands of his business and his addiction to high-tech toys, it was the only vehicle that would suffice. In addition to the armored doors and windows, he'd also equipped it with the latest in communication technology. He'd even thought to include a cipher-activated vault below the center console, in which he kept a supply of cash in case of emergencies. Right now, the vault held $25,000 in hundred-dollar bills. Boxers called it the Batmobile.

The hard-lined telephone mounted on the dash was an encrypted satellite phone that allowed him to freely discuss anything with anyone who had similar technology on the other end. Predictably, Boxers called it the Batphone.

And it was ringing.

A wrong number was impossible, but Jonathan nonetheless answered it on speakerphone with a noncommittal, "Yes."

"Digger, it's Venice. We've got a problem."

He waited for it.

"The Hugheses are a family of murderers."

* * *

As she drove toward Muncie, Gail Bonneville wasn't sure what she expected to glean from the scene of the quadruple murder there, but when so many people were dead, and the single name of Hughes was tied to their murders, it was a lead that needed following.

This latest twist was a stunner. What had seemed so clearly to be an altruistic act of bravery on the part of her shooter in Samson suddenly looked like something else entirely. Three people murdered in the rescue of the son of murderers. What could that possibly mean? Every one of the conclusions she'd prematurely drawn to this point was now in question.

The trill of her cell phone annoyed her. One of the good things about long drives was the time it afforded for quiet thought. The caller ID showed her it was her office, but that somehow only heightened her sense of annoyance.

"Bonneville."

"Collier." Jesse matched her tone exactly, making her smile. "You in the mood for entertaining news?"

"I'd prefer 'good' to 'entertaining,'" she said, "but I'll take whatever you've got."

"When were tracking down all that flight information a while ago, I made some good contacts," Jesse explained. "One of them just called to tell me that the Perseus Foods jet has filed a flight plan for a return trip to Indianapolis."

CHAPTER TWENTY-THREE

The murder scene on Detweiler Avenue in Muncie was as gruesome as faux FBI Agent Jonathan Grave had ever seen. The bodies were gone—shipped off to the morgue hours ago to be split open and rummaged through—leaving behind the dried pools, smears, and spatters of gore that were somehow more awful by themselves than they would have been with the corpses still present. The milling presence of crime scene technicians helped to take the edge off the creepiness, but the heavy infestation of flies turned Jonathan's stomach.

And the odor. Dear God, the odor.

The house itself was otherwise clean, obviously the object of its owners' affections. At about 2,300 square feet on two levels, it was exactly the kind of house that middle-class Americans think of when they think suburbia. Outside, the place was likewise well kept, even if the grass was a little long—the fact that prompted a neighbor to realize that something might be wrong in the first place. In the eighteen hours since that poor Samaritan had peeked in the window and called the police, thousands of footsteps by dozens of police officers and emergency workers had destroyed the lawn, and the dozens of feet of crime scene tape had ruined the innocence.

Stan Hastings of the Muncie Police Department was lead detective on the case. Five-eleven and trim, with signs of gray in what was left of his elaborate comb-over, he looked to be about forty-five, and seemed none too pleased to be walking through the scene yet again. He'd asked the usual jurisdictional questions when Jonathan arrived with his FBI credentials, but was easily convinced that he was investigating a link between the Caldwells and the theft of classified information.

As he conducted the tour, Hastings clearly avoided looking at the gore. "Angela Caldwell and her two children, one six and the other three, and their nanny, Felicia Bourdain, a French citizen, all murdered," Hastings explained. "The nanny was killed right here in the foyer," he said, indicating the lake of dried blood on the tiled floor and the spray that reached all the way to the ceiling in spots. "We figure she was killed answering the door. One slash across her throat, and she just dropped."

They moved through the living room into the tiny dining room with its hideously stained blue- and pink-flowered wall paper. "We found Angela, the mom, tied to that chair there at the head of the table. She was the worst one, by far. From what we can tell, she was tortured pretty brutally. Lots of deep cuts, and signs of beating, but only one fatal wound— another slashed throat."

Jonathan saw the picture in his mind, and wished that he could make it go away. "What about the children?" he asked. Even as he spoke, he regretted asking. That he *needed* to know didn't mean he *wanted* to.

Hastings's eyes reddened, and he cleared his throat. "It looks like the baby was killed right away, too. But the little boy, well, we think the killer was hurting him to get information out of the mother." He fell silent after that, and Jonathan could see his jaw muscles working hard. "Jesus, let's get out of here, okay?"

He didn't wait for an answer before he made a beeline for the back door and the rear deck. Jonathan followed closely behind. By the time he caught up, Hastings had his hands shoved deeply into his pants pockets and he was looking very sheepish.

"You okay, Detective?" Jonathan asked.

He laughed and rolled his eyes. "Sorry about that," he said. "It's been a long time since I've been bit by a case."

Jonathan smiled and shrugged. "It happens."

He snorted. "Yeah, well, people see you being soft, and they'll expect you to start being human and shit. God only knows what would happen then."

Jonathan gave the cop a few seconds. A barking dog next door filled the silence. "So, how do you tie Stephenson Hughes to this murder? Just the fingerprints?"

"Him and his wife both," Hastings corrected. "Neighbors saw their car parked around the corner about the time the murders occurred, and one of them even gave us a positive ID off Stephenson Hughes's drivers permit. Plus, the family has disappeared. That's enough for me."

It would be enough for anyone. "Any idea on motive?"

Hastings helped himself to a nylon-strap chair in the shade. "Not yet. All we know is that they were coworkers. At Carlyle Industries here in Muncie. They were both in the program office, whatever that means. It's too early to know much more than that. I tell you what, though. A murder like this had better turn out to be something more than a love gone ugly. I'm thinking this has something to do with that other bloodbath down in Samson."

Jonathan wasn't going to bring it up if Hastings didn't. "We'll be looking into that, too," he bluffed.

Hastings smiled. "Then I'm pleased to offer one-stop shopping."

"Excuse me?"

"Sheriff Bonneville from Samson is here. Out front, last time I saw her. I'm surprised you didn't see her when you came in."

The news landed like a punch, but Jonathan showed nothing. "Maybe I did," he said. "There are a lot of people out there. I don't think I've ever met her to recognize her."

Hastings stood and hooked an elbow around Jonathan's shoulder, guiding him toward the steps that led from the deck to the ground. Obviously, he was avoiding another trip through the house of horrors. "Come on," he said. "I'll introduce you."

Jonathan saw the sheriff standing at the front door to her unmarked cruiser, back pressed to the window, arms folded across her chest. Trim and athletic, with all the hair of a model, and none of the corn-fed look of so many female law enforcers, she struck him as pretty hot. She wore expensive blue jeans and a white blouse, covered with a dark blue blazer that was cut just a little larger than it needed to be, no doubt to conceal a weapon. The smirk on her face read, "Gotcha."

Hastings led him across the lawn. "Hey, Sheriff, I've got someone here wants to meet you." When they were within a few feet, Hastings spread his arms. "Special Agent Leon Harris with the FBI, this is Sheriff Gail Bonneville of Samson, Indiana."

They shook hands. "Pleased to meet you, Sheriff."

She held his eyes in an amused glare. "The pleasure's all mine, *Special Agent* Harris." The way she leaned on the words brought an icy breeze.

Hastings caught it, and he became uncomfortable, as if he'd walked into the middle of a lovers' spat. "Can y'all spare me?" he asked. "I've got a lot to do."

"Of course," Jonathan said, turning to shake his hand as well. "Thank you very much for the tour."

Gail answered the detective with a dismissive shake of her head, and Hastings wasted no time disappearing.

"You must be pretty busy, too," Jonathan said.

"Do you mind if I take a look at your creds?" Gail asked.

"Sure," Jonathan said. His FBI credentials were impeccable—and occasionally real. Yet another perk of calling Uncle Sam a customer from time to time.

Gail examined the contents of the leather case carefully, taking care to note the details, and dedicating special attention to matching the photograph to the face before her. That was when Jonathan knew she was bluffing. Even the most amateur forger could handle the photograph.

"You don't look much like an FBI agent," she said, handing back the creds case and eyeing his casual clothes.

"Says the small-town sheriff with the hot body." Jonathan delivered the line with a smile that successfully kept the humor and removed the smarminess. He tucked the case into his back pocket, not at all concerned that his weapon showed as his jacket bloused. In the uncomfortable silence that followed, his mind raced to deliver his next move. He hadn't counted on this at all, but now that he was face-to-face with the last person in the world he wanted to meet, he realized he had a role to play. In for a dime, in for a dollar, right? "Have you got a few minutes to review the details of the shootings in your town?"

"Why not just talk with Vince Medina?" she asked.

"I don't know him," he said. *The old name-recognition trap,* he thought. He relaxed even more, confident that she was merely on a fishing expedition. If she'd had facts to back up her suspicion, she'd have come with a posse, and he'd be wearing handcuffs.

"He's in the Chicago Field Office," she clarified.

"I'm not," Jonathan said. He intentionally did not elaborate. Real Bureau agents were all about power plays, so he thought he'd live up to the role.

"What office are you from, then? I was Bureau for fifteen years."

Jonathan hardened his gaze, and placed his hands on his hips. "Have I offended you, Sheriff? I meant the 'hot body' thing as a compliment."

"Where were you on April twentieth?"

Time to show real annoyance. "Where were *you*?"

Gail shrugged. "I was home in bed. The next morning, though, I was investigating a triple murder."

Shock. "And you think *I* had something to do with it?" Jonathan laughed. "What the hell is wrong with you, Sheriff?" He made a waving gesture between the two of them. "Good guys," he said. He made a sweeping motion toward the rest of the world. "Bad guys. It's not that complicated."

"I don't believe you're who you say you are," Gail said.

Confusion. "Then who might I be?"

Her eyes narrowed and she cocked her head. In different circumstances, Jonathan would have been throwing down some of his best charm. "I don't know yet," she said. "Not by name, anyway. But I suspect that you're the guy who shot up my town, which puts you on the list as an associate of the people who shot up this house." She placed a forefinger on the center of her own chest. "Good guy," she said. Then she pointed at Jonathan. "Bad guy."

Jonathan pointed back. "Crazy sheriff. If you're planning to arrest me, you'd best plan for a hell of a battle."

She tensed.

"Not a gun battle, a *court* battle," he clarified. "I'll own you for that kind of false arrest." He turned to walk back toward his rental car. "I'll do my checking with the field office," he grunted as he tossed off a dismissive wave.

She called after him. "Harris!"

He turned.

"I've got a face now," she said. "With that, I can get all the proof I need. Then I'm going to put you away." Her smile chilled him.

"Good guy," he said, pointing at his face.

As he pulled away in the Avis rental, he watched the sheriff in the mirror. She glared at him all the way to the turn at the end of the street. When he was out of sight, he called Boxers and told him to get the hell out of town. "Leave Lydell's plane where it is, and find a way home," he said. "We're hot."

Chapter Twenty-Four

As director of corporate security for Carlyle Industries, it was Charlie Warren's job to know things that he wished he didn't. He knew who looked at pornographic Web sites from their work computers, and through that access, he knew to marvel at the sheer number of perversions out there. He knew from security camera footage who was boffing whom in corners where people thought there were no cameras. He knew who had credit problems, whose kids were sick, and who was using the company's copiers and e-mail accounts during off hours. It was way more information than any sane man would want to know.

As he hung up the phone, he steadied himself with a deep sigh. He knew now that the GVX incident had grown to a new level—that their containment efforts had sprung a new leak. For the next step, he'd need to speak again with Rocko Bunting, Carlyle's president and chief operating officer, despite the man's orders that he be kept out of the loop as much as possible. He called Rocko's secretary to make the appointment, and as he expected, Rocko agreed to see him right away.

The walk was a long one, from the basement of the

west end to the penthouse of the east end. At a good clip, it would take him every bit of ten minutes. On his way out the door, he told his assistant that he probably would not be back for a couple of days. She nodded and made a note, knowing better than to ask for specifics. Charlie's position frequently required sudden departures for long periods, and details were neither sought nor supplied.

He decided to take his time today, strolling rather than striding as he sorted out his presentation to the boss. Charlie had known from the beginning that this was going to be a complicated problem, but he hadn't dreamed that it would blossom to this size. And he had no one to blame but himself. He should have listened to Ivan Patrick when he'd first raised the warning flag.

But that wasn't really being fair to himself. Ivan never presented an issue or a challenge in which he did not have a stake, or from which he did not extract a percentage. Nine times out of ten, to ignore an opportunity from Ivan was to avoid an inevitable headache. No one could fault Charlie for avoiding that.

Who was he kidding? It was Charlie's job to keep things like this from happening. Rocko was going to be pissed beyond measure.

According to Ivan, the plan by that nut job Fabian Conger to extort the delivery of GVX by kidnapping a project manager's kid had been of Conger's own making, born out of a genuine if misguided attempt to save the world. Charlie wasn't sure he believed it, but by the time he'd found out about it, that particular genie was way out of the bottle. By then, it was time for damage control.

According to Ivan, Fabian Conger had for years pressed Stephenson Hughes—himself an active student protester during the Vietnam years—to sell out his employer, but, as reported through Ivan, Hughes had repeatedly "put his head in the sand" and refused to believe that his longtime employer was involved in the programs that Conger alleged. It wasn't until Conger snatched his kid that Hughes got religion and started to dig deep for the information he didn't think existed.

By then, Charlie had known there was a security problem, but by the time he responded to Ivan, they had fallen woefully behind the power curve. He knew through analysis of computer records that Stephenson Hughes had figured out that Angela Caldwell was the project manager for PATRIOT—the code name for the GVX project—and that shortly after he'd pulled that information from the system, Hughes disappeared. When Ivan subsequently paid a visit to Angela at her house, at Charlie's request, and on Carlyle's payroll, she'd initially claimed that she'd never talked with Stephenson Hughes.

But Ivan and Charlie both knew better. They had the e-mail in which Angela invited Hughes to her house. She stuck with her story far too long, with terrible consequences to her family. By the time she revealed to Ivan that she'd shared with Hughes the details he'd needed to obtain the ransom for his son, one child was already dead, and the other was screaming for the pain to stop. The thought of the torture sickened Charlie, but he hadn't hired Ivan because he was kind; he'd hired him because he was effective.

Yet still they'd been behind the Hugheses.

The GVX was stored at an old Nike missile facility that Carlyle had owned for decades. Their reinforced concrete underground structures made them ideal for civilian operations with secrets to keep. By the time Ivan and his team had arrived at the storage facility, two security guards were dead, and a dozen canisters of GVX were missing.

It was a nightmare. It was *the* nightmare, come true.

Charlie Warren entered the final elevator on his way up to executive country and tried to anticipate what Rocko's reaction was going to be to the latest news. There'd be anger, and there'd be shouting, and, no doubt—

What?

Charlie felt his spine stiffen. Just what the hell could Bunting do to him at this point? Fire him? Not likely. Hell, not possible. They were so far down the path of misery that there was no turning back. In fact, Rocko himself had approved Ivan's plan to recover the stolen GVX. He'd been excited, as a matter of fact, when Ivan proposed that the only way to get the genie back into the bottle was to allow the ransom transfer to occur.

"Think about it," Ivan had said during the meeting in the parking lot of the old Hotel Roberts in downtown Muncie. "Hughes will have no choice but to show up with the GVX he's stolen. He'll need it to make the transfer to save his son's life. Those idiots Fabe has got watching the kid down in Samson are losing patience with all the delays, and Hughes knows it. If he wants to see the kid alive, he's got no choice but to bring the stuff. When he shows up, I kill them all, and the world is back on its axis."

Charlie marveled now that murder could sound like such a rational choice when you're scared and your options are limited.

"What's the rest?" Bunting had asked. "What's in it for you?"

"A fee."

"No doubt one that's higher than usual," Charlie had guessed.

"Not in terms of cash, no," Ivan had said. He let the silence hang for dramatic effect, then explained, "I have some North African connections who would love to get their hands on exactly what the Hugheses have stolen. They'd pay me millions for it."

Charlie had searched Bunting's expression for a sign of horror—or even anger—but had seen nothing but resolve.

"A few million doesn't mean anything to a company like you," Ivan had said. "But that's retirement money for me."

The deal was sealed when Bunting nodded and headed for his car.

Charlie found it hard to believe that that had all transpired in the last month. Hell, less than a month.

The elevator opened on the vast expanse of the executive suite, where two hulking stuffed grizzly bears towered menacingly on hind legs. Trophies bagged by Rocko years ago during an Alaskan safari, the twin trophies served as a none-too-subtle warning for weak-hearted managers who dared to make the trip. Bunting was famous for his temper, and those who progressed to Charlie's level within the company had endured more than a few tirades that made them wonder if the hairy beasts with their splayed claws and exposed teeth were not in fact blood relatives of the boss. He walked across the plush maroon carpeting to the smoked glass double doors, beyond which lay the showplace that was Executive Country.

Katie Fallon, Rocko's busty assistant, was already waiting on the other side, poised to greet him with instructions to wait in the CCR, Carlyle-speak for the Chairman's Conference Room. She led him to the door, opened it for him, and then closed it behind him. Charlie knew from experience that Rocko would enter from the door on the far end, the one that connected to his office. The room was a study in stained teak, sporting an ebony-inlaid conference table that would easily seat thirty in the overstuffed leather chairs that surrounded it. Teak paneling lined the walls between the floor-to-ceiling windows, and on the wall opposite, Charlie knew that the elaborate painted Carlyle logo opened to reveal a screen onto which images from a drop-down projector could be viewed. In these days of government contraction, Charlie Warren often wondered how the bosses could get away with this level of opulence when they preened for the rock stars of the military and their civilian handlers.

He didn't bother to choose a chair. He would wait for Rocko to enter and take his cue from the boss. After about three minutes, the door opened up on the far end of the room, and Rocko Bunting entered. He was a big man, though not particularly tall, with a pug face and broad shoulders that left no doubt that his stories of stardom on his college rugby team were not exaggerated. He took the chair at the far end, and motioned to his left. "Sit," he commanded.

It took a good ten seconds to cover the distance. Charlie lowered himself into the indicated chair and waited for the command to give his report.

"You know he set us up for this, right?" Bunting said.

The non sequitur startled Charlie. "Excuse me?"

"This Ivan guy. You know he set us up." Bunting's normally ruddy complexion was unusually red as his indignation rose. "I've been giving it a lot of thought, and I realize now that Ivan was probably the impetus from the beginning. His friend Rock Star didn't come up with that kidnapping plot on his own. I'm coming to think that that was all Ivan from the beginning. Some Machiavellian plot to make a fortune off our product."

Charlie had drawn a similar conclusion two days ago, but he'd never mentioned it. At this point, motivation was irrelevant. From here out, all that mattered was containment. He chose not to rise to the bait. "We've got one more complication," he said.

"Well, what the hell is one more?" On a different day, his comment might have caused a smile, but definitely not today. "Has Ivan found the GVX yet?"

"No, sir. The Hugheses seem to have completely disappeared. Apparently, Ivan was so confident in his plan at the ransom transfer that when it went south, he had no backup. But I know he's working hard to find them."

"How?" Bunting asked.

Charlie felt an odd sense of relief that he knew the answer. "He's got tags on Hughes's credit cards, his phone records, everything. The moment he makes a mistake—the moment he peeks his head out of whatever hole he's hiding in, Ivan will know about it."

"And then what?"

"And then he'll take care of business."

Bunting's eyes hardened. He had famously low tolerance for empty words.

"He's at his headquarters—"

"His cult commune?" Bunting interrupted.

"Exactly." Again Charlie opted not to sniff the bait. "He's assembled a team, on his own dime, I might add. As soon as he knows where Hughes is, he's going to move. Stephenson got the drop on him by surprise the first time. There's no way Ivan will let that happen again."

Bunting was shaking his head. Clearly, he had less confidence in their contractor's abilities.

Charlie went on, "At least the police have connected the Hugheses to Angela's murder. That'll keep them from seeking help from the law. That'll buy us some time. We just have to hope they don't act against their own best interests and call them anyway."

Bunting scowled and shook off the possibility. "That won't happen," he said. "Or if it does, he'll wish he didn't."

Charlie waited for the elaboration.

"Turns out we're not alone in this," Bunting said. "I spoke with a friend of mine on the Senate Armed Services Committee. I explained in general terms what we were facing, and he understood the political fallout if details of PATRIOT were to leak out. He spent the day making calls of his own, and it turns out that the Justice Department is on our side, too. If Hughes surfaces, he'll be disappeared before he can say a word."

Charlie realized that his mouth was open, and he hurried to close it. When the word *disappeared* is used that way in a sentence, it only means one thing. The image of Guantanamo materialized in his head. "My," he said. "How . . . fortunate."

"What's the plan if Hughes never gets stupid?" Bunting asked. "What's Ivan's plan then?"

Again, Charlie knew the answer. "Depends on how long it takes," he said. "If it goes on for more than a week or two, I'm guessing he goes on the run himself."

Bunting raised an eyebrow, confused.

"Seems he already accepted payment from someone who wants to buy *his*"—Charlie used finger quotes—"GVX. All I know is it's a *North African*"—more finger quotes—"client who is quick to think he's been double-crossed. If Ivan doesn't deliver what he's already been paid for, it's likely to get ugly."

Bunting smiled. He clearly liked the idea of Ivan Patrick getting a taste of his own medicine. Then the smile went away. “So, what’s *this* meeting about? What’s this new complication?”

Charlie steeled himself with a deep breath. “The sphere of knowledgeable people has expanded.”

“What the hell does that mean?”

A beat. “It means that a private investigator from a place called Fisherman’s Cove, Virginia, hacked into our e-mail server this afternoon and downloaded the precise e-mails that detail our initial conversations with Ivan. The security office was able to shut them out before they got everything, but they got enough to worry me.”

The redness in Bunting’s ears deepened, but his demeanor remained calm. “Do you have a name and an address?”

“I do. The e-mail account where the information was forwarded belongs to Venice Alexander, who is an executive with a firm called Security Solutions.”

“What do they specialize in?”

Charlie shook his head. “I don’t know. I did a search, but all I got was Chamber of Commerce stuff. Apparently, they’re one of those companies that runs mostly by word of mouth.”

The tone of his response triggered another scowl from Bunting. “That seems to disturb you,” he said.

Charlie nodded. “Well, it does. Private investigating firms that operate under the radar are the kinds of operations that do . . . *specialty* work.”

“Please stop speaking in code,” Bunting growled.

Charlie sighed. He hated going out on a limb like this, but he’d been in the security business long enough not just to speak in codes, but to understand the codes when he heard them. “They’re the kind of firms that specialize in what they call special projects, or executive services. Typically, that means mercenary work.”

When that didn't seem to score a direct hit with Bunting, he added, "Hired guns."

He saw the recognition he was looking for. The boss's eyes got big.

"Exactly," Charlie said. "The kind of firm that you would hire if your kid had been kidnapped and you wanted to get him back quickly."

Bunting stared. You could see the significance of it all settling on his shoulders. "Are you talking theory or fact, Charlie?"

"Strongly held theory," he hedged.

"Well, then," Bunting said, rising from his chair. "Looks like you need to get on a plane and find Fisherman's Cove."

Chapter Twenty-Five

Father Dom D'Angelo needed to take a walk. Between the human drama of the students they admitted to Resurrection House and the childhood burdens that were unveiled to him during counseling sessions, he needed the fresh air and the calm of Fisherman's Cove to remind him of the grace that God had bestowed upon the world. Man did what they could to screw it up—and they took special care to damage the world of children—but a walk in the spring air could always restore him to peace.

This was the time of year he loved most. The last vestiges of winter had blown away, and spring was coming on strong. Countless flowers perfumed the air, yet the oppressive humidity of summer had yet to arrive. Fisherman's Cove was a special place any time of day, but in the evening like this it held a special magic for Dom. With the storefronts dark and the traffic nonexistent, the village had an Old World quality that brought peace. Tonight, with the breeze blowing in off the water, he could hear the creaking and gentle bumping of moored boats in the marina two blocks away.

Evening was a time when a priest could walk down the sidewalk without the perpetually pleasant look that was expected by his flock. We all have roles to play, and his allowed little room for moodiness. At this hour the streets were always deserted. He was startled, then, when a shadow spoke to him near the concrete walkway to St. Kate's main entrance.

"Good evening, Father."

"Venice." She was sitting on the concrete steps, hugging her knees. She looked cold. "Are you all right?"

She didn't answer.

"Would you like to walk with me?" he offered.

She sniffed. "I'm sure you need your alone time."

Dom held out his hand. "Please come with me," he said.

Venice stood, using Dom's hand for assistance. He let the silence hang.

"I worry about Digger," she said.

"Don't we all."

"No, I mean I *really* worry about him. I think he's gotten himself in over his head." She relayed the results of her search at the Archives. "That's *seven* murders, all related," she finished. She went on to explain Jonathan's confrontation with the sheriff who most wanted to see her boss put in jail. "He just scares me to death."

Dom considered the details. "He's always been a daredevil, Ven. Ever since college. In his mind, if he's not pushing the envelope, he's standing still."

She gave him a look. "You sound like you admire him."

He shrugged. "Of course I admire him. He's the closest friend I've ever had."

"Then you should talk some sense into him."

Dom laughed. "Yeah, right after I cure world hunger, and figure out how to keep the tide from coming in, I'll get right to talking sense into Digger Grave." A beat. "So, when does he get in?"

"His flight arrives at ten-something at Dulles."

Dom laughed again. "Digger flying commercial. I wonder if he even knows how it works."

Venice allowed herself a laugh as well. "What about Box? How'd you like to be in the center seat next to him?" As if Boxers would dream of traveling in coach.

They walked for the better part of a block in silence, ascending the gentle slope away from the river before finally turning onto Pine Avenue, the world becoming a dark tree-formed tunnel where the only illumination came from porch lights receded in the blackness on either side.

"How comfortable are you with this notion that the Hugheses are a family of killers?" Dom asked.

"Not even a little," Venice answered. "Intuitively, I can't make it work in my mind. People who care that much about their child aren't going to murder two children. It just doesn't make sense to me."

"Maybe it didn't happen that way," Dom offered.

"You know what Digger says about coincidences," Venice said. "They don't exist. All events are linked all the time."

Dom nodded. He could hear Jonathan's voice saying it. "Okay," he said. "Let's accept that as gospel. There are no coincidences. Let's also agree that the Hugheses would never kill two children. That means that the coincidence is linked, but we just don't know how."

Venice stopped. Her eyes had grown huge as Dom's logic hit home.

The wideness of her eyes made him laugh. "Would you mind terribly if I helped?" he asked.

* * *

Fifteen minutes later, they were in the third floor of the firehouse, Dom perched in a chair behind Venice, watching over her shoulder. They worked without a break for three hours, uncovering exactly the kind of details they were hoping for. When Jonathan arrived from the airport, they'd blow him clear out of his shoes with the tidbits they'd been able to find. Dom had never seen Venice so animated.

Then Mama Alexander called from the mansion, and everything changed.

All things considered, the flight to Dulles passed quickly. For good or ill, Jonathan and Boxers both ended up on the same flight out of Chicago, direct into Washington Dulles International Airport. They both sat in coach, nowhere near each other in order to avoid security concerns. Gail Bonneville knew what to look for in Jonathan, but as far as she knew, Boxers did not even exist. By keeping separated, any spies that she might have been able to place on the plane would be unable to link them. The chances of such a thing were remote, but considering the chances of coming face-to-face with Gail Bonneville, he was all about caution now.

He'd probably carve out his tongue before admitting it to Venice, but she'd been right about his playing fast and loose with long-standing security protocols. He'd done a foolish thing in Muncie, and he'd damn near gotten himself caught. Wolverine would protect him if Bonneville decided to pursue his identity, but his cavalier attitude had cost him. If nothing else, he'd lost access to Richard Lydell's jet. At least someone would be happy.

The other casualty was his weapon. To avoid security issues at O'Hare, he'd had to stop at a FedEx facility to ship his .45 and its ammo. He'd have it back in two days, and he had more than enough replacement weapons in the short term, but he hated traveling without a sidearm.

Throughout the two-hour trip to Washington, the mystery of the Caldwell murders consumed his thoughts. He didn't believe that the Hugheses were capable of such a thing. Plus, the torture element had Ivan Patrick written all over it. But why? What did Fabian Conger, Tibor Rothman, Angela Caldwell, and Ellen all have in common? What would warrant such violent treatment, all presumably from the same man?

Given the close environs of aircraft cabin, Jonathan fought the temptation to make notes as he thought his way through the logic. He closed his eyes and tried to visualize the links.

Angela Caldwell, Stephenson Hughes, and Fabian Conger all shared Carlyle Industries and the GVX that they manufactured. That was their connection. Hughes and Tibor shared Thomas Hughes, each in their own way. Venice's research showed that Conger and Hughes were also connected through Carlyle. He could throw Tibor into that mix as well, if only as a reporter who was likely contacted by Conger at one point or another as he jousted at his publicity windmills.

He squinted his eyes tighter. The answer felt close. He drew a Boolean diagram in his mind, connecting all the logic gates. He knew for a fact that Thomas Hughes was kidnapped as a means to extort GVX from Carlyle via Stephenson Hughes. He also knew for a fact that the exchange was *this close* to being completed when Jonathan stepped in and rescued Thomas.

Was that the critical moment when everything went to hell for the good guys? The thought chilled him. If the 0300 mission had failed, Thomas and Stephenson and Tibor all would have doubtless been killed, but then what?

His breath caught in his throat as he closed the loop. If he hadn't done his job so well in Samson, then there would have been no video chip to mail. And without that, there would have been no reason to torture Ellen. She wouldn't be lying in a hospital right now. She wouldn't be on the feather edge between survival and death.

But for Jonathan, the people he loved would be healthy and fine. But for him.

Jesus.

The impact of the wheels on the tarmac startled him. He'd been so absorbed in his thoughts that he hadn't heard the flaps and landing gear come down.

Jonathan and Boxers ignored each other as they filed out of the airplane into the C Concourse, and from there into the crammed bus that shuttled them to the main terminal. After that, they walked separately through the lower level, out the doors past the baggage carousels, and toward the ramp that would take them to their separate taxis.

Jonathan never got as far as the ramp. He saw Venice as he was passing the first carousel. The sight startled him, and his stride hesitated. It wasn't until he saw Dom there with her that his blood turned to ice. Never in all the years that he'd been running missions—whether for Uncle or for himself—had Dom D'Angelo shown up to greet him at the airport. There was no waving, no smiles. Venice looked as if she might have been crying. Dom looked as if he were about to. The priest stepped ahead to get to Jonathan first.

"What is it?" Jonathan asked, knowing the answer already.

Behind Dom, Venice started to cry in earnest. "Let's sit down," Dom said quietly.

"Nope, right here," Jonathan said.

Dom reached out for Jonathan's elbow, urging him toward the chairs. "Sitting is better," he said.

"Is it Ellen?" Jonathan asked. It was written all over their faces, but he had to hear it. Even better, he had to hear that he was wrong.

Dom cast a look to Venice, and then locked his gaze with Jonathan. "She died at 9:30 this evening, Dig. She never regained consciousness. I'm so sorry."

Jonathan stared, unblinking, as the words moved in slow motion. It was exactly as he had feared, but expecting and realizing were nowhere near the same shade on the emotional color chart. One did not prepare you for the other. As the frigid fist clutched more tightly at his guts, he locked his jaw and forced his emotions back into the depths where they belonged.

Dom cocked his head. "Dig?"

Venice moved closer, her arms outstretched to offer a hug. "Digger, I'm so, so sorry."

Jonathan stopped her with a raised palm. "I'm okay," he said. "It's not exactly a surprise." Something caught in his voice, but he was able to speak past it. He turned and started walking toward the exit. "Let's go. We've got work to do."

"Dig?" Dom called.

He kept walking. He didn't want to talk to people right now. He didn't want to be anywhere near people right now. Well, maybe one person. Come to think of it, he couldn't wait to be *very* close to Ivan Patrick.

"Jon!" When Jonathan didn't slow, the priest trotted to catch up. "Look, Dig, I really think we need to talk."

Jonathan forced a smile. "Is that your priest hat or your shrink hat talking?"

"It's my friend hat. And I'm tired of you walking away from me when I'm trying to help."

Jonathan turned on the priest. "Gonna analyze me, Father? Gonna take my confession? Gonna hold my hand, kiss my boo-boo, and make it all better?"

Dom's eyes reflected the anger projected toward them. "Yeah," he said. "A little of all of the above."

"Well don't bother. I've seen death before. Hell, I've wallowed in it."

"A superhero," Dom mocked.

"A realist. Ellen's dead. I got it. And she'll still be dead tomorrow and a year from now. If I need a psychiatric couch along the way, I'll look you up." In his peripheral vision, he could see Boxers arriving and pulling up short next to Venice.

"Jon, for God's sake—" All around them, other passengers swerved to avoid them, a human current flexing to avoid rocks in the stream. Those who were observant enough responded to the obvious tension with a concerned second look.

"Do you want me to walk you through all the stages of grief, Dom? I know about the anger and the guilt and the denial. I've lived 'em all before, and I'm sure I'll live them all again. Don't crowd me."

"You loved her, Dig."

That one got him. A simple sentence; so short and so true. He felt the stitching that held his emotions together starting to strain. He turned and started walking again.

Dom reached out a hand to touch Jonathan's shoulder, but he shook it away. "Dig, come on. Please. You loved her. Don't try to match anything that's happened in your past with this. Don't even try."

"Dom, stop."

"Damn it, Jon, look at me!" Dom yelled, startling

everyone. The waters parted widely now to give them as much room as possible. Fifty feet away, a pair of uniformed cops took notice and moved their way.

Jonathan's eyes grew hot, a look of untamed rage. He grabbed a fistful of the priest's shirt and twisted it, bringing their faces within inches of each other. "What do you want from me, Dom? You want tears? A breakdown, maybe? You want me to get all sad and cuddly for you? It's not going to happen."

Dom said nothing.

As a look of pained horror passed across Digger's face, he let go of the shirt and made a half effort to smooth out the wrinkles he'd left behind.

"Sorry," Jonathan mumbled.

"Is there a problem here?" asked a cop, still fifteen feet away.

"No, we're fine," Dom said.

The younger and shorter of the two officers gave a concerned scowl. "You sure, Father? I saw him grab you."

"I said I'm fine," Dom repeated.

The tone seemed to piss the cop off. "Whatever it is," he said, "take it outside." They walked away, glancing back to make sure that the embers of the argument didn't reignite.

"Look," Jonathan said, settling himself. "I don't know if I can explain this to you, but in my world, emotion is useless. It gets in the way. I deal with hard facts and soft theories. I understand action and reaction. Cause and effect. That's where sanity lies with me. The rest of it . . ." His voice trailed off. "The rest of it doesn't mean anything."

Again, Dom let the pause hang in the air, waiting for it to fill itself.

"This is my fault," Jonathan said finally. "I put the

events in motion to get Ellen killed, and I'll set it right again."

"You can't," Dom said.

"Don't make another speech, Dom. Please. At least do me the favor of sparing me that."

"Vengeance is the Lord's, Digger, not yours. Let Him and the police do their jobs."

"They don't know what I know. They can't trace the evidence in the same direction."

"Then share it with them."

"You know I can't do that."

"Then share it with Wolverine. She's got the clout to make it all right."

Jonathan paused before coming clean. "I don't want to," he said. "I want the son of a bitch to see me killing him."

Chapter Twenty-six

Boxers drove Jonathan home in the Batmobile while Venice drove Dom in Glow Bird. For the first forty-five minutes or so, no one said a word in the Hummer. Jonathan could feel Boxers' discomfort with the silence, his need to say something to lighten the mood, but he didn't care. They all had burdens to bear, and Boxers would just be stuck with the awkwardness of it all.

"You okay, Boss?" the big man asked.

Jonathan pivoted his head to look at him, but he said nothing.

Boxers sighed. "I'm sorry you're hurting like this."

"You didn't even like her," Jonathan said. He could hear the whininess in his own voice and it embarrassed him.

"No, I never did," Boxers confessed. "I never came close to liking her. And the way she treated you when she left, well, that didn't help. But that don't mean I don't hurt when you hurt."

This time, when Jonathan turned to face the big man, he allowed himself a gentle smile.

"You're my friend, Dig. That makes you a rare friggin' breed. I hate seein' you in pain."

A feeling of warmth washed over Jonathan. He didn't think he'd ever heard a more heartfelt expression of empathy.

"There's somethin' else you should know," Boxers continued. "Time comes you want to get revenge on the asshole who killed her, you know I'm there."

Glow Bird beat them home, and when Jonathan and his chauffeur entered the firehouse, Venice, Dom, and JoeDog were already in the living room, waiting for them. Jonathan paused in the entryway and sighed as the dog scrabbled off the sofa and charged to meet him. He knew they were there to see him through his emotional crisis, but he was not in the mood.

"Not tonight, guys. I really want to be alone."

"I don't think you do," Venice said.

Jonathan scowled.

Dom elaborated, "Before we got the news about Ellen, we did some brainstorming."

"We?"

"Dom and I," Venice said. "We were trying to make the pieces fit. And I think we did."

Jonathan waited for it.

"We know that Stephenson Hughes needed the GVX as ransom," Dom began.

Venice quickly interrupted, "And that Ivan Patrick worked for Carlyle in a special capacity for something called Special Projects."

Dom leaned back in his seat, and let her have the floor.

"So, working from the assumption that there are no

coincidences in the world, since Angela Caldwell worked for Carlyle, too—"

"She was the one who knew how to get their hands on it," Jonathan said, connecting the dots for himself.

"So, the Hugheses *did* kill her," Boxers said. "They tortured her to get the information."

Venice shook her head. "No, I don't think so. She had a family. She was a mother. I think all they had to do was tell her what they were up against, and she gave them the information. Somehow, Ivan Patrick must have found out about it, and then *he* was the one who tortured and killed them to find out what she'd told the Hugheses." Her eyes bored into Jonathan, seeking assurance that her logic was sound.

"It certainly explains the brutality—Ivan's MO," Jonathan agreed. "If that's the way it went down."

"Tell him about the other shootings," Dom prompted.

Venice leaned forward, her eyes wide. "No coincidences, right? Well, using this hunch, I did a little more poking around the ICIS network and I found even more activity around the Muncie area. Well, okay, eighty miles from Muncie, but still."

"Another murder?" Boxers asked.

"No, but a shooting—sort of. A half of a shooting." Jonathan's face showed his waning patience, so Venice picked up the pace. "A 9-1-1 call reported a shooting at a place called Apocalypse Boulevard in a town I don't remember. Then, while units were still responding, the call got canceled. The caller called back and said that they were mistaken, and that everything was okay. The dispatcher turned the ambulance around, but the cop car went on in anyway just to check things out. According to their report, the people they met there at the gate—employees of a security firm—seemed agitated, but they swore that everything was fine, and the cops had no grounds to press their suspicions any further."

"But you don't believe that things were fine," Jonathan concluded for her.

Venice nodded. "Exactly. Because there are no coincidences. I did a Zillow search on the address." Jonathan recognized the name of the real estate search engine. "Care to guess what that address used to be?"

"An Indian burial ground," Jonathan grumped.

"A Nike missile launch facility. It's all in the public record. Back in the eighties and nineties, we got rid of all our Nike missiles, and the sites went up for sale. This one, on Apocalypse Boulevard, was bought by Secured Storage Company out of Wilmington, Delaware."

"Interesting company name," Boxers poked. "I wonder what they do."

"*Delaware*," Venice stressed. Clearly, she was frustrated that they hadn't already leaped to where she was going. "Carlyle is a Delaware company."

Jonathan coughed out a laugh. "Jesus, Ven, half the companies in the world are Delaware corporations."

"Which makes it that much easier to do the search," she countered. "Secured Storage Company is a subsidiary—several steps removed, of course—of Carlyle Industries. They're the same company!"

Finally, Jonathan got it. "Missiles mean underground storage magazines," he said. "That's where Carlyle was storing the GVX."

"When the Hugheses went there to get it, there must have been an exchange of gunfire," Dom said.

"So what's with the phone call to 9-1-1?" Boxers asked. "And if there someone was shot, why *un*-call?"

"Because they didn't want the publicity," Jonathan explained. "Every state requires gunshot wounds to be reported to the police, mandating some kind of investigation. That's the last thing a company like Carlyle would want."

The room grew silent except for JoeDog's snoring as they each put the puzzle together for themselves.

Finally, Jonathan test-drove his own theory aloud. "Desperate to get their kid back, the Hugheses reach out to Angela Caldwell. She points them in the right direction, and pays for the decision with her life. Obviously, they visited her at her house, or else their fingerprints wouldn't be all over the place. Then they went to this Apocalypse Boulevard place and took what they needed for ransom."

"Shooting the place up while doing it," Boxers said.

"Right," Jonathan agreed. "So now the Hugheses are hiding somewhere. They can't call the police without walking into a murder charge, and they've either stashed their GVX somewhere, or they're still hanging on to it. It's their curse and their bargaining chip." He looked to each of them. "We need to find Stephenson Hughes and his family."

Venice beamed. "I already did."

CHAPTER TWENTY-SEVEN

Gail Bonneville's chair squeaked noisily as she leaned all the way back and stretched to relieve the kink that now owned space between her shoulder blades. With her feet up on her desk, she moved her wireless mouse along her thigh and cued up the video footage yet again. The first few seconds featured Leon Harris entering the arrivals lounge at Washington Dulles International Airport. It was hard to tell because of the high angle, but she thought he looked tired as he walked out of frame lugging only a computer case.

There was an edit blip, and then she watched him emerge from another door, this time into the baggage claim area, where he was greeted by a priest and a woman. Clearly, they knew each other, but there was tension, especially between Leon and the priest. There was no audio track, but emotions were running high as they confronted each other. At one point, Leon even grabbed the priest's shirt. As a lifelong Methodist, she didn't know the precise teachings of the Catholic Church, but she was pretty sure that hell awaited anyone who attacked a priest.

But it was only a flash of anger, dissipating and ending in body language that looked a lot like an apology, even before the two cops stepped in to intervene. Finally, it all ended with the arrival of a fourth player in the drama, this one a thick, towering brute who likewise was warmly welcomed.

All told, the video record ran less than ten minutes, but Gail remained convinced that the drama on her screen held the key to the answers she sought.

The police work that brought this video to her was a bit of brilliance, she thought. She didn't for a moment believe that Leon Harris was with the FBI—despite the confirmation she received from the Bureau—any more than she believed that Leon Harris was even his real name. The fact that she had footage of him exiting a flight on which no one named Leon Harris was registered only proved the point. With his Perseus Foods cover blown, he couldn't risk being spotted returning to the parked jet, which would leave him with two options: chartering a different private jet, which would be traceable, or disappearing into the river of passengers on a commercial flight.

On a hunch, she contacted the Transportation Security Administration and talked them into sharing the security camera images from the arrival lounges of all the Washington-area airports that had flights arriving from any airport within five hundred miles of Indianapolis. Turned out to be a hell of a lot more flights than she'd anticipated, so she narrowed it to a slightly more manageable population by throwing in the variable of a tickets purchased within ten hours of the flight.

Then she'd lucked out and found Leon's image in the fifth video she'd watched. Once she found him in the arrival lounge, it was a fairly simple task to trace his every step through the airport by cross-referencing the time stamps on the hundreds of cameras that continually recorded every second of airport life.

But what did it mean? Why was the man who was not Leon Harris so interested in protecting the Hughes family? She sensed that if she could find the answer to that one question, she would single-handedly solve seven murders.

A rapid two-knock on her door told her that it was Jesse even before he walked in without waiting for an invitation. His face seemed electrified with a just-ate-a-canary look. He carried a file in his left hand, and as he approached her desk and helped himself to the guest chair, he waved it like a lady would wave a fan at the opera.

"Pay dirt, Boss," he said; but he didn't open the folder. "Facial recognition software turned up bupkis on your pal Leon Harris. Absolutely nothing. So, I decided to run the other faces. This is what I got."

Gail waited for him to open his file and select a facedown piece of paper. She turned it over and saw a mug she vaguely recognized. She scowled and waited for her answer without asking the question.

"The priest," Jesse said. "From the video. You are looking at one Father Dominc D'Angelo, pastor of St. Katherine's Catholic Church in a place called Fisherman's Cove, Virginia. Don't ask where it is, because I don't have a clue. The picture you're looking at is from a fund-raiser for something called Resurrection House. It's an orphanage, sort of, for kids whose parents are serving time in jail."

"How sweet," Gail said.

"Hey, it's a start," Jesse said. Then he smiled. "But it's only the beginning. Clearly Leon and Father D'Angelo know each other, right? So I thought I'd search the Internet for the cross section of Dominic

D'Angelo and Fisherman's Cove. Actually, there were more hits than I would have thought. For a priest, he really gets around on the rubber chicken circuit. He's like a fund-raising machine. He's also a psychologist, for what that's worth."

"Is it worth anything?"

Jesse shrugged. "I suppose if you're crazy, but not so much for us right now."

"Then why—"

"Stay with me. I'm getting there. I wasn't finding anything to link him to Leon, and I traced him back as far as I knew how to trace. Finally, I found an alumni newspaper from the College of William and Mary from sometime in the mideighties. They were running some kind of a retrospective of the Good Old Days, you know?" His smile broadened, and he slid another sheet face down to Gail. "And look what I found."

With a sense of real anticipation in her gut, Gail turned the sheet over and found a picture of two clearly intoxicated college students. The clothing styles spoke of the last days of disco. These two boys were laughing heartily, hanging off each other in that way that you never see in guys who are much beyond their teens.

"Don't you see it?" Jesse prompted.

Then she did. The caption identified them by name. The dark-haired, dark-eyed beauty on the left was a younger version of Father D'Angelo. And the shirtless blond Adonis on the right was a very young Leon Harris—only his name on the page was Jonathan Gravenow.

"Oh, my," Gail beamed. "Look what you found. Nice work, Jess. Wonderful work. Now we have a name for the face."

Jesse shook his head. "Actually, we don't," he said. "Jonathan Gravenow doesn't exist. Nowhere in the world."

"But I just saw him."

Jesse's smile got even broader. "No," he said as he slid a third sheet of paper across the desk, "you just saw Jonathan Grave."

This new sheet of paper looked to be articles of incorporation for a company called Security Solutions, a Virginia corporation headquartered in none other than Fisherman's Cove.

"This one was a little tricky," Jesse said, exuding pride. "Jonathan Gravenow was the only child of Simon Gravenow. Does that name ring a bell, Miss FBI?"

It didn't ring a bell, it bashed a gong. Simon Gravenow was one of the great racketeers. "Organized crime, right?"

"Exactly," Jesse said. "The Dixie mafia. As soon as Jonathan Gravenow graduated college, he changed his name to Jonathan Grave, and he joined the Army. Twenty years later, he owns a private investigation company. Now, what kind of investigation firm do you suppose a former Army guy might run?"

This time, Gail saw it immediately. People like that were exactly the folks who would get into the paramilitary business. The kind of business that might specialize in rescuing wayward hostages. It was time to find Fisherman's Cove on the map and make a plane reservation.

She was about to say something to that effect when her phone rang. Even as she reached for the receiver, she had the sense that she should have ignored it.

Thirty seconds later, she cursed herself for not listening to her instincts.

Venice didn't try to conceal her pride for what she'd accomplished. "I knew you'd want to track the Hugheses," she said, "so I worked the problem. I was hoping that they'd done something really stupid like using their credit cards, but obviously they haven't, or the police would have been all over them. They've been pretty smart. The only record of unusual behavior is their withdrawal of twelve thousand dollars and change from their savings account. Pretty much wiped out their cash supply."

"That's their traveling money," Boxers said.

She continued, "I tried tracking the cell phones owned by each of them, but they've either turned them off or thrown them away. Either way, there's no signal to triangulate on."

Jonathan asked, "What about the number I called at the end of the 0300 mission?"

"That's one of those prepaid disposable jobs—thank God you called it, or we'd have nothing even to look for—but it's turned off, too. Even so, it got me thinking. If they know enough to keep their cell phones off and to use prepaids, then they'd probably buy more than one of them, right? One for Stephenson Hughes and one for his wife, Julie." She waited for the nods. "So, with a little help from a friend of mine in the telephone company, I did a search on the telephone numbers that were called by Stephenson's prepaid, and guess what I found?"

Jonathan feigned patience because it was easiest. "What?"

"That he called another prepaid disposable phone."

"The wife?"

"That would be my guess. Anyway, those calls—there were three of them altogether, beginning shortly after your call to Stephenson, with the last one about thirty hours ago—gave us a routing to look at."

"Where the signals began and ended," Dom explained.

Venice nodded. "Exactly. And it got interesting. The other end of the call—the receiving end in every case—was from different locations, starting in Indiana, and moving in a rough line north and east. The originating end of the calls all came from the same tower combinations in southwestern Pennsylvania."

"Pittsburgh?" Jonathan asked.

"Not Pittsburgh per se," Venice said, "but from that general area. In the mountains." She reached under the coffee table and found the atlas that Jonathan always kept there, and searched for the appropriate page. To Jonathan's eye, it looked a little staged. When she pointed to the map, she did it with a swirling motion that involved all of her fingers. "In here," she said.

Boxers gave a low whistle. "That's a lot of territory," he said. "Can you sharpen that pencil a little?"

She gave him a sideward glance. "Of course I can," she said. Her voice became even more animated. "That part of the state is in pretty tough shape economically. You don't have neighborhoods like we know them. Up in the mining country there are lots and lots of old homesteads, but they tend to be on big tracts of land. Dozens of acres, if not hundreds."

Jonathan found his patience waning, but he hung in there.

"I know, I know," Venice said, reading his body language. "Get to the point. Well, I am, believe it or not. Because the land tracts are so large, there are only a few that could possibly be the source of Stephenson's signal."

"Unless he's decided to bivouac," Boxers said.

Venice waved a dismissive hand. "Trust me," she said. "He didn't. He decided instead to use an old family home up there in the woods."

"*His* family?" Boxers asked.

"Why haven't the police found him?" Jonathan added.

She beamed. "Because it's deeded to Alistair DuBois," she said. "Not to Stephenson Hughes."

Jonathan recoiled. "Who the hell is Alistair Dubois?"

"Stephenson Hughes's mother's father."

"Holy shit," Boxers barked.

Dom laughed. "Isn't she amazing? Honest to goodness, it only took her about forty-five minutes to piece all of this together. I watched her do it."

Jonathan's mouth gaped. "What kind of twisted logic gets you to places like that?"

She shrugged. "I cheated. I started with the assumption that he had a plan that made sense." She shot a look to Boxers. "One that made more sense than *bivouacking*, anyway, which meant that there was probably some property that they had access to. If that were the case, then I figured that it would be family property, else how would they know about it? Based on that assumption, I started with the tax records for the most likely tracts, and then I worked backward through a genealogy search. The answer came pretty fast."

Jonathan gaped. "You never cease to amaze me."

She beamed.

"You up for doing some more magic?"

Her face fell. "Like what?"

"Like finding me everything you can about a place in West Virginia known as Brigadeville." It took less than a minute to share the spotty information he'd learned from Andrew Hawkins.

Venice scowled. "That's not much to go on."

"You saying you can't?" Jonathan asked.

"I'm insulted," she said.

"I thought you might be." Jonathan looked at his watch. "It's seven-fifteen now. Let's meet again in three hours and see where we are."

Now she looked shocked. "You know it's seven fifteen in the evening, right?"

Jonathan stood. "Three hours and fifteen minutes, then. You, Box, and I will meet up in the office at ten thirty." He looked to Boxers. "That work for you, big guy?"

He stood, too. "Doesn't feel like there's a lot of choice."

"Then I'm communicating," Jonathan said. "Now, if y'all don't mind, I'd like some time alone."

The mood in the room plummeted. It was as if they'd all forgotten about Ellen. Venice shot to her feet, startling JoeDog. "Oh, God, Digger," she said. "How rude of us."

Jonathan herded them toward the steps at the base of the fire pole that led to the one-way door to the office corridor on the second floor. "No need to apologize. You did great work."

"Do you want company?" Dom asked, triggering a panicked look from Boxers, who relaxed right away when he saw that he wasn't a part of the offer. The big guy wasn't long on soothing words.

Jonathan smiled. "I'm fine, Dom," he said. "Really, I'm fine."

"You're sure?"

"Git," Jonathan said. "You've wasted enough time on my soul for the night."

Dom didn't look comfortable with the order, but he couldn't come up with a reason to stay. He exited the firehouse through the back door.

As they walked away, Jonathan stooped to rub Joe-Dog's ears, turning his back on Venice and Boxers. He waited for the sound of the office corridor door latching shut again, then stood to his full height and fished out his cell phone. He opened it, scrolled through his Contacts list to the name he was looking for, and pressed Send.

The man on the other end answered after the first ring. "Chief Kramer," the voice said, all business.

"Doug, it's Jon Grave. I need a favor."

Chapter Twenty-Eight

Even in civilian life, when the agent in charge of the FBI's Chicago Field Office delivers an urgent message, you listen. "You need to go home," Vincent Medina had said. "And you need to go alone." When Gail had pressed for more details, his tone took on a pleading quality as he told her that he was not authorized to share any more than that simple directive.

"I don't work for you guys anymore," Gail had said.

Medina had let the comment just hang there. Authorized to say no more meant say no more. "I can't tell you what to do, Gail. For what it's worth, I don't even know what this is about. But the fact that Headquarters called me directly and made a point of ensuring that I be the one to make the call to you tells me that it's something big."

"And I have to go alone."

"That's what they told me."

"I don't suppose you can clarify who the 'they' is."

"Gail. Sheriff. Please."

So, here she was, driving alone toward the unknown. She pushed away the paranoid thoughts that this would be a terrific setup for a hit. A single shot out of nowhere. Boom. Dead. It was ridiculous on its face. Even if they'd wanted to do such a thing—and the Bureau never did, not anymore—they certainly wouldn't have set it up with a phone call.

As she made the last turn to cruise up her long driveway, her heart rate doubled. It doubled again when she saw a Chrysler with rent-a-car tags parked in front of the garage. Steeling herself with a deep breath, she threw the transmission into Park and opened her door. As she climbed out, she made a special effort to keep her right hand poised on the grip of her pistol. If this did turn out to be some sort of trap, the person on the other end of it was going to suffer.

She saw movement on her porch. Her weapon hand twitched, but she didn't yet have cause to draw down. "Show yourself, please!" she shouted, but the *please* part was in no way a request.

The shadow hesitated, then raised its arms in an amiable gesture to show that its hands were empty.

"Into the light," Gail commanded.

Her next thought was, *holy shit.*

Chief of Police Doug Kramer drove. It was the single condition on which he'd hung his decision to grant Jonathan's request. He wouldn't allow his friend to make this trip on his own. During the long drive north, the men barely spoke beyond the required statements of condolence. What was there to say under the circumstances?

Jonathan knew what the others thought of Ellen. He knew that they all thought he was naïve to still have feelings for her, that at one level they all though less of him for his loyalty to her. He'd never tried to set the record straight, because it had never made sense to try.

It took about an hour. I-95 to the Beltway to Gallows Road. As the edifice of Fairfax Hospital loomed, his heart started to pound. They made the left into the sprawling complex, and then swung an immediate right, passing the helipad on their left and disappearing down the hill until all notion of architectural interest gave way to the pure efficiency of Dumpsters and loading docks. By the time a patient's stay took him to these parts, aesthetics meant little.

Doug pulled his cruiser to a stop at the base of stairs that led to a nondescript metal door that serviced two of the closed loading docks. "You're sure about this?" he asked.

Jonathan nodded, even though he really was anything but.

"Want me to stay here or come with?"

The oddly Midwestern sentence construction amused Jonathan. "I need to go in by myself," he said, "but I don't want to burden you with sitting in a dark alley. Want me to call you when I'm done?"

"Nope," Doug said without thought. "I'll be here. Wish we'd brought Father Dom."

Jonathan gave a wry chuckle as he opened the door, bathing them in the glow of the dome light. "Absolutely not," he said. "I love that man like a brother, but he's never learned the value of a good silence. You have." He paused, hoping that Doug had heard the thank-you he'd intended. Then he got out and closed the door behind him.

At the top of the stairs, he punched a three-digit code he'd been given into the 4 x 4-inch intercom. A second later, a young male voice said, "Speak."

The abrupt cheerfulness caught Jonathan off guard. "Um, good evening. This is Jonathan Grave. I believe that Chief Kramer called to gain permission to view my wife's body."

A pause. "Yes, sir. Of course. Come on in and I'll be there to meet you." Jonathan envisioned this night shift kid kicking himself for his cavalier attitude.

The lock buzzed, and Jonathan pulled the door open. Inside, tiled floors and walls created a tableau of beige.

A redheaded beanpole appeared from a doorway halfway down the hall. Somewhere between eighteen and twenty-five, the kid stood six-one, and weighed maybe a hundred thirty-five pounds if you kept a thumb on the scale. Consumed by a green scrub suit, he was all arms and legs and had a neck like a giraffe. He also had a smile like the dawn. "I'm Jimmy," he said, extending his hand as he strode deliberately up to Jonathan. "I'm the night tech."

Jonathan shook his hand. "Jonathan Grave," he said. He wanted to be gruff, but was having a hard time pulling it off in the light of the young man's sincerity.

"I'm really sorry about the attitude on the intercom. Some nights, we get kids who like pushing buttons—" He stopped himself. "Anyway, I'm sorry for your loss."

"Thank you," Jonathan said.

"Are you here alone?" Jimmy asked.

Jonathan tossed his head toward the metal door. "A friend is waiting for me out there."

Jimmy winced. "You sure you don't want them in here with you? This viewing stuff can be sort of tough, and—"

"I was in the military, son," Jonathan said. "There's not much you can show me that I haven't already caused myself, one way or the other."

Jimmy's face reddened, but not nearly to the shade of his hair. He started walking down the hall. "Okay, then, follow me." The kid led the way past the alcove from which he'd emerged, then took a left to face an otherwise nondescript door that was marked, plainly enough, MORGUE. UNESCORTED ACCESS PROHIBITED.

A desk sat inside the door, abandoned, but piled with all manner of office flotsam. Even in his fleeting glance, Jonathan saw boxes of tissue paper and latex gloves, countless reams of stark white copy paper, and an array of yellow #2 pencils that had somehow come to rest in the near perfect shape of a sunrise.

Jimmy paused in the anteroom, just on this side of the large refrigerator door that led into the next room. "You know I need to stay with you, right?" he asked.

Jonathan scowled. No one had told him anything of the sort.

"It's a procedural thing," the kid explained. "Chain of evidence. I don't want to intrude, but I also can't let you touch the . . ." He cut himself off. "You know. Her. I can't let you touch her."

Jonathan cocked his head. For the first time, he found himself coming to grips with the reality that to the authorities in charge, Ellen was evidence now, to one day be used in the trial of the people who killed her. The people that Jonathan would have somehow failed to kill himself.

"I understand," Jonathan said.

Jimmy eyed him, then turned toward the doors. "If you feel faint or anything—"

"You don't have to worry about me," Jonathan assured.

Jimmy mumbled, "I had a nickel for every time I heard that . . ."

The temperature dropped twenty degrees on the far side of the refrigerator door. In here, the tile was blue-green, or maybe green-blue. Aqua? It was a color that struck Jonathan as a desperate effort to make this vault of death somehow less horrifying than it really was, yet in the process somehow trebled the awfulness. The bodies—dozens of them, as if there'd been some natural disaster that Jonathan hadn't heard about—lay shrouded in white on gurneys that were stashed at odd angles.

Jimmy motioned for Jonathan to stay put as he navigated through the horizontal forest of corpses checking toe tags that were in fact attached not to toes, but rather to the ears of black plastic body bags that were covered by tightly tucked white sheets. Jonathan stuffed his hands in his pockets as he steeled himself from a shiver.

The kid stopped at the far right-hand corner. "Here she is," he said.

Jonathan started to walk forward, but then stopped when he saw that Jimmy was going to wheel the gurney to him. It only took a few seconds.

Jimmy fixed Jonathan with an are-you-sure-you-want-to-go-ahead look, then pulled the sheet down and unzipped the body bag down one-third of its length. He separated the edges of the bag, and there she was.

Actually, no. There was what she'd been turned into.

This long after death, her always fair skin should have been a yellow-white, lying slack against her delicate features. Her eyes should have been closed—or nearly closed, with perhaps a half-moon of iris showing above or below her eyelid. The flaccid flesh of her face should have brought her thin nose and high cheekbones into sharp relief. In Jonathan's mind the dead never looked at rest so he didn't expect that, but he did expect a look of peace. With the frowning muscles as lifeless as their smiling counterparts, he expected a deathly smoothness to her face.

Yet he found none of that.

Ellen's face was barely a face at all; it was a bloated purple eruption of battered tissue. On her left side, the one closest to Jonathan, the cheekbone, eye socket, and brow had merged into a blood-filled globe. In the middle of the mass, the slit that was once the opening between her lids appeared to be glued shut. The angle of her jaw told him that it had been badly broken and wired back, and the odd cast of her lips was a clear indication that her teeth had been broken.

Looking at her like this, Jonathan understood why no one wanted him to be here. No one should ever have to see a loved one in a condition like this. Emotion blossomed behind his eyes, but it wasn't driven by sadness. There was some of that, sure, but the redness of his eyes was all anger, as was the tightly locked jaw and the fists that he didn't realize he'd clenched. He inhaled deeply and noisily, suddenly aware that for a long while he hadn't been breathing at all.

"Sir, are you all right?" Jimmy asked. He looked terrified that he might have to care for the living instead of the dead.

Jonathan glared at him, at the long thin neck. Inexplicably, he thought how easy it would be snap it. One blow was all it would take. Or one violent twist. In his mind he could see himself doing it.

He shook the thought away. This wasn't a time for violence. Certainly not against this clean-cut kid who'd tried every way he'd known to keep Jonathan away from this very moment. No, the time for violence would come later.

"I'm fine," Jonathan said, returning his gaze to Ellen.

"You don't look fine," Jimmy said.

Jonathan didn't answer. Instead, he turned on his heel and left the only woman he'd ever loved behind him on the gurney. He didn't want to watch as Jimmy pulled the zipper shut again.

On the other side of the heavy door, in the paper- and equipment-strewn office, he nearly collided with Detective Weatherby of the Fairfax County Police Department.

CHAPTER TWENTY-NINE

Gail had never met the woman who stepped out of the shadows on her porch, but she recognized her on sight. "My goodness," Gail stammered. "Director Rivers." She extended her hand to the highest ranking law enforcement officer in the country. "What an honor."

FBI Director Irene Rivers returned the handshake warmly and smiled. "The honor is mine, Sheriff Bonneville."

Gail flushed. She found herself oddly speechless in the presence of the woman whom she admired perhaps more than any other. "Madame Director. Why are you here?" she asked, and then winced at the seeming rudeness.

"Please dispense with the 'Madam Director' and call me Irene."

Gail smiled. "I'll try, but no promises. You look well."

"Thank you." Irene absently touched the spot on her head where her auburn hair concealed the ragged scar left by the bullet that nearly killed her a few years ago. "I'm sorry to hear about the shootings here the other day. That must be very unsettling in a community this small."

"I'd think it's unsettling in any community," Gail said.

Irene gestured up the steps toward the front door. "May I invite myself inside for a chat?"

Gail gave a little start and headed for the steps. "Where are my manners? Yes, please come inside."

They settled at the kitchen table because that was the only room that was furnished. Irene Rivers told her that she loved the place. Gail smiled and offered a soft drink, which the director refused, and they settled in to the business at hand.

"I know how difficult your last few days have been," Irene started. "I've run high-profile cases myself over the years, and the pressure to produce results can be overwhelming."

Gail crossed her arms and leaned them on the table. As her head cleared from celebrity shock, she decided to resist small talk. This was not a social call, after all. "Does this meeting have something to do with the shootings?" she asked.

Irene ignored the question. "Can I trust that what we discuss here in the next few minutes will remain in this room?"

"Absolutely not," Gail said, surprised to hear her own words. "Not until I know what you're about to say. My first allegiance is no longer to the Bureau."

Irene arched her eyebrows and smirked. It was a look of admiration, not derision. "Why am I not surprised?" she said. She regrouped her thoughts. "Okay, then, tell me who *you* think the killer is."

Gail hesitated, but she wasn't sure why. "By name?"

Irene cocked her head. "*Could* you answer by name?"

The sheriff nodded. "I think so."

"Then no," Irene said. She looked a little embarrassed. "You'll see when we're done that I'll need plausible deniability. Tell me instead where your deductive path has led you."

Deductive path, Gail thought. *How very Bureauspeak.* Her eyes narrowed as she weighed her options. "I must confess, Madam Dir—" She cut herself off. "I'm not entirely comfortable sharing those details. Not at this stage of the investigation."

"Because the Bureau has a history of, what, screwing people over?" Irene ventured. "Because we have a history of hogging credit when things go well and of passing the buck when they go sour?"

The director's bluntness startled Gail. "Well, yes," she said.

"I don't blame you. As you might imagine, when you sit in my chair in the Emerald City you learn to trust your instincts on whom you trust and whom you don't. In this case, I'm asking for the benefit of reasonable doubt."

Gail liked this woman. She had always respected Irene Rivers, and after the shoot-out that involved the death of her predecessor in the job, the whole world had come to admire the woman's courage under fire. "Okay," Gail said at length. "I think that our shooter is a professional of a very high order. I think that he has advanced tactical training, perhaps Special Forces, perhaps HRT or SWAT. He knows how to make a big entry, and he knows how to shoot extremely well. He also did not work alone. He appears to have arrived by helicopter."

Irene nodded and pinched her lower lip as she listened. "So you suspect that he was an assassin hired to come in and shoot these three people?"

Gail hesitated. Was she *supposed* to be thinking that? She felt self-conscious as she shook her head. "No, I don't. I believe that his primary mission was to save lives, not take them. I think that the Patrones kidnapped a college student named Thomas Hughes, and that our shooter team was hired to come and rescue the victim. How am I doing?"

Irene's expression never changed. She stopped pinching her lip and pushed herself away from the table just far enough to allow her to cross her legs. "You're very close," Irene said. "But let me ask you this. If you believe that the shooting was merely collateral damage from a hostage rescue, how hell-bent are you on aggressive prosecution?"

Gail was receiving a jumble of mixed signals, and the effect was unnerving. "My job is to follow leads wherever they take me," she said. "I find the people who commit crimes, and the district attorney does the rest."

"That's a civics lesson, not an answer," Irene said. Her expression remained pleasant. "How important is it to you to find the people who killed a group of kidnappers?"

Gail sighed. Game time was over. "Irene, you flew to Indiana from Washington to meet with me, and clearly you have an agenda. Why don't you just get to it?"

Irene considered for a second, then said, "I want you to suspend your investigation."

It was as Gail had anticipated. "You're crazy."

"We'll make all the evidence mesh with a solid cover story. We'll make sure your constituents see you as a hero."

"I won't walk away, Irene. Not after a triple murder."

"Not murder. Rescue attempt. The people who did this have been great friends to the U.S. government over the years. They're very, very good at what they do, but in this case, things went awry and people were killed—but only because they were about to kill their hostage. The rescuer was in fact waiting for a peaceful moment to make his entry when the Patrones tried to castrate their hostage. He had no choice. The Patrones took a shot at the hero, and the hero dropped them." She paused to make sure Gail had had a chance to absorb it all. "Does your evidence so far support what I've told you?"

Gail churned it all and nodded. "They were going to use long-handled pruning shears."

"There was a vehicle shot up on the premises, too, was there not?" Irene asked.

"Shot up and burned."

Irene recapped how that came about, demonstrating her complete knowledge of the incident. "You can see, then," Irene concluded, "that these were good people doing the work of the angels. To prosecute them would be a crime in itself, don't you think?"

"It doesn't matter what I think. Even if things happened exactly the way you describe them—"

"They did, I swear to you."

"Okay, they did. What you described is still homicide in this state. Perhaps even premeditated murder. My God, they invaded a private home and shot the owners to death. I *want* that to be a crime. Otherwise, we'd have chaos."

Irene considered a new course. "I think I read on the plane that you were with the Hostage Rescue Team. Is that correct?"

The non sequitur startled Gail. She became cautious. "I was HRT in Chicago for three years."

"And what happened in that farmhouse is no different than what happens in any given raid. If people put their hands up, they live. If they have a gun in their hand, they die. It's just the way things work."

"It's not the way things work," Gail protested. "When I crash a door, or when SWAT does it, it's with a legally obtained warrant, acting with the authority of the entire community. This is just vigilante—"

"Oak Brook Liquors, Gail," Irene said, cutting her off. "December of 2004, I believe. You were there?"

Heat flooded Gail's face. She felt verbally slapped, and she set her palms on the tabletop, as if ready to pounce. "How dare you," she seethed. She could hear the tremor in her voice.

Irene was unmoved. "You were SAC on that, I believe, in charge of a hostage-taking in a liquor store off Butterfield Road. Surely you must remember."

Gail rose from her chair, scooting it backward against the hardwood floor with the force of her knees. "You know what? I think it's time for you to leave."

Irene didn't move. "You had a critical situation, according to the incident reports, and you handled it perfectly. You got a commendation from your field office SAC. I remember reading about it at the time. You got the bad guy without hurting him, and you got five of seven hostages out safely. The other two were killed while you were waiting on the warrant, which, paradoxically, turned out not to be necessary after the bad guy pulled his trigger."

The words were like heated fishhooks, tearing away the patches she'd sewn over the single most horrible moment of her life. She sagged back into her chair. The killer had been a veterinary student named David Jackson, and the two DOAs had been fourteen-year-old twin sisters who just happened to have accompanied their father on his mission to lay in the supply of Christmas cheer. The girls had been duct taped together at the neck and murdered at point-blank range by a single bullet through both of their brains. They'd fallen sideways when they'd died, their shoulders resting across their father's knees. That's where they lay when Gail and her team made their breach entrance. Gail still awoke some nights with the image of their father in her mind. Jackson had bound him just like he'd bound everyone else, and the look of desperate emptiness in the dad's face as he helplessly absorbed his daughters' blood into his clothing redefined for Gail the meaning of pain.

"You did everything by the book," Irene remembered. "If you could dial back the clock and do it again without the book, wouldn't you say to hell with the warrant and go in earlier?"

Gail measured her words. By thinking about each syllable, she could resist the urge to strike this woman. "It's not a reasonable question. Who wouldn't go back in time and undo every bad thing that's ever happened to them? Life isn't like that."

"But violent people are always violent people."

"And the law is always the law." She chuckled at the absurdity of this conversation. "There is no minor violation of civil rights, Director Rivers—they're all major. It's why we have laws in the first place. When people play this game of bullshit Bingo, it always turns to the ultimate hypothetical. Wouldn't it have been great if someone had had the courage to murder Adolf Hitler in 1936 and saved millions of lives?"

Irene arched an eyebrow. Perhaps she was thinking that very thing.

"My answer is no," Gail said. "Individuals don't get

to decide who lives and who dies. Even if he's a good friend of the U.S. government."

"He saved a young man's life," Irene said through tightening lips.

"And killed three others in the process." Gail sighed. "Look. You may be right—I'll stipulate that you probably are. If I were anyone else but the sheriff—the woman elected to be the voice of the law—I might even agree with you. But as it is, I will pursue this killer with vigor, and I will chase him to ground. The rest will be up to the jury." She stood again. "And in fairness, ma'am, I should tell you that you'll be relaying this story one more time to a grand jury as soon as I get the subpoena put together."

Irene didn't move.

"Director Rivers, I think it's time for you to leave," Gail said. "Now."

Irene gestured for Gail to resume her seat. "We're not done here," she said.

Gail laughed reflexively. "I beg to differ. And inasmuch as this is my home—"

"Sheriff Bonneville." Irene shot the words like a bullet. "Sit."

Gail felt in Irene's glare the heat that had wilted so many others. She sat.

"I wanted to keep this meeting friendly," Irene began. She steeled herself. "You can't win this one, Sheriff. The personalities involved in the operation at that farmhouse are valuable assets to me. I won't let you take them down."

"Are you telling me that the murder of the Patrone brothers was a government operation?"

Irene shook her head. "I'm not telling you anything of the sort. I'm telling you that these rescuers were on the side of the angels in what they did. They save lives. Your constituents would not have been killed had they not posed a clear and present danger to the rescuers."

Gail coughed out a humorless laugh. "Do you hear yourself? You're underwriting vigilante killings."

"I'm underwriting nothing. Be honest with me, Sheriff. If they had called and tipped you to what was going on, what could you have done? Do you honestly believe that your deputies could have pulled off the surgical precision that you saw out there at the farmhouse?"

Gail considered the question, then looked away.

"Gail, you were part of the most elite rescue team in the world. How many times were you inclined to seek assistance from a sheriff's department? Is never a pretty close guess?"

Gail knew that she should be offended, but the director spoke the truth.

Irene kept going. "Without your own capabilities, you would have had to wait for the state team to make their way out to the farm. How long would that have taken? An hour, maybe ninety minutes on a good day? Three or four hours if someone was on vacation?"

Irene was correct on every point but one. "There still are rules," Gail said. Even she heard the naïve weakness of her words.

"Yes there are." Irene softened her tone. "And you know what? I can't tell you how much I admire your commitment to them."

Gail rolled her eyes, angry again.

Irene recovered. "No, I know that sounded patronizing, but I didn't mean it to. These days, commitment to principle is a rare commodity."

"But it has to be tempered with practicality, right?"

A beat. "Well, yes."

"History is filled with terrible injustices fueled by practicality. Tour Eastern Europe or the Deep South. There was practicality there up to your neck."

"The slippery slope," Irene said, smiling. "Bullshit Bingo chapter two."

Gail massaged her forehead, hoping to stave off the boomer that she knew was on the way. This was exactly why she'd left the Bureau. She couldn't stand the hypocrisy. Nowhere on the planet was there a group more dedicated to standard operating procedure and strict adherence to rules, yet the agents whose careers hit the stratosphere all shared the cowboy trait; they all flouted the rules when it suited their purposes—Irene Rivers included. If you took a chance and things went right, then you were a hero. If you took a chance and things went to hell, so did your career. Worst of all was to be in the third category of doing everything by the book and having things go wrong anyway. That was called a lack of initiative.

She knew what the scuttlebutt at the Chicago Field Office was. They'd assumed that she'd left the Bureau because of the dead hostages—that she couldn't take the sight of two dead kids. Well, they were partially right; the brain-pierced children were horrific. But the criticism she'd taken on that day and the weeks that followed, first in the press, and then from her superiors, had felt like a knife to the kidneys. She didn't like being anyone's scapegoat when she was doing what she was hired to do, but when the music stopped, *somebody* had to be blamed, and the on-scene commander was always a better choice than the top dog himself. So she got her commendation with one hand, and a punch in the career with the other. Faced with that, what other choice was there but to leave?

Gail leaned back in her chair, feeling tired. "So, what aren't you telling me, Irene?"

"Excuse me?"

"You said that I *can't* win this one. That was your word—can't. What happens if I fight you?"

Irene cocked her head. "We'll make our guy impossible to find. Then we'll use that fact against you to make sure that you never get elected again. Details about your departure from the Bureau will leak out. We'll do everything we can to make you a punch line on Letterman."

Gail could see it playing out as if it had already happened. "And I still won't get my killer."

"And you still won't get your killer." She let it hang. "You know that we're very good at this sort of thing."

Some of the puzzle pieces fell into place. "You've already made him impossible to find, haven't you?"

"I don't know what you're talking about," Irene said, but her eyes betrayed her.

"Sure you don't. It's just an accident that my chief suspect, Jonathan Grave, has no fingerprints on file?"

Irene shrugged. "All I'm doing is protecting people who snuffed some sociopaths. I'll say it again. We're on the side of the angels."

Gail stood. She had to stand or she'd blow up. She walked to the front window. Watching her own reflection in the glass, she chuckled again. "I guess if I'd just agreed with you from the start, I wouldn't feel like such a pawn right now."

Irene remained silent. What was there to say when the truth was put so elegantly?

Gail turned to face the chief law enforcer in the United States. "So, what lie do I tell?"

Irene was ready for the question. "The Patrone brothers were scheduled to testify in a terror trial, and friends of the terrorist found out about it. There was a gun battle, and people died. My people are already working on the paper trail. No one ever has to know."

"What about all the other people at the crime scene? They're going to try and match the evidence to the cover story. It won't fit."

"Of course it will fit. I say again, we're very good at this."

This is what Alice must have felt like as she stepped through the looking glass. "And the perpetrators? I still have my constituents to answer to."

"Of course. They've left the country. You should be furious about that, by the way. You should be over-the-moon pissed that the FBI didn't clue you in on the operation they were performing, and I'm willing to go on the record telling the world what a pain in the ass you've been dragging information out of us. That should play well here, don't you think?"

"You'll make me look like Superman."

Irene shook her head. "Not at all. I'll use a little fiction to reinforce what we both know is the truth. You're the best law enforcement professional that this community has ever seen."

Gail laughed. "Oh, now you sweet-talk me. You'll help to lock in my career, and all I have to do is sell my soul."

Irene folded her face into a concerned frown. "A career is a poker game, Gail. You can't expect to win every hand. Sometimes you have to fold to preserve resources for the future."

Gail studied Irene. "How do I know you're not bluffing?"

"You don't," Irene said. "But I'm not. I've got it all—the cards, the cash, and the table. You really, truly want to sit out this hand."

"And what about the other murders?" Gail asked.

"The Caldwells? I can link Jonathan Grave to those deaths via the Hughes family."

The news clearly startled Irene, and Gail was sorry that she'd said anything. "I don't believe you," she said. "How are they linked?"

Sensing the upper hand and loving it, Gail smiled. "I don't believe I'll share that with you," she said.

Irene shook it off. "I don't know who this Jonathan person is," she lied, "but whatever you think you know, I guarantee you're wrong."

"Yet you'll stipulate, I assume, that Stephenson and Julie Hughes are connected to the Caldwell murders."

Irene hesitated. Gail could almost see the gears whirring in her head as she tried to work for position.

"I've already spoken to the investigating officer in Muncie, Irene," Gail said, sealing the deal. "He wants to nail the Hugheses. His Hugheses are the parents of Thomas Hughes. Jonathan Grave rescued Thomas Hughes and killed the Patrones in the process. That links them all."

Irene stood. Her features iced over. "Sheriff Bonneville," she said as she walked toward the front door, "I'm going to offer one last bit of advice, and I'm going to beg you to listen to it carefully." She turned.

Gail suppressed a shiver.

"Know when it's time to stop pushing," she said. "There are some answers to which you simply are not entitled."

She let herself out.

Chapter Thirty

Detective Weatherby sat on the front corner of the ancient metal desk, one foot on the floor and the other swinging in an exaggerated display of patience. Doug Kramer stood next to him, red faced with his thumbs tucked into his Sam Browne belt. Jonathan got the impression that he'd interrupted an unpleasant conversation.

But that was past. Now they were silent, staring at Jonathan as he stared back at them.

"I told you it was bad," Weatherby said, breaking the stalemate.

"I tried to talk him out of this," Doug said to Jonathan. "I told him that this wasn't the right time to talk to you."

Weatherby's gaze never strayed from Jonathan. "Never any time like the present, I always say. You holding up okay?"

Jonathan locked down every emotion and he kept his face impassive. "How can I help you, Detective?"

"I told you that I'd check up on you after Tibor Rothman's body was found, didn't I?" Weatherby asked.

Jonathan said nothing.

"Cat got your tongue, First Sergeant Jonathan Grave?"

Weatherby asked. It was an attempt to startle, but it fell short. "Interesting what you find out about a man when you go looking. Criminal's kid turned Army Ranger. A lifer who quit after serving only seventeen of his twenty years. One of those locked-down service records that tells me you did some spooky stuff in your day."

Jonathan decided to maintain his poker face until Weatherby had shown his hand. "You seem to be waiting for me to deny something," he said.

"Confirm would work, too," said the detective.

"I'm sure it would. Are we done?"

Weatherby shook his head. "No, sir, I don't believe we are." He crossed his arms, causing his navy blue sport coat to pull tight across his back. "A man like you has the skills and wherewithal to do a lot of violence, wouldn't you say?"

Jonathan narrowed his gaze. "Skill and motivation are entirely different things," he said. "And if you're on the edge of accusing me of doing the kind of damage that I just viewed, I think you should draw your weapon. Otherwise you'll see my violent capabilities firsthand."

Doug Kramer stiffened and put his hands out to intervene if a fight broke out.

Weatherby didn't move.

Neither did Jonathan. But he was ready to. If Weatherby uttered the words Jonathan knew were on his mind, he'd lose his teeth and jaw with the first blow, and his nose with the second. After that, it would just be a brawl.

The detective drew his fleshy face into a scowl, which then dissolved into a humorless smile. "I hope you understand that I had to check my instincts about you," he said. "When I got the call that the chief here had arranged a special viewing, I figured that this would be the best venue to see where you're coming from."

Jonathan cocked his head.

"Stand down, Mr. Grave," Weatherby said. "I don't suspect you of any of this. Your reaction just reassured me that I was right. You can tell a lot about people when they're under stress, you know? If you'd been all defensive or started shouting at me, then I might still wonder. But your quiet threat to kill me was all I needed to hear." His smile became genuine.

He went on, "You know, in the academy, they'd say that you are the quintessential suspect. You're the ex-husband who's involved in a lawsuit that completely goes away with the deaths of the two people who broke your heart. Christ, it doesn't get any more obvious than that."

Jonathan waited for the rest.

"I see you as a killer, Mr. Grave. I see that as well within your capabilities. But I don't see you as a torturer. I think that's a line you wouldn't cross."

Jonathan scowled. "Um, thank you?"

Doug sighed noisily and relaxed his stance.

"I really am sorry for your loss," Weatherby said, and he extended his hand.

Jonathan accepted it, and the detective's grip closed like a talon. "But about that killing thing," Weatherby said, trying to pull Jonathan in closer but damn near getting pulled off the desk himself. "I meant what I said before. Vengeance is mine, saith the Fairfax County Police Department. You start hurting people, and I guarantee I will become your very worst enemy."

Doug put a hand on each of their chests and pushed them apart. "Enough!" he commanded. "Jesus, Weatherby, what's with you?"

"I just want your friend to know that we don't need his help."

"I have no intention of helping you," Jonathan said. "You have my word."

The detective's grip relaxed and he scowled again at the double meaning buried in Jonathan's words.

Doug Kramer said, "I don't know who you think this man is, Weatherby, but he's not your enemy. Hell, as far as I know, there's no one alive who thinks of him as an enemy."

A double entendre of his own, Jonathan thought. Just how much did Doug Kramer know about his business?

"You need somebody to vouch for his character," Doug went on, "you just ask me. I've known him since we were kids. He's not someone for you to worry about."

Jonathan pulled his hand away. "It's time for me to go," he said. "Thank you for your kind words, Weatherby."

The detective stayed behind while Jonathan led the way back to Doug's cruiser. When they were inside and on their way, the chief asked, "As bad as you feared? Ellen, I mean?"

Jonathan looked at him across the console and sighed. "Worse."

Doug kept his eyes on the road. "I'm really sorry, Dig."

Jonathan nodded and joined him in watching the lane stripes on the Beltway zoom past. They remained silent all the way to the I-95 turnoff before Doug started talking again. "You know, Jon, there's not a soul in the Cove who's not hurting for you over what happened to Ellen. It's just not right." His voice was at once serious and soft. Jonathan wasn't sure he'd ever heard that tone before.

He felt his throat thicken. "Thank you."

The cop's eyes shifted from the road to bore right through his passenger. "I'm not done yet. If there's anything I can do to help you—I mean, *anything*, you just let me know, and it's yours." He started looking at traffic again. "I've never known much officially about the work you do, but most people in town know about the work you used to do. There's been talk about why you quit early, but the Cove is proud of you, Dig. Proud and pleased to call you their friend. You know what I'm trying to tell you?"

Jonathan shook his head. "I'm not sure I do."

Doug sighed. "And I'm not sure how to tell you, because it's not something I *can* tell you, if you catch my drift. I just wanted you to know that under circumstances like this, a man's gotta do what a man's gotta do, and whatever that means, you've got friends who'll back you up."

Jesus, Jonathan thought, Doug just offered to cover up a murder.

Gail opened her front door and found Jesse Collier standing there, slightly out of breath. "Thanks for coming," she said, and ushered him inside.

"Thanks nothing." He stepped into the foyer. "I've been going crazy since you left. What the hell's going on?" He looked around. "Nice house."

Gail closed the door, embarrassed that this was the first time that Jesse had ever been to her home. "The director of the FBI just visited me," she explained.

Jesse's mouth gaped. "Irene Rivers? Herself? Here? You're shittin' me."

Gail pointed the way to the kitchen, to the same spots where she'd met with the dragon lady just a half hour ago.

"What did she want?"

"For me to save my career and quit looking for the Patrones' killers." It took a few minutes to fill him in on all the details.

When she was done, Jesse gaped some more. "So, what are you going to do?"

"What do you think I should do?"

He hesitated, and then he laughed. "Okay, Sheriff, you've got to give me a hint here. Is this one of your quiz questions where I'm supposed to give you the answer you expect, or do you really want to know my opinion?"

She deserved that. During the months that they'd worked together, she'd done an awful lot of loyalty testing with Jesse, and she realized now that it had all been unnecessary. He'd lost the election fair and square, and he'd never given her a single reason to suspect that he was anything but one hundred percent behind her. "I want your opinion."

He waited a beat. "I look at it this way," he began. "I'm all about enforcing the law, but I'm also all about justice. I think I've made it pretty clear from the beginning that I think this Leon character—or Jonathan Grave, if that's his real name—is more hero than villain."

Gail's shoulders sagged. She'd asked for an opinion, but this one disappointed her.

"Don't go all droopy on me yet," Jesse admonished with a grin. "But I've been humbled enough times in my life to know that when the sun sets on our earthly adventure, the one thing we'll have that's all our own is our integrity. It's one thing to turn our backs on a case because it's our decision, but I'll be goddamned if I'm going to do it because some hotshot from Washington tells me I have to."

Her shoulders elevated again.

"I say we keep going. The job's not worth having if you don't do it right." His grin got bigger. "Besides, I already lost an election to a girl. That was humiliating enough. I'm not going to lose my soul to another one."

Gail laughed.

"The one condition is I get to go to Virginia with you," he said.

"I wouldn't have it any other way. When can you leave?"

Jesse shrugged. "How's now?"

Chapter Thirty-One

Jonathan, Boxers, and Venice reconvened at ten-thirty in the War Room. Even as he entered, Jonathan could sense a pall.

"Was it awful?" Venice asked.

Jonathan nodded to the big screen on the wall. "What did you find out?"

"You okay, boss?" Boxers asked.

He pointed to the screen. "You show me what I want to see, and I'll be fine," he said.

Venice and Boxers exchanged glances, then she got on with it. "Based on what little we had to go on—"

"With as little preamble as possible," Jonathan clarified.

"Fine," she said. She tapped her keyboard and the screen filled with an aerial photograph. "This comes from the SkysEye network," she said, "and it's only about an hour old. I think this is Ivan Patrick's playground. Brigadeville, right? It's the only patch of real estate that came close to fitting what your friend in the alley told you."

"Andrew Hawkins," Jonathan reminded her. SkysEye was a commercial mapping company that anyone with the financial means could access for the going rate of twenty grand a year for an open license, plus a usurious tasking fee every time they wanted a picture. The private satellite network was a recent startup headed by Lee Burns, one of the original Unit members who hadn't seen action in two decades. At various high and low orbits, SkysEye satellites could count the dimples on a golf ball anywhere on the planet. Lee's largest customers came from the petroleum industry, which used the network to locate the kinds of geological formations that looked like money. Given the founder's background in Special Forces, Jonathan worried that Lee might have sold his services to a few bad guys over the years—after all, finding geological formations wasn't a lot different than precision targeting—but he'd have never stated his concerns aloud. He owed that much to a brother in arms.

What was most remarkable about the SkysEye imaging—what set it apart from other commercial sites—was its ability to provide real-time imaging that refreshed every four minutes. Through extrapolation and a little guesswork, you could determine whether a particular piece of real estate was currently occupied, how many vehicles were there, whether or not there was an active power plant, and a host of other details that were of value to an invader. It was nowhere near as helpful as the SatCom images he'd used back in the day, but it was a close second.

Accessing the pictures was only the beginning. The real trick lay in manipulating the images to deliver the highest resolution. The raw images were little more than a tableau of treetops, the thick foliage making ground details difficult to discern. To learn useful details, Venice superimposed a thermal imaging view that showed the presence of three dozen individual buildings of varying size and shape. Using that data, a smart CAD system was able to make an accurate sketch of the entire area. The overall layout reminded him of old Army posts from the days of the Indian wars. An open space anchored the middle of the complex, with most buildings arranged in concentric ovals. In the back corner, far from the other structures, two buildings stood alone.

"They look like munitions storage," Jonathan observed, pointing to the screen.

"They've got themselves a damn city," Boxers said. "We can't take that. Not the two of us."

Truer words were never spoken.

The next step in building the computer image was to superimpose data from the public record onto the satellite image. That way, they could locate the known roads, as well as—if they were so inclined—the location of the septic fields, the aquifers, and even family burial plots. If it was in an accessible database, they could put it on the map.

Finally, with the entire infrastructure in place on the screen, the program used data from the U.S. Geological Survey to add elevation data. When Venice was done, they had a three-dimensional rendering of the area that could be rotated in any direction, for either a plan view or a more useful elevation view.

"No fuckin' way," Boxers said.

And it wasn't just a matter of real estate. The map showed the heat signatures of several dozen people sleeping in the various buildings, and twice that number who seemed to be up and about.

"Revolution must be a full-time job," Boxers mused. "But seriously, if that's where they took the weapons, we can't possibly take it down."

"You keep repeating the same thing," Jonathan observed.

"That's because I want to hear you say something sane. Like, 'Hey Box, don't worry, I wouldn't dream of taking on a place like that.'"

Jonathan kept staring at the screen. There had to be a way. There was *always* a way. He'd built his entire life around the concept. The memory of Ellen's beautiful features filled his mind, and then they morphed into the pulpy mess that lay zipped inside the rubber bag in the basement of the hospital. He thought of trying to go on with his life while the monster who did that to her still walked free, and he simply couldn't imagine it.

But Boxers was right this time. There was no way to take Ivan at Brigadeville; not without raising an army of his own, anyway, and he'd have a hard time doing that merely for a mission of vengeance.

For vengeance, you got a team of thugs. If you wanted professionals, the goal needed to be loftier than that.

The phone rang, and as Venice checked the caller ID, Jonathan said, "I'm many things, but suicidal is not one of them. We can't take them there."

Relief filled the room like a cool breeze on a hot day.

"It's Dom," Venice said, and she lifted the receiver. "Hi, Father," she said into the receiver. Instantly, her face darkened. "Whoa, okay, hold on a second. No, I know, he's standing right here." She handed the phone to Jonathan with a look that told him a crazy man was on the line.

Jonathan brought the phone to his ear. "Yeah, Dom, what's up?"

"When I hang up, you'll have Wolverine. She's pissed, Dig. I don't want anything to do with this."

"That's not the protocol," Jonathan protested.

"You think I don't know that? I'm out of the middle here." With that, there was a click, but Jonathan could still hear an open line.

"Is this Scorpion?" said Irene Rivers' familiar voice.

"The one and only," Jonathan said. Venice and Boxers craned their necks to hear what was being said, but he shooed them away.

"I just got back from visiting your friend in the Midwest," she said, each word clipped to make her anger clear. "I covered your ass. Now I find your teeth marks in mine. How dare you not tell me that you were working with these Hughes idiots?"

"Be careful, this is an open line—"

"I know what kind of line it is! I placed the call. Now are you or are you not in cahoots with Stephenson Hughes and his family?"

Jonathan felt heat rising in his face. "I don't think that 'cahoots' is the right word. Their kid was—"

"Let it go, Digger," she said. "Whatever you're thinking of doing, don't. Do *not* get in the middle of this. You won't be able to get out, and I won't be able to protect you. There are forces in play here that can't be stopped, and they're all coming from the very top."

Jonathan said nothing, but he believed he saw pieces coming together. Uncle Sam wanted his secrets kept, and he was willing to get wet to make sure he succeeded.

"Are you there?" Irene snapped.

"I'm here."

"Well?"

"I've got nothing to say. You made a speech and I listened. It was a nice speech, though."

"Promise me, Dig," Irene said. Perhaps she sensed that anger wouldn't work on Jonathan, so now she gave pleading a shot. "Promise me that you won't get into this. Promise me you won't do something to intervene on behalf of those murderers."

Jonathan hesitated. "I promise," he said. The words churned his stomach.

"Say it."

Another hesitation. This must really be huge for her to push this hard. "I promise that I won't intervene in what's going to happen to the Hugheses." Venice and Boxers recoiled in unison.

It was Irene's turn to drop a beat. "Can I trust you?"

"Can't you always?" he responded. "Good night, Wolverine." He handed the receiver to Venice, who placed in on its cradle.

They both gaped at him as if he'd gone mad. "You really changing your mind, Boss? I mean, I don't know what she said to you, but I heard—"

"I lied," Jonathan said, and those words drew even greater gapes of surprise. It was something he just never did. "Hey, I told her what she wanted to hear, and what she wanted to hear was unreasonable."

He caught them up on their conversation. "The FBI might despise what Ivan is doing," he concluded, "but with the horse not just out of the barn, but screaming toward town, they can't afford to stop him. If the Hugheses show their faces anywhere public, the police will nail them and the Bureau will make all problems go away. Otherwise, they'll just stay out of Ivan Patrick's way."

They waited for more. When it didn't come, Boxers asked, "So what does this mean for us?"

"It means that we have to fight Ivan on our own turf," Jonathan replied. "Or at least on turf of our choosing." He turned to Venice. "Re-task SkysEye to find the DuBois homestead in Pennsylvania."

Venice reared back and shot her patented have-you-lost-your-mind glare. "What for?"

Boxers' eyes grew wide. He got it right away. "You're going to bring them into the fight, too!" He laughed.

Venice was still confused. "How do you know they'll want to?" she asked.

Jonathan shrugged. "What choice will they have after Ivan attacks them?"

Charlie Warren shifted in the shotgun seat of the rented Mercury and tried yet again to find a position for his legs that would allow adequate circulation. Next to him in the driver's seat, Bob Garino sipped from a cup of Dunkin' Donuts coffee, and together, they ignored the sound of Gary Glick's juicy snores. As much as Charlie envied the man his nap, he couldn't think of a decent reason to wake him up. How many people did it take to watch a window, for God's sake?

"Kind of a nice little town," Garino said through a slurp of coffee.

"Only if you like living in Norman Rockwell paintings," Charlie grumped. Keep your small towns, he thought. Muncie was too tiny for him as it was. Whenever he got around to retiring, it was going to be in a *real* city. New York, probably, but maybe Chicago if he could hypnotize himself out of remembering that February does in fact come every year. There's something about being able to eat at four in the morning that he found immensely appealing, even though he rarely found himself awake much past the eleven o'clock news.

Another slurp, followed by another snore. "What exactly are we waiting for?" Garino asked.

"Something interesting," Charlie replied.

Slurp. Snore.

"Suppose they just left the light on?" Garino pressed. "Suppose everybody's at home in bed? We gonna just—"

Snore.

"—stay here all night and watch a damn window?" Slurp.

"Stop!" Charlie boomed. Beside him, Garino jerked coffee all over himself. The car jumped as Glick was startled back to life and kicked something.

"What the fuck—"

"You two!" Charlie snapped. "The noises. Jesus."

"Like to give me a heart attack," Glick groused. "What the hell happened?"

"Nothing happened," Charlie said. "Not a single fucking thing in the last two hours."

"Then what are you shouting for? Give me a heart attack, swear to God."

Garino looked over his shoulder. "You were snoring like an old man," he said. "If you'da died, you'da waked yourself."

Charlie more sensed than saw Glick raise himself to a sitting position. Bald on top, with a middle-age paunch, he looked more like a computer programmer than the tradesman he was—a sharp contrast to Garino, whose bulky build and S-shaped nose clearly stated their case at first glance. "So she's still up there?" Glick asked.

"If she was ever there to begin with," Garino observed. "I think we shoulda followed the big guy."

"What big guy?" Glick asked. "I thought you said nothing happened."

Charlie explained, "A guy left the building about a half hour ago and walked up the hill. Bob thinks we should have followed him."

"Why didn't you?" Clearly, Glick would have done the same.

"Why would I? He's not the one we're after. It's

some chick, not the Incredible Hulk. I always say, never pick a fight with a mountain when you don't have to."

Garino still wasn't convinced. "Look, I'm just sayin'—"

Charlie silenced him with a raised hand, then pointed toward the firehouse they'd been watching. "Light just went out," he said. "Whoever's in there will be leaving in a couple of minutes." He opened his door and started to get out.

"Wait a second," Garino said, grabbing his arm. "Where are you going?"

"I'm going to follow her," Charlie said. "According to the records we pulled up, she lives just up the street. I'll follow to verify, and then we can take the rest of the night off."

"Suppose she drives away?" Glick asked.

Charlie shot his an annoyed glare. "Which part of 'lives up the street' proved too hard for you?" He didn't bother to wait for an answer. Instead, he stood in the chilly night air and reached below his jacket to turn the knob on the radio that was clasped to his belt. He thumbed the wrist mike—identical to the brand used by the Secret Service—and whispered, "Radio check."

Garino's "Loud and clear" came loud and clear through his earpiece.

From this spot midway up the block from the marina, Charlie could see both the front and back doors of the firehouse, but he opted to walk up the hill away from the water to separate himself from the parked Mercury. A strange vehicle was suspect enough in the middle of the night, as is a stranger walking along the street. The two of them together would undoubtedly spook his prey.

He didn't have to wait long. Within a minute, he

heard the sound of a door opening and closing, followed a few seconds later by the sound of a substantial lock being turned. A moment later, he saw the woman he'd been waiting for. She turned the corner to walk up the hill where he was stationed, but on the opposite side of the street. She walked hurriedly, with her head down. She looked preoccupied to Charlie, oblivious to him or his car or the night air or anything else that was not going on inside her head. He waited for her to get fifty yards ahead, and then he followed. He stayed on his side of the street; he never tried to close the gap between them.

He thought about how easy it would be to wreak havoc in a town like this. Watching her navigate the night as if there were no danger lurking, he thought about how easy it would be to take her. To have her. No doubt about it, she was hot in her own right. All he'd have to do, he wagered, would be to walk up to her and ask her for the time. She'd stop to help and then he could make her pay for the mistake. He imagined it was that way for everyone in this little burg. People who've never known violence never stop to think about it. It was the kind of naïveté that conquerors dreamed of.

But tonight, his mission was not conquest; it was intelligence gathering. This was the night when he would come to know his enemy.

His earbud buzzed, "How's it going?"

"Keep the channel clear," he hissed, hoping that his annoyance came through. If he needed help from Frick and Frack, he'd ask for it. Meanwhile, he just wanted them to quietly do their jobs.

He was across the street from a church now, St. Katherine's Catholic. It was a big place with spires and the kind of traditional architecture that you just don't see much anymore. As the Alexander chick walked past, she slowed and looked across the vast lawn, as if hoping to see someone.

Her pace slowed even more as she approached the walkway that led across an even bigger lawn and then to the wraparound porch of a mansion that made Tara from *Gone with the Wind* look like a guest cottage. The place had to be 12,000 square feet, and it seemed to stretch forever. It was difficult to make out details in the darkness, but the house painted a hell of a stain against the sky.

Charlie found himself staring in disbelief as he watched his prey climb those stairs, navigate the walk, and then disappear through the front door. "Just how successful can the private investigating business be?" he mumbled aloud.

Gail Bonneville had to admit that she loved the town. Fisherman's Cove was the kind of place she thought of when she thought of a quaint riverside refuge. She loved the fact that New World efficiency had not yet run off Old World charm. She could see why a man like Jonathan Grave would be drawn to a place like this, even if she couldn't begin to wrap her mind around why a town like this would want a man like Jonathan Grave as a resident.

"I wish I knew what those guys were up to," Jesse Collier said yet again. When they'd arrived in Fisherman's Cove forty-five minutes ago, they'd noticed the Mercury parked across the street from the firehouse that served as the offices of Security Solutions and according to the public record also doubled as Jonathan Grave's residence. From that very first moment, they'd assumed that someone else was surveilling the place, but they couldn't be certain if they were working for Grave or against him.

Rather than litter the street with a second suspicious car, Gail had opted for a more aggressive surveillance strategy and urged Jesse to park the car and climb with her to the roof of the marina across the street. "This can't be legal," he'd hissed as he followed his boss up the ladder they'd found stowed along the back wall of the marina office, no doubt for use helping people up to the dock during low tide.

"Of course it's legal," Gail had quipped. "We're police officers."

Now, thirty minutes later, they sat on the rough shingled roof, watching from behind the three-foot-high decorative parapet that seemed to be the architectural standard for Fisherman's Cove. The view from up here was perfect, but it was tough as hell on the knees and back to stay so low all the time. They agreed to take turns watching. Presently, it was Jesse's turn, and quiet time that exceeded three minutes seemed to disturb him.

"Whoa!" he whispered. "Look, look, look they're moving!"

Gail scrabbled to her hands and knees and turned to peer over the low wall, using her hands to support her and provide her with a reference point to ensure that only her forehead and eyes showed above the level of the roof. It occurred to her that the two of them looked like a pair of the Kilroy drawings from World War II. The image made her smile.

Then the activity below made the smile go away. They watched as man in a suit got out of the Mercury and walked briskly up the hill away from the water, and then sank into a shadow to wait. An attractive young black woman left the firehouse, locked the door, and started her own walk up the hill.

"Is he waiting for her?" Jesse whispered.

Gail answered with a nod. The real question, she thought, was whether he was waiting to meet her, to hurt her, or merely to watch her. The answer became obvious when the woman reached the level of the man and he let her pass, only to stroll after her a few paces later, all the while staying on the opposite side of the road.

Gail never did see where the woman turned off. When she was still halfway up the hill, the Mercury's doors opened again, and this time two men climbed out, one from the front seat and the other from the back. These two were nowhere near as well dressed as the other one, and they moved as if they were in a much bigger hurry.

"Looks like they're not done," Jesse said. Captain Obvious still on the job.

Gail ducked below the wall again and fished through the dark for her bag, from which she removed an expensive digital camera with a 15-power zoom. She rose again, rested it on the top of the parapet, and looked through the viewfinder.

Jess placed a hand on her shoulder. "You're up awfully high, Boss."

"I know," she whispered. "But I want some pictures of this." Even with the magnification from the zoom—probably because of it when she thought about it—details were difficult to discern in this light, but she kept pressing the shutter button anyway.

The men each carried what looked to be a gym bag that didn't weigh very much. They hurried to the door from which the woman had just exited and placed their bags on the ground at their feet. The angle prevented her from seeing what was in the bags, but the men worked quickly in the dark. They stooped low on their haunches and concentrated first on the door, and then on the alarm panel on the wall next to it.

"Can you make out what they're doing?" Jesse whispered.

"Actually," Gail said, "I know exactly what they're doing."

APRIL 23

CHAPTER THIRTY-TWO

The trick was to keep your head down and the ball cap pulled just so. That way, the security cameras could never get a good shot. An empty black rucksack—a big one—hung limply from his shoulders.

Jonathan walked through the Wal-Mart hesitantly and avoided eye contact. When people eventually looked at the security video and talked to witnesses, he wanted everyone to remember a nervous man. The point was to draw enough attention to be memorable, yet not so much as to frighten people real-time. He'd already walked a quarter mile before he arrived at the store—they'd parked the Hummer in a different lot to avoid the cameras in the Wal-Mart lot—so he already glistened with sweat, making the nervous-guy ruse even more convincing.

He wasted no time. He grabbed a cart and headed toward the groceries aisle. There he picked up an assortment of canned goods, including powdered milk and powdered energy drink. Next he bought toilet paper and then, from the camping section, a can of white gas—the kind you use in camp stoves and lamps.

He said nothing to Carol, the chipper checkout clerk,

and when she announced his total, he whipped out a credit card that Venice had manufactured for him the night before and allowed the clerk to scan it. After the receipt was printed, Jonathan moved like a man who realized he'd made a mistake. "Wait," he said. "My wife didn't want me to use that credit card. Is there a way to void it and pay with cash?"

But of course there was. As a line started to build behind him, Carol pushed a flurry of buttons and printed out a new receipt. Jonathan paid and thanked the clerk.

"Not at all, Mr. Hughes," Carol replied, glancing at the receipt. "Thank you for shopping at Wal-Mart."

Thank God for a big engine and four-wheel drive. No mere mortal of a vehicle was designed to pull two adults and three hundred pounds of equipment up roads that were this vertical. Nearly eight hours and two tanks of gas had passed since they'd pulled away from the firehouse in the wee hours, and now that they were closing in on the last mile, even the Batmobile's engine was beginning to show the strain.

"You'd think that somebody could at least pave the road," Boxers grumped. He fought with the steering wheel to keep them on some semblance of a course. The road, such as it was, was recognizable only as parallel ruts partially overgrown with weeds and scrub growth. "In the rain or snow you're screwed."

Jonathan shook his head. It was beyond imagination. "What was Old Man DuBois thinking? Of all the places in the world, why settle here?"

"A hundred acres of get-away-from-it-all," Boxers grumped. "I'd have to have my scotch delivered by airdrop."

The woods out here were as thick as Jonathan had

ever seen, outside of the tropics. This was as close to wilderness as the twenty-first century had to offer on the East Coast. Hardwoods towered above the forest floor, many of them hundreds of years old. The canopy of leaves overhead, while broken in places, choked out much of the sunlight, bathing them in the aura of perpetual dusk.

Boxers slowed the vehicle to a crawl as they approached a ravine that was twenty feet wide and channeled a substantial creek fifteen feet below. The only access to the other side was via a wooden bridge that looked as if it had been built by Boy Scouts. Supported by 6 x 6-inch pilings that disappeared into the water, the plank surface had no guardrails, and looked barely wide enough for the truck's wheelbase. He pulled the Hummer to a stop.

"What do you think?" Boxers asked.

"I think we've got no choice," Jonathan replied. "But go slow." It's a reality of physics that defies instinct: when driving over a bridge of questionable strength, it's safer to move as slowly as possible than it is to listen to your gut as it screams at you to floor it and get it over with.

"Maybe you should get out first, make the load lighter," Boxers offered.

"What the hell am I gonna do here alone after you and the equipment drop to the water? Drive on." He glanced at the satellite image on his laptop. "Once we get to the other side, I figure we'll be about eight hundred yards from the cabin. We should be able to see ourselves when the picture refreshes."

Boxers took his foot off the brake and let the Hummer inch forward. "I never did like to look at myself on television," he grumbled.

The front wheels rolled easily onto the wooden

planking, but the instant that the rear wheels crossed over from solid ground to the bridge deck, a loud *crack* startled them both.

"Slow and steady, Box. As far as I can tell, we're both still here."

"Do you feel the sway?"

"I'm pretending I'm dizzy. Just keep it slow and steady."

It took forever. The Hummer swayed back and forth as if driving against a stiff wind, but they both understood that the sway came from the shifting of the entire bridge structure.

"You know, Boss," Boxers quipped, "I don't often tell you how much I enjoy all the stupid shit you put me through."

The Bat Phone buzzed on the dash.

Boxers laughed. "Perfect. Venice can be here with us as we plummet to our deaths."

"Who says we'll die from the plummet?" Jonathan said, reaching for the phone. "It's entirely possible that we'll drown in the creek or burn to death." He pushed the speaker button. "Hello, Ven. Ignore any crashing sounds you hear. Or screaming."

"Dig, I just got off the phone with Lee Burns at SkysEye." She was all business, not interested in the banter. "He marked every vehicle he could see at Brigadeville, just like you asked him."

Another *crack*, and this time it registered as a shudder through the truck. They pretended to ignore it, and Boxers stayed concentrated on the slow and steady. They were past the halfway point, which in Jonathan's mind meant that they were at least past the weakest point of the bridge.

Venice continued, "He wanted you to know that they're moving."

"Excellent," Jonathan said. "Are they headed in the right direction?"

"He thinks so. But he also wants you to know that he can't track them continuously for the hours it's going to take for them to get to you. He doesn't have the capability. He says once they commit themselves to a compass direction, he's going to have to shut down the active tracking."

The front wheels found terra firma. Boxers said, "Fuck it," and gunned the engine just to get it over with. Nothing collapsed.

Jonathan said, "Looks like our credit card trick worked. Tell Lee that I appreciate anything he can do for us."

"He also said that this is going to cost you an effing fortune," Venice said. "Those were his words."

Boxers laughed. "Lee Burns has never said, 'effing,' in his whole life."

"Okay, that part was mine," Venice confessed. "But you know what I mean."

"What's the point of being rich if you can't buy access to cool technology?" Jonathan said. "Thanks, Ven. Anything else? We're about to get into the thick of it here."

"I can see that on the sat image. You just appeared." Venice hesitated. "So do you think it'll go down tonight?"

"I do," Jonathan said.

The silence from the other end caused Jonathan and Boxers to exchange glances. "You there?" Jonathan asked.

"Promise me you'll be careful," Venice said.

"How about I promise to do my best to win?" No one ever won a firefight by being careful.

"I guess it'll have to do." She was trying to keep her

voice light, but Jonathan heard the worry anyway. "I'll be here all night monitoring things."

"I never thought otherwise," Jonathan said. "Look, I'm sure we'll talk again before things go hot. We've got to get to work. I gotta go."

He pushed the disconnect button before Venice had a chance to get emotional. Over the years, he'd known warriors who thrived on thoughts of home and loved ones—who were better at their profession because they fought to get back to them. For Jonathan, sentiment had always been a burden. You concentrate on the mission and keep your head away from any emotional distraction. It was the only way he knew to keep the odds in his favor.

"How do you want to handle this, Boss?" Boxers asked. "You want to unload here and hump in, or do you want to drive closer?"

"The Hugheses are going to be terrified after hunkering down for this long," Jonathan said. "I don't want to spook them with a vehicle, or even the sound of a vehicle. I say we park here and go in with a light load."

That was fine with Boxers. He threw the transmission into Park. He flopped down a tiny plastic door on the dash near his left knee and punched in the eight-digit code that would allow the keyway in the tailgate to operate. Jonathan left him to his work and walked around back. The code allowed the key to turn easily, but it was always an effort to lift the heavily armored tailgate. Boxers gave him a hand as he came around.

Ten large duffel bags of equipment formed a rough and uneven pyramid on the carpeted truck bed. Jonathan reached for the duffel farthest to the right and pulled it toward him. He spun it so that it was perpendicular to his body, and unzipped it, revealing a stack of firearms.

Next to him, Boxers was working an ammunition bag. As Jonathan lifted an M4 carbine out of his duffel and handed it to Boxers, Boxers passed a 30-round clip to Jonathan. Jonathan took an M4 for himself. He inserted the clip, chambered a round, and looped the combat sling over his shoulder.

"So we're gonna shoot back if they start shooting at us?"

"I don't see we'll have a lot of choice."

"Sorta counterproductive, don't you think?"

Jonathan smiled. "Ya think? We need to make sure it doesn't come to that."

"You're talking about diplomacy, aren't you?" Boxers growled. "I hate that shit."

"But you're so good at it," Jonathan quipped. Fact was, Brian Van de Muelebroeke—a.k.a. Boxers—was the quintessential Special Forces professional. Jonathan had seen him defuse countless situations through the very kind of diplomacy that he pretended to hate. He'd also seen him wreak a special kind of havoc after the other side failed to realize that the "negotiation" was in fact the terms of their surrender. Boxers was the wrong guy to point a gun at.

Glancing at his GPS locator, Jonathan pointed up the hill and they started walking.

"Suppose they don't want to fight?" Boxers asked.

"Then we're carrying way too much firepower."

"No, I don't mean now. I mean at all. Suppose they're not up for this battle you're planning?"

Jonathan had thought about that. "Everybody'll fight if the stakes are high enough," he said.

"But not everybody's good at it."

Jonathan shrugged. "If it falls that way, we'll all share a righteously shitty day." He could speak this bluntly because it was Boxers. Both of them had stopped worrying about death a long time ago. "We'll have to train them, and hope they can shoot straight."

Thomas Hughes was living a nightmare.

Over the course of a single week—no, *less* than a week, six days—he'd gone from getting his knob polished by Tiffany or Christine or whatever the hell her real name was, to getting kidnapped, shot at, and now living out here in the middle of nowhere. Just the three of them—like the happy family they'd never be.

And if that wasn't a thick enough shit sandwich, the police thought they were murderers. Oh, yeah, and his dad was some kind of WMD trafficker.

They called this special corner of hell "the lodge," but it was really a cabin. Built of hewn heavy timbers, and designed to look a hundred years older than it actually was, the place had a certain Abe Lincoln look to it. The lodge itself sat on a footprint of 20 by 30 feet, and was more or less an unadorned rectangle. A second floor had been raised somewhere along the way on the back half of the house, providing additional sleeping space. When Thomas was little, Mom and Dad took the upstairs for themselves while he was consigned to the sofa in the "living room," which was separated only by an imaginary wall from the "dining room," which in turn sat adjacent to the way-out-of-date kitchen in the back of the house. Without gas or electricity, cooking power came from the logs that they piled into the wood stove.

It was stiflingly hot in the summer, and freezing cold in the winter (kerosene heaters and fireplaces couldn't touch the February chill). Thomas hated this place. Once he'd gotten his driver's license and access to his own car, he'd stopped coming. Keep your primitive and your rustic; give him new and shiny any day of the week. At least give him running water. And a toilet that was more than a hole in the ground.

Presently, Mom and Dad were at it again, blaming each other for all the crap that was going wrong. They kept screaming at each other about a plan. They needed to have a *plan.*

Well, Thomas had mapped out a pretty nifty plan for himself: he was getting the hell out of here. He was done with Chef Boyardee and boredom. He was done with hiding. He didn't have a dog in this fight. Even if he did, wasn't it way harder to hit a moving target than a stationary one?

The barn full of synthetic smallpox complicated things for his parents, but the more he thought about it, the more he realized that he didn't care about what happened to everybody else—not even to the poor bastards that got sprayed with the shit if that's what came down. He'd sacrificed enough to this madness as it was, thank you very much. Last time he checked the chart of family responsibilities, he didn't see anything about putting his whole life on hold so that his parents could stay in hiding forever. He was twenty-two years old, for God's sake. After graduation in May—the graduation that now wouldn't happen because he'd missed two projects and an exam while being trussed up in that basement—his plan had been to flee. He thought he'd try New York for a while and see if he could put together some kind of street-playing trio or maybe a quartet. One of his fellow music majors had done that a couple of years ago, and he'd made some pretty good coin.

To have any kind of a future at all, Thomas had to get the hell out of here. He'd been telling himself every morning that today was the day, but then each today had drained away, and he hadn't moved. Already, too much of this today had slipped by.

For sure, tomorrow.

Meanwhile, he needed air.

He stood from his sofa bed and walked to the front door. The light that managed to peek through the ripply windows did little to diffuse the oppressive darkness of the lodge.

The instant the door opened, he more felt than saw his mother whirl from her argument with his father. "Where are you going?" she snapped.

"Out," he said, and he pulled the door shut behind him.

"Let him go," Dad said, and that launched a whole new argument.

Truth was, he had no idea where he was going. For a walk, he supposed, but there was nowhere to go. There were no destinations out here. He knew from experience that an hour in any direction merely took you into more woods. Maybe that was the reason why he hadn't yet made good on his promise to flee.

The thought angered him. Fear of the unknown was the worst form of cowardice. At his age and his station in life, the fact that he didn't know where he was headed should have been the inspiration to take the trip. He remembered the lame poster on his freshman year roommate's wall: *A journey of a thousand miles begins with a single step*.

A thousand miles should just about do it.

As he pondered his options, he realized that getting out was only the beginning. He could wander forever and none of this would change. What he really wanted was to be anonymous again. To disappear into nothing and play his music and be alone with the things that were really important to him—his friends, when he wanted them around, and his solitude when he tired of their company.

The front yard—all five acres of it—was the only part of the family spread that had been cleared of trees, and he could remember a time when it was gorgeous. As much as he hated the trips up here, he had to confess to beauty when he saw it. But it had been at least two years since anyone had visited, and in that time, the grass had grown hip-high. The once-cleared acreage now sprouted scrubby oaks and maples and pines that looked more like big weeds than little trees, and illustrated how aggressive Mother Nature could be when she wanted to reclaim the land. It needed to be bush-hogged, but because they couldn't afford to show themselves to anyone, there was no way to get the gas to fill the tractor.

Everything about this was a nightmare.

He started walking. A problem addressed in fresh air and sunshine was always less daunting.

He forced himself to concentrate on Beethoven's Quartet in E Flat Major, the concert that he and three school buddies were preparing for a performance at graduation. As the tune filled his head, he heard every part, and he could feel his left hand on the neck of his cello; his right hand balancing the bow in his fingers. For as long as he could remember, he'd been able to read a musical score the way most people read books. The dots and spaces on the page converted directly to music in his head. His parents and friends called it a blessing, but to him it was equal parts curse. By reading the music, he was blessed to hear a perfect performance every time. When he performed, however, there were always flaws, most never heard by the audience, but they resounded like errant cymbal crashes in Thomas's mind.

The peace of the music couldn't dislodge his anger, though. Not today. And the anger was the thing that could break him. Intuitively, he knew who the real evil-doers were in all of this. He knew that the focus for his anger should be Christine Baker and Fabian What's-his-name—the people who started it all—but he found himself reserving his ugliest thoughts for his own father. He was the conduit through which all of this awfulness had flowed. But for him, Thomas would still be blissfully stressed over academics. But for his involvement in this weapons bullshit, things would be normal. If those guys had just managed to kill his dad at the time of the ransom transfer—

He hated himself.

Movement.

He didn't know if he'd heard it or seen it, but something happened in the tall grass over to his right. The music went away, and he was one hundred percent tuned into reality. Could it have been a snake? A cougar, maybe? They'd found evidence of a big cat up here, and—

The man launched himself with the speed of a lightning bolt, rising out of the grass—out of the ground itself, it seemed—and hitting Thomas hard in the middle, knocking him backward and driving the wind out of his lungs. He tried to yell, but before words could form, a gloved hand attached itself to his mouth, killing the words and threatening to extend the favor to the rest of him.

He arched his back and tried to defend himself when his attacker said, "Thomas, stop."

The familiarity startled him. He stopped squirming as he tried to place it. No, it couldn't be.

"It's Scorpion," the voice said. Right away, Thomas's gaze shifted to the man's eyes—the feature he remembered most from that night. Holy shit, it really was.

A new panic bloomed.

"I'm here to help," Scorpion said, as if reading his thoughts. "I'm not here to hurt anyone. Well, not you, anyway. Not your family."

Thomas stopped moving.

"I'm going to take my hand away now, okay?"

He nodded.

True to his promise, the hand lifted. Scorpion smiled. "So, how've you been?" he asked, his tone filled with irony.

Thomas's head whirled. "What the hell," he said. It was the best he could do.

"Turns out we've got more work to do," Scorpion said. "I had—"

"GUN!" The voice boomed from nowhere—from everywhere. Scorpion prostrated himself on the ground and covered Thomas with his body.

In a horrible flash of realization, Thomas knew exactly what was happening. "No!" he yelled.

But his voice was drowned out by the gunshot.

CHAPTER THIRTY-THREE

A rifle discharged from the area of the cabin, launching a bullet that skimmed the grass within inches of Jonathan's back. A millisecond later, a second rifle barked from the tree line.

A woman screamed.

"Stay down," Jonathan commanded, and he rolled to his side. "Sitrep," he said into his mike, demanding a situation report.

"They fired on you," Boxers said.

Thomas was way ahead of both of them. "What did you do?" he shouted as he jumped to his feet. "Ah, Jesus, what did you do?"

On one knee now with his M4 to his shoulder, it all came clear for Jonathan. A man lay sprawled on the steps leading to the front porch, a woman crouched over him, screaming. She had blood on her hands, but Jonathan couldn't determine the source.

"You shot him!" Thomas yelled, and he launched a roundhouse open-handed slap that Jonathan easily deflected with his forearm. "You fucking shot my father!"

"He's okay," Boxers said in Jonathan's ear. "It's a leg

shot. Through and through." He emerged from the tree line and moved forward. "It's not fatal. Not even crippling."

Thomas hurried toward the house, moving as quickly as his flip-flops would allow in tall grass. At least the kid had been able to change out of the dead man's clothes.

Jonathan rose to his feet and followed, his rifle hanging on its sling, but his hand still on the grip, just in case. The woman—he recognized her from Venice's intel work as Julie Hughes—was screaming unintelligibly and stroking her husband's face as he gripped his thigh. As he got closer, he saw the blood leaking through the man's fingers.

Thomas got to the porch first, and when Jonathan was about twenty feet away, Julie Hughes snapped back into sanity, and she looked right at him. He saw the clarity return to her eyes as she spun and scrambled for the lever-action .30-30 rifle that Stephenson Hughes had dropped when Boxers' round dropped him.

Jonathan dropped to a knee and shouldered his weapon. "Don't!" he commanded. "Don't pick up that weapon."

She was screaming again.

"Thomas!" Jonathan shouted. "Save your mother's life. Get her to put that weapon down." If the muzzle leveled on him, he would have no choice but to shoot her. At this range, the ballistic damage done by the sheer force of the bullet could be fatal, no matter what nonlethal target he picked.

"I've got her," Boxers said in his earpiece.

"Hold fire," Jonathan said. "Thomas!"

The kid leapt to his feet, and snatched the rifle away from his mother by its barrel. "They're friends," he said.

She looked stunned. "They shot your father."

"He shot at me, ma'am," Jonathan said. As if that would convince anyone whose loved one had just been cut down. Rising again to his feet, he stepped forward and held out his left hand, even as his right remained on the grip of his M4. "I'll take that weapon, Tom."

"Don't," Julie said.

But Thomas didn't hesitate. Still holding the rifle by its barrel, he eased sideways down the three stairs from the porch and handed it to Jonathan. The way he kept the weapon upright and pointing away from anything told Jonathan that the kid had some experience with firearms. That could prove helpful.

Julie made a halfhearted lunge for the rifle, but Thomas stopped her with an outstretched arm. "These are the people that rescued me," he said. "They saved my life."

She didn't get it. Her eyes remained wild.

"They shot me, goddammit," Stephenson said. He held both hands gripped around his thigh. "They shot me."

"You fuckin' shot at us," Boxers said as he strode to the wounded man. He let his M4 fall against its sling and he ripped open a large pocket on his combat vest. He pulled out two large white paper packets and put them on the step.

"Leave him alone!" Julie commanded.

Boxers ignored her.

"He's going to dress the wound," Jonathan explained. He recognized the packets as HemCon, a chemical-coated gauze that Jonathan believed was responsible for saving more lives in modern combat than any other technical advancement. You stuff the HemCon into a wound, and the bleeding stops. Just like that.

When Boxers unsheathed his K-Bar knife, Thomas jumped as if to intervene, but then he seemed to remember the last time he saw one of those blades. "They're okay," he reassured his mom. "They know what they're doing."

Julie shot a withering look to Jonathan. "Who are you?" she demanded.

"Call me Scorpion," Jonathan said. "My friend is Big Guy."

"Those aren't names," she growled.

Jonathan shrugged. What could he say?

Boxers slipped the blade of his K-Bar into the bloused leg of Stephenson's trousers and sliced upward, ankle to crotch. The fabric fell away, exposing a perfectly round puncture in the flesh on the inner side of the man's left leg.

"You could have killed him!" Julie accused.

"Woulda, coulda, shoulda," Boxers growled. "But didn't. He'll be fine." With the wound exposed, he poked around the rest of the leg and gave a satisfied nod. "Damn, I'm good," he said. "Bone's fine. No arterial bleeding." He winked at Jonathan. "Bullet went just where I put it."

Thomas's jaw dropped. "Nobody's that good a shot."

Jonathan smirked.

Julie slapped the back of Thomas's head. "Don't admire them," she snapped. "They tried to kill us."

Boxers laughed.

Julie's eyes grew hotter.

"All respect, ma'am," Jonathan said. "When we try to kill, people die. You're not dead."

Boxers ripped open a HemCon package. "I ain't gonna bullshit you," he said to Stephenson. "This is gonna hurt like hell." He didn't wait for a response, moving with skill and purpose to stuff the gauze into the hole made by the bullet.

Stephenson howled in agony. He squirmed and kicked, but there was no refusing Boxers, who held his patient down with his hips and his left arm while he used his right pinkie to cram the HemCon into the wound.

"Stop!" Julie commanded. "You're hurting him!" She took a step to intervene, but again Thomas was able to stop her.

"Let them do their thing, Mom," he urged. "They're the good guys. Really."

"They're *hurting* him!"

"We're helping him, ma'am," Jonathan said. "It'll be over in a few seconds."

"There," Boxers said, sitting upright. "We're done. Only took one pack. Still with us, Steve?"

"It hurts," Stephenson said.

"Of course it hurts," Boxers said. "You've been shot, for God's sake. It's supposed to hurt." Mister Bedside Manner. "Now try not to move. I need to put a dressing on it and we'll be done."

"Who the hell are you?" Stephenson said.

"Asked and answered," Boxers grumped. "Welcome to the party, though. Better late than never." His hands slippery now with Stephenson's blood, Boxers replaced the remaining HemCon package into his vest pocket, and pulled out four standard 4 x 4 dressings and a roll of Kling wrap. The dressings went over the entry and exit wounds, and the Kling held it all in place. When he was finished, the bandage looked like it might have come from a doctor's office.

As he stood, Boxers used a larger dressing to wipe the blood from his hands. "Never let it be said that I don't fix what I break." He extended a hand to Stephenson. "There's no need to baby the leg," he said. "It'll hurt like hell one way or the other, but if you don't exercise it, it'll tighten up and it'll all be tougher than it needs to be."

Confused and exhausted, Stephenson Hughes looked from face to face, trying to decide what the next move should be. In the end, he grabbed Boxers' extended hand in a powerful thumb-grip and used the leverage to stand.

"Somebody want to tell me what the *hell* is going on?" Stephenson said.

They sat around the scarred, wooden dining table in the kitchen, four of them gathered in matching chairs as if playing a game of poker, while Boxers sat on the outside of the square on a carpet rocker a few feet away.

It took only twenty minutes for Jonathan to explain their situation, and another twenty for Stephenson Hughes to tell his side. Jonathan was forthcoming about everything—much to Boxers' consternation—prompting Stephenson Hughes to be open with his own details. After driving all the way out to the lodge in the truck that he'd stolen from the Nike silo, Stephenson had stashed the still-loaded truck in the barn out back. Along the way, he'd managed to avoid further confrontation with the people he now understood to include someone named Ivan Patrick.

Jonathan noted the lack of emotion when Stephenson learned that Fabian Conger was dead, but was a little startled by the depth of dismay shown at the announcement of Tibor Rothman's death. "How did you and Tibor hook up anyway?" Jonathan asked.

"We were friends in college," Stephenson explained. "He was always up for a good fight, a good exposé. I had the idea that if we made some kind of permanent record of all that was transpiring, then we'd have some leverage." He looked down as his voice dropped. "In retrospect, I guess I was a little naïve." He raised his eyes again. "How was he killed, do you know?"

"Badly," Jonathan said, and he let it go at that. "I assume that it was through him that you made contact with me?"

Stephenson shook his head. "Not really. In fact, until this moment, I had no idea who you were. Tibor said he knew someone who might be able to rescue Thomas. He wouldn't tell me how he knew you, or where you'd met. I asked what the charge would be, and he said for me not to worry about it. He always was a good friend."

Jonathan kept his features flat and avoided eye contact with Boxers as he heard this. The fact that Tibor Rothman could have had close friends was hard for him. And how the hell could Tibor know about his covert work? He wondered if maybe the next round of legal wrangling might have included a bit of blackmail.

"Why the video?" Jonathan asked.

Stephenson shrugged. "To have a record. It was a tiny little device. Tibor had the camera in the brim of a hat he was wearing, and the recorder itself was stuffed into his sock. No wires or anything. We figured that if everything went wrong and we didn't get out alive, maybe someone would find the chip and there'd be a record."

"Why did you tell them you had it, then?" Boxers asked. His voice dripped condescension.

Stephenson's eyes flared, but then the anger turned to embarrassment. "I don't have an answer for you. When that phone call came in that Thomas was safe, I guess I felt like we'd won everything. I shot off my mouth. It was stupid."

"Stupid doesn't touch it," Boxers spat. "That little slip of the tongue is what got Scorpion's ex-wife killed."

Stephenson's expression morphed to horror. "Is that true? How?"

Jonathan waved it off and shot an angry look to Boxers. This was neither the place nor the time.

"Of course it's true," Boxers said, ignoring the silent order to shut up. "They tortured and killed her because they thought she had the recording chip that they never should have heard anything about."

Stephenson gaped. "Jesus. I'm so sorry. I don't get—"

"The past is past," Jonathan interrupted. "Let's not get into that."

"How dare you lay that on us?" Julie spat. She pivoted in her chair to glare at Boxers. "We're in the middle of this nightmare, you shoot my husband, and now you try to make us feel guilty? How dare you!"

"Mom, stop," Thomas admonished.

"Don't tell me what to do," she snapped. "Don't any of you tell me what to do. I'm tired of being told."

Jonathan felt his ears reddening. This was the time for team building, not agitation. Boxers was out of line. Accidents happened all the time. People with the best of intentions—or with no intention at all—do stupid things, and once the events are set in motion, there's no pulling them back. It's just the way things worked.

"You said you had a plan," Stephenson prompted, clearly trying to change the subject.

"I do," Jonathan confirmed.

"Will it put my family in jeopardy?"

Jonathan crossed his legs. "You and your family are already in jeopardy. No matter what happens, your chances of being alive next week, let alone next year, are minuscule. Surely you know that."

Stephenson smirked, then winced as his leg twitched.

"I'm surprised I'm still around today, if you want to know the truth."

Jonathan went on, "One way or another, you're going to have to fight these people. If we do it here, we can have some measure of control, and I'll be here to help you."

Julie leaned into the table and shook her head. "Don't listen, Steve," she said. "We don't need to fight. We can leave." She looked to Jonathan. "You'll let us go if we want, won't you?"

"I'm nobody's jailer," Jonathan said.

Julie stood, ready to head for the door. "See? Let's just go. If they want to fight a battle, let them do it without us."

Jonathan remained impassive. Boxers kept recrossing his legs in the chair that was clearly too small for him.

"She's right on one count," Jonathan said. "With you or without you, I'm staying to take care of unfinished business."

Her face brightened and she grabbed Stephenson's hand, ready to go.

Stephenson remained seated, his eyes locked on Jonathan, who returned his stare. "I can't," he said. He turned to Julie and covered her grasp with his other hand. "You can. You should. And take Thomas with you."

"I'm not going anywhere," Thomas objected.

Stephenson faced his son. "This isn't your fight, Tommy."

"The hell it's not."

Julie's voice took on a pitiful, pleading tone. "We've had enough of this nightmare, Steve. I can't take anymore."

Stephenson eyed Jonathan. "We can off-load the truck and the two of them can drive away together."

Jonathan shrugged.

"I can't go without you," Julie whined.

"You have to."

"*I can't.*"

Jonathan interjected, "Where will you go?"

Julie shot him a glare. "This is none of your concern," she snapped.

"Yet the question remains. Where will you go? You're a murderer, remember? Sooner or later, you're going to be recognized. Then what? With your bank accounts frozen, you won't be able to hire a lawyer. That is, if you even get the chance. You have exactly zero friends and fewer resources past the threshold of that door."

She opened her mouth to answer, but seemed to have lost the words. "Steve?"

He shrugged. "Think of the evil these people represent. I have to stay."

Julie's face showed raw betrayal. "Do you hear yourself? You're buying into this insanity. You're going to get yourself killed. I'm going to be a widow. For what?"

"For everything," Stephenson said.

"We'll go to the police," Julie begged. Her voice rose, and her words came faster. "We'll tell the whole story. Every detail. They'll have to believe us."

Jonathan stepped in. "They won't. They can't. They've got to keep you quiet. There's plenty of evidence against you for the Caldwell murders, and what they don't have already, they can manufacture. I'm telling you, Mr. Hughes—"

"Steve."

"You have no option."

"What about the video?" Stephenson reasoned. "Won't that exonerate us?"

Jonathan shrugged. "If I were the prosecutor, I might just use it as evidence of your desperation to get Thomas back. I'd argue that a desperate man wouldn't hesitate to kill the Caldwells and their nanny as a means to learn the whereabouts of your son."

"You see?" Julie said, her voice full of hope. "At worst, they'd see a case of justifiable homicide."

"No, they wouldn't," Thomas said. His face and his tone showed anger. "They'd see premeditation." He glanced to Jonathan. "Right?" You don't watch as much *Law & Order* as he did without learning something.

"That's the way they designed this thing," Boxers chimed in. "These guys we're after, they're very damn good at what they do. We either stop them, or they keep going. They keep going, your family never gets to rest."

"You don't know that," Julie objected. "You just want your vigilante justice. You want to avenge your wife."

"That doesn't make me wrong about the rest," Jonathan replied.

Julie's cheeks flushed with color.

"I'm staying," Thomas said. He left no room for negotiation.

"Think it through, Tom," Jonathan warned. "These are bad people. There's going to be shooting, and the bullets are going to be real. There's no video game do-overs."

"I don't want those bastards chasing me for the rest of my life."

Julie shouted, "Stop it! All of you stop it! This is crazy!" She started to cry, but Jonathan sensed more anger than sadness. After a few seconds, the tears dissolved to sobs. She buried her face in her hands. Her shoulders heaved with the force of her emotions.

Stephenson moved to her, kneeling at her side as he tried to comfort her. "Honey, there's no choice," he cooed, but she shook him off.

"Don't talk to me!" she shrieked.

Jonathan and Boxers stood together. "Let's unload the equipment," Jonathan said, striding toward the front door. Boxers fell in step three feet behind him.

"Wait!" Thomas said, also rising. "I'll give you a hand."

Boxers started to object, but this time backed away from Jonathan's admonishing glare. Clearly, the kid wanted to get out of there. Probably needed to. What was the harm?

"Don't you think you should be staying with your folks?" Jonathan asked as they walked. "They probably don't need any more worry than they've already had."

"Shit," Thomas scoffed. "Worry is all they've got. And they've earned every bit of it."

"Watch the attitude, kid," Boxers scolded. "Those people went through a lot for you."

Thomas glared. "They didn't do anything for me. They didn't even think of hiring you."

Jonathan gave a disapproving scowl. "They tried their best."

"And that worked well, didn't it?"

"It's not their fault."

"Their way would have gotten me killed."

"They were *trying*, Tom. Sometimes, that's the best you can hope for."

Thomas stopped short in the middle of the tall grass. "Are you really that blind?"

Jonathan and Boxers exchanged looks. "I guess I am."

"Dad knew what his company was making. He knew about this germ crap. He had to."

"He says he didn't."

"It doesn't matter whether he knew about the GV whatever. They were making bombs or missiles or some such bullshit murder machine, and he never once stopped to ask himself what the fuck was going to happen with what they rolled out. It's all about killing. Good guys, bad guys, Arabs, Americans, what difference does it make? It's still about killing people."

Boxers seemed to grow taller as his defenses kicked in. "Makes a hell of a lot of difference when you're the one being shot at."

"As I'm going to find out, apparently," Thomas conceded. "I got kidnapped because my dad worked for a company that manufactures shit that kills people. If he was working at a drug company, or at a lawn chair manufacturer—"

"Then there might have been some nutcase who objected to animal testing, or an idiot with a jones for lawn chairs. These people are crazy. Your parents are as much the victims as you are."

Thomas walked faster.

"I feel for you, Tom," Jonathan said. "You want this to make sense. When there's this much violence involving so many people, you want it to be for a reason you can point to. More times than not, it just doesn't happen that way."

Thomas stopped and turned on Jonathan. For the first time in all their hours together, the kid seemed on the edge of losing control. "You don't get it!" he shouted, punctuating each word by driving his forefinger into Jonathan's chest. "I'm a musician! I'm a poet! I write songs! I don't want any of this shit! I never did! When I left my house to head off for school last summer, I told myself I was never going back. I told the *world* that I was never going back."

He made a wide, sweeping gesture back toward the lodge. "Don't you see them in there? Don't you see how they are? They don't give a shit about me. They never did."

"Coulda fooled me," Boxers said.

"They fool *everybody*! Hell, they fool *themselves*. How twisted is that? Now I'm stuck in their fucking nightmare, and I've got no choices left."

They finally reached the wood line. The Hummer was still at least three hundred yards deeper into the woods. Jonathan said, "You do have choices, Tom. Nobody expects you to stay here. You don't have to be a part of what's coming."

"Bullshit."

"You don't!"

"I do!"

"No!"

"Yes!"

"Why, for Christ's sake?"

Thomas held Jonathan's gaze. "Because you saved my life."

Chapter Thirty-Four

"Scorpion, Scorpion, this is Mother Hen."

As often was the case when radio traffic had died but the bud remained in his ear, the sound of a voice in his head startled him. Boxers, too. Thomas sensed the urgency, but had no way of knowing what it might be.

Jonathan pressed the transmit button on his vest. "Go ahead, Mother." He suppressed a smile as he spoke to Venice. He was the one who assigned radio designations, and she hated hers.

"Scorpion, you are not alone. I repeat, you are not alone."

Jonathan motioned for the others to get off the road, such as it was, and they all dove for the foliage on the left side of the overgrown path. Jonathan took a knee and lowered his voice to a whisper. "Okay, you've got my attention."

"There's another vehicle near yours at the bridge. Looks like a light truck. Maybe an SUV, but a small one. Details are hard to see through the trees."

"Just the one?" Jonathan whispered.

"I think so. It's definitely not the Green Brigade. They're still hours out."

Then who the hell was it? He looked to Boxers and got a shrug. "How long ago did they arrive?" he asked.

"I can't say exactly," Venice advised. He could hear the embarrassment in her voice. "Once you got to the cabin safely, I stepped away for a while. No more than ten minutes."

Jonathan did the math in his head. Whoever the visitors were, if they'd only had ten minutes, they couldn't have accomplished very much. "Any sign of people?" he asked.

"Negative. Again, the trees are pretty thick, and it's too warm for the infrared imaging to do much good."

Jonathan sighed. Translation: she had no friggin' clue. "Okay, Mother, thanks for the info. Advise if you see any more detail." Jonathan motioned for Thomas not to move, and then moved slowly and carefully toward the kid while beckoning Boxers to join them. "We have company," he told Thomas.

The kid gasped. "Oh, my God. Is it them?"

"I don't think so," Jonathan said.

Boxers added, "It couldn't be. They haven't had time."

"Who else?" Thomas asked. "Who else would know?"

Boxers shrugged. "If we could figure it out, I guess others could, too."

Jonathan shook his head. "Our key was the disposable cell phone number. No one else had access to that."

"That we know of," Boxers said.

Jonathan rejected the notion. "I think we were followed," he said.

Thomas's jaw dropped. So did Boxers'. "We've never been followed," the big guy said.

There's a first time for everything, Jonathan thought, but he didn't say anything.

"So what do we do?" Thomas asked.

Jonathan inhaled and danced his eyebrows. "We improvise," he said. Boxers got the joke and smiled. "Improvise" was the catchall term for "hope for the best."

"I figure they've got to use the road here, right?" Boxers reasoned. "I'll go to the other side and we'll set up an ambush."

Jonathan liked it. "No shooting unless *absolutely* necessary," he said.

Boxers winked. He brought his rifle up to a ready position, eased to the side of the road cut, and peered down its length. "It's clear," he whispered, and he launched himself. Five seconds later, he was invisible in the bushes on the other side.

"I don't get it," Thomas said. The edge in his voice sounded more like excitement than fear, Jonathan thought.

"I don't either. But I think we'll all figure it out together here sooner than later."

It didn't take long at all.

"I see movement," Boxers' voice said in Jonathan's ear. "I see two heads."

From his side of the road, Boxers had a better view than Jonathan, able to see farther down the leftward curve of the roadbed. "Keep down," Jonathan whispered to Thomas. "People are coming."

"I'm tired of keep down," Thomas muttered.

Jonathan smiled. Who could blame the kid? He'd for sure been doing a lot of cowering these past few days.

Boxers' voice said, "Boss, you are *not* going to believe this when you see it."

"Good news or bad?" Jonathan hated riddles at times like this, and Boxers knew it.

"You tell me."

Ten seconds later, he saw for himself: a man and a woman moving cautiously but abreast in the middle of the road cut. Each carried a shotgun at a loose port arms, and they both wore visible sidearms. Jonathan recognized the silhouette of the woman before he saw her face.

"Well, I'll be damned," he muttered. He pressed the transmit button. "Wait for it," he whispered. "We don't shoot police officers. Remember that." Then again, he'd never been a position to trade shots with them before. At least not on American soil.

The prey got closer. "Anytime for me," Boxers radioed, meaning that they were now in front of him. If they needed a crossfire, they would have one.

They were too close for Jonathan to dare a reply. He squatted near the berm at the side of the road, his legs coiled. Twenty feet. Fifteen. Ten.

He rocketed to his full height, his rifle leveled at Sheriff Gail Bonneville and the guy he assumed must be her deputy. "Freeze, Sheriff!" he commanded.

The guy to her right reacted by swinging his shotgun around, and Jonathan stitched the dirt in front of his feet with a three-round burst that made them both jump back.

"Freeze means freeze, goddammit!" he yelled.

And they froze.

"Weapons down!" he commanded.

Gail lowered her Mossberg shotgun by its barrel to rest its butt plate on the ground and let it fall like a tree. The deputy didn't move.

"I do *not* want to shoot you," Jonathan said. He saw in the deputy's eyes that daring should-I-or-shouldn't-I look that had gotten so many people killed over the years.

"I don't want to shoot you either," Boxers said, emerging from the woods behind them.

The daring look went away. The deputy knew that he'd been beaten. He let his Mossberg fall.

"Sidearms next," Jonathan said. "Two fingers and slowly, please."

Using exaggerated movements, they unfastened the straps that secured their weapons in their holsters, and then stooped to ease them onto the overgrown path. Handguns cost too much these days to go throwing them around the way they did in the movies.

"Well done," Jonathan said. "Now put your hands behind your backs, please, while my big friend zips you guys up."

It all went as if they'd rehearsed it. Boxers approached from behind and produced two set of zip ties from his vest. They were much more convenient than handcuffs, and more secure. Given the right conditions, ballpoint pen fillers could be used to pick handcuff locks. Without a knife or a good pair of snips, zip tied prisoners stayed zip tied until someone decided to let them go free. Besides, there were no keys to lose.

When they were both secure, Jonathan let his weapon fall against its sling and stepped closer. He gave his most charming smile. "Well, hello, Sheriff Bonneville. What's a nice girl like you doing in a place like this?"

"Taking you down," said the deputy.

Jonathan allowed his smile to fade as he shifted his gaze. "I don't believe we've met."

The man just glared.

"This is Jesse Collier," Gail said. "My right hand."

Jonathan took his time evaluating what he saw. Middle aged and a little thick of middle, the guy had a life-hardened look about him. Jonathan assessed him as zero bullshit and dangerous. "He looks like a loyal deputy," he said. "A *smart* one, who knows when he's no longer in control and needs to do what he's told."

Jesse spat a wad of phlegm that nailed the shoulder of Jonathan's vest. Boxers dropped him with a savage punch to the kidney. The entire transaction went down with such speed that they all jumped.

"Enough!" Jonathan commanded.

"The *fuck* do you think you are?" Boxers yelled at the contorting deputy. "That's my friend you just spit on."

"Big Guy!" Jonathan said, more soothingly this time. "It's okay."

"Nobody spits on you."

"Apparently not," Jonathan said. "Did you rupture anything?"

"No, I'm fine," Boxers said.

"I meant him."

"I know what you meant. Fucker." He spat a wad of his own onto Jesse.

"Hey," Jonathan admonished.

"He'll be fine," Boxers said. But he clearly wished otherwise.

When Jonathan made eye contact again with Gail, she still looked shocked. "Speaking of loyalty," she said. "You seem to inspire a bit of that yourself."

Jonathan smiled. "Yeah, how about that. Big Guy, this is Sheriff Gail Bonneville from Samson, Indiana. Sheriff, this is Big Guy."

"That's a name?"

"It'll do for now," Jonathan said. "My name is Scorpion now. Leon Harris is so yesterday."

Gail's eyes remained hard. "And what about Jonathan Grave? You don't like that name anymore either?"

He smiled. "Whoa," he said. "Good for you. That couldn't have been easy to find."

"Not as hard as you'd think," she said. She pointed with her forehead to a place behind Jonathan to his left. "And who's that?"

Jonathan glanced. "Ah, yes. This is one of the murderers you're looking for." He beckoned for Thomas to step closer. "Thomas Hughes, college senior and music major, allow me to introduce the intrepid Sheriff Bonneville."

The kid smiled and nodded an uncomfortable hello. "Okay, this shit is getting very weird," he said.

Jonathan gestured toward Jesse Collier. "Tom, would you please help Deputy Collier to his feet?" As Thomas did just that, Jonathan planted his fists on his hips. "Well, I confess that you're a variable I hadn't planned for."

"I'll take that as a compliment," she said.

"Weren't you told by some pretty powerful people to let this case go?"

She shrugged. "It was that whole 'being told' part that didn't sit right. When people are killed in my town, I take a personal interest."

Jonathan smirked. "So how's that working for you today?"

"You've stepped right into my trap," she quipped.

He laughed, and the look of fear triggered in Thomas made him laugh even harder. "And a hell of a trap it is," he said. "Welcome to paradise." With Jesse upright, Jonathan asked, "How are you?"

"Didn't hurt a bit," he grunted.

"Tom, do me a favor and search the deputy's pockets for a set of keys, will you?"

"They're right there in his front pocket," Thomas said. "I can see them through the fabric."

"Good. Now, I want you to pick up these weapons from the ground and take them and the keys down to the bridge with Big Guy and then drive the sheriff's vehicle back up to the cabin."

"What are you gonna do with *them*?" Boxers asked as Thomas recovered the keys.

Jonathan moved to the side of the roadbed and gestured with his chin for his prisoners to start back up the hill toward the cabin. "I thought we'd take a little walk," he said as he keyed his mike to bring Mother Hen up to date.

Chapter Thirty-Five

Julie and Stephenson Hughes were still going at it when Jonathan pushed open the front door and ushered his prisoners inside. He got the shocked expressions he'd been expecting. Julie jumped to her feet, startled; Stephenson might have if he hadn't been hurting so badly.

"Gail Bonneville and Jesse Collier," Jonathan said, "allow me to present the rest of the Hughes family—Steve and Julie."

"What's going on?" Julie demanded.

Jonathan explained the confrontation on the road as he helped the newcomers into dining table chairs.

"Why are they here?" Stephenson asked.

"If you want the short version," Jonathan began, "Sheriff Bonneville is better at her job than I had anticipated. When I rescued Thomas, it was from a farmhouse in her jurisdiction."

"So you admit it now," Jesse said.

"Not much sense denying at this point," Jonathan conceded. "Anyway, she's been hunting for me ever since." He turned one of the remaining dining chairs around and sat with his chest resting on the cane back, facing Gail. "I do hope, however, that you'll tell how you connected the final dots. I know it didn't come from fingerprints—we've already established that."

Gail smiled as she shook her head. "When you unstrap my hands, I'll fill you in."

Jonathan smiled. He liked this woman. He even liked her deputy, although of the two of them, he was the one to be feared.

"What was your plan?" Jonathan asked. "Were you going to arrest us single-handedly?"

She shrugged. "If the opportunity arose, I suppose we might have. But really, it was more about recon. Once I got the lay of the land, maybe I would have taken my pictures to the state police and put together a plan to take you out."

"In spite of your directive from the FBI."

"*Because* of my directive from the FBI."

She had guts, he had to give her that.

Stephenson looked confused. "So, your only interest here is to arrest Scorpion for shooting up your town?"

"And to arrest you for killing the Caldwell family," Gail replied evenly.

"So you don't know about the rest?" Julie asked.

Gail and Jesse exchanged looks. "What rest?"

Stephenson laughed heartily and paid for it with a muscle spasm. "Boy, do we have a story for you," he grunted through the pain.

It took every bit of a half hour to tell the story again—thirty minutes that they could ill afford. By the time they were done, the Hummer and Gail's Kia Sorrento had both arrived in the front yard, and Thomas and Boxers had joined the confab in the main room.

"So, Sheriff and Deputy, you've stepped into the middle of a war that's about to happen," Jonathan concluded. "And to tell you the God's honest truth, I don't know what I'm going to do about it. You've proved yourself to be just crazy enough not to be trusted if I let you go, but it doesn't seem right to keep you trussed up like a couple of sculptures once the shooting starts. The third option—giving you a gun and asking you to help—doesn't do much for me, either."

"Well you sure as hell can't give Deputy Dawg there a weapon," Boxers said, pointing at Jesse.

Jonathan stood. "Enough chatting," he said. "Let's get to work. Once it gets dark, we'll be on borrowed time. We've got to get that grass cut down out front, and we've got to get an ambush set." He looked at Stephenson. "How about we start with a tour? Are you up for a little hobbling?" He held out his hand and helped the man to his feet.

"What about them?" Boxers asked, indicating the captives. "We gotta do *something*."

He had a point. "Zip them to the chairs."

"I have to go to the bathroom," Gail said.

Boxers froze. He shot a panicked look to Jonathan. Everyone has strengths and weaknesses. For Boxers, the Achilles' heel was excretory functions. He could wallow to his elbows in blood and brains and not even wince. Pee and poop were entirely different matters.

Trying not to laugh at the look of horror from the big guy, Jonathan's eyes narrowed as he assessed Gail's angle. "Okay," he said at length. "Tom, escort the sheriff to the outhouse."

"No way!"

"You just have to walk with her," Jonathan said. "You don't have to wipe her."

Gail was blushing. "You know I'm right here, right?

And, not to get too graphic, there is the matter of my pants."

"Yeah," Thomas said. "Who's gonna do that?"

Jonathan rolled his eyes. "Julie?"

She stood. "Sure," she said, and she helped lift Gail to her feet with a hand on her biceps. "Come on, Sheriff, I'll help you."

Before they'd had a chance to move, Jonathan said, "Tom, you go, too, to help your mom."

Thomas made a slashing motion with his hand—a definitive denial. "No. I am not—"

"Tom, I want you to stay with your mom." This time, his tone conveyed his real message, and everyone in the room caught the subtext. Jonathan didn't trust either woman.

Thomas conceded, even as Julie's back stiffened.

"Let's not argue, okay?" Thomas said, getting ahead of his mother's inevitable complaint. "Let's just do this and get it over with."

Jonathan's tour of the DuBois property started by heading up the stairs. The steps led directly to the master bedroom, where the ceiling was barely high enough to allow him to stand upright in the parallel troughs between the rough-hewn oak beams. A sagging double bed and a small table filled the space.

"Cozy," Jonathan said.

Stephenson chuckled. "As a kid, I used to think this place was huge."

"I guess it helps to be four feet tall." He knocked on the nearest beam with his fist. "Solid."

"Family lore has it that my grandfather built the place with his own hands. Not sure how he got the three-hundred-pound beams up."

"Not a man to be trifled with," Jonathan said. "I need to know if your wife is going to be a liability." He launched that last part like a torpedo.

"Excuse me?"

"Do I need to watch my back when she's around?"

Stephenson waved off the notion as foolish. "She's not a violent woman. That's part of why she's being so . . . difficult. You have nothing to worry about."

"You're sure."

"I'm better than sure. She's just terrified. Hell, so am I."

Fair enough, Jonathan thought. "Next I need see the GVX."

Boxers came along. As barns go, the one on the DuBois property was small, but built to the same standards as the house. The heavy timber pillars looked brand new even if the fifteen-foot peaked roof they supported needed considerable repair. An ancient John Deere tractor stood in the far corner, still hooked up to the enormous cutting deck that clearly hadn't been used in a while. "There you go, Big Guy," Jonathan said, pointing. "Fill that baby with fuel from the spares on the Hummer and mow down all that free cover out front."

"On it," Boxers said, and he headed out the door to get things moving.

The barn in general smelled of mud and old gasoline, and light leaking through spaces in the walls cut pinstripes through the dust that stirred as they entered. Stephenson explained, "It's a place to store stuff we never use. As a kid, it was my retreat. My fort. I used to hide out in the loft."

Next to the tractor sat a relatively new three-quarter-ton truck. "Is that the vehicle you helped yourself to?" Jonathan asked, pointing.

"That's the one."

"And how much germ juice is in there?" Jonathan slipped a mini-Maglite out of a loop on his belt and twisted it on, launching a piercing white beam across the floor. "Show me," he said.

Stephenson hobbled to the back of the truck and pulled open the back door. All they could see were five wooden crates, each of them three feet square. The one closest to the rear of the vehicle had clearly been opened, and its lid hastily replaced. "That's the one I took the cylinders out of on the night we were trying to free Thomas," he explained, pointing.

Jonathan hoisted himself into the truck for a closer look.

Stephenson continued, "Tibor met me at a truck stop outside of Shepherdstown that night. I left the truck there and took the three canisters that Conger wanted and we went the rest of the way by car."

The canisters themselves were about the size and shape of a salami, and constructed of what appeared to be stainless steel. Jonathan hefted one and guessed the weight to be maybe six pounds.

"Not much to them, is there?' Stephenson said.

"A couple of pounds is a *lot* of germs. Why do you think Tibor Rothman agreed to come along with you?"

Stephenson pursed his lips and shrugged. "I really don't know. My begging helped, I think." He meant it as a joke, but it fell flat. "I talked myself into believing that the only way to have a chance long-term, if everything went right, was to have an eyewitness from the press to report what had happened."

Jonathan put the canister back in the crate and closed the top. "That wouldn't make them all the more anxious to kill you?"

"Maybe, but for a different reason. In that case, they'd be killing me because they were pissed. Everybody would know who did it, and for what reason, and because of that, I figured they'd be less inclined to go to the trouble."

Jonathan smiled. "Good old-fashioned reverse logic. Why did you and Tibor split up after you bolted from the drop-off site?"

"Harder to catch two moving targets than one. I ended up taking a bus back to the truck stop where I left this beast." He patted the side of the truck. "By the time I got back to it, I figured the story would have broken and it would have been over. But the story never broke. I guessed that meant Tibor was missing and I decided to go into hiding."

"Let me get down outta this," Jonathan said. "Shit gives me the creeps." He lowered himself back down to the ground, then asked, "How did I get involved?"

"You personally? I don't know. Tibor said he knew a guy. How he knew you, I don't know. For a guy who exposed so many other people's lives, he didn't say much about his own. Thank God he did, though. My original plan was to just meet their demands and hope for the best. With Tibor knowing you, we had a second plan. We had hope for a way out." He extended his hand. "Thank you, by the way. For my son. For all of us. In all the confusion, I think I might have forgotten to say that."

"So, I take it that you two are not necessarily on board with this whole shoot-out idea," Gail said. She tried to keep her tone even, nonconfrontational, but she realized that she had very little time with Julie and Thomas alone.

"There's no other way," Thomas said.

"There's always another way," Julie corrected. "When it comes to violence, there's *always* another way."

"I think you're right," Gail said. She realized as she traipsed through the grass that she'd never walked without the use of her arms, and she found it difficult to keep her balance. "Is there a way I can help?"

"I think you shouldn't be talking about this," Thomas said.

"I don't see why we can't just go to the police," Julie said, ignoring her son.

"As it is, the police have come to you," Gail countered. "If you want us to help, we can."

"Stop!" Thomas commanded; but he did it at a whisper, and he checked over his shoulder, as if to see if anyone might be listening.

"What can you do?" Julie asked.

"Nothing, as long as my hands are tied like this. If you could set us free—"

"No!" Thomas declared. "We are not trusting you. We are not trusting any of the police. Scorpion told us—"

"His name is Jonathan," Gail interrupted. "Jonathan Grave. He's from a little town in—"

"I don't care where he's from!" Thomas said. "And I don't *want* to know his real name. All I need to know is that he saved my life when no one else was even trying." He glared at his mother. "*No one*. If he says we're in danger, we're in danger. If he says he's our friend, he's our friend."

"He's a killer," Gail said, lowering her voice in hopes that Thomas would lower his.

"He's a *rescuer*," Thomas countered. "If he was all

about killing, none of us would be alive. You didn't hear, but before they got you on the road, the last order he gave was to not shoot you under any circumstances. He said they never would shoot a cop." As the last sentence escaped his throat, he wished he hadn't said it. It felt disloyal to repeat what he'd overheard.

"Can you really help us?" Julie said.

"No, she can't!" Thomas said. He was yelling now. "She said herself that she's here to arrest us. They brought guns to do it with."

"I thought you were killers then."

"But you don't anymore?" Julie asked.

"How could I, after the story you told? When a jury hears that—"

"There!" Thomas accused. "A jury. She just said it. She *does* want to arrest us."

Gail kept her voice calm. She needed this kid to shut up. She needed to get Julie alone. "There's a matter of propriety here," she said. "The kind of arrest we're talking about isn't what you're thinking about, Thomas."

"Do you put us in jail?"

"Just for safekeeping. For holding. Not as part of a sentence or anything."

"Just long enough that we can't move around at will anymore," Thomas said. "Just long enough to make us easy targets."

"It's really not like that," Gail said, but she knew she was lying. The idea was to get these people into custody without a struggle.

"I believe you," Julie said.

"I think she's a lying sack of shit," Thomas countered. He turned and faced the distant barn. "Scorpion!" he yelled. "Scorpion, I need you!"

Jonathan appeared in the doorway of the barn, and then started walking toward them.

When Thomas turned to face his mother, her features were red, her eyes hard. "How dare you betray the family," she growled.

Chapter Thirty-six

They'd been at the homestead for four hours now, and according to Venice, the caravan from Brigadeville was still about an hour away from the Wal-Mart where Jonathan had used his false credit card. Soon it would be time to take the final step to lock in their future. In the meantime, they'd cut the grass in the front of the house to ankle height, thus removing places for attacking forces to hide while likewise limiting the possible attack strategy of simply burning them all to death. Strapped now to their chairs, Jesse and Gail had been positioned on opposite ends of the long porch, close enough to be kept an eye on, but distant enough to be out of the way.

Presently, the five of them stood in the front yard, the Hugheses in a rough line with Jonathan in front and Boxers pacing nervously behind. Each of the Hugheses held an unloaded Colt M4 carbine. From the way Stephenson handled his, Jonathan knew he'd had some training. Thomas kept shifting the weapon around, as if trying to find the coolest pose.

Then there was Julie. She held her own rifle as if it were a dog turd—something foul. "You're holding one of the most reliable weapons ever created," Jonathan instructed. "If you aim it correctly, what you're shooting at will fall down every time. We don't have time for a complete course in weaponry, but we do have time for the basics. Rule one. Watch where you point the damn thing. Rule two—" He held his own rifle vertically to show off the left side of the weapon. With his other hand he pointed to the fire selector switch near his thumb. "Keep the selector on 'safe' until you're ready to shoot. And even then, make sure the selector is on single-shot, not three-round burst." He demonstrated by moving the switch to the position perpendicular to the barrel.

"Why not fully automatic?' Thomas asked.

"Two reasons," Jonathan said. "The first is that the weapon won't let you. Spray-and-slay is out of fashion these days."

"You think that's *funny*?" Julie growled. "It's not funny, it's sick. Spray and slay."

Thomas suppressed a giggle.

"The second is a matter of accuracy. A bullet's no good unless it's aimed, and once the first bullet clears the muzzle the recoil kicks in and you're not aiming anymore." Moving on, he continued to hold his rifle high as he demonstrated how to adjust the butt stock. "I only slide it out to the first click," he explained. "Somebody the size of the Big Guy might take it to two. But you want to keep it short enough so that you can shoot it with your elbow tucked in tight."

"I learned to shoot a rifle with my elbow out like this," Thomas said, holding the weapon the way most people do, his elbow extended at a right angle to his body.

"Way to give your enemy a target," Boxers said as he slapped the elbow down. "You make a bigger sight picture and you get too easily knocked around by your own guys."

Jonathan nodded his agreement and went on with his lesson, showing them how to insert and eject the ammo magazines. "When you need to reload, just let the empty mag drop and insert a new one."

"How many will we have?" Thomas asked.

"Plenty," Jonathan replied. "I brought a couple thousand rounds of five-five-six ammo. You'll each have two mags loaded. That's sixty rounds apiece. That should be more than enough."

"Suppose it's not?"

He shrugged. "Then you'll have to start loading additional mags. But I really wouldn't worry about that. The op we've planned will ambush the bad guys well away from here. I think there's a really good chance that none of you will even have to fire a shot." He forced himself not to look away as he spoke that last part, maintaining eye contact so that he would appear to be as sure as he pretended to be.

"Okay, now let's load up and see how well you can actually shoot these things. Julie, you're first." Might as well start with the toughest challenge.

She turned to her husband. "You're really going to allow this to happen?" It was a bald accusation. She glared, waiting for an answer, then dropped the rifle into the grass, and stalked back to the lodge.

Stephenson hurried after her, rifle in hand. "Come on, honey, don't be that way."

"This whole plan is crazy!" she shouted. She never looked back. As she stormed into the house, Jonathan made eye contact with Gail Bonneville, who returned his gaze with a look that said, "Having a good time?"

"She's not going to change her mind," Thomas said. "She specializes in never changing her mind."

"You should ship 'em all home," Boxers grumbled.

"I already told you I'm not going anywhere," Thomas said.

"Nobody's going anywhere they don't want to go," Jonathan said. Julie's outburst had injected real concern, though. Not being helpful was one thing, but now he worried about her actually doing harm to the mission. Her attempt to conspire with Gail Bonneville was to be expected, he supposed—else, why would he have insisted that Thomas go along with them—but now that everything was about to go hot he was beginning to wonder if he shouldn't tie Julie up as well.

"My turn to shoot," Thomas announced, bringing everyone back on point. He squared, chambered a round, and brought the rifle to his shoulder.

Jonathan stepped out of the way as he said, "Keep it in tight to your shoulder. There's not a lot of kick, but you don't want it to be more than it needs to be."

"I've shot before," Thomas assured.

"Then shoot," Jonathan said. "You gonna pick the target or am I?"

Thomas pointed downrange. "See that big tree down there?" A drooping oak loomed thirty yards away. "That branch coming out of the right side?"

Jonathan nodded approval. "Gutsy choice."

Thomas braced himself, his left leg ahead of his right. He settled himself with a deep breath and tightened his whole hand around the pistol-grip stock as he tucked his shoulder in. When the weapon barked, the kid seemed ready for it. Even without binoculars, Jonathan could see the white gouge that the bullet carved into the bark of the tree.

"Very nice," he said, meaning it. "Give me another."

Thomas set himself and fired again. More wood flew.

Jonathan grinned. "Excellent. Where'd you learn to shoot?"

"A buddy of mine at school has a farm. I've killed hundreds of bottles in the last four years."

"Bottles don't shoot back at you," Boxers growled. "Ever shot anything that was alive?"

Thomas had had it with Boxers' grousing. "What the *hell* is your problem with me? I'm on your side."

"I don't need you on my side," Boxers said.

"But he's here, isn't he?" Jonathan said. "He's volunteered to put himself in harm's way, and we're going to need the extra manpower."

"Against these yahoos that are on their way? Bullshit."

"That's *enough*!" Jonathan snapped.

"It's *crazy*!" the big man snapped back. "Can we talk privately?"

"We don't have time," Jonathan said. What was the point? He knew where the conversation was going to go. "Just say what's on your mind."

Boxers shook his head. "Not in front of the kid."

"Hey!" Thomas barked. "What is with—"

"You don't know shit, kid. You don't even know what you're getting into."

"I know enough," Thomas said.

"No you don't! And the fact that you think you do is even scarier." He turned to Jonathan. "You don't have the right to expose them like this. It's wrong, and you know it."

Jonathan stared, stunned.

"I'm good for this, Scorpion," Thomas said.

Piss and vinegar, Jonathan thought.

"What are you gonna do, *Scorpion*?" Boxers pressed. "You want me to speak freely, I'll speak freely. You got the only two people who actually know how to shoot tied up on the porch, you got one who's ready to surrender to anybody who'll listen, you got an old guy with a bad leg, and a kid who thinks we're gonna be attacked by bottles. What in that picture looks anything but crazy to you? If these Brigade yahoos are good enough to make us need what we've got, then we're completely screwed. You're gonna get them killed."

Jonathan didn't know what to say. Andrew Hawkins's description of Ivan Patrick's demagoguery echoed in his head. If Boxers was right—if he was asking too much from people who had no chance to deliver—then Jonathan and Ivan had something terrible in common. He said nothing as he turned and started walking toward the tree line.

"Where you goin'?" Boxers wanted to know.

Jonathan kept walking. He needed to think. A knot had formed in his stomach. Say what you like, package it as you wish, this was a revenge mission—a murder mission—and he realized now that it was a poisonous one. Dom and Ven were both right. Boxers had even seen it, for God's sake, and if that didn't translate to totally fucking obvious, what did?

"What do you want me to do?" Thomas called. "Do I keep shooting?"

"Sure, kid," Boxers said. "Just keep your aim away from me and your own foot."

Jonathan heard Boxers's heavy footfalls on his right. "Dig, you're scaring me," he said, a little breathlessly.

"Not here," Jonathan said as another report from Thomas's rifle ripped through the afternoon. He was buying time, trying to think of a way to undo a plan that was already in motion.

Boxers kept with him step for step as they strode

deeper into the woods. "Are we off to actually do something, or are you just having one of your Digger moments?"

Jonathan kept walking. When they were out of sight of the house, he stopped and leaned his back against a tree. The adrenaline and lack of sleep were beginning to catch up with him. He felt eighty years old. "The torpedo's in the water, Box," he said. "It's too late to put it back in the tube. Ivan and his people are on their way. They'll be here tonight. If we're not ready, then you're right. I'm going to get all of these people killed."

Boxers stood a couple of yards away with his hands in his pants pockets. He never liked it when Jonathan showed weakness. "We've beaten armies before, just the two of us. It's about weapons and skill. We've got both—we've certainly got more than what's coming at us."

"Never underestimate your enemy," Jonathan said, quoting from a thousand different combat texts.

"And never overestimate your allies," Boxers countered. "I'm not saying that the fight shouldn't come. I'm just saying we don't need the Hugheses."

Jonathan scowled. "You *were* listening, right? They've got noplace to go."

"When the shooting starts, anyplace will be better than here. Not getting arrested is no reason to get killed."

"That's the problem. If they get arrested, they *will* be killed."

"At least it won't be your doing, Dig. That'll be worth something at the gates of hell."

Jonathan forced a laugh. "This one's all on me. I'll make sure St. Peter understands."

"Call Wolverine," Boxers said.

"For what?"

"Hell, I don't know. She's director of the FB fuckin' I. At least she has clout. Maybe she can send reinforcements. It's worth a try, isn't it?"

Jonathan shook his head. "She made her intentions clear. When the Bureau gets involved in this one, we're all going down. Uncle Sam's got a secret he wants kept, and everything is secondary to that."

Boxers shrugged. "Then the battle's gotta come," he said. Analysis complete, decision made. "Let's get on with it. We got shit to do." He took two steps back toward the house and waited for Jonathan to follow. He sighed. "Okay, Boss, while you're in your mood, I do have one other question for you."

Jonathan waited.

"When we win this thing, what's our next step after that?"

"Our next step?"

"Yeah, the bad guys will be dead, but there'll still be a secret that needs keeping. How are we going to get past that?"

"There's a way," Jonathan mused.

"Any idea what it might be?"

"Not a clue."

"But you're working on it. Cool. Good enough for me. Now let's get ready to kill some bad guys."

This time as Boxers led, Jonathan followed. As he walked, he thought about Boxers' question. The coming fight would go as it would go. Far more difficult was the next step. Irene Rivers could not have been more direct in her warning: the weapons they had in their possession were a Homeland Security issue now, meaning presumption of guilt and suspension of all civil rights. It meant disappearing. Poof. It meant never having existed at all.

Jonathan had learned years ago that it was a mistake

to second-guess the past, but under the circumstances of the last week, he found it impossible not to. The ripple effect of Thomas's rescue was staggering in its scope, the number of ruined lives and people killed—with more to come tonight.

All because of . . . what? Greed, he supposed. That was the common denominator. The Patrones and Carlyle Industries had been greedy for money, Fabian Conger had been greedy for attention, and the agencies that had funded the project in the first place were greedy for power. All the rest were soldiers, pawns, or merely collateral damage.

There had to be a way to stop the juggernaut of destruction. There had to be an exit strategy that would allow them to win this for real. All Jonathan had to do was find the right handle to pull.

Good old-fashioned reverse logic.

A fully formed plan came to him just like that, out of nowhere. He jerked to a stop and Boxers turned.

"What's wrong now?" Big Guy asked.

"Not a thing," Jonathan said with a grin. "I've got the answer."

CHAPTER THIRTY-SEVEN

Jonathan gathered the crowd into the dining room for another chat. With two of the chairs taken by Gail Bonneville and her deputy, Thomas sat on the sofa topping off the magazine he'd fired from. Stephenson and Julie took the remaining chairs while Jonathan and Boxers remained standing. Jonathan had a little speech prepared in his head, but before he could say anything, Stephenson preempted him. "I think you need to share your plan," he said. "And tell us how we can help." As he spoke that last sentence, he shot a glare at Julie, as if daring her to start up again.

Jonathan exchanged glances with Boxers, then leaned forward with his forearms resting on the table. "I've looked over the latest satellite imagery of this place, and from what I can tell, access is limited to that bridge we came over yesterday. Is that right?"

Stephenson nodded.

"You're sure?" Jonathan pressed. "No fire roads, deer trails, hiking trails, nothing like that? Nothing where a four-wheeler can gain access?"

"I'm sure," Stephenson said. And right away he

backpedaled, "Well, I guess if you want to get into a place badly enough, there's always a way."

Jonathan conceded the obvious. "Of course. But we want to make it as difficult for them as possible."

"What about the fire road on the top of the ridge?" Thomas asked.

Stephenson scowled. "That's hardly access to the property."

Jonathan pulled a USGS map of the area from a flap pocket in his pants and spread it out on the table. "Show me."

It took a few seconds for Stephenson and Thomas to orient themselves to the map and reach agreement. "About in here," Stephenson said, tracing his finger along a section that was half a mile north of the lodge.

Jonathan noted the closely packed contour lines. "That's a hell of a steep slope."

"Have you *seen* the backyard?" Julie said.

Jonathan forced a smile. God, he didn't like that woman. There was indeed a fairly steep slope to the backyard, but apparently just beyond the tree line, it went nearly vertical.

"Why isn't the road on the map?" Boxers asked. "These things are usually pretty accurate."

"There's really not much to it," Thomas said. "It's not really even a road. More like a wide trail."

Jonathan asked, "How do you get to it? Where does it begin and end?"

Stephenson and Thomas looked to each other for answers, then both shook their heads. "I have no idea," Thomas said for both of them. "I've never hiked it from beginning to end. I only know it's there because that's where you end up when you go out back and start climbing."

Jonathan turned to Stephenson. "You either?"

"Nope. I've probably gone a mile in each direction over the years, but I've never found the end. It's in pretty rough shape."

It was inconceivable to Jonathan that anyone could grow up here and not know. He looked to Boxers. "What do you think?"

"It's a weakness. Our Achilles' heel. If we had a platoon, we'd cover it. As it is, I think we have to live with it."

Jonathan agreed. "Okay, that brings us to our various roles for when the war comes." Julie recoiled from the term, but Jonathan didn't back down. "The key to survival once the shooting starts is for you guys to spend as much time as possible here inside the lodge. These timbers in the walls will stop just about anything they can throw at us. They're just about bulletproof."

"What about the windows?" Julie asked.

"Not bulletproof," Jonathan said. "We're going to spend the next few hours making this as sturdy a fortress as possible. We need to block access to that bridge out there to slow them down and hopefully even keep them out. Big Guy and I will set up an ambush at that spot, so if everything goes perfectly, you won't even have to worry about firing a shot up here."

"Are you going to take the bridge out completely?" Stephenson asked.

Jonathan shook his head. "I think we'll rig it, but I don't want to blow it unless we have to. When it's all over, it'd be nice to have a way to get out again."

"I presume you'll want some of us out there to help you with the ambush," Stephenson said.

This time the head shake was vigorous. "Absolutely not. Ambushes are tricky. After the first shot, they tend to go to shit, and it's very damn easy to kill your team members. Besides, even the best-planned ambush is a dynamic event, and with that wounded leg, you won't be dynamic for a while. If Big Guy or I get hit, then this place becomes the Alamo. You'll need to be here to defend it."

"Everybody died at the Alamo," Julie said. Ever the voice of optimism.

"So what's next?" Thomas asked.

"Big Guy and I are going to take care of business down at the bridge and out around the house. I need you guys to practice reloading your weapons in a hurry. Over and over again. Load 'em up and then jack out the rounds and load 'em up again. You'll be doing it for real in the dark, so make sure your hands know what to do."

"Won't we have to expose ourselves to a window to shoot?" Julie asked, another inquiry from Captain Obvious.

He didn't bother to answer. "Steve, when you get a chance I need you to rig a lightproof space upstairs where we can monitor the satellite images without the glow providing an easy target."

"Will do," he said.

Jonathan stood. "Let's get to it, then."

"What about us?" Gail asked.

Everyone stopped; everyone turned to face them. "What about you?" Jonathan asked.

"Being quiet would be a good first step," Boxers offered.

"We can help," she said.

Boxers laughed. "Yeah, 'helpful' is exactly the vibe I've been getting off of you all day."

Jesse Collier gave it a try. "We talked during your target practice. This arrangement here, with us all trussed up, makes no sense at all. Y'all are in a box. You can't call for help, and hell is coming to pay a visit. Like it or not, we're in the box with you, and we're going to be in the middle of all the shooting. If these Green Brigade people you're talking about kill you, they're sure as hell going to kill us, too. However it comes down, you'll be wishing you had additional hands, and here we are. It only makes sense that we'd want to help."

Boxers laughed.

Jonathan didn't. His eyes narrowed as he considered Jesse's words.

"You're not thinking of saying yes, are you, Boss?"

Jesse pressed harder. "We came here to arrest you for the crimes committed in Samson. I didn't even want to do that, to tell the truth. Seems to me, the Patrones got what was coming to them. This fight here? We got no dog in it."

"But you're offering to fight with us anyway?" Stephenson asked.

"It beats getting shot while tied in a chair," Gail said.

Jonathan gave Gail a hard look. "And what about those charges in Samson? You still intend to pursue them?"

She took a long time answering. When she did, she looked a little ill. "It's my job," she said. "I'll have to."

Jonathan smiled. His question had been a test. If she'd said she would drop the charges, he would have known that they were playing an angle—telling them what they thought they wanted to hear. He nodded to Stephenson. "Cut them loose and put them to work," he said.

Jonathan spent an hour with Boxers on the near side of the bridge, using two-foot lengths of detonating cord to drop trees across the road. Few toys were more fun than det cord. Thomas hung around as their shadow, watching the process so carefully that Jonathan let him set the detonators. Finally, with the three of them huddled a safe distance away from the current shot, Jonathan handed Thomas the wireless trigger. "You do it," he said.

The kid looked like he'd just gotten a bike at Christmas. "Really?"

Jonathan ignored Boxers' angry glare. "Remember what to do?"

"Just put in the battery, move the switch to Arm, and push the button, right?"

"After shouting what?"

Thomas nodded. "Oh, yeah." He shouted, "Fire in the hole! Fire in the hole! Fire in the hole!" Then he inserted the AA battery, moved the safe/arm switch to the proper position, and pressed the button. The earth shook with a satisfying *crack*, and up ahead, a thirty-foot pine jumped and slowly arced to the earth, gathering momentum as it crashed through its coniferous siblings.

Thomas grinned. "That is so cool." He handed the trigger back to Jonathan.

"The technical term is KFB," Boxers said, rising to his feet.

"KFB?" Thomas asked, taking the bait.

"Ka-fuckin'-boom."

They laughed, Thomas harder than the others. "Can I ask a question?"

"Do you do anything but?" Boxers grumped.

Thomas was learning Boxers' crankiness. "We kept the bridge so we can get out, but aren't we still cutting off our own escape with the trees?"

"We're not here to escape," Jonathan said without hesitation. "We're here to prevail. If we don't prevail, escape won't be an option. If we win, we'll have time to clear a path."

Thomas's eyes narrowed. "You don't really think we might get killed here, do you?"

"*Might's* a pretty tough bar to clear," Jonathan said. "They're gonna be shooting back."

"But we're better than them, right?" he pressed. Anticipating Boxer's inevitable barb, he added, "I mean you. You're better than them."

"It's not about being better. Half of it's just about being lucky. Once a bullet's in the air, it's on its way to where it's going. The best you can hope for is to stay out of its way." It wasn't what Thomas wanted to hear.

"You still got time to skedaddle," Boxers urged.

Thomas shook his head, but he looked peaked. "I said I'd stay. I'll stay."

Jonathan clapped him on the shoulder. "Big Guy and I have both seen our share of shoot-outs. We haven't lost yet."

Thomas tried to smile, but reality was settling in. "What's it like?" he asked. "You know, *after*."

Jonathan cocked his head. "After a battle?"

"After killing someone."

Jonathan's eyes narrowed as he decided not to answer. "We should head back," he said.

"I want to know."

"Soon enough, you will."

"I'm serious."

"I don't have an answer for you. It affects different people different ways. It changes you, sure, but people all handle it differently."

"How did you handle it?"

Jonathan sighed. Talk like this never came to good. "I guess it didn't hurt me enough to make me unwilling to do it again."

"But we're ultimately talking more murder charges, aren't we? Only these'll be real."

"Don't worry about that, either," Jonathan said.

"Why?"

Boxers guffawed, "Because they can't charge you with nothin' when you're already dead."

CHAPTER THIRTY-EIGHT

Father Dom smiled at the little girl on his office sofa and tried to make her feel at home. She'd arrived only an hour ago, and she was struggling to be brave. Her feet dangled in the air, and she sat with her hands crossed demurely on her lap. One of St. Kate's staff social workers, Annie Horvath, sat next to her on the sofa, a respectable distance away.

"Well, Elena," Dom said, closing out his initial assessment, "We're going to do everything we can to make sure things get easier from now on. Have you met Mama Alexander yet?"

Elena did not respond, but Annie knew her cue. "We haven't been there yet."

Dom leaned back in his chair. "Oh, my goodness! You haven't had the cookies yet?"

"We thought about going there first, Father, but we were running short on time—"

"Annie, Annie, Annie," the priest railed, much too dramatically had Elena been even a year older. "I hear that this afternoon's batch of cookies is the best *ever*." For the first time, the girl's eyes moved. She didn't yet dare happiness, but the interest was there. Dom used the brief eye contact to his advantage. "I don't know about you, but I have a thing for chocolate chip cookies. When I was a little boy, people used to tell me that I was going to *become* a chocolate chip cookie when I grew up."

The hint of a smile.

He continued, "Mama Alexander makes the very best chocolate chip cookies in the world. And you know what else?"

Elena shook her head.

"Father Timothy, the other priest here, loves sugar cookies as much as I love chocolate chip, and he tells me that Mama makes the best *sugar* cookies in the world, too. She's like a cookie queen."

"Cookie queen," Elena repeated.

He looked to the social worker. "Miss Annie, do you think you could escort beautiful Elena to visit the cookie queen?"

Without a knock, his office door opened, and a dark, weathered face peeked in. Mrs. Morales had been the secretary at St. Kate's since the days of Pope Paul VI, and she now served as Dom's administrative assistant. She wasn't particularly good at her job, but she did it with passion and commitment. At the moment, she seemed frightened.

"Excuse me, Father," she said. "The police are here."

He rose from his chair, and Anne did likewise, but Elena's eyes grew huge with fear. This was exactly the wrong kind of news to deliver in the presence of a child. "I'm sure it's nothing," he said, careful to keep a lilt in his tone. "Certainly nothing bad."

"I don't know—"

Dom cut her off. "*Nothing* bad." If his glare had had

the power to start fires, she'd have lit up like a sparkler. He placed his hand gently on Elena's shoulder, and told Annie with his eyes to get moving. "You tell Mama that I said hi, okay?"

Elena wasn't yet a true believer, but she seemed willing to take a chance. Such was the magical power of chocolate chips.

When they were gone, Dom turned to Mrs. Morales. "Don't ever bring stress into this office in the presence of a child."

The old woman's shoulders seemed to contract, and she dropped her gaze to the floor. "I'm terribly sorry, Father."

And now he felt like shit. "Don't worry about it. Remember for the future. Now, the police?"

"It's Chief Kramer. Something happened at Resurrection House."

Thirty seconds later, Doug Kramer was in Elena's spot on the sofa. "I don't even know if it's that big a deal," he said. "I just thought you should be aware."

"Of what, Chief? What happened?"

"There was a guy there this afternoon talking to some of the kids, Roman Alexander among them. Mama called me just to give me a heads-up, but if Mama is disturbed enough to call the cops, then I think it's worth looking into."

Dom steeled himself for news he knew he wouldn't like. "And because Mama called, I'm going to guess that the talking was more like touching?"

"Not exactly, but she seemed to think he crossed a line. The guy asked questions about Venice. About where she worked and what she did there. I don't know if he knew that Roman is her son, but Roman didn't know any better, so he just answered with the truth.

About the time Mama saw them together and intervened, Roman was about to go with him down the hill to show him the way."

"Who was this guy?"

"Nobody'd ever seen him before. Well dressed, they said. Suit and tie."

Dom's stomach tightened. *There are no coincidences.* Dom pinched his lower lip and scowled. "Didn't touch him, though?"

"Nope. Didn't do anything I could arrest him for, even if I knew who he was or where he went."

"Did he ever show up at Venice's office?"

"Not that I know of. I asked Mama to check that out and call me if he did. I haven't heard back from her, so I can only assume . . ." He didn't bother to finish the sentence. "Frankly, Father, I'm not as concerned about Venice as I am about strange guys hanging around an orphanage talking to little boys."

"It's not an orphanage." It was an important distinction in Dom's mind.

"Still, I think you can see my point."

"I do. What do you recommend?"

The chief shrugged. "I don't know. I was hoping that maybe you could shed a little light on what your friends at Security Solutions are up to. Does this have something to do with that?"

Dom didn't like the tone of the question any more than he liked being stuck in the middle. "It wouldn't hurt to be more vigilant over the next few days," he said.

CHAPTER THIRTY-NINE

"Claymores?" Stephenson gasped. "I haven't seen one of these in years." They were out in the front yard of the lodge, making the final preparations for their defense.

Jonathan couldn't tell from the man's tone whether he was impressed or appalled. "One of the best antipersonnel weapons ever invented," he said. "But they're only a last resort, understand?"

"So if we see someone in the clearing, we just blow them up?" Jesse asked.

Jonathan shook his head. "No, if you see *a lot* of someones, and you know they're all OpFor—excuse me, opposition force—then you can use them, and then only if they're close. Effective range is only about eighty yards."

"I've heard of claymores," Thomas said. "Didn't they use them in *Platoon*?"

Jonathan chuckled. The modern military was looking more and more like a video game every day. "Claymores have been around forever." He lifted the wedge-shaped plastic box and displayed it to the group. "This baby has 700 steel balls in front of about a pound and a half of plastic explosive. When they detonate, they send a wall of buckshot out in a sixty-degree pattern that makes living damned difficult." He tossed one to Thomas, who almost turned himself inside out bobbling it in the air.

"Jesus! What's wrong with you?"

Jonathan grinned. "They're stable until you put a detonator in the back."

"We called that soldier-proof back in the day," Stephenson said.

Thomas turned the mine over in his hands, examining it. He chuckled. "Is this soldier-proofing too?" He displayed the business end of the device to the others. "'This side toward enemy'?" he said, quoting from the label.

"It's a mistake you don't get to make twice," Boxers said. "A little signage is a good thing."

Stephenson said, "When my dad was in 'Nam, they had a problem with sappers sneaking into compounds before nighttime assaults and turning those things around. Some nervous picket would blow the detonator and kill himself and his buddies."

"All's fair," Jonathan said ruefully. He extended the collapsible legs on the bottom of the device, and arranged it just so, about five inches above the dirt.

"How do you set them off?" Thomas asked.

Jonathan walked back to the Styrofoam packing box from which he'd removed the mine. The packaging looked like something from RadioShack. Jonathan displayed a device that looked oddly like a four-inch beetle with a tail of electrical wire. "This," he said, "is the clacker." He squeezed it as a demonstration, and sure enough, it clacked. "Each claymore has one. To set one off, you clack the initiator three times. Like this." He squeezed it the way you would squeeze one of those grip strengtheners from Sports Authority, three clacks in about two seconds. "It'll go *clack, clack, kaboom!* The detonation will happen on the third clack."

About ten yards away, near the far corner of the front of the lodge, Boxers was setting his own mine. "I'll thank you not to make that noise while I'm setting these!" he called.

"How many do we have?" Stephenson asked.

Jonathan said, "Only four. I'm going to put two in the front here, and then one each on the on the sides. That steep hill out back won't let the weapon work on the black side. Remember. Once you shoot them, you're done. If you waste the big stuff on the first wave, settle in for a very long and painful second wave."

"*Waves?*" Stephenson gasped. "How many people are you expecting?"

Jonathan kept his attention focused on the business of inserting a detonator in the back end of the claymore.

"What you expect and what you prepare for are entirely different numbers," Gail said, ending a long period without a word from her.

Stephenson pressed, "Okay, let's try this. How many *waves* do you expect?"

"At least two," Jonathan said. He stood up and threaded initiator wire back toward the cabin. "Our intelligence shows that Ivan Patrick is well trained. Army Ranger. No one with that background would commit all of his forces on a single attack. If I were him, I'd send in half on the first wave to see what happens, and then correct for weakness on the second wave."

Thomas looked troubled. "Where does he find his troops? I mean, I always wondered about that in the old

TV shows on Nick at Nite. Where did KAOS or THRUSH find people to take on Maxwell Smart and Napoleon Solo?"

Jonathan chose not to address the woeful mixing of TV classics. "Ivan Patrick's got a pocketful of zealots. Some of them probably believe they can save the planet through violence, while others just like to fight. I imagine a good handful will disappear as soon as the first bullet passes their head. The ones who are the most frightened will become the most fearless fighters."

Jesse cocked his head. "Do I hear admiration in your voice?"

Jonathan continued working while he talked. "Respect is a better word. I respect anyone willing to die for a cause."

"Even terrorists?" Thomas asked.

Jonathan nodded. "Even them."

"But they're the enemy," Jesse protested.

"And my goal is to help them die for their cause. But I still respect them."

"So, what's next?" Stephenson asked.

Shadows were getting very long now; it would be dark soon. The explosives were set, the weapons were loaded, and the satellite link was established. His troops and his camp were as prepared as they were going to get. "I guess it's time to make your phone call," he said.

Stephenson's expression didn't change as he heard the words, but color drained from his face. He turned away and hobbled up the steps into the cabin.

"What phone call?" Gail asked.

"The one that's going to bring hell to the front porch," he said. "We alerted Ivan and his gang to our location by using Steve's credit card at the Wal-Mart back in town. We wanted to get them on the road in the correct general direction. When Steve turns on his cell phone and makes a call, they'll be able to zero right in on us. We're at the point of no return."

Gail cocked her head. "Why are you really doing this?" she asked.

"I'd like to know that myself," Jesse said. The facial twitch that followed from Gail announced her wish that he would wander off somewhere.

Jonathan wished that himself. "Want to take a walk?" he asked.

"To where?" Jesse protested.

"I wasn't talking to you," Jonathan snapped. He looked to Gail for her answer.

"Sure," she said. This time, Jesse read her glare perfectly. He was staying behind.

Jonathan led the way toward the front tree line, his hands in his pockets, his rifle hanging from its combat sling like an exclamation point down the front of his body. When he felt far enough out of earshot, he said, "You go first. Why are *you* really doing this?"

She chuckled. "You really have the whole story. I didn't want to get shot tied to a chair. You wouldn't do the sensible thing and call the authorities, so I had only one choice. I had to pick a side, and as scary and hopeless as you and your little army are, the other side seems worse."

"I guess next time, you need to listen to Irene Rivers when she tells you to butt out."

"Next time."

They walked awhile in silence. "You know we have a chance of winning this thing," Jonathan said. "A good chance."

"Okay," Gail said. Another silence, then, "You haven't told me why yet."

Jonathan looked toward the treetops as he said, "The

lofty answer is duty. The tawdry one is revenge. Just like any war anywhere."

Gail wanted more, then realized he'd said a lot. "What did Ivan do to your wife?" she asked.

"He killed her."

"There's got to be more than that."

"There is."

"Then tell me."

Jonathan shook his head. "Nope, those details are mine. You can access the reports when we're done."

When they got to the tree line, they hung a left and waded together through the scrub growth on the leading edge. "When we're done," Gail said.

"Excuse me?"

"You said 'when we're done.' Are you really going to let Jesse and me go when it's over?"

He smirked. "The phrase, 'turn myself over to you' seems more appropriate."

She didn't get it. "You're really just going to let me take you in?"

He shrugged. "That was the deal, right? You help us fight, and I turn myself in."

"That makes no sense."

"Sure it does. A deal's a deal. You caught me outright. I made mistakes and you capitalized on them. To the victor belongs the spoils."

Gail stopped. She looked shocked.

Jonathan gestured with his head for them to keep walking. "When there's a lesson like this to learn, someone needs to learn it. That someone's me. Like you said, with extenuating circumstances and all, maybe I'll be acquitted."

She was still befuddled. "I don't know whether to believe you."

"Always believe me. Especially when I make a deal. I'm really not very complicated."

"How can you speak for your big friend?" she asked.

Jonathan laughed. "I don't speak for my big friend," he said. "In fact, you need to leave him alone."

"Why?"

"Two reasons. First, he didn't have anything to do with those shootings. All he did was lift me and the kid out of trouble. I did all the shooting."

"What's the second reason?"

Jonathan looked right at her. "He'd kill you if you tried."

Chapter Forty

Night fell inside the lodge a good half hour before it fell outside. They'd carried the kitchen chairs upstairs into the master bedroom and draped blankets to create a lightproof nook in which they could operate their laptop without creating a beacon for the bad guys. The computer was set to continually monitor the SkysEye satellite images of their corner of the world. They'd configured the screen view in such a way that the cabin was in the middle of the frame, with outer margins calibrated to show a one-mile radius from the center point.

"We've got a great signal, Mother Hen," Jonathan said into his satellite phone. "Looks like we're all set here."

Back in Fisherman's Cove, Venice sat in her office scanning her three large computer panels. In the middle, she watched the same SkysEye image that Jonathan saw. On the left screen, she tracked the progress of the Brigadeville caravan as they moved ever closer to her boss's location. True to his word, Lee Burns had not been able to provide constant video of the vehicles as they moved, but he had been able to mark them electronically by their heat signatures through the SkysEye network. As long as the engines were not stopped for more than a few minutes, and the heat signatures remained constant, their position appeared on her screen as white dots on a map. She kept the right screen available for obtaining further information.

She keyed her microphone. "Scorpion, the caravan is approaching the Wal-Mart now. If they turn and head in your direction, we'll know that they picked up on the cell phone signal. If they do, they'll be on you in forty minutes."

"Roger that," Jonathan said.

Venice watched her screen as the lead dot stopped in the parking lot of the department store, and then waited as the other seven dots converged. None of them moved.

"Okay Scorpion, they've stopped at the Wal-Mart." Knowing how much Jonathan obsessed about brief radio traffic, she didn't add her concern that they might not have picked up the clue from Stephenson's cell phone signal. Since there was no way to tell, there was no reason to say anything.

Her true concern was that they might turn off their engines. As long as the heat signatures stayed at their nominal levels, the SkysEye passive sensors could follow their progress and transmit their map coordinates for interpretation by the computer. If the heat signature changed dramatically—particularly if it cooled—the passive sensor would lose contact, and be unable to reacquire it without re-tasking the satellites, which Lee had already told her they could not do.

Venice had long ago decided that if she died young it would be because of these moments. The waiting was unbearable. Excrutiating. She wondered sometimes if the anticipation of danger—especially when you knew without doubt that it was on the way—was more stressful on a person than facing the danger itself. Here she was hundreds of miles away from the battle, and while she was glued to her seat as a critical component of all that was to follow, she felt powerless to have any real impact. She could observe and report and keep tally, but she couldn't save anyone.

She'd been watching the screen for seven minutes when the first vehicle disappeared. Fifteen seconds later, a second one was gone, and about ten seconds after that a third.

She reached for her microphone. "Scorpion, this is Mother Hen. We've got a problem."

By the time Jonathan answered, all but one of the eight dots on her screen had disappeared.

"Well, we're blind," Jonathan announced to the room. He caught them all up with the events reported to him by Venice. "One of the incoming vehicles still has his engine running, but there's no telling if he's going to keep it that way."

Julie looked horrified. "So we'll have no idea when—or even if—they're on their way."

"The if isn't in play," Jonathan said. "They'll be here. And if our one guy keeps his engine warm, we'll at least know where that vehicle is. When they get within a mile of here, we'll see them on the satellite picture on a four-minute update. It's not what I was hoping for, but it's not a nightmare, either. No need to panic."

Julie made a snorting noise. "The time to panic passed

a long time ago," she mumbled loudly enough to make her point.

"Sure did," Boxers growled. "It passed the minute you said you were staying here."

"There's still time to drive away," Jonathan reminded. "You might pass them on the road, but there's a chance."

"I'm not leaving my family," she said.

"Then why don't you stop complaining?" Thomas said. "Honest to God, Mom, you're embarrassing us."

"Don't talk to your mother that way," Stephenson snapped.

"Hey!" Jonathan was sick of the bickering. "How about everybody just can it for a while, okay? We've got final preparations to make yet, and we don't need the infighting. We're to the point where you're either on board, or you're a liability. Just let it go."

He sent Stephenson upstairs to monitor the computer screen and take some of the stress off his leg. Then he directed the others to gather all the furniture into a pile in the center of the room downstairs. With the walls free from obstruction, there'd be easy access to the windows, and they'd be able to maneuver quickly in the dark to secure better fields of fire. The windows themselves were all open wide to keep from having to break out glass when they came into service as gun ports. On Jonathan's instructions, Jesse Collier had fastened all of the doors to their jambs with two-inch screws.

He gathered them all upstairs in the bedroom for one final pep talk. With the draped-blanket light lock taking up one-quarter of the tiny space, Julie and Stephenson sat together on the bed while Thomas sat on the floor at the base of the tiny window. The rest stood where they could, with Gail and Jesse tiered on the stairs. In the light of the kerosene lanterns, their faces showed variations of dread and anger. All except for Thomas, who seemed ready to avenge his days in captivity. Boxers listened from the first floor at the base of the steps.

"Okay, folks," Jonathan began. "Our friends will be with us soon, probably within the next few hours. Listen to me. From this point on, until the shooting is over, the only way in and out of here is through the windows. It's slower than the doors, but the inconvenience largely favors us. I've put the clackers for the claymores on the floor in front of the front door. They are arranged as they are arranged out in the yard. The two middle initiators are for the mines out front, and the outboard initiators power the mines on their respective sides of the building. Do not—I repeat—do *not* activate any of the explosives until you hear Big Guy or me say, 'claymore, claymore, claymore.' We'll say it three times if we need them. Remember, these are weapons of last resort, and if you screw it up, we can be in a world of hurt. Especially me and the Big Guy."

Stephenson scowled—a good sign that he was paying attention. "Why especially you?"

"Because we won't be in here with you. We'll be out there." He tossed his head toward one of the windows.

"Oh, fine," Julie erupted.

Thomas squirmed. "Mom."

Jonathan looked at her patiently. "Remember the plan. If we can maneuver well and if the pieces all fall into place, this lodge will never come into play. That's the goal. But if they send a lot of people, or if we get hit early, you need to be prepared to defend yourselves.

"Steve, I want you to stay on the second floor. The

elevation improves the satellite link, and I don't want you tearing open that leg. The rest of you will spread out downstairs. If they get past us at the ambush site, they'll come up the main road and fan out along the tree line before making their assault across the lawn. Use the NVGs I gave you—night vision goggles. The instant you hear shooting in the distance, put them on and keep them on until this thing is over. If you see anyone approaching and you don't recognize them, shoot, understand? Remember there are six sides to this building—you can't forget the roof and the crawl space underneath—and you've got to keep all of them covered. Don't get so wrapped up in defending one side that you just let people walk in another. When you shoot, go for the center of mass—a body shot. Shoot to kill, not to wound."

"Suppose they're wearing body armor?" Stephenson asked.

"They should go right through. At least they'll leave a hell of a dent. If they get back up, shoot them again."

"My God," Julie said. Her voice trembled as she spoke. "Do you hear yourself? You talk as if this is just another day at the office. Those people you're shooting and then shooting again have heartbeats and souls." She slashed Stephenson with her glare. "And you're with him."

Jonathan had reached his saturation point. "Mrs. Hughes, shut up. These people are on their way to kill you. Everybody seems to understand that except you. With all respect, it's time for you to cowboy up or just simply shut up."

Then to the rest: "Battles are won when warriors make the decision not to lose. Folks, you need to understand that surrender is not an option. We're not defending some strategic objective that can be surrendered to the enemy in return for mercy. You *are* their strategic objective, so there will be no mercy. Do you understand this?"

The Hughes family just stared, stunned.

"It's a real question, people. Do you understand what I just told you?"

"I understand," Thomas said.

"So do I," Stephenson agreed.

All eyes turned to Julie, whose mouth was set in a narrow, angry line.

"Answer him, honey," Stephenson urged.

"I'm not an idiot," she snapped. "Of course I understand." She turned her attention to Gail Bonneville. "Why aren't you stopping this?"

"Because he's right," she said. "Some fights are inevitable. This is one of them."

"But the fight's not yours," Julie said.

"It will be," Jesse said from behind and below his boss. "As soon as the first person takes a shot at me, it becomes my fight, because they brought it to me."

"So you're not willing even to take a chance at peace?"

Jonathan inhaled to fire off an answer, but Gail gestured for him to be quiet and he obliged. Gail cocked her head slightly and softened her tone. "Mrs. Hughes, loving your neighbor is a wonderful concept, but when that neighbor is running at you with a meat cleaver, love doesn't help you. You meet violence with violence, and when it's over, the winner gets to enjoy his peace, but only until the next time it's threatened. If Grave is right—and he seems to be—this will be a peaceful place in the morning. We just have to decide who'll get to enjoy it."

As Julie listened to Gail's words, something changed

in her eyes. Maybe hearing it from a woman made it easier to digest. She just nodded once and looked to Jonathan to hear whatever else he might have to say.

Jonathan nodded his thanks to Gail. "Well said. We're the good guys here and it's time we started thinking of ourselves that way."

Thomas raised his hand to be recognized. "I have a question. If you and Big Guy are outside when the shooting starts, how are we going to know you from . . . the bad guys?"

"Good question," Jonathan said. "When I yell beer, you yell, balloons, and vice versa. Those will be the passwords."

"Beer and balloons?" Apparently Thomas wanted something more exotic.

"You've got to make it a tough link for the enemy to put together," Stephenson explained. Jonathan got the sense that the man was aching for a little attention. "Use something like thunder and lightning and anybody might get it."

"Can we at least be beer and *you* be balloons?" Thomas groused.

"Hell no," Jonathan laughed. "I don't want anybody thinking *I'm* the pussy."

Boxers called from downstairs, "Hey Scorpion, it's time to go. I want to set up the ambush while there's still a little light left."

Julie's horror deepened. "Ambush," she repeated.

Jonathan's radio crackled, "Scorpion, Mother Hen. They're moving. I don't know how many, but the one I can still see is moving, and it looks like he's coming your way."

Boxers was right; it was time to go.

* * *

They'd stacked their tactical gear at the end of the living room farthest from the windows. Jonathan pulled Dragon Skin vests from one of the duffels and passed them out to the Hugheses. "Wear these," he instructed. He handed a second one to Thomas and added, "Take this one to your father, and make sure he wears it. If he objects kick him in the leg." The two that remained were originally for himself and Boxers, but that would leave Gail and Jesse without any. He picked up the remaining two and handed them to the cops from Samson.

Jesse took his, but when Gail shook her head, he hesitated. "You're the ones who'll be out there exposed," she said. "You keep them."

Jonathan shook his head. "No, thanks, I move better without it. Besides, you're my guest."

"I won't do it," Gail said. Jesse looked like he wanted to shoot her.

Jonathan wouldn't budge. "My war, my rules," he said. "Besides, if the time comes when you need these, you're *really* going to need them."

She hesitated.

"Please," Jonathan insisted. He leaned in close and whispered, "I'm serious. If the bad guys break through, you two will be the only ones with your heads about you. If you go down, everybody's got a lot worse chance of coming through alive."

That won her over. She accepted the vest and slipped it over her head. Jesse was way ahead of her.

"Besides," Jonathan said, "I've got this." He turned his attention to his load-bearing tactical vest. Constructed of a lighter Kevlar material that provided some limited protection against small caliber handguns and shrapnel, the tactical vest would do nothing to slow down a rifle bullet. On the positive side, it was ten pounds lighter than the Dragon Skin, and made running a hell of a lot easier. Plus, it had huge storage capacity for ammo.

Boxers was delighted to see that the vests were no longer in play. He never liked the damn things anyway. If it weren't for the standing orders from Digger, he'd never even pack one.

"Remember the night vision," Jonathan reminded as he stuffed the pouches of his vest with as much as they would hold. "Put them on your heads now, and then turn them on when you hear the shooting. Remember what I taught you this afternoon. Julie, if you're not going to be shooting, you've got to be reloading mags. Meanwhile, if things go to shit, Sheriff Bonneville here is in charge. Any questions?"

He almost laughed at the blank expressions. Yeah, there were questions. Too many to verbalize. Jonathan looked Thomas in the eye. "Beer."

Thomas gave a nervous smile. "Balloons."

"Don't worry, kid, you've got what it takes. Just don't give up. Whatever you do, don't give up."

Jonathan looked to Gail to see if she had caught that last bit of coaching, and when the sheriff responded with a nod, it was time to go. "Equipment check, Big Guy."

This was a ritual before every engagement, no matter how large or small. They wore all black, from head to foot, including black Nomex gloves with leather palms for extra grip. Their Kevlar helmets supported their own NVGs as well as their commo gear. A transceiver ran from radios in Velcro pockets on their shoulder into their right ears. The radios could be set to voice-activated or PTT (push-to-talk) mode, and Security Solutions' SOPs required the latter, with the microphone triggered by a button in the center of their chests. Jonathan pushed his. "Radio check, one, two, three."

Boxers gave a thumbs-up. "I'm good."

Jonathan looked to Gail, who realized with a start that she hadn't yet turned her radio on. Jonathan repeated the three-count, and she nodded. "I can hear you," she said, just to make it official.

"Mother, are you on the air?"

"I'm here, Scorpion," she said. "Be careful."

In sheaths mounted on their left shoulders, they each carried a K-Bar knife, and on their chests they each carried two fragmentation grenades. Around their bellies, their ammo pouches carried 400 rounds of ammunition for their M4s, 40 extra rounds for their sidearms, and 18 twelve-gauge rounds for their specially modified pistol-gripped Mossberg shotguns. They carried the M4s across their chests in combat slings, with the Mossbergs dangling by bungee slings from their armpits. The sidearms—Boxers still preferred the new Beretta standard issue over Jonathan's Colt 1911 .45—were strapped to their thighs.

Believing that it was never possible to have too many weapons in a battle, Jonathan also carried a backup snub-nose .38 in the left-hand thigh pocket of his Royal Robbins 5.11 trousers. With the checkoff lists complete, they were ready to go.

"Jesus, look at you," Thomas said. His voice floated with admiration. "You're ready to take on an army. Leave a couple of bad guys for us."

Julie gasped, "Thomas Hughes!"

Jonathan smiled. This Hughes kid was not the stereotypical music major. He had fight in him. It's a shame his mother saw that as a bad thing.

Only twenty minutes of daylight remained as they slid out the window to the porch. "One more thing," he said, looking back inside. "Keep an eye on the computer. As soon as you see vehicles, take your places." They nodded, but they were unfocused.

"Hey," Jonathan said, "look at me. When this is over, we'll have a hell of a story to tell. If you want victory, we can have it. I'll see you all on the other side."

Chapter Forty-one

Charlie Warren felt Garino shift uncomfortably in the driver's seat. He knew what question was coming before the driver had a chance to ask it. "You sure you want to keep waiting?"

Charlie checked his watch. It was 9:20. "Ivan set H-Hour for 10:30. We go in at 10:10." It was the third time he'd answered the same question. "The plan hasn't changed. The plan isn't going to change."

"I just don't want to be late," Garino said.

Glick concurred from the backseat. "He's got a point, Charlie. We wait too long, we run the risk of something going wrong. We slice the clock too thin and Ivan loses his surprise."

Charlie's determination remained unshaken. "If you guys did your jobs properly last night, twenty minutes will be plenty of time. If we go too early, Grave is gonna get spooked and start to adapt." While his research into Jonathan Grave's background had turned up nothing useful, the very fact that the man could remain that invisible told Charlie that he was a man who could seize even the smallest advantage and put it to devastating use.

Charlie knew—as Ivan knew—that Ivan was charging into a trap. The gaffe of using the credit card might have been written off as a stupid rookie mistake, but when the cell phone went live there was no question that they were being lured. Thing was, it was a perfect trap. Even with full knowledge that he was acting as Jonathan Grave's puppet, Ivan had no choice but to go in anyway. Ivan's North African customer had made it crystal clear that his patience had evaporated. He wanted his GVX, or he wanted the blood of the man who failed to deliver.

For every trap, though, there's a countertrap. Warriors become complacent when they think they've successfully pulled a fast one. Often they are the most vulnerable to stunning defeat. Once it became clear to them what Grave's plan was, the counterplan was a slam dunk.

Charlie couldn't begin to guess how Grave had put the pieces together the way he had, but now that he understood that Security Solutions was running things, the details had fallen in place pretty easily for Charlie and Ivan. Charlie proposed that Grave was using some form of tracking technology to follow Ivan's moves, and from that theory, Ivan quickly connected the dots to something called the SkysEye system, which apparently was run by a former Special Forces guy. Ivan didn't know him personally, but he knew of him, and he apparently was a straight shooter. That was bad news for Ivan.

Not that it mattered. It was well known within the Special Ops community that SkysEye had developed technology that built on black programs from the Cold War era to passively track vehicles by their unique heat signature. The weakness, knew those in the know, lay in the fact that the civilian version of the technology required relatively consistent temperatures. Once a target was acquired, the software could extrapolate for minor variations of 100 degrees or so, but if the engine block cooled, the sensors would lose their lock and the vehicle would be invisible.

Glick's and Garino's visit to Security Solutions' headquarters last night had verified Charlie's suspicions: that logistics for the fight would be run from here via satellite link. This Alexander chick would be Jonathan Grave's eyes during the fight.

By turning off all but one engine in the Wal-Mart parking lot, Ivan had blinded them in one eye. At 10:10, Charlie would turn out the lights completely.

It was a classic ambush design. They knew that eight vehicles were on the way, and they knew the route they had to take. The war would begin here at the choke point—the pile of felled trees 800 yards from the cabin. The attacking vehicles would reach the deadfalls, Boxers would blow three more trees thirty meters behind to block off retreat, and then the turkey shoot would begin. Between the two of them, they could create a kill zone of 5.56 mm ammunition that would make survival virtually impossible.

With so many moving parts in the plan, it was ridiculous to expect a hundred percent success once the bad guys started shooting back, but of all the potential complications, the one that most bothered Jonathan was the outside chance that some Boy Scout troop or other group of innocents might somehow wander in. Because it was so ridiculous, it was exactly the kind of complication that a professional warrior had to prepare for.

Jonathan flexed the muscles in his arms and legs to keep them from stiffening. He checked his watch and pressed his transmit button. "Still awake, Big Guy?"

The big man replied cheerily, "Can't wait."

"Gail? How about you in the house?"

"We're okay. We've got the night vision gear on, and we're nervous as cats."

Jonathan appreciated the candor. "And how about you, Mother?"

"I'm fine," Venice said. "I don't yet have a visual on my screen, but the one vehicle I can still track seems to be coming right at you. Just a few more minutes, I think."

Now it was just about the wait. The endless, crippling wait. Jonathan's mind drifted back to the minutes and hours that preceded the countless Unit missions he'd participated in. He thought of these moments as the Magical Hour. Preparations were completed, he was competent and well trained, and all he needed was a bad guy. Like all elite soldiers, he'd lost his fear of dying decades ago. It's going to happen to everyone sooner or later, so why sweat it? Thanks to Dom, his faith in the existence of something—*anything*—beyond this life had been revived, but even his burdened soul didn't bother him. The God he knew had a sense of humor and understood Jonathan's world.

His earpiece crackled. "I've got a visual!" Venice announced. "Eight vehicles on the access road, coming straight at you."

Stephenson was more direct. He shouted, "I've got vehicles in view! I've got five—no, eight—vehicles in view. Jesus, they're almost on top of you!"

"Got it," Jonathan said. "Talk to me, Mother." Nothing Stephenson said would have any weight until Venice confirmed it.

"They're too close for me to call. This four-minute delay is killing me. They should be really, really close, Scorpion. Oh, God, please be careful."

He didn't bother to respond, but he did allow himself a smile. He keyed his mike. "Box, do you see anything?"

"Yeah," Boxers replied with his signature growl. "I see a whole friggin' column. Looks like tanks, in fact. I just thought I'd keep it to myself."

Smart ass. "I copy that," Jonathan said, playing it for real. "Tell me if you see any muzzle flashes."

A moment passed. "You know I was kidding, right?"

Thomas's heart pounded in his ears. The world glowed green in the altered light of the night vision, looking like the television footage from war zones that had been covered by the media. Kneeling at the far left-hand window on the second floor, he'd folded a rubber-backed fuzzy throw rug from the master bathroom into a cushion to ease the pressure against his knees. On the other end of the long room, his father had just taken his post in the other window, choosing to sit in a desk chair and rest the grip of his rifle on the windowsill. Behind them both, Mom sat concealed in the lightproof shelter for the computer.

The clarity of the night vision surprised Thomas. Television added graininess that didn't exist in real life. What he saw was as clear as daytime, only green and drained of contrast. He scanned the tree line, zeroing in on tree trunks and individual rocks to practice his aiming skills. The goggles really didn't change much.

"Thomas, get away from that window," his mother hissed from the darkness.

"Leave him alone," Stephenson said. "He's where he needs to be."

"Steve, you get away, too."

Thomas idly wondered if psychologists would be put out of business if every victim of a violent crime got to shoot at the people who victimized them.

In the third floor offices of Security Solutions, Venice watched her screen and wondered why the attackers hadn't moved. Through three four-minute refreshment cycles, they'd just sat there, barely within the periphery of her visual imagery.

"I've got a heat signature," Boxers said over the radio. "No lights, but a heat signature. They're moving."

She gasped and covered her mouth with her hand. On her screen, everything remained the same. Four minutes was an eternity when you desperately wanted information.

"I see it, too," Jonathan said. "We're coming up on it, people. Stay alert."

Venice closed her eyes and settled herself. Good Lord, how she wished that she could compartmentalize moral issues the way Digger could. Or even Dom. She wanted to live in their world, where all issues were sharply divided between black and white, right and wrong.

Finally, the image refreshed. She let out an audible gasp and reached for her radio.

Before she could press the transmit button, she felt cold steel pressed into the base of her skull.

"Don't move," a voice said.

* * *

Jonathan tucked the butt stock of his carbine into the soft crook of his shoulder and settled the reticle of his 4-power sighting scope. The vehicles were SUVs, and in Jonathan's mind that translated to as many as eight attackers. He pressed his transmit button. "I see two vehicles. Hold your fire until my command."

"I copy two vehicles, and I concur," Boxers replied.

Where the hell was everybody else?

Jonathan didn't like it. By all accounts, Ivan Patrick was an experienced fighter, and smart. It only made sense that he would split his forces, but where would the others go? "Steve, are you there?" he whispered into his microphone.

Stephenson Hughes whispered back, "Right here."

"Check that fire road. We're missing too many people here."

After a long pause, Stephenson said, "Let me get back to you."

"Get back?" Boxers hissed. "How 'bout you fucking *hurry*?"

"Stow it," Jonathan snapped. "Mother, where are the other vehicles?"

No answer.

"Mother, I need a report on the other vehicles. I've only got two in sight. Where are the others?"

Still nothing.

Shit.

The nearest SUV navigated the bridge without lights, and when it reached the deadfall, it stopped. Jonathan watched as five men, all of them armed, dismounted. While the second SUV hung back on the safe side of the bridge, three of the dismounts took up defensive positions on circumferential compass points, while the other two examined the roadblock. The invaders were all within sixty meters, easily within the kill zone. He watched intently as they examined Boxers' handiwork at the felled tree, and he continued watching as they drew their forces back to the driver's window for a battlefield powwow.

"Want me to shoot the other trees?" Boxers whispered.

"Not yet." *Where the hell were the others?*

Jonathan tried to put himself into their heads. Did they smell the trap? God forbid, were they setting one of their own? One thing was certain: If they tried to back up or drive away, he'd have Boxers shoot the remaining trees. They would not get away.

Then the driver of the SUV opened his door and stepped out, and all of the contingencies were pushed to the side. "Stand by," Jonathan said.

Boxers acknowledged without a word by breaking squelch, a silent "Roger."

Stephenson's voice came over the radio, sheepish and hesitant. "Um, Scorpion? A bunch of them found the fire road. I see a bunch of them. Six vehicles. Maybe twenty people. You need to get up here."

The goddamn fire road. The one that no one knew about. Somehow Ivan had gotten his hands on a better map, or a newer map, and he'd set up a trap of his own. He remembered Boxers calling it their Achilles' heel, and he cursed himself for not having taken it more seriously.

"Scorpion?"

Jonathan watched the line of fighters approach in their ragged single-line formation. They each carried a rifle—Jonathan saw a couple of M16s, and what might have been an AK-47, but it was hard to tell through the trees. He saw clearly, however, that they likewise were equipped with night vision gear. But there were only two vehicles' worth. It was a feint, and Jonathan had fully committed himself to it. He had to take care of these skirmishers before he could return to the lodge.

Stephenson's voice crackled in his ear, "Scorpion, are you there? What do you want us to do?"

"Try shutting the fuck up for a few minutes," Boxers hissed. "Wing it."

Jonathan didn't argue. "We'll be there as soon as we can," he said.

The approaching enemy moved too noisily, but otherwise their discipline disturbed him.

"Gettin' awful close, Dig," Box whispered.

With Jonathan and Boxers on either side of the primitive roadway, there was a trade-off on how long to wait before engaging the enemy. Closer meant an easier fight, but too close increased the likelihood of the ambushers shooting each other.

Jonathan steadied his forestock on a deadfall and fixed his sight on the man in the lead. "Stop where you are!" he yelled. "State your business!"

At the sound of Jonathan's voice, the leader whipped his weapon around. He was still moving when Jonathan dropped him with three precisely aimed bullets. Even in the green light of the night vision, he could see the brains fly.

"Shoot the charges, Box!"

The world erupted. The tree charges fired in rapid succession, a ripple that pummeled the air with crisp, bright concussions.

The invaders scrambled for cover, most firing wildly as they scampered and slid behind whatever they could find. One of them made a break for the lead SUV, but Boxers dropped him with a burst before Jonathan could react. As the rear vehicle threw its transmission into reverse and tried to escape, Jonathan fired three rounds into the vehicle's engine compartment and another four into the wheel well to disable it. He did the same for the lead vehicle. In the light-enhanced view, bullet hits registered as white-hot flashes.

"Stay together!" someone yelled. "Do not retreat! Return their fire!"

Boxers fired another burst at the source of the sound, and Stonewall Jackson shut up.

Jonathan could see all kinds of movement, but he resisted the urge to shoot until he had a defined target. Each pull of the trigger launched a muzzle flash that told an opponent your exact location. The spray-and-pray approach of the movies was suicide in real life, as was running and ducking. In low light, a moving target was easier to detect than a stationary one. It's why ambushers have the advantage over ambushees.

"Over here, assholes!" Boxers yelled, and he emptied half a magazine toward the spot where the enemy had last formed a line. It was a damned risky way of getting your enemies to reveal themselves, but Boxers had never been averse to risk.

The attackers opened up with everything they had, ripping the night apart with noise and light, thus sealing their fate. Jonathan knew his cue. A shooter's face resided three feet behind a muzzle flash. He picked a flash, and squeezed off a burst. When that rifle dropped, he found another flash and repeated the process, although without a hit, he thought.

Predictably, the rifle fire turned, and Jonathan dove to the ground under a storm of bullets that shredded the foliage around him. He tried to make himself disappear into the ground behind a hardwood. He could feel the impact of bullets through the trunk.

* * *

Moments earlier, in the lodge, the Hughes family had gathered around the computer screen to watch. The heat signatures from six separate vehicles lined up along the ridge that ran behind the cabin.

"How could he have left us like this?" Julie railed. "We even talked about it. How could he do this?"

Thomas barked, "What the *fuck* difference does it make now?" She looked like she'd been slapped, and he enjoyed it. "They're there and we're here."

They'd taken off their night vision to keep from whiting them out with the computer screen, and in the blue glow, Thomas watched his father rub his neck the way he always did when he was contemplating a problem.

In the distance, they heard three quick shots, and then a second later, three explosions that seemed to trigger the rolling fusillade that was Jonathan's firefight.

Thomas climbed from behind the blanket-formed light lock and darted to the front window. He replaced the goggles and looked toward the shooting. "Sounds like they're tearing 'em up," he said. He looked back to his family. "It's really happening." He brought his rifle up and waited.

Behind him, Julie huddled with Stephenson, and that pissed Thomas off. He wanted his father to quit coddling her and take command. He wanted him to step up like Scorpion and issue orders for everyone.

Thomas hated the fact that they were hiding—cowering—as Scorpion did the dirty work. It was shameful. When this was over—

"Oh, God," Stephenson said from the light lock. "They're swarming down the hill in the rear. The picture just refreshed. My God, there are so many!"

Thomas moved back to the light lock to see for himself. He could see people now. His eyes went first to the fighters who were engaging Scorpion, frozen in time as they faced off almost nose to nose. Then he saw the swarm of images on their way down the hill.

He counted them. Jesus, could that possibly be right? Could there possibly be twenty attackers, plus the ones with Scorpion? They were still a long way off—a half mile or more, probably—but they were on their way in a wide loop that looked like a noose around the cabin. "We need to get ready," he said. "We need to get downstairs." He shouted, "Gail! Jesse! They're on their way!" He started for the stairs.

Julie grabbed him to make him stop. "No! They said to stay up here where it's safe."

Thomas pulled away. "The attack is coming from behind," he said. He slapped the heavy timber wall. "There are no windows up here that face backward." Neither his mother nor father moved. To hell with them. He spun and bolted for the stairs, catching his shoulder in the blanket that formed their light fort and bringing all the equipment crashing to the floor. He'd killed SkysEye, but he didn't care. It was time to fight.

Jonathan scooted to his right, parallel to his enemy and away from the spot where they'd last seen his muzzle flash. They kept shooting at that spot, just as he had hoped. When people thought they had you pinned, they got sloppy and exposed themselves to return fire. Jonathan would make them pay for the mistake.

Across the hill, Boxers opened up again.

A deafening *crack* got Jonathan's attention as a bullet passed inches from his right ear, slapping his head with its shock wave. Instinctively, he rolled to his right and dove for cover behind a deadfall, just a heartbeat ahead of a second bullet that would have killed him. Christ, he thought. The last thing he needed was a shooter who knew his craft.

Jonathan had to move. Pressing his belly into the ground, he crawled as quickly as he dared to the base of an upright tree, where he raised his head just enough to peer through the underbrush. Silence had engulfed the battleground, a noise far more unnerving than the actual sounds of war. Silence could mean too many things. In the best of conditions, it meant that your enemy was dead and that the engagement was over. More times than not, however, it meant that he was moving for advantage.

His mind revisited a Unit op in El Salvador when he had lain like this for seven hours, trying to remain perfectly still while outwaiting the patience and training of his opponent. Back then, he'd three times talked himself into believing that the bad guy was dead and had nearly stood when he'd decided to give it just a little longer. When he was finally, *finally* convinced that he was waiting for a dead guy, his enemy had dared to trust his own instincts. As the enemy rose oh-so-cautiously, Jonathan had shot him through the throat.

Tonight, lying in the weeds, light enhancement wasn't doing him any good, so he moved his left hand to his helmet, where he switched his NVGs to infrared mode. The picture was far less vivid, but it allowed him to read heat signatures through the shrubs and undergrowth. Close to the ground like this, virtually everything was warm, though—from the mulch floor to the rocks and even the trees themselves. In this kind of environment, the trick was to find the abnormality, the thing that stood out as different. Nature was made of random patterns—mottled light, drooping branches, swaying grass—and that randomness formed its own pattern. What you looked for was the *absence* of randomness. You looked for the bush that swayed less in the breeze, or the pattern of leaves that didn't quite match the surrounding foliage. You looked for a mound of dirt that moved, as if to breathe.

But there was nothing out there.

Off to his left, and now behind him, he heard another burst of rifle fire from Boxers' segment of the battlefield. He heard a yell as someone was hit, and then the return fire began all over again. Muzzle flashes appeared as fireflies in the infrared view.

Jonathan did not react to the explosion of noise, but the prey he sought couldn't help himself. Jonathan saw movement from a mere ten meters away. He fired.

CHAPTER FORTY-TWO

"Why are you doing this?" Venice demanded.

The intruder refused to answer. At gunpoint, she'd been forced to bind her own ankles with duct tape to the legs of a guest chair in her office, and then to tape her own left wrist to the arm of the same chair. When the intruder was satisfied with her work, he then bound her right wrist and revisited the other three points of bondage with much tighter, more aggressive loops. Finally, he fastened her elbows, eliminating movement.

When that was done, the man, whom she now recognized from her Internet searches to be Carlyle Industries' security chief and from Mama's description as the man who'd approached Roman, slid behind her desk and squinted at her computer screen.

"For heaven's sake!" Venice barked. "Would you please say *something*?"

Charlie Warren's head didn't move as his gaze shifted to her. "Watch the attitude, Ms. Alexander. You are two strips of tape away from suffocation." A smile bloomed on his handsome face. "There's also that fine son of yours to worry about. Much too young to die."

Something inside Venice dissolved. "You wouldn't."

"Maybe I already have." He transformed his voice to a mocking falsetto. "Ow! Ow, you're hurting me! Please stop! Mommeee!"

Enraged and terrified, Venice pulled at her bonds.

Charlie Warren laughed. "You know I'll just shoot you if you wriggle free, right? Go for it." He squinted as he watched the images on the screen. "Ooh, looks like they're in trouble."

The world tilted inside Venice's head. The image of Roman yelling out to her was so real, so vivid. Could this man really do such unspeakable things to a child?

Of course he could. Look what they did to Tibor and to Ellen. When the stakes were high enough, she realized, cruelty had no limits. This man in her chair, behind her computer screen, was a monster.

Why hadn't he killed her already? He *needed* her to be alive. But why?

Her role was a tactical one, she realized. He needed her alive for a specific reason. She reran the events of the past week and she landed on her answer. "I'm your insurance policy," she announced.

His gaze shifted again from the screen.

"You need me alive as a bargaining chip in case Ivan Patrick fails. If Digger—if Jonathan lives through the attack, you're going to use me to get your weapons back."

The man tried to maintain a poker face, but she could see that she'd nailed it.

In an unexpected burst of bravado, she added, "And you are Charles Warren, security director for Carlyle Industries. Your picture is on the Web site. That's probably not very smart."

"I'd be careful," Charlie warned, looking back to the

screen. “Start thinking too hard and I’ll have no choice but to kill you.”

“You’re going to kill me anyway.” She wanted to sound bold, but angered herself with a tiny catch in her voice.

The man smiled. “Maybe I should get it over with.”

Venice smiled back. “You can’t. Not yet. Jonathan wouldn’t do anything to help you unless he had—what does he call it? Proof of life. Like the movie.”

“Pretty smug for a condemned woman.”

She looked at him hard, as if trying to see through him. “You know he’ll kill you, right?”

The man laughed. “And cocky, too.” He nodded to the screen. “What I see, I won’t have much to worry about.”

“He’s very good at what he does,” she said.

“So am I.”

By denying nothing, he’d just confirmed everything. She asked in a strong voice, “Do your bosses know that you’re committing murder for them, Mr. Warren?”

His eyes narrowed to slits. “You talk way too much.”

“I just wanted to be sure that my suspicions are correct.” She nodded to the blinking light on the telephone near Charlie’s elbow. “Are you going to answer that?” she asked. “I keep the ringer silent.”

He eyed the phone, then looked back to the screen. After twenty seconds, the light stopped blinking.

“Bet you didn’t think we’d be here doing this tonight,” Jesse quipped. He’d stationed himself on the far right side of the kitchen, leaning both forearms on the sill. Something about his appearance in his NVGs made Gail think of a kid playing soldier.

"Not in a million years," she agreed. "Sorry about getting you into this."

He chuckled. "Oh, don't worry about it. I'd've probably done something stupid with my night if I wasn't here. You know, gone to bed early or something."

"I shouldn't've pushed you to come along."

He pulled in from the window to look straight at her. "Don't you go getting all guilt-laden on me now. I'm the one who insisted I was coming." He leaned back into the window. "Not that I wouldn't go for a do-over with twenty-twenty hindsight."

Jesse asked, "You still gonna bring your man in for the shootings? And these people for the Caldwell murders?"

It was the question of questions. She'd sworn an oath to the people of Samson, and now she was cursing the day that she'd raised her hand to God.

It turned out that the question was rhetorical. "You know, I never shot at anyone before," Jesse said.

"Most people haven't," Gail said. "Consider yourself fortunate."

"I just wanted you to know. I don't know why, but . . . Well, I just did."

A crash from upstairs startled them both, and they whirled to see Thomas pounding down to the main level, one hand gripping his rifle and the other the railing. As he reached the hardwood at the bottom of the stairs and slid to a halt, he slapped his NVGs down in front of his eyes and addressed them both. "They're here," he said. "And they're attacking from all sides."

He hurried to Gail's window on the left-hand side of the kitchen and slid into place next to her.

"No, I've got this," she said. "You cover the front."

He shook his head aggressively. "This is where they're

going to hit us," he argued. He described the picture they'd just seen on the computer upstairs.

Gail appreciated his zeal to repel the attack, but she shook her head. His logic was flawed.

"Just because they parked at the top of the hill back there, it doesn't mean that's the direction they're going to attack from," Jesse said, stealing her thunder. "Certainly it doesn't mean that will be the *only* direction of attack."

"You don't have to protect me," Thomas protested. "I'm not going to wuss out on you."

Gail put a hand on his arm. "Remember what Scorpion said about six sides. We have this one covered. You and your family need to take care of the front."

Thomas scoffed, "Yeah, me and my family." He pulled away from the window. "It's gonna be awful lonely."

Stephenson hobbled into the doorway. He leaned against the doorjamb favoring his left leg by putting all his weight on his right. "I'm not the coward you seem to think I am," he said. "I'm just a little slower than normal today." Julie appeared next to him.

Thomas's shoulders slumped. "I didn't mean that the way it sounded," he said.

His father smiled. "Yeah, you did, and that's okay. Emotions are running a little high all around."

The family drama thing puzzled her. Clearly, there was a lot of history there that she couldn't begin to understand, and about which she truthfully didn't much care. She sensed Jesse's gaze, and she turned, expecting one of his signature smirks. They'd just made eye contact—lens contact, really—when his head exploded with a horrifying *whop.* Bone and brain tissue erupted in a gruesome wet cloud, spattering every nearby surface.

He fell without a sound.

Gail screamed, "Jesse!" and rushed to him.

She heard Julie scream, and someone said "Holy shit!" People started running. More shooting erupted. The stench of blood and gunpowder brought her back to that liquor store in Oak Brook, Illinois, when she'd done everything by the book and caused a death there, as well.

With the memory came the pain.

With the pain came a commitment to even the score. To even a lot of scores, in fact. Not to avenge Jesse's murder, but that of the little girls in Illinois, and of Angela Caldwell, and of every other victim of every other crime who found themselves caught in a system that cared more about process than results.

She was about to become what she loathed.

Thomas just stood there, trying to take in what he'd just seen. Trying to ignore the blood that he'd felt hit his cheek. It was as if Jesse's death took everything away—oxygen, light, sound, everything. Nothing moved.

Then everything moved, all at once. He started for the front windows, and his mother grabbed his arm. "No, Thomas," she said, "don't you see? I don't want that to be you."

He yanked his arm away. "Then fight, goddammit!"

"Thomas—"

"I'm not dying here!" he shouted. He dashed into the front room and slid on his knees to the left front window. He rested his forestock on the sill as he scanned the darkness. Behind him, from the kitchen, the rate of fire increased as his father took the place vacated by Jesse, and the attackers started firing back.

Thomas forced himself to ignore that battle, however. Having seen how simple it was to kill a man who was not paying attention, he vowed not to let that happen to the rest. If there was a threat out there in the front, then he was going to see it and engage it. Even in the dyed light, details of the yard were clear. Over there to the right was the fake wishing well that covered the real wellhead. Surrounded by chairs, it was positioned to view the setting sun. Off to the left, he saw the empty water bottles left behind from the afternoon's shooting lessons. A few feet from that, the wooden swing set that had once been the only cool thing about visiting this place swayed gently.

But there were no people.

An upsurge in shooting down the hill startled him. In all the excitement here in the lodge, he hadn't realized that Scorpion's battle had stopped for a while.

Something moved in the starlight shadows cast by the trees on the edge of the yard. He almost hadn't seen it. Then he saw it again, definitely movement this time. He pressed himself closer to the protection of the heavy timber wall and pulled the rifle in closer to his shoulder. He squinted for a better view, but it didn't work that way with the goggles. You got the view you had, take it or leave it.

Now there was more than one.

"We've got them in the front yard!" he yelled.

Three shadows emerged as people, and they moved cautiously but quickly toward the house. It was as if they'd heard Thomas's warning (and why wouldn't they?).

He settled on the figure farthest on the right and he pulled the trigger. The gun bucked with a deafening report, but the three figures kept coming. "Shit!" He fired again. And again. Jesus, why didn't they fall?

Then the return fire started. Chunks of wood erupted from the window frame, peppering his face with chips as bullets burrowed into the timbers. Behind him, on the opposite wall, decorative plates disintegrated as the hutch that supported them was torn apart. With his face pressed against the heavy timbers of the lodge's outer walls, he could feel the wood humming under the onslaught, as if infested with enormous angry bees.

Keeping the rifle close, he rose to take another shot, trying to ignore the incoming bullets as he exposed only enough of himself to take aim.

He yelled reflexively as he saw that there was an attacker only ten yards away, nearly at the front porch. The man saw him, too, and raised his weapon. Thomas jerked the trigger and the man toppled backward into the grass as the unaimed bullet hit its mark. But he wasn't dead. On his side and clutching his belly, the faceless attacker howled in agony. Somehow, the sound of his pain rose above the thunder of the gunfight.

Pleased with himself, yet horrified at the result, Thomas ducked to the floor again, his back to the outer wall, and squinted into the void of the cabin. Out of the shadows, a man came right at him, lumbering at a crouch across the living room from the kitchen, clutching a machine gun and ammo vest in his fist.

Thomas raised his rifle, but hesitated. And by hesitating, he spared himself the anguish of killing his own father.

As the battle raged up the hill, the fight down in Jonathan's and Boxers' sector seemed to have ended. "Box, are you okay?"

"Hale and hearty. I got three confirmed kills."

Jonathan waded through the bushes and scrub growth to address the body of the shooter who'd nearly taken him out. Jonathan's rain of bullets had torn the man apart, opening gaping wounds in his chest and head, and completely severing his right arm at the elbow.

Good fight, he told the man silently.

"I got two more," Boxers announced. "These guys died in each other's arms. Ain't that sweet?"

Sometimes, Jonathan couldn't stand his friend. He enjoyed this part of the job way too much.

Jonathan didn't bother to report his one confirmed kill. "Time to get back into the fight," he said.

Dropping the spent mag out of his M4, he slapped in a new one from his vest, and took off at a run back up the hill toward the lodge. To his right and behind, he could hear Boxers trying to keep up, but he knew he'd lose him soon. Between the extra weight and his titanium thigh, Boxers was built more for endurance than speed.

"Steve, give me a situation report," Jonathan panted into his radio. When he got no reply, he tried again. "Gail, how are you holding out up there?"

Still nothing. What the hell was going on with the radios? First it was Venice and now the Hugheses. Without either of them, he was blind out here.

It sounded like they were locked in one hell of a war.

Chapter Forty-Three

Dom hated being outside the loop on Digger's escapades. Tonight in particular, he had the sense that his old friend was in over his head, and he wanted to *do* something. The fact that Venice was ignoring her phone made it even worse.

He stayed out of it because Digger wanted it that way, probably to save him from the burden of the violence, but Dom sensed that there was also an element of shame. Noble rationale notwithstanding, he hated being left outside the circle.

He couldn't take it anymore. As a *Seinfeld* episode reran on the rectory television, he realized that he no longer cared what Digger thought. Dom's rightful place tonight was at the firehouse helping Venice cope with the stress of being Digger's link to the world. If that pissed her boss off, then let him be pissed.

Grabbing a gray jacket to ward against the chilly evening, he called to Father Timothy and told him he was going for a walk.

The breeze off the water made the night feel more like March than April. He shot the collar of his jacket and stuffed his hands into the front pockets as he made his way down the hill toward the firehouse, two blocks away. Scanning the dark, empty streets, it was hard to imagine the madhouse it was going to be in two short months when the tourists returned. He made a mental note to remind the Town Council to repair the streetlights. On a moonless night like this, footing was treacherous for anyone who didn't know the lay of the land. After years of practice, Dom knew to expect the loose bricks in the sidewalk near the corner at Second Street, and he adjusted his stride accordingly.

Passing the darkened silhouette of St. Kate's on his left, he fought the urge to double-check the sanctuary doors. He wasn't a fan of locked churches anyway. If the fear of mortal sin still prevailed in society, he'd have left the doors open to serve the homeless. He considered it a failure of the modern church that such kindness was no longer possible in today's world.

Just past the church and its grounds rose the six-foot colonial-style brick wall that surrounded the parking lot and back doors of the firehouse. Jonathan had erected the wall within months of purchasing the property as a means to keep people from turning into his parking lot from Church Street, and to provide some element of privacy.

Approaching First Street at the bottom of the hill and the marina that lay across, the temperature dropped another five degrees. Dom had always loved this view of the water through the forest of darkened masts, swaying in the gentle waves of the river.

He turned the corner and knew that the peace would not last. In the otherwise deserted streets, a heavily jacketed man sat across from the firehouse on a public bench in the tiny Veteran's Park among last summer's flower carcasses. The newspaper he held spread above his lap could not possibly be legible in the yellow glow of the single streetlight across the street.

"Hello," Dom said with his most priestly smile.

The man looked startled at first, then grunted a quick, "Good evening, Father," before he returned to his paper.

Dom noted the formality and concluded he was at least a Catholic.

There are no coincidences.

It all felt very wrong. Over the span of a second or two, he inventoried the status quo, beginning with the fact that Digger was in the middle of an uncontrolled shit storm. Add to that the fact that Venice didn't answer her phone—Venice *always* answered her phone—and cap it with a stranger sitting in a place where no reasonable man would be, reading in light that allowed him to see virtually nothing.

Something bad was about to happen.

No coincidences.

Maybe something bad was already happening

Dom said nothing more to the man. He just kept walking. He turned left at the corner of Gibbon Creek Road, at the far end of the firehouse, and fought the urge to quicken his pace as he turned left again and entered the alley formed by the portion of Jonathan's brick wall that separated his parking lot from St. Kate's. The night felt suddenly colder, and Dom found himself wishing that he'd grabbed a heavier jacket.

At the height of the workday, there would be as many as fifteen cars parked in the lot on the back side of the firehouse; at this time of night, it was usually barren. Tonight, however, the lot hosted a single vehicle, parked as far from the security light as possible. He thought he could see a silhouette behind the steering wheel, as if someone was watching the back door. He paused there in the mouth of the alley before continuing his stroll back up the hill toward the church.

Dom glanced up at the third floor as he strolled, hoping to see some sign of activity, but the blinds were all pulled, as they so often were when Venice worked alone at night.

Maybe he was overreacting. Jonathan was paranoid as hell that his friends and his staff might be victimized as a result of his work, and he'd years ago insisted that Venice and Dom both have sensors implanted under the skin near their armpits that would allow for easy tracking if the worst happened. He also insisted that they both carry panic buttons—Dom's in the form of a crucifix, and Venice's in the form of a gold pendant—that would kick emergency procedures into gear if needed. Venice had a panic button in her desk that would accomplish the same thing. If she were in the kind of trouble that Dom suspected, wouldn't she have activated the system?

He decided he didn't care. His father had once bestowed upon him some great advice: sometimes, if there is doubt, then there really is no doubt at all.

Dom took a deep breath and found a shadow where he felt most invisible. He pulled his cell phone from his pocket and dialed the number for the police department. He briefly thought about calling 9-1-1, but decided against bringing too much attention to what was fundamentally a gut feeling.

The smoky voice that answered the phone could have been male or female. "Fisherman's Cove Police Department. Is this an emergency?"

"No emergency," Dom said. "Is Chief Kramer in his office?"

"Who's calling, please?"

"This is Father D'Angelo with St. Katherine's Parish. I'd like to speak with the chief if I could."

"Good evening, Father. I'm sorry, sir, but the chief is not available at the moment. It's a little late."

Of course it was a little late. After ten-thirty, for heaven's sake. He should have thought of that. "I'm sorry, I don't know what I was thinking. I'll give him a call at his home."

"You can try, Father, but I don't think you'll have much luck there, either. He took off early this afternoon to head into the District to visit his mother. Would you like to speak to the duty officer?"

And say what, he wondered. It was one thing to bring Doug Kramer into the mix—he'd already pieced together the fundamentals of Security Solutions' larger mission—but he felt uncomfortable confiding in any other cops. "Chief Kramer's really the one I need," he said. "Did he mention when he might be coming back?"

"The duty board shows him in tomorrow, but other than that I don't know. Do you want me to page him?"

"No, that's okay." If he was in downtown DC, there'd be no way for him to get back anyway. "It's just a personal matter. Thanks for your help."

The dispatcher started to make another recommendation, but Dom had already signed off. What was he supposed to do now?

He tried calling Venice one more time, but after six rings and no answer, he ended the call and found himself facing the same dilemma as before.

He narrowed his options to one: he had to go check on Venice himself. If she was in trouble, he'd do what he could to help, starting with a call to 9-1-1. But how was he going to get inside? If there was in fact someone in that car, he couldn't let himself in through the back door, and the guy on the bench took the front door out of play.

Good thing there was another door that no one knew about. As he approached closer to the church, he started to jog.

"Dammit, Gail, answer me!" Jonathan barked into his radio. The whole world was coming unzipped up there, and no one would talk to him. He knew they weren't all dead yet, or else the shooting would have stopped. For the whole of his uphill run—to the half-way point—he kept trying to reach someone, *anyone* who could clue him in on what the hell was going on.

"Venice, answer up," he said, changing tacks. "What do you see?"

Again, all he got in return was silence.

Gail snapped a three-round burst, then ducked behind the protection of the timber wall. The volume of return fire startled her. Long volleys smashed into the house, tearing chunks of wood away from the edges of the window. Incoming rounds from the front of the house eroded the inside wall to her right, while behind her, the incoming fire through her window tore up the inside of the front room. The result was an internal kill zone that made rising higher than a crouch a capital offense.

They couldn't possibly sustain this onslaught for much longer, and the rapidly diminishing supply of ammunition shortened their survival clock even more.

Something had to change or they'd all be dead in a few minutes. Stephenson took the initiative to gather magazines from Jesse's body and redistribute them among the surviving friendly shooters, but it was nowhere near enough.

In the far corner of the living room, tucked in a corner that provided the maximum cover, Julie Hughes was doing her best to become invisible. "Julie!" Gail yelled above the din. "You need to reload the empty mags. And you need to do it quickly!" She picked up two empties from the floor at her feet and threw them across the expanse of the room. "Thomas! Steve! Slide your empties to Julie!"

She hoped that by not soliciting a vote, she could force Julie to handle the chore without argument.

Soon, it wouldn't matter.

"Use the mines!" Julie yelled from her shelter. "There are too many of them! Use the mines!"

"No!" Thomas and Stephenson answered together.

"Scorpion might be out there," Thomas added.

He realized they were losing. Throwing Scorpion's instructions to the wind, he'd changed the selector on his rifle from single-shot to three-round burst. The improved volume of fire slowed the attackers down, but as the breech on his weapon locked open for the third time and he inserted his fourth and final magazine, he realized that he was thirty rounds away from being in real trouble. Even as the thought passed through his mind, he fired another two bursts. Make that twenty-four rounds from a world of hurt.

He slid the empty mags across the floor to his mother. "Hurry, Mom!" he shouted. She moved in slow motion, as if in a trance.

There were no targets, per se, to shoot at. Instead, he found himself targeting the sparkles of muzzle flashes along the tree line and in the grass. His father had repositioned to the rear of the house again, where he apparently had all kinds of targets to shoot at, emptying clip after clip of automatic weapons fire through the two windows he commanded.

Out front, the man Thomas had shot would not shut up. He screamed like a wounded animal, begging for someone to help him. If it hadn't been so unnerving, it would have been sad. Twice, as Thomas stuck his weapon through the open widow to take another shot at the tree line, he'd considered helping the poor bastard to a bullet to his head, but both times he stopped himself. What was the point of wasting a bullet on someone who was already hit?

He fired two more bursts. "Mom! Hurry on the reload! I'm almost out! You've got to work faster!"

But she'd either gone deaf or was ignoring him, because she just kept her head down and continued to fumble with the rifle he'd already slid to her. "Jesus, Mom! Hurry." She was unmoved. It was as if she'd set a pace for herself, and was by God going to stick to it.

A two-man team charged forward, and he cut them down.

His breech locked again. Unarmed now, and facing a yardful of attackers, just what the hell was he supposed to do? As the wounded man continued to scream, Thomas heard his father fire another six or seven shots through the back window.

"This is fucking crazy," he mumbled, and he scrambled on hands and knees across the wooden floor to his mother, who was crying as she struggled with the bullets.

"I'm sorry," she snuffled. "I'm trying, I'm really trying."

He snatched the magazine from her, along with the

box of bullets, and scooted back toward the window. It felt about half-full. There had to be a better way.

Wait. There *was* a better way.

No, it was crazy.

No, it was the only answer.

Spinning like a propeller on the smooth pine floor, he scrambled back to his mother and grabbed her arm. "Mom, come with me," he said.

She looked horrified. "I can't."

"You *have* to." He tightened his grip and dragged her toward his window.

"Ow!" she hollered. "Thomas, you're hurting me!"

He ignored her, even as he heard his father boom his name from the other room.

Once again at the window, he peeked up long enough to fire again into the night, and then he ducked down again. He was back to single shots again. He snapped the NVGs out of the way and stared at the lens of hers. He shoved the rifle into her hands. "You've got to shoot."

She tried to pull away, but he wouldn't let her. "No!" she whined. "Someone has to reload. *I* have to reload. I promise I'll do it faster."

"Mom, goddammit, shut up and listen to me. All you have to do is fire out the window. Just for a few seconds."

"I can't."

"And try not to hit me."

That last part flew right by her, unnoticed. "I can't do it, Thomas. Please don't make me."

He leaned in and kissed her on the cheek. "Then don't," he said.

He snapped his night vision back into place, and hefted himself up and over the sill into the night.

The rate of fire outside doubled.

Chapter Forty-four

Dom entered the sanctuary through the side door and locked it behind him. He made a beeline for the space behind the confessionals where a semiconcealed door led to the concrete stairway into the basement. As intimidating an underground space as Dom had ever seen, the cavernous basement under St. Kate's had been blasted out of solid rock during construction back in the thirties, and as far as Dom knew, it still contained every item that had ever been deposited there. Boxes of old bulletins and stacks of broken furniture lined the walls, and in the middle, stoutly constructed metal shelves held all manner of old toys, tools, gardening equipment, and even three cases of beer that might have dated back to Prohibition. Even with the overhead lights turned on, you needed a flashlight to find anything. Over the years, Dom had considered assigning children to the task of cleaning the place up as a form of particularly aggressive penance, but always backed off in the end.

He hurried to the far side and pushed an ancient Nativity scene out of the way to gain access to the mostly blocked heavy door that would take him into Jonathan's tunnel. A crooked picture hid the keypad, which was recessed into the concrete wall.

Dom settled himself before entering the code, knowing that he only had three shots at getting it right. He punched the 14 numbers carefully, using the ridiculous mnemonic that he'd never shared with anyone. "TRA HELEFUNT BOX" produced the numeric code, 8-7-2-4-3-5-3-3-8-6-8-2-0-9, an entirely random cipher. He pressed Enter, listened as the locks slid out of place, and then pushed the heavy panel open. Using the green glow from his cell phone, he found the light switch. Fluorescent light tubes flickered to life, revealing the passage.

Once inside, he didn't bother to close the door on his end. Instead, he took the eight steps to the tile floor in two strides, and ran the distance to the other end, where another heavy door stood between him and the basement of the firehouse. As he entered the identical code, it occurred to him that he'd never passed through this portal without Jonathan at his side. In fact, be believed that this was the first time he'd even been in the tunnel alone. What would be the point? When the locking pin cleared, he pushed on the door to open it.

It resisted him. It felt as if something on the other side was in the way. He pushed harder, and when the door still pushed back, he gave it everything he had. The door gave way, and as it did, Dom realized what had been holding it back.

He'd forgotten about the empty oil tank that Jonathan used to camouflage the entrance on his side. It fell onto its side with all the stealth of a cymbal crash.

Charlie Warren's head whipped from behind the screen as the building shook with a rattling *bang*. He shot an angry look at Venice, but whatever it was had startled her, too.

He snatched his cell phone from the desk and pushed a button. "What the hell was that?" he asked. He spoke into it as if it were a walkie-talkie.

"What was what?" a voice asked.

"That bang. I heard a big bang."

"I heard nothin' out front," the voice said.

"What about you, Garino?" Charlie asked.

A different voice said, "I didn't hear anything either."

Charlie scowled. "You seen anything unusual?"

"I've seen nothin'," the first voice said. "Not even any people, for Christ sake. This is one dead town. Only thing I saw was a priest out for a night stroll."

Venice's heart jumped.

Charlie's eyes narrowed as he looked straight through her. Into the radio, he said, "Garino, I want you to come in through the back and check out the downstairs."

"What am I looking for?" Garino wasn't being difficult; his question sounded heartfelt.

"Anything," Charlie said. "A priest, maybe." As he said that, he watched Venice and smiled. "And if you see one, shoot him."

"You want me to shoot a *priest*?" He sounded horrified.

"A little late to worry about hell, don't you think?" Charlie jabbed. "Let me know whatever you see."

Thomas fell hard onto the wooden porch, and as he did, the tree line became a light show of flashing strobes. Bullets slammed all around him, pulverizing the wall and the floor and peppering him with shredded wood.

Moving faster than he knew he was capable of, he rolled two times to his left and dropped from the porch onto the ground, where a long divot caused by years of rain-water erosion along the front edge of the porch provided some shelter.

"Thomas, get in here!" his mother shouted.

"Jesus, Mom, shoot!"

This was a really, really bad idea. He was in the middle of a war without a weapon, with the whole world trying to shoot him. Paralyzed by terror, he tried to figure a way to move either backward or forward without getting torn to pieces. Pressing himself into the ditch, he inchwormed backward, parallel to the porch, until he was even with where he thought the now-silent screaming man had fallen.

Suddenly the man's gun and ammunition seemed less important. With remarkable clarity, he decided that he was fucked. The moment he raised his head, he would die.

Then he heard the rapid fire of a machine gun from behind him, and his father's voice yelled, "Go get it, Thomas! I'll keep their heads down."

It was his best chance. Thomas closed his eyes, made himself as skinny as possible, and hoisted himself out of the trench onto his belly. He kept his butt low as he crawled like a frightened lizard toward the lump that was the fallen attacker.

A giant crescendo of incoming gunfire made him cringe, but the piercing impact of a bullet never came. In fact, the bad guys' aim seemed to have worsened. His dad's distraction was working, drawing fire away from him toward the front window.

Quickening his pace, he dug his fingers and toes into the cold hard ground, filling his sinuses with the smell of dirt and his own fear. Then there was something else, a horrific stench that brought images of rotted dog shit. The ground grew damp, and within a few feet, it became wet and slippery. With each inch forward, the awfulness increased by a factor of ten, until, as he finally was upon the body—and that's clearly what it was now, with its open eyes and lolling tongue—he realized that he was lying in the man's spilled intestines.

The horror of it hit Thomas hard. Without thought or preamble, he vomited all over both of them.

Jesus God, what had he done to this man?

Two bullets slammed into the dead man's side, and two more whizzed past Thomas's head, their supersonic whip crack pounding his eardrums.

Fuck this. Now was not the time for reflection or regret. It was time to load up with ammunition and make more of these bastards look like their friend here.

The dead man's rifle—an M16, Thomas remembered from the History Channel—lay on the ground next to the body. He snagged it by its sling with his right hand, and pulled it in close. But a rifle by itself was no good without the ammunition to feed it, and this dead man carried his ammunition all over his body, the way that Scorpion did. Thomas started to remove the man's vest, until another near hit changed his mind. Grabbing the man by his collar, he dragged him back toward the shelter of the divot. He ignored the long rope of entrails that snaked along behind them.

Jonathan tried one more time to raise someone on the radio, and cursed at the continued silence. He considered that the Hugheses might be dead, but if so, then who was everybody shooting at up there? Given the heat of the battle, he was willing to forgive Stephenson for losing track of his radio, but there was no excuse for Venice leaving her post like this.

He crossed the final rise and saw the scale of the assault being mounted against the lodge. This really was a war.

Ivan's strategy was obvious. The attackers had formed a wide V-shaped formation, coming at the lodge from its front and right. He imagined that there were attackers in the rear, as well, but that part of the house was invisible from his angle. Jonathan cursed himself for having underestimated his opponent. There wasn't much he could have done differently, short of reading Ivan's mind, but that didn't change the fact that their tactical situation sucked.

He keyed his radio. "Hey Box, are you close?"

"Right behind, you," he said, inches away from Jonathan's ear.

He damn near shit his pants. "Goddammit, don't do that."

Boxers laughed. "This doesn't look good for the good guys," he said.

"Yeah, well, just wait." He explained what he wanted to do.

To Dom's ears, the crash of the oil tank was louder than an explosion. It reverberated off the concrete walls, echoing like a gunshot in the Grand Canyon.

Running was out of the question. If Venice was in trouble, he had to help her out. And staying put was out of the question, too. The words of a long-forgotten football coach bloomed in his memory: *If you're not moving forward, then you're going backward.* Reborn in the acid bath of panic, he heard the advice as, *If you don't get out of this basement, you're going to die.*

Again using the light of his cell phone as a guide, he navigated through the assembled junk and glided up the stairs into the old hose tower, and from there, through the utility room. He held his breath as he cracked the door to the living room open an inch and looked around. Everything looked as it always did: neat, organized. In the glow of the street light that painted parallelograms of light through the old bay doors, he could make out the outlines of the furniture. There were no signs of a break-in or struggle.

Heart pounding, Dom stood in the threshold of the hose tower, waiting to see the response to his cacophonous entry. He inched his way into the cavernous living space. His feet sank into the thick Persian carpeting as he headed for the ancient brass pole and the stairs that surrounded it. He'd nearly cleared the cluster of sofas and chairs in the middle of the living room when he heard a scraping sound at the back door. He froze.

Dom had a clear, unobstructed view of the back door's mullioned half-window, and through the fabric of the sheer curtains, he watched the shadowy silhouette of a man who seemed to be peering back at him. The man turned his shoulder to the door and pushed. It creaked against the jamb, but it didn't move.

Dom cursed under his breath. He was in the open. Frozen in place, he watched as the silhouette backed off and then threw itself into the door. The impact reverberated through the concrete floor. Once more, and the intruder would be inside. Father Dom D'Angelo, man of peace, crouched low and prepared to defend himself. In the space of a heartbeat, his army training flooded back.

The third attempt at crashing the door did the trick. Glass and wood splinters flew as the beefy thug stumbled through the door with a pistol in his hand.

Dom raced straight at the man, slamming him hard in the face before he had a chance to recover his balance. Dom clamped the intruder's gun hand in a crushing grip while he thrust his right elbow into the center of the man's throat and drove him backward into the fractured door. The pistol fell to the floor.

The man made pitiful gurgling, coughing sounds, but Dom wasn't finished. Moving with speed and gracefulness that he didn't know he possessed, Dom's grip on the now-empty gun hand never loosened as he wrenched the attacker's arm up and out and back, then broke it across his knee at the elbow. The crack and the agonized scream felt like victory as the man fell, but the noise was a liability. Dom silenced him with a savage kick to the head.

The whole fight had lasted less than ten seconds.

Chapter Forty-Five

The combined stench of blood and shit and fear was crippling. In the trench along the front porch, it settled around Thomas like a cloud, flooding his sinuses and soaking his clothing. He just wanted it to be over. Keeping low to the ground and close to the gore, he worked with trembling hands to pull ammunition magazines from the pockets of the dead man's equipment vest and stuff them into his own. As his hands slickened with blood, the process became more difficult. Above him, the lodge vibrated in the onslaught of violence.

He stopped after he'd stolen six magazines. He just couldn't take the company of a corpse anymore.

He crawled along the length of the ditch toward the far end of the porch. From there, he'd . . . *what?* How the hell was he going to get out without getting shot to pieces? It's one thing to roll over and flop down into a ditch, but how was he going to reverse the process? He'd be helpless and fully exposed.

"Thomas!"

The sound of his name above the din startled him.

"Thomas, are you all right?" It was his father

"I'm here!" he shouted. "I got a gun and bullets!"

"Get back in here!"

"How?"

"Thomas, just stay down!" his mother yelled.

Dad shouted, "Come around to the back! From the end of the porch you can run around—"

A fusillade of bullets ripped at the floor of the porch just above Thomas's head. They'd locked in on his position. He needed to move. Now. His only viable plan was to emerge from the trench as fast as he could, then dash around back and hope that there weren't a thousand bad guys waiting for him.

"Thomas, did you—"

"I heard you!" he shouted. *And so did everybody else*, he thought. Where the hell was Scorpion?

He rose to his knees, with his elbows still pressed to the ground, butt up, then raised his head to take a look. The flashes in the trees had become people now, and they were moving toward him in a wide line that ran parallel to the front of the cabin. With the distorted vision, he had no idea how far they were, but it couldn't have been more than forty or fifty yards.

On impulse, Thomas brought his new rifle to his shoulder, rested the forestock against the ground, and picked a target. He squeezed the trigger just as he'd been taught, and jumped as the muzzle spit out a long burst in full-automatic mode. The target he'd picked flopped like a rag doll onto the ground, and the four or five attackers closest to him dove for cover.

His hidey hole became the battleground's most popular target. Bullets shredded the wood and churned the turf at the edge of the porch. Thomas heaved himself out of the trench onto the open ground, falling forward into the grass and eating a mouthful of turf. Behind him, the section of ground he'd just left was consumed by a sustained burst of incoming fire. Scrambling to get his balance, his feet found traction and he ran for the nearest corner of the house.

Three steps later, a sharp jolt slammed him hard and he yelled in horror and pain as his leg hinged up at mid-thigh and his own foot kicked him in the face.

Venice could see the fear in Charlie Warren's eyes and hear it in his voice as he tried unsuccessfully to raise his people on the radio. He glared at her. "What's going on?"

Completely immobile, and at the whim of this man who seemed intent on killing, Venice opted to say nothing.

"Do you know a priest?" Charlie asked.

"We live next to a church," she said. "This is a small town."

"What would he be doing here?"

She shook her head. "I have no idea."

"Call out to him. Tell him that you're busy and can't be disturbed."

That didn't even make sense, she thought. Why would she say such a thing?

"Say it," Charlie repeated. This time he pressed his pistol to her head. "If I see anyone, I'm going to shoot."

"Dom!" she shouted. "Is that you?" If nothing else, maybe she could save his life.

No one responded.

"Is that the priest's name?" Charlie asked. "Dom?"

Venice nodded.

"Tell him to stay away."

She took a breath. "Dom, if that's you, I don't have time for you. I'm busy."

Again, no reply.

"Maybe the noise was nothing," Venice offered. "A picture fell off the wall."

Charlie flashed her an angry look. "Pictures don't scream," he said. He moved away from her, closer to the door. He adjusted his grip on the pistol. "Whoever it is, is about to be shot." He placed his hand on the knob and turned it.

Even in the cacophony of the gunfire and above the piercing sounds of Stephenson's shouting, Gail heard the bullet hit Thomas, a wet snapping sound. They all heard it. Julie screamed, "Oh, my God! Thomas!"

Stephenson scrambled for the window.

Gail yelled, "Steve! No! I'll get him!"

"He's my son," Stephenson said. And that said everything. He heaved himself over the window and onto the porch with a clattering thump.

Julie reached for his ankle, but he was already gone.

The volume of fire outside crescendoed. But for the heavy timber walls, they'd have all been torn to pieces.

Gail started to crawl across the cabin to Stephenson's window, then realized that a chance to hit a second target at the same spot would spell disaster for her. Acting on pure impulse, she turned and vaulted out of her own window into the tall grass that still rimmed the foundation in the backyard.

She braced herself for a brutal fusillade.

Alone now inside the cabin, Julie felt blinded by a terror she'd never known. Thomas and Stephenson both were out there being raked by bullets. She couldn't lose both of them.

Where was Scorpion? And his obnoxious sidekick?

How could they leave her like this? Even her own family had left her. She didn't want to die.

Her gaze fell on the detonators. The clackers. Giant shotguns. Their last resort. Their Alamo position.

The only way to save her boys' lives.

But Scorpion might be out there among the attackers.

"Don't do anything unless you hear me say . . ." Whatever. Something. How was she to know if Scorpion was even alive anymore?

She didn't care.

Dom knew from her voice alone that Venice was in distress. Her message was out of character. She needed him.

Yet here he stood, paralyzed by indecision. He knew it was a trap. If he walked through that door, God only knew what might come next. He'd get shot, probably. But to stay out here while Venice was in danger in there was . . . *cowardly*. How could he—

The turning doorknob settled it. Dom darted to the hinge side of the door and waited. When the tongue of the latch cleared the strike plate, he launched his full weight against the heavy panel.

As he'd hoped, his explosive entrance caught the intruder off-balance. He backpedaled to keep from being propelled to the floor, but unlike the man downstairs, this one was agile and light on his feet. As Dom clutched fistfuls of the man's suit jacket and tried to drive him to the floor, the intruder effortlessly pirouetted free. His hands were empty, though.

The intruder struck a martial arts pose, and Dom knew right away that he was in trouble. Army training notwithstanding, Dom could not prevail in a hand-to-hand confrontation. He prayed for a weapon, and in that instant saw the intruder's pistol on the floor. That was his only hope.

The intruder moved first. He seemed to have read Dom's mind as he struck like a snake to throw a punch at the left side of the priest's head—the side closest to the weapon on the floor. Dom dodged it, but in so doing leaned into the path of a left hook that caught him square on his cheek, in front of his ear. He heard a snapping sound, and instantly his sinuses filled with the smell of blood.

Reeling from the blow, Dom staggered backward into the coffee table, which caught him behind his knees and sent him tumbling to the floor. He knew without doubt that his jaw had been broken. And he knew that the pistol was still on the floor. He could see it. If his arms were four inches longer, he could have touched it.

If only he could move. But he *had* to move. He had to save Venice or die trying. Rolling to his side, he stretched his arm to its full length and beyond, a lunging reach stretched his shoulder nearly to dislocation. He might even have made it but for the kick to his forehead. Lights flashed behind his eyes, and he felt himself balanced in a sickening netherworld between consciousness and coma.

When his vision cleared, he saw the pistol in the intruder's hand.

Then he heard the gunshot.

The Green Brigade advanced on the lodge. They moved out of the tree line, shooting constantly, laying a deadly volume of fire on the cabin.

There was nothing nuanced or subtle about Jonathan's plan. He and Boxers split left and right and came at the line fast and hard from their right flank. Jonathan circled to the left to come in from behind, while Boxers circled to the right to hit them on an oblique angle from the front. If the plan worked, they would close in on the attackers in a quickly advancing V-formation and roll them up to their left.

He advanced in a walking crouch, his weapon to his shoulder and set to fire three rounds with every trigger pull. When he saw a bad guy, he shot him, center of mass, and moved on to the next. No time to confirm the kill or worry about him hopping up again.

There are rhythms to war, ebbs and crescendos that no one plans, but that nonetheless give audible clues about what was happening. Presently, as he closed in for his third undetected kill, Jonathan heard a shift in the action, a peak in shooting that seemed less random, more focused. He looked to his right, through the trees, in time to see someone dart out from the cabin, only to be cut down.

He spat an obscenity and nearly turned back to reacquire a target, when more movement from the front of the cabin triggered an even more intense fusillade. Jesus Christ, one Hughes was trying to save the other.

Jonathan needed to support them. He brought his rifle to his shoulder, sighted on a muzzle flash, and fired a three-round burst. A weapon spiraled off into the darkness.

A brilliant flash near the lodge startled him, followed by the distinctive *wham* of a claymore. Whatever lay in the woods to the left side of the lodge was now torn to bits.

In his earpiece, Jonathan heard Boxers' shout, "Who the fuck—"

* * *

The fusillade never came. Even as Gail was airborne, tumbling out of the window, she'd expected to be torn apart by incoming fire, but somehow she was still here.

She didn't pause to wonder why, or to thank God, or to even give it much of a thought. One of her team was dead, two were wounded, and she had to bring them to safety. She didn't think any of these things, she just knew them; sensed them as her duty.

Gail belly-crawled on elbows and knees to the back corner of the house, and then around to the left-hand side. In the near distance she saw Thomas on the ground writhing in agony, screaming curses to the night while his father covered him with his body. They were alive. Beyond them, she saw the attackers closing in. They were charging now, at a full run, closing the distance with remarkable, terrible speed. Their formation had taken the form of an L, closing in from the front and left sides.

So much violence here, yet no more shooting in the rear. Finally, she understood the violence of the initial attack. They'd been raining covering fire in the rear to mask the joining of the two skirmish lines.

But there was even more to it than that, she realized. They were protecting the true target of their assault. "Oh, my God," she said aloud. "They're—"

A blinding, white-hot flash took the world away.

The echo of the first claymore was still rolling across the yard when a second one erupted, this one on the left side of the front of the house. Ahead of him, through the green light of his NODs, Jonathan saw people and vegetation shredded by the high-velocity pellets as they shrieked through the night, destroying everyone and everything.

In his three decades as a warrior, he'd never been on this end of a claymore, and it was orders of magnitude louder than he'd expected. *If you hear the explosion, you're okay.*

But not for long. Since he was just outside the arc of that claymore, he could count on being just *inside* the arc of the next.

He slapped the transmit button on his chest. "Box, get—"

The last word was cut off by the explosion.

Inside the lodge, Julie had nearly forgotten that it took three clicks to detonate a mine. On her first try, she'd squeezed the initiator only once. When nothing happened, she quickly squeezed it twice more, and was again disappointed. Third time, she squeezed it three times rapidly and screamed as the explosion ripped the night.

She'd thought it through as best she could. She remembered that the danger zone behind the mines didn't allow you to be very close. If she didn't shoot them now, she didn't know when the attackers would be behind the kill zone or when Steve and Thomas might be in front of it.

Moving without pause to the second detonator, she did it right on the first try, and this time, the detonation flashed within her peripheral vision: a brilliant light, then a cloud that obscured everything. The punishing concussion came an instant later.

She moved to the third, wrapped both hands around the clacker and cowered behind the timbers as she squeezed and counted aloud. "One. Two. Th—"

This blast was a hundred times louder than the first two, but only for an instant before her ears shut down from the pounding. The inside of the lodge erupted in splinters and broken glass.

Then she felt nothing.

Dom thought he was dead. He *had* to be dead. How could the killer have missed? He felt a pair of strong hands on his shoulders, and a vaguely familiar voice saying, "Father? Father! Jesus, are you all right?"

The voice crystallized before the images did. It was Doug Kramer.

"I'm alive?" Dom asked.

"Are you shot?" the chief asked.

As much as he hurt, he might have been, but he honestly didn't know. He was on the floor of Venice's office, on his back, and to his left, he could see the contorted face of his attacker flush with the carpet, twisted in obvious pain. "I can't feel my legs," the man cried, but Kramer seemed unmoved. On the far side of the prone intruder, Dom saw that Venice was still bound tightly to her chair.

"I got your message," Kramer explained. "I got here in time to see some guy trying to break in through the front door. Him and his unconscious friend are handcuffed to the stairs down there. I came up here when I heard all the commotion."

Venice wriggled against her bonds, making her chair jump. "Cut me loose," she said, and then, as if catching herself, she added, "Please. Digger needs me to be at the computer."

Kramer cocked his head, then looked around. "Digger."

"You gotta help me," Charlie whined.

"Ambulance is on the way," Kramer said. "Digger's here?"

Dom scooted across the floor to tend to Charlie's injury. He pushed the man's tie out of the way and ripped open the front of his shirt. He found the exit wound first, just above and to the right of his navel. The entrance wound was square in the spine. "Can you tell them to hurry?" Dom slurred through his fractured jaw. "He'll bleed out without help."

"I can only call 'em, Father. I can't drive for 'em." In the distance, sirens grew louder. A lot of them. A shooting in Fisherman's Cove was the biggest of big deals.

Kramer pulled a Swiss Army knife from his pants pocket and slit the tape on Venice's arms first, and then the loops on her ankles.

She leapt back to her keyboard. "Please let there be something left to do," she prayed under her breath.

CHAPTER FORTY-SIX

"Holy fuck," Boxers exclaimed over the radio. "They turned the claymore on the cabin! They had sappers!"

Again, a more advanced, more daring move than Jonathan would have expected. "BDA?" he asked. Boxers would recognize the acronym as Battle Damage Assessment. From Jonathan's vantage point, the view was still obscured by dust.

"Heavy to extreme," he replied in the detached monotone of a warrior. "I'll get you more in a minute."

Heavy to extreme. That said it all, even as it said nothing. And it fit the tableau of destruction that stretched out in front of Jonathan. The night had gone silent again, and as Jonathan advanced on the skirmish line that no longer was, his stomach tightened. In her panic to stop their advance, Julie—and it had to have been Julie—had unwittingly exposed the one critical flaw in Ivan Patrick's training regimen: the attackers were jammed too close together. It was instinctive among humans to seek community in the presence of mortal danger, an instinct to be overcome on the battlefield. A single claymore had killed or maimed what looked to be over a dozen Brigadiers.

As his hearing returned to normal, the silence gave way to the agonized cries of the wounded. He saw bodies and parts of bodies everywhere. Where he encountered attackers who were still alive, he disarmed them and let them be. "We'll get help on the way as soon as we can," he said, over and over again, even as he walked on. He wasn't interested in prisoners, and he had neither the time nor the resources to guard them. If they lived, good for them; if they died waiting for help to arrive, such was the price of being a Bad Guy.

His earpiece crackled as a radio broke squelch, and he heard Venice's voice. "Scorpion, this is Mother. Do you copy?"

"Where the hell have you been?" Jonathan growled.

"Too complicated for the airwaves," she said. "What's your situation out there?"

"Unclear. At least one friendly is down. Many OpFor. We're still securing the scene."

"What about Big Guy?"

Before Jonathan could reply, Boxers said, "Couldn't be better. Thanks for asking. Scorpion, the kid's bad. We need to get him to a doc pronto."

"What about inside the cabin?"

"Haven't checked yet. Getting the kid's bleeding under control first. Any sign of Ivan?"

It was a reasonable question, but it was too early. "So far, no sign of him. I got a lot of body parts out here need to be matched up, though."

"Be careful of stragglers with attitude," Boxers warned.

Another good point, but Jonathan didn't reply. He figured that everyone who could was running full-tilt toward someplace safe.

Venice said, "We have transportation ready if you're up for it."

"And our special guest?" Jonathan asked.

"Last I checked, he was scared and ready to go."

"Start them on the way. When they're ten minutes from touchdown, make the second call and bring the world."

"Roger." Coming from Venice, the military jargon always sounded stilted and forced. There was a lot of commotion in the background on her side of the transmission.

Jonathan keyed his mike. "What's going on there? I hear noise."

She hesitated. "Worry about you," she said. "We'll talk about us later."

"Us? Who's 'us'?"

"I just got a refreshed satellite image," Venice said, dodging his question. "On infrared, I see . . . My God, Digger, what happened there?" Infrared records heat as a paler color than background. Spilled blood has its own signature, registering as great splashes. He wagered that Venice was looking at one hell of a mess.

"Just get the help on the way."

Standing among the carnage, his rifle once again to his shoulder, Jonathan turned a slow pirouette, scanning each minute of the compass for some movement, some indication of danger, but he saw nothing that he hadn't already noticed. The scene was as secure as he could make it.

He started toward the lodge.

The right-hand side of the building had been ravaged by the explosion. The porch was gone, reduced to splinters on the side farthest from the door. A small fire burned from the newly created woodpile along the front edge. From the blast pattern on the ground, he could see that the sapper hadn't just turned the mine on the building, he had moved it to within ten yards of the porch, to devastating effect.

As he closed the distance even further, though, he saw that front wall had held for the most part. Heavily scarred and gouged, it appeared that the timbers had repelled the main brunt of the claymore's deadly assault. The exception was the area around the front window on the right, directly in front of the mine, where a huge chunk had been torn away, a divot along the upper edge that was maybe a foot in diameter. Whatever pellets made it into the inside of the cabin would have caused one hell of a mess.

"Julie?" Jonathan called. "Are you in there? It's safe to come out now." Nothing.

Dreading what he was about to see, he waded through the wreckage of the porch and positioned a half-consumed two-by-four as a bridge from the grass to the top of the pile. With his weapons dangling, he gripped the bottom sill and pulled himself up to chin-height, and then used his shoulders and forearms to wriggle through and onto the floor of what only an hour ago had been a quaint living room.

Now, it was a demolition zone. Nothing remained whole. Very little remained even recognizable. The claymore pellets had savaged everything, if not on their initial impact, then undoubtedly as they ricocheted from wall to wall

"Julie?" he called. "Julie Hughes! Are you here?"

He kicked broken furniture and glassware to the side as he walked to the spot where he'd left the initiators. And there she was.

She lay on her right side facing him, her head oddly skewed by its angle against the timbers of the front wall. A smear of blood masked her ear and matted her hair. He approached quickly, dropped to his knee, and pulled off his Nomex glove to check for a pulse in her neck. He smiled as he felt her carotid artery strumming solidly under his fingers. He pressed his palm to his transmit button.

"All units, this is Scorpion. I found PC-Three and she seems okay. Unconscious, but a good strong, regular pulse." Boxers would be able to fill in the blanks, and maybe Venice. Barring an unseen, serious head injury, Precious Cargo Three would be okay. He stood and walked toward the kitchen and noticed the body on the floor in there. Jesus, they'd had themselves a hell of a time. "How's PC-One?"

Boxers answered, "He hurts like hell, but his vitals seem strong. Gonna have a leg like mine, though."

Jonathan inhaled deeply, held it, and let it go. All things considered, it all went better than—

"Hey, Scorpion," Boxers added. "The sheriff is down, too. Unconscious. I don't know her status."

Something moved in the yard out back. Jonathan was certain he'd just seen someone running, from right to left.

"Big Guy, Scorpion," he said into his radio, getting Boxers' attention. "PC One and Two with you?"

"Affirmative."

"You on the black side of the lodge?"

"Negative. We're on the green side. Problem I should know about?"

Jonathan headed for the back window and climbed through. "Thought I saw something out back. Gonna check it out."

"Tough for me to join you, boss. I'm still workin' on the kid."

"It's okay," Jonathan said. "If you're not there, I don't have to worry about shooting the wrong guy."

Jonathan dropped to the ground on the other side of the window. He rolled to his feet, in a crouch, and tucked his M4 into his shoulder. He scanned for targets.

More corpses littered the ground, but nothing moved. He pressed his transmit button and whispered, "Mother, this is Scorpion."

"Go ahead," Venice said.

"What does your latest satellite image show?"

A pause. "No change that I can see," she said. "But with these four-minute updates . . ."

She didn't need to complete the observation. A lot of ground can be traveled in four minutes.

He ran scenarios through his head. Maybe the guy was just running away, trying to get the hell out. He dismissed it out of hand. First of all, he was running in the wrong direction to escape. Out here, with the narrow yard and the steep, bald embankment, there was precious little cover, and it would be hard as hell to run uphill fast enough to get away from anyone.

Then he got it. "Big Guy, I think he's going for the GVX."

"Five minutes," Boxers said. "Give me that and I can join you."

"Maybe it's Ivan," Jonathan said.

"Four minutes, then."

Jonathan liked the idea of a one-on-one with Ivan. Could he possibly be that lucky? It made sense, though. What need was there for Ivan to lead the attack when the odds were so stacked in his favor? Why take the risk, when all he wanted in the first place was the germ juice?

"Scorpion?" Boxers asked over the radio.

"Stay put," Jonathan said. "I'm going in."

"Don't take chances, man," Boxers said. There was a pleading tone that Jonathan rarely heard. "It's probably just one of the soldiers. You don't know that it's Ivan. Even if it is, he's trapped in there. You don't have to do anything unless he tries to get out. We'll lay a siege on his ass until we get reinforcements up here."

Reinforcements—if you could even call them that—were an hour or more away. Too much could happen. Jonathan pulled the transceiver from his ear and let it dangle on his chest. He knew the risks. He knew that a one-man search of a building the size of the barn was stupid. He'd taught the courses, for Christ's sake. He could recite the doctrine. But none of that mattered when you got a chance to face down your wife's murderer. Her torturer. Maybe he didn't want help because he didn't want anyone to witness what he was about to do. Maybe he didn't care about the danger because he worried more about the thought of Ivan Patrick living free.

Or of him living at all.

Having crossed the yard undetected, he paused at the heavy door to cobble together a plan. All things considered, Jonathan actually had a sliver of advantage. Having seen the interior in the daylight, he knew the basic layout, while Ivan could not. He also knew for sure where the GVX was hidden, while Ivan could only guess.

Okay, it was a narrow sliver of advantage. And it didn't come into play until Jonathan was safely inside and behind cover. In that first second after entry, though, framed by the open door, even on a dark night, it was like having a "shoot me" sign on your chest. And these particular doors opened out, making it all the more difficult. At least they weren't latched shut.

He let his M4 fall against its sling, and brought up the pistol-gripped Mossberg to take its place. The Mossberg's buckshot loads would do all the damage that needed doing at close range, but had much less likelihood of passing through his target into the nasty shit.

With his weapon at the ready, he stood and steeled himself. *Get in, and get to cover*. That was the entirety of his plan.

He used the fingers on his left hand to throw the heavy door open and he dashed through the slot into the darkness. Three steps in, he heard the staccato burp of a suppressed submachine gun—a Mac-10, he guessed, just from the outrageous rate of fire. With the silencer in place, the weapon sounded like riffled playing cards. The impact of the bullets in the wall behind him made twice the noise of the explosions that launched them on their way.

Jonathan dove for a patch of dirt behind one of the barn's massive support structures. In the three feet when he was airborne, he felt a bullet tug at his shirt-sleeve, and one tear a chunk out of the heel of his boot. In the shadow of the pillar, he drew himself up to create as small a target as possible. "That you, Ivan?"

His answer came as another long burst, this one stitching up the other side of the pillar.

"Whoa!" Jonathan taunted. "I was hoping for better marksmanship."

He waited for the next burst, which was shorter than its predecessors, signaling an empty clip. Jonathan took it as his cue to move. He found his feet and dashed deeper into the shadows, closer to the truck, placing the vehicle between himself and the shooter. If his enemy had been looking down to change clips, he wouldn't know where Jonathan was anymore. It was time for silence. Time to listen.

On the far side of the truck, he heard rustling, the sound of feet moving across the dirt floor. He lowered himself to the ground so he could peer from under the truck. If something moved, he'd shoot it. He waited for a shadow. A noise. Anything.

Another rustle, this one farther to the left. The shooter was moving toward the pillar that Jonathan had just abandoned. Or maybe he was moving to position himself behind Jonathan. From the direction of the noise travel, either scenario was possible. Jonathan faced a choice: He could remain still or he could reposition himself to better cover on the far side of the truck. The latter would effectively corner him.

He opted to wait a little longer, hoping not to squander his advantage. He resisted the temptation to shoot at the noise because it would be a rookie mistake. The chances of hitting your target were nil if you couldn't see what you were shooting, and in trying, you'd announce your location to the world.

The third time he heard the rustle—it was really more of a scrape this time—it was still farther to the left, well past the location of the pillar. That confirmed that the shooter was moving for position. If Jonathan could remain still enough for long enough—

A soft *pop* startled him, and an instant later, a blinding white light consumed the darkness. Jonathan slapped his night vision out of the way, but it was too late. The illumination flare had whited out his NVGs, and the glare dug into his eyes like spikes. Temporarily blinded, and completely vulnerable, he fired the Mossberg in the direction of the last noise, then jacked another round and fired slightly to the left, and then another slightly to the right before scrambling for cover under the truck.

With his ears and eyes all ruined for the short term, he rolled again to the far side of the vehicle and whatever cover it could provide. He was sickeningly aware that a stray bullet through one of the containers inside the truck would render a gunfight moot. Blinking rapidly, *frantically*, to erase the white blur on his retinas and regain some semblance of night vision, he moved toward the front of the barn. Until his senses returned, or until he knew where his opponent was, his only chance lay in his ability to keep moving.

But the same rules applied to his enemy. Sure, he no doubt looked away and shielded his vision from the erupting flare, but even now, as his eyes adjusted, Jonathan would still be invisible on the far side of the light. To get a bead, the attacker would have to cross to Jonathan's side of the truck.

Would it be from the right or the left? He backed off from the truck to open up his peripheral vision, and to see the front door, in case the gunman pulled a fast one and tried to make a straight run for it. Two steps more and he was flat against the cowling of the tractor, directly under the overhang of the . . . loft!

He more sensed than heard the second attacker over his head. Maybe it was an errant shadow cast by the illumination flare, or maybe it was a creaking board, or maybe even a sixth sense, but in a flash, he realized where the next attack was coming from. He raised the shotgun to a vertical position and pulled the trigger, but the man dropped onto him in time to be inside the sawed-off barrel. The powder and flash got them both though, singeing Jonathan's eyebrows and raising a welt on his cheek. The attacker fell over the cowling of the tractor, but he never really lost his balance, landing on his feet in a power stance with a Beretta 9 mm pistol closed in his fist and ready to fire.

Jonathan reacted without thinking, calculating instinctively that he didn't have time to jack another round or to draw his .45. Instead, his fist found the handle of the K-Bar knife on his shoulder. He drew it in a fraction of an instant—in less time than it took to aim a pistol—and he slashed at the attacker's weapon hand, severing tendons and nerves in his wrist and causing him to drop the Beretta onto the floor. He took a step closer to the man and slashed in a wide arc up his belly and across his throat. In the shadows cast by the flare, the erupting fan of blood appeared black. The man fell like a stone.

Jonathan whirled for a second attack, but nothing happened.

"Dig, are you okay?" It was Boxers, calling from the other side of the door. "I'm coming in."

"Box, no—"

The big man dove through the door and to the right, just as his boss had done a few minutes before. "Did you get him already?"

"Not all of them."

"You look like hell. Was that Ivan?"

Jonathan shook his head and pointed to a spot along Boxers' wall, toward the back of the building. He let the Mossberg fall back against its sling, and traded out for the M4 again. Facing this direction, he didn't have to worry about accidentally hitting the truck.

The two of them moved as one, as they had so many times in the past, in so many foreign lands, Boxers high and to the right, Digger low and to the left.

Boxers saw it first. He rose to his full height and tightened his grip on his rifle. "You in the corner! Don't move! Not a muscle!"

Jonathan darted ahead to get a glimpse around the corner of the pillar. A man who looked remarkably like the attacker whose throat Jonathan had just cut lay on the floor in a lake of his own blood. Boxers flipped on the tactical light on the muzzle of his rifle, and in the glare, it was easy to see that Jonathan's snapshot Mossberg blasts had pounded at least five holes in the man's neck and left shoulder, so large and ragged that he knew they had to be lethal.

Boxers poked the man with his weapon. "Hey, you alive?"

"Feel for a pulse," Jonathan said.

"I ain't stickin' my fingers in that mess."

Jonathan rolled his eyes. He stepped into the blood and squatted low to lift the wounded man's chin. His eyes were open and focused, and neither one of them bore the awful scar that defined the man Jonathan wanted most to kill.

"Where's Ivan?" Jonathan demanded.

The man smiled. Then his eyes lost focus as his life soaked into the filthy floor.

Chapter Forty-seven

The transfer went smoothly. Including Thomas and his parents and all of the surviving attackers, the Blackhawk took off just six minutes after it had touched down with a load of only eight civilians in the cargo bay. For enough money and the right connections, there were confidential solutions to every kind of problem. In about an hour, they'd all be off-loaded at an Army medical facility outside Cincinnati whose physicians and staff were used to providing outstanding medical care to people about whom it was their responsibility to know as little as possible. For Jonathan, access to the network of clandestine medical facilities both domestically and abroad was one of the great perks of his connection to the Unit.

Jonathan watched the loading process only as long as it took to make sure that the Hugheses were aboard, and then he turned to Boxers, who still held his M4 at the ready, slung across his chest. "You too, Big Guy," he said.

Boxers didn't even look at him.

"Box, this is it."

"I'm staying," he said.

Insubordination from Boxers was more startling than sniper fire. “The hell you are,” Jonathan started to say, but he pulled the words back and opted for a softer approach. “It’s the plan,” he said.

“Plans change all the time. I’m not leaving you here to take the heat by yourself.”

Jonathan sighed. “Look, I appreciate the loyalty—”

“Then shut up and send the chopper on its way. We’re running out of time.”

Jonathan stepped around to stare him straight in the eye. Well, straight in the Adam’s apple anyway. “You’re medic trained. You can help the kid and his mom.”

“The bird is full of medics as it is. They don’t need me. I’m not letting you take the fall, Dig.”

“It was my mission, Box. And my fuck-up, and now this is my recovery plan. You’ve done—”

“I’m not going.”

Honest to God, they didn’t have time for this. Jonathan made one last try. “Tell you what. If things go wrong, and they end up taking me to jail, you can lead the mission to get me out.”

Even in the darkness, he could see the sparkle of interest. “Out of a jail here in the U.S.? No way.”

“If it goes that way, I’ll be counting on you.”

Boxers shifted his gaze back to the distance as he considered it. “You know that’s impossible.”

“I know no such thing. Not with you in charge.”

Boxers snorted, “You are so full of shit. What about her?” He nodded to Gail Bonneville, who held both hands to her head, which had obviously not yet cleared of the cobwebs caused by the blast wave of the claymores.

Jonathan smiled. “You know I’m a sucker for a pretty woman.” When he didn’t get the chuckle he was hunting for, he added, "The next call is hers. I made a deal."

Boxers rose to his full height, gaining a couple of inches as he drew in a deep breath and then let it go as a noisy sigh. "I'm staying," he said, but as the words came out, he stammered a little. He didn't make a habit out of saying no to his boss.

Jonathan was stunned. He'd heard excuses before, and objections, but he couldn't remember the last outright mutiny.

"If we need to break out of anywhere, we'll do it from the inside," Boxers said. He let his rifle fall against its sling. "I've made up my mind, so don't bother to say nothin' more."

There it was. You didn't get much less negotiable than that. As the Army chopper piloted by old friends powered up, Jonathan turned his back to the rotor wash and approached a vaguely familiar middle-aged man who looked like he'd been ripped out of bed and shoved into a pair of jeans and a gray sweatshirt. Boxers kept his distance. The newcomer's expression showed equal parts horror and bewilderment.

"Will Joyce," Jonathan said, extending a friendly, blood-spattered hand. "Nice to see you again."

The man's body didn't move, but he cocked his head curiously. "Do we know each other?"

"Know each other overstates it. But we've met. In the front yard of Tibor Rothman's house just a few days ago."

Will's right eye squinted with the effort to remember. "You're the ex-husband."

"I am."

It wasn't nearly enough explanation. "What the hell happened here?"

Jonathan abandoned the attempt at a handshake and stuffed his hands in his pockets instead. It was a gesture designed to be nonthreatening. "Only one ground rule before we begin. You either agree to it, or I call that chopper back and I send you home. You can write whatever you want about what you see, but you can't use any of the names of people that you talk to tonight. Agreed?"

Will recoiled. "I can't agree to that."

Jonathan made a show of pressing the transmit button. "Rescue Flight, Scorpion."

He'd unplugged his earphone jack, so Will could plainly hear the pilot reply, "Go ahead, Scorpion."

Jonathan looked to Will. "It begins here or it ends here. It's your call, and you don't get a second chance. Do we have a deal or don't we?"

You could almost see the thoughts racing through the reporter's head. "Just the names?"

"Scorpion, do you have traffic for Rescue Flight?"

Jonathan keyed the mike. "Stand by." To Will: "All parties remain anonymous. We'll be a whole nest of Deep Throats. No names, no personal descriptions, nothing to make us identifiable to the outside world. And I warn you not to make a promise that you're not willing to keep."

Will stood there and sort of vibrated as he thought through his options. "Who's she?" he asked, nodding at Gail.

"I got people waiting, Will. You either want this story or you don't."

Clearly against his better judgment, Will let go with a giant sigh. "Fine," he blurted. "I agree."

Jonathan scanned for signs of insincerity, then keyed his mike again. "Rescue Flight, disregard. Have a good night." He flashed a smile to Will. "Where were we?"

"You were about to tell me what the hell is going on."

"First tell me what you already know."

Gail wandered up to stand next to Jonathan. She nodded in response to his glance to tell him that she was on the road to okay.

Will pulled a penlight out of his pocket and clicked it on, casting a beam into the night. It settled on a corpse. "Jesus," he whispered. He brought his gaze around to Jonathan. "I got a call at home a few hours ago telling me to meet a driver at the front door if I wanted to snag the story that would make me famous. I had two minutes to make my decision. They said it had something to do with Tibor, so I threw on some clothes, and a guy who didn't say much took me to a farmhouse in Middleburg, where that big chopper was waiting for me. For a while, I thought I'd walked into my own kidnapping.

"We were airborne for a half hour or so, and then we set down in another field, and just waited for instructions. I still don't really know much about what's going on, but they kept telling me that if I hung in there, I was going to get a hell of a story, and that no one else was going to have any piece of it." He paused, as if pondering whether there was anymore to tell. "Is that enough?"

Jonathan nodded. "I think that sounds about right." He took a deep breath and prepared himself for the coming monologue. "See, we had us a bit of a war out here tonight . . ."

Once he got started, it didn't really take all that long to tell the story—at least the essence of it; the details could come later, in future interviews.

Will Joyce listened, checking his recorder from time to time to make sure that there was still space on his chip. When Jonathan was done, Will said, "And this GVX stuff is here?"

"Right over there." Jonathan pointed toward the barn.

"And the reason you're sharing this with me is . . . ?"

As he asked the question, the sound of an approaching helicopter began a long, lazy crescendo.

Jonathan nodded toward the sound. "That's the reason up there," he said.

The night erupted in brilliant white light, and a million-candlepower searchlight swept the trees in the near distance.

"Who's that?" Gail asked, her first words since the blast that knocked her out.

"That will be the FBI," Jonathan explained. He looked at Will. "And I warn you that they're gonna be seriously pissed about all this. Uncle Sam is embarrassed as hell that this secret leaked out, and he'll go to great lengths to keep it from spreading any further."

"What kind of great lengths?" Will asked, raising his voice to be heard over the rotor blades. The flood light found them both and locked them into a blinding circle.

"Fabian Conger had one thing right," Jonathan shouted, turning his head and shielding his eyes from the rotor wash. "The truth is a powerful weapon. Once a secret is revealed, there's no reason to fight to keep it anymore. That's why I invited a reporter to the party."

Boxers stepped up next to his boss. "Looks like it's gonna get interesting," he said.

They could no longer see the chopper through the blinding light and the windstorm, but as it lost altitude, the angle of the chin light shifted from overhead to full-on. A loudspeaker—it could have been the voice of God, given the volume—said, "Lie on the ground on your faces, arms and legs spread, and don't move."

A look of horror settled onto Will's face. "Jesus, they're going to think I'm a part of all this."

Jonathan held his arms out to his side and slowly and deliberately sank to his knees. "At this second, yes, they do," he shouted. "And you should do exactly what they say."

Gail was already way ahead of them. "Listen to the man," she advised.

His eyes terror-set, Will Joyce threw himself onto the ground and formed a human X. The move was so quick and jerky he was lucky he didn't get shot. Since Jonathan was the one festooned with weapons, he didn't have the luxury of that kind of mistake. When his own cheek was against the ground, he called to the reporter, "Trust me, Will. Give this ten minutes, and you'll see how the plan works."

Jonathan felt the vibrations of boots pounding the ground as the FBI assault team swarmed them. He endured the shouted threats, and complied with all the orders not to move. He didn't even resist as his arms were pulled back way too forcefully and his wrists were enclosed in zip cuffs. Off to his side, he thought he heard Will Joyce crying, and he knew for a fact that he heard him apologizing. For what, he hadn't a clue. To Jonathan's left, Boxers allowed himself to be subdued—a decision that doubtless saved everyone a lot of ammunition.

Jonathan mostly kept his eyes closed during the ordeal, an instinctive protection against dust getting kicked into his face, but he did get a glimpse of rubber-encased boots. There was no mistaking the Darth Vader sound of the respirators. These guys had come in biohazard suits. That meant that Dom had relayed his message properly.

Once he'd been properly restrained, the team members cut away the combat straps that attached his rifle and shotgun to his shoulders and relieved him of the weapons. The .45 and K-Bar went next, and then they found the .38 in his leg pocket. Finally, they snatched his radio away from him and left him alone.

A female voice, familiar even through the distortion of the respirator said, "Sit them up."

His handlers seemed gentle as they guided him by his armpits into a sitting position. He was impressed, though not particularly surprised, that the FBI used the same Level A chem suit as the Army. For Will Joyce, it had to be terrifying to find himself surrounded by what looked to be a troop of aliens.

Jonathan flashed his cockiest smile. "Is that you, Wolverine? I love the outfit. You don't need it out here, though. The GVX containers were never compromised."

The alien in charge looked to a subordinate who held a multimeter—an air survey instrument designed to test for multiple chemical and biological hazards.

"I'm reading zeros on all scales," the minion said.

Wolverine said, "Go to Level D, but keep the suits handy." With that, she pulled her hood from her head and shook out her shoulder-length hair. Jonathan knew it to be red, but right here, in this light, it could have been any color.

"Holy shit," Will Joyce exclaimed as he recognized the woman's face.

Jonathan smiled. "Will Joyce, reporter with *The Washington Post*, allow me to introduce Irene Rivers, director of the Federal Bureau of Investigation."

Neither offered a hand in greeting. Will cocked his head. "Wolverine?"

"We go way back," Jonathan said with a shrug. "She likes it when I call her animal names."

Irene tucked her hood under one arm, and planted the other on what was probably a hip, somewhere under the baggy green suit. Jonathan saw the anger in her eyes. "A reporter?" she said.

"Not just *a* reporter," Jonathan said. "Tibor Rothman's friend. Reporting on his death."

Irene's jaw set as her eyes shifted from one man to the other. "You killed a lot of people tonight, Dig," she said.

"They shouldn't have shot at me."

"You set a trap. That's first-degree murder. I should arrest you."

Jonathan smiled. "You probably should," he said. "Let's get the attorney general and my lawyer in a conference room and talk that out. Go ahead and plan that press conference."

"You should have called us in," Irene said. She glared at Gail. "And you *certainly* should have called. What the hell are you doing here anyway?"

"The very question I've been asking myself three times a minute for the last eight hours," Gail replied.

"I did call you," Jonathan said, drawing them back on topic. "How do you think you knew to be here? Welcome, by the way."

"You should have called us in earlier. Where's the GVX?"

He gestured with his head. "Over there in the shed."

"Is that all of it?"

"It's all that I'm aware of."

"And where is the Hughes family?"

Jonathan paused. "Not here."

"Where?"

He arched his eyebrows and waited for her to connect some dots. These really weren't details that she wanted to be discussed openly in front of her subordinates.

Irene nodded to an agent. "Let them loose, please."

Jonathan caught the hesitant glance from the agent, but noted that he didn't question the order. He felt the cold point of wire cutters against his flesh. Two snips and he was free. Two more, and so was Will Joyce. Gail came next, Boxers last.

"And I need my radio back, please." He knew better than to ask for his weapons.

Irene nodded, and his radio reappeared. He reconnected himself to the earpiece.

"Leave us alone," Irene said to the nearby agents. "Suit back up to Level A and inventory that shed."

The agent hesitated again. "Ma'am, I don't think—" Then he saw the glare. "Yes, ma'am."

"Let's walk," Irene said, heading down the hill toward Jonathan's original ambush site.

"You come, too," Jonathan said to Will. That Gail would follow was a given. To Irene, he said, "So, how does it feel being back in the thick of things again?"

She switched on a flashlight to illuminate a path. "It's been a while. I like it, but it makes the field agents nervous as hell."

"Nobody wants the director to get in trouble on their watch," Jonathan said.

After thirty yards or so, Irene brought them to a stop and lowered her voice. "Okay, let's hear it. I know you have a plan, and that it's carefully choreographed, so let's just get to it."

Jonathan had always appreciated Irene's bluntness. He turned to Will. "Remember your promise," he reminded. Then to Irene, he said, "Step one. You make sure that the Hughes family is left alone, and that the pursuit to find them guilty of murdering anyone ends now."

Irene shook her head. "I don't think you—"

"I'm not done," Jonathan said. "Step two. You prepare whoever you need to prepare for the fact that my friend Will here is going to write a blockbuster story about Carlyle Industries and their secret contract to produce bioweapons in violation of God only knows how many treaties. Once that secret is out, there'll be no need to kill people to keep it."

Irene glared at the reporter, who seemed newly energized as he hovered a microtape recorder in the air between them. "Anything else?" she snarled.

"Oh, come on, Irene, you know you find this to be as much a relief as a pain in the ass. The truth will set you free."

"Anything else," she repeated, this time more as a statement than a question.

"Two more," Jonathan said. "First, you make known to the world what the Green Brigade was up to, and how it was transformed by Ivan Patrick from a well-meaning environmental group into the self-serving paramilitary wolf pack that it is today. If you dig a little, I guarantee that you'll find a history of illegal weapons sales, and I'll bet you a hundred dollars that that very kind of sale was what ultimately created this mess."

"Which leaves one more," Irene prompted.

"Yes, it does. I want you to treat my friend Will here as the designated historian for all that transpires from this. Let's see about getting him a Pulitzer."

Hands on both hips, she shook her head in disbelief. "All this havoc, all these dead bodies, and no accountability. That's what I'm hearing."

Jonathan chuckled, knowing he'd won. "Your glass is always half-empty, Irene."

Irene appealed to Gail. "And what about you Sheriff Law and Order? What are you going to do?"

Gail took her time answering. She looked at Jonathan, and then she turned to survey the carnage. When her gaze returned, she'd made a decision. "I'm going to go back to Indiana and bury a good friend." Her eyes reddened and she locked eyes with Jonathan. Under different circumstances, he'd have felt compelled to reach for her hand. "And I'm going to work with you expert alibi-makers to make Jesse Collier one of the great terrorist-fighters of our time."

Jonathan smiled. No more lives would have to be ruined.

Irene tried to look angry, but ended up with a rueful laugh. "Digger, you're a piece of work."

"So did you just agree?" Will asked Irene.

She answered slowly. "I guess I did."

Jonathan's earpiece crackled to life. "Scorpion, this is Mother Hen. We've lost a truck."

His hand snapped to the transmit button. "What truck?" he asked, drawing concerned looks from everyone around him.

"One at the top of the hill," Venice said. "I thought we were done, and I stopped monitoring the sat photos. When I looked back just now, it was gone."

"As in it drove away?" Jonathan asked. A nightmare scenario was blooming in his mind.

"What else?" she asked. "Scorpion, I'm so sorry. I should have—"

The night turned to day as the barn erupted in a roiling ball of fire and debris. When the concussion hit, it knocked all four of them off their feet.

CHAPTER FORTY-EIGHT

If you hear the boom, you're okay.

That's a standard rule of thumb for anyone who works with explosives, so Jonathan knew even before the chunks of wood and steel and rubber started falling to the ground that he'd lived to see another day. Another minute, anyway. He also understood what had happened. Ivan hadn't gotten away, and he hadn't died here. If ever he'd planned to engage in the battle that Jonathan had staged, the plan had changed along the way.

The whole firefight was merely a screening maneuver to grab some GVX and run for it. And for that he'd sacrificed God knew how many of his followers.

And with the trees blown across the bridge, there was no way to catch him.

"He's stealing the GVX!" Gail shouted. "I figured it out just before the claymore went off. I realized that they were laying down covering fire, and then when I saw their skirmish lines—"

She continued to explain, but Jonathan tuned her out as he helped Irene Rivers to her feet. "Are you okay?"

She was already on her radio, spewing orders to her

people to count heads and to suit up in Level A garb again. Clearly, she had her hands full.

Behind her, he saw Boxers hurrying forward. He looked fine, and he looked angry. "What the hell is going on?"

"I'll explain in the chopper," Jonathan said, pointing to the idling Blackhawk.

Boxers smiled as he sensed the birth of a new adventure. As they jogged up the gentle slope toward the bird, Jonathan sensed, then saw that Gail was coming with them. Under any other circumstance, he'd have objected. But here and now, what would be the point? Watching her friend get killed was plenty enough ante to buy into the game.

They were five steps from the aircraft when the pilot stepped forward and drew down on them. "Stay where you are," he commanded.

Boxers decked him with a single punch. Poor guy actually bounced when he hit the ground.

"He's a federal officer," Gail snapped. "You can't do that."

"Sure you can," Boxers said as he climbed into the pilot's seat. "Just don't hit him in his badge."

Jonathan pushed Gail along to the open cargo doors, where she threw herself onto the deck and he followed right behind. "Get it off the ground in a hurry!" Jonathan yelled. Twenty yards away, the feds hadn't yet figured out what was going on, but as soon as they heard the engine spool up, they were going to become very interested very quickly.

Boxers didn't even bother to strap in as he dropped his hand to the collective pitch lever and throttled in the power. The blades started to turn, and as they did, they made the pop-pop sound that was so characteristic of the Blackhawk. As Jonathan predicted, the FBI team took an immediate interest. Jonathan more saw than heard orders being shouted, and then they came running.

"Up, Box!" Jonathan yelled.

The Fibbies were only twenty yards out now, and they had their weapons drawn, trained straight at Jonathan. He threw himself to the floor to lower his target profile. The rotors found their grip in the air, and as the engine howled, they lifted off the ground, but the agents were only ten yards away now. Someone fired, but he had no idea where the bullet went.

Jesus, he thought, they're going to shoot down their own bird?

Five yards.

The chopper was four feet off the ground when the first arriving agent flung himself at the doorway. He got an elbow and a hand on the floorboard, but as they lifted higher, he didn't have a foothold. The tactician in Jonathan's head celebrated a shield that would keep them from taking another shot. The humanitarian, though, saw an overzealous and shortsighted kid who'd made a really stupid decision, but didn't deserve to die for it.

Boxers hesitated in midair. "Are we taking him?" he shouted.

"We've already got him!" Jonathan shouted back. "Go!"

As they lifted higher—past the fifty-foot mark, and then a hundred feet—the look on the agent's face turned steadily more desperate. His eyes were hot with fear, his skin pale with it. When they were far enough up and away to avoid making himself a target, Jonathan rose, leaned out into the night and hauled the terrified agent in by his belt. He landed in a heap on deck, with his legs still hanging out into the night, and scrabbled for his side arm.

Jonathan put a boot on his neck. "Hey, dickhead," he shouted over the noise. "I just saved your life. Don't give me second thoughts."

Gail scooted over and relieved the agent of his Glock .40 caliber pistol, then zip-cuffed him with his own ties. "Do you have any more weapons?" she asked.

The kid went the stoic route even as his eyes screamed for his mommy. That was fine with Jonathan. Stoic meant quiet.

Jonathan lifted a headset from its hook on the bulkhead, and then handed Boxers' to him as Gail donned a set of her own. Blessedly, the cacophony disappeared. He pressed the intercom button. "You on, Box?"

"Right here, Red Rider," he said. "We just joyriding, or are we goin' someplace?"

"Do we have FLIR in this thing?" He knew Boxers would recognize the acronym for Forward Looking InfraRed, a passive tracking system that can see in the dark.

"We've got it and it's on."

"Find me a vehicle running away," Jonathan said. "Might have as much as a ten-minute head start on us."

"Doesn't mean much when there's only one way in, does it?" Boxers heaved the machine into a turn that would follow the access road that they'd driven earlier in the day. At this altitude, they could see several miles of road length, so it couldn't possibly take long.

But as Jonathan watched over Boxer's shoulder, the screen betrayed nothing.

"Wait a second," Jonathan declared, landing a hand heavily on Boxers' shoulder. "Go back."

"To where?"

"To the cabin. To the trail at the top of the ridge. The Hugheses said they didn't know where it went. Maybe Ivan does."

"Or maybe he sees this as the perfect time to find out," Gail added.

Boxers didn't bother to reply. He kicked in a load of tail rotor and spun them around like a top to head in the other direction, damn near throwing them all to the deck. As the passengers yelled their protests, the pilot laughed. "God, I love my job," he said.

They rose to 500 feet as the nose dipped and the rotors pulled them faster and faster back toward the cabin. As the house and the barn passed below them, Jonathan saw the scope of the destruction. The blood had cooled enough to become less visible, but the bodies had not. He fought the urge to count them. That seemed somehow wrong.

Soon the tableau of destruction was gone, and they were again cruising over the unending expanse of trees.

Jonathan and Boxers saw the truck at the same instant, and they pointed together. "There," they said in unison. The truck was driving faster than was prudent, given the road conditions. Even from this altitude, with very little magnification of the image, they could see the SUV barely hanging on as roots and potholes bounced it around.

"Any ideas how to stop it?" Boxers asked. "Looks like he's got a real road to connect to in about three miles. At his speed, that gives us about seven minutes to think of something."

Jonathan and Gail looked at each other. Her shrug matched his absence of ideas.

He turned to survey the equipment they had available. The seat and deck of the Blackhawk were strewn with the flotsam of the raid on the cabin. He saw helmets and a few extra Kevlar vests. Like good soldiers in any outfit, of course, no one had left a weapon behind; but at least they had Captain Courageous's Glock. It was something. Not much, but something. He slipped it into pouch pocket on his thigh.

His eyes settled on a pile of coiled rope, and then he knew what he had to do.

"You know this is crazy, right?" Boxers asked over the intercom as Jonathan made his final preparations.

"Welcome to today," Jonathan mumbled. In the roar of the rotor noise, no one heard him. He looked to Gail. "You've got to be his eyes," he said.

Gail nodded, but her expression belied her wholesale agreement with Boxers. This was crazy.

Jonathan went on, "He can't look ahead and down at the same time."

"I've fast-roped before," Gail said. "HRT, remember?"

"Humor me," Jonathan said. "Given the stakes, I want to say it all out loud. Watch for speed and altitude. Box should be able to keep me in the slot, but the rest will be up to you."

"I'll handle it," she said. But she wished she could think of a better way.

"You can't second-guess my hand signals," he said. "If I signal to release the rope, you release it, understand?" He'd already set the rope to release on its own if it got snagged. Since it was his crazy idea, it didn't seem right to kill them all if it went wrong.

"For God's sake, Grave, I understand all of it."

Boxers broke in, "We're down to about three minutes before we get to the road. If you're still committed to suicide, you'd better get on it."

"Roger that," Jonathan said. He started to take off his headset, but hesitated. "Call me Digger," he said to Gail, and he winked. With that, he pulled the muffs off his ears and tossed them onto the deck. He stood, walked to the open cargo door, and grabbed the heavy 40 mm rope that he'd clipped to the receiver inside the door. Facing the night, he swung himself out into the rotor wash, gripped the rope with his legs and boots, and started his ride down.

The violence of the windstorm surprised him. Between the rotor wash and the forward momentum, it was like hanging onto a floppy flagpole in a hurricane. Below his crossed feet, beyond the end of his fifty-foot section of rope, tree canopies sped by as a black blur. He could have been over solid ground, or over water, for all his visual reference told him. That was a problem with fast roping, in fact, as it was with all aerial insertion techniques. Looking straight down disorients the hell out of you; you don't know you're going to slam into the ground until it's too late to do anything about it. To counter the effect, you look out at a forty-five-degree angle, where the horizon gives you an additional point of reference.

As Jonathan looked out, he saw the truck up ahead, moving with reckless speed through the slot created in the trees by the fire road. From the erratic driving alone, he figured that Ivan—he was sure now that it was Ivan—had heard them approaching and had entered panic mode. Instead of driving a straight line, the truck was cutting quick S-turns, which Jonathan deduced from the bouncing pattern of the headlights meant that the vehicle's suspension was being pummeled by the road surface.

He slid farther down the rope. When he was still a good five feet from the end, he looked up to see how the Blackhawk was doing. Normally, fast-roping is done from a hover; this was the first time Jonathan had ever attempted it at velocity, and he was impressed by the distance by which the rope trailed the chopper. He wondered if there was even the remotest chance of success here.

Gail found herself shouting into the intercom, even though she knew that the noise-canceling boom mikes made it unnecessary. "Faster," she said. "He's still trailing the truck."

The chopper increased its speed.

Below, Digger's rope swung farther backward, giving the impression that they were driving away without him.

"He's crossing over top of the truck now," she said, watching the silhouette that she knew to be Scorpion blot out a man-shaped stain across the top of the lighter-colored SUV. "He's ahead now," she said. "Reduce your speed."

The plan was to match the speed of the fleeing vehicle, but with Scorpion keeping pace in front of the SUV. As it was, they'd overshot by quite a lot.

"Not too much," Gail warned as the distances between them started to close.

She saw muzzle flashes from the truck.

"They're shooting at him!" she shouted.

* * *

It was an amusement park ride of which no mother would approve.

The force of the wind made hanging onto the rope difficult in its own right, but when you combined the wind pressure with the progressively more horizontal orientation of the line, gravity had become Jonathan's enemy. He was still secure on the rope with his legs wrapped tightly around and locked, but the whole thing had become an endurance contest. His left hand and forearm trembled from the sustained effort, so he hooked the rope deeper into his armpit to bring relief that he knew would last mere moments.

Boxers' piloting was a thing of beauty, he thought as he overtook the SUV and lowered Jonathan even farther. When he flew past, though, and pulled way ahead, he silently cursed Gail for her lack of skills as a crew chief. Then he felt himself slowing again, and he knew that the time had come for him to act.

Still slicing through the night at treetop level, Jonathan pulled open the Velcro flap on the pocket on his right thigh and fished out the Glock he'd taken from the FBI kid. He grabbed it tightly in his fist, all too aware of the fact that this was his only weapon, and of the unusual sensitivity of the trigger mechanism on this weapon that essentially had no safety—at least not one that Jonathan felt comfortable with. He kept his finger outside of the trigger guard as he pulled the weapon free, and—

A searing pain tore through his gut on his right side, barely at his belt line. It slammed him hard, knocking the breath out of his lungs and nearly lurching the rope out of his grasp. He knew even before he saw the muzzle flashes from the truck that he'd been shot.

"Fuck!" he yelled. It was a skilled shot—or a lucky one—and that son of a bitch had taken first blood. He yelled. He roared. It was a guttural thing; pain and rage combined into something animalistic. Raw.

Extending his right arm, he pointed the Glock at the front of the approaching truck and he pulled the trigger. He pulled it over and over. Six shots. Ten. He didn't aim as much as he willed the gun to act as an extension of his hand as he drilled round after round into the windshield and the engine block. Even in the dark, he could see steam rising from the ruined engine. Fire blossomed from a torn fuel line.

Boxers slowed, and the SUV sped past, under his feet, covering maybe fifty feet before the S-turns became violent, and the vehicle slammed into a tree and then flipped twice before stopping in the middle of the fire road on its roof. The engine compartment was fully ablaze, and then Jonathan whipped past again, moving much slower now. He felt the heat on his ass and his legs as he passed over the fire.

The ground started to fall away again as Boxers clearly assumed that their work was done.

"No!" Jonathan yelled. He craned his neck to look up the rope at Gail and he waved violently, bringing the agony in his gut to new levels. "Put me down!" he shrieked. "Down! Now!"

Above him, he thought he saw Gail shaking her head. They were saving him from himself. It was a nice thought. He hated them for it.

He was ten feet above the trees when he kicked his legs free of the rope and let go.

"Oh, my God!" Gail shouted. She watched in horror as Scorpion dropped into the trees. "He fell!"

"The hell he did," Boxers barked. "We've got to set this fucker down."

The roar of the engine became deafening as the pilot poured on the power, and the G force of the acceleration made her knees sag. The chopper pitched violently, and the world became a blur.

The bird skidded to a halt in the air, and then dropped, reversing the G forces to make her feel nearly weightless. It was like riding in a blender. She felt a thump and when she looked outside, she saw they were in the middle of the road, with three vehicles heading right for them.

"Jesus!" she shouted. "Get out of the way!" Instead of applying more power, however, Boxers chopped the engine completely. "What are you doing!" Out the starboard side cargo door, she watched, horrified, as the lead vehicle skidded sideways in the road, and the one behind it T-boned it hard. Together, their momentum carried them into the side of the chopper with barely a bump.

The trussed-up FBI agent's eyes were the size of hockey pucks, somehow befitting his skin, which was the color of ice. "He's fucking crazy!" the agent yelled.

Gail was about to agree when she realized that she hadn't seen the half of it. Boxers heaved himself out of the pilot's seat and out onto the road, where he strode to the third car in the approaching line—a Nissan pickup that hadn't hit anything, but had stopped sideways in the road nonetheless—and opened the driver's door. She could neither see nor hear the negotiation, but the driver seemed more than happy to surrender his seat.

Gail understood what was about to happen, and she scrambled out of the chopper to join him. Until the very last second when he stopped to let her in, she wondered if Boxers might just run her over.

* * *

To keep his arms and legs from being broken, Jonathan hugged them close to his body, like a cannonball off the high dive. The very, very high dive.

Branches tore at him and buffeted him as he fell through the canopy, but even as his gut screamed at him with every impact, he reminded himself that they were keeping him alive. Without something to break his momentum, a fall from this height offered little chance of survival, and virtually none of escaping without injury.

When the ground slapped him, he howled with agony. He'd been torn by bullets before, but the mind mercifully takes the edge off memories like that. It felt as if someone had packed his appendix with hot coals. He paused at the base of his tree and tested his legs. Everything seemed to be intact. Somehow, he'd managed to hang on to the Glock all the way to the ground.

He forced himself to his feet, listing to his wounded side, and tried to get his bearings. Out here in the dark, the burning truck might just as well have been a lighthouse on a calm sea. He headed that way.

He didn't want Ivan Patrick to burn to death. That would be too easy. He wanted the man to suffer, but he wanted to be its cause.

Fewer than a hundred paces brought him to the edge of the road cut, close enough to the SUV to feel the heat from its fire. The vehicle reminded Jonathan of a dead bug on the floor, on its back with its feet in the air. He squinted against the intensity of the light as he approached the cab. As he got to within a few feet, he forced himself into a low crouch, where he could see through the shattered windows, grunting noisily at the effort. The first thing he noticed was four GVX canisters strewn across the roof, which was now the floor. The second thing was that the vehicle was empty.

He was as much the hunted as the hunter now, and the hairs on his arms and neck rose to attention. A gunshot boomed from behind him and he dove right, blowing a bellows on those coals in his gut and stirring them with an ice pick. He rolled again as a bullet slammed into the spot he'd just left, and then he rolled back to that spot just to be unpredictable and screw up the shooter's aim. A third shot missed.

Jonathan cursed his stupidity. Anger, pain, and blood loss together offered no excuse to create a perfectly backlit target. If he died here, he deserved it. This was a rookie mistake, and it rightfully came with a death penalty.

Scrambling on the ground, he found his feet and scurried for the woods line he'd come from, only to dart left at the last moment to put the burning vehicle between him and the gunman. The maneuver would make him invisible, but only temporarily. Standing in the light was standing in the light. As soon as Ivan repositioned, he'd be as vulnerable as if he were standing on a stage.

He needed cover. Keeping low, he half walked, half staggered to the opposite wood line, where he climbed the slight incline and disappeared into the trees. He crouched low and took inventory.

The odds were horribly stacked against him. He'd been counting on a kill shot through the windshield of the truck, and hadn't considered the possibility of Ivan drawing first blood. He switched his weapon to his left hand and used his right to probe the spot where he'd been hit. He didn't like how wet the fabric felt at the point of entry. He was bleeding badly. With an escalating sense of dread, he dared to bring his hand around to examine his back, and sure enough, there was the exit wound. Finding it made the wound hurt even more, adding a steel cinch to the coals and the icepick.

"Okay," he breathed aloud, barely even a whisper. "Get a grip. Inventory what's good." Even though Ivan wasn't dead, there was a high likelihood that he was at least wounded. In fact, that would explain why he missed the backlit shot a minute ago. Next, there was the margin of the exit wound. It was hard to tell exact measurements in the dark just by feel, but it felt about the same size as the entry wound. That meant that it was truly a through-and-through shot. If it had hit bone or any of the fragile solid organs, the bullet would have tumbled or fragmented, and left his body through a gaping crater. That it didn't was probably the best news.

On the shitty side of things, Ivan probably still had night vision, while Jonathan did not. That tilted the odds significantly in the wrong direction.

Or did it?

His thoughts returned to the burning vehicle. As long as he stayed near the fire, Ivan's night vision would be more burden than benefit. The heat and brightness of the fire would white them out.

He slid closer to the edge of the road cut, staying in the shadows, but capitalizing on the fire. "Hey Ivan!" he called to the night. "How bad did I get you?" He scanned the surrounding landscape for movement. Or a muzzle flash.

He heard nothing but the crackling of the fire.

"I'm giving you an advantage here, asshole!" he yelled. "Follow the sound of my voice and take your best shot. See if you can be lucky." In his mind, Jonathan could see the disapproving glare he'd be receiving if Boxers were here to witness this. By any measure, the smart play would be to stay put and outwait the opponent, but the one thing Jonathan had in short measure was time. He could already feel the cold seeping into him, and he was thirsty as hell—both signs of blood loss. If he didn't force the situation, he'd end up being unconscious when Ivan killed him.

Ivan could be anywhere now. There'd been plenty of time for him to circle around. Catching movement in the dark was becoming less and less likely. There were only so many compass points that you could watch at one time.

"Nice of you to leave all your men to die up there, you cowardly piece of shit!" Jonathan yelled. "I understand now why you couldn't make it in the real army. Never had the guts for it, did you? Not unless you got to torture little girls and boys! Did you know that your name became a fucking joke in the Community after you washed out? Everybody knew you were– "

He saw the muzzle flash half a second before he heard the bullet pass through the leaves to his left. The son of a bitch was directly across the road.

Jonathan didn't hesitate. Screaming like a wounded animal, he lunged out of his cover and charged straight at the blinking flashes, leading with his extended weapon and shooting the magazine empty as he ran.

Gail kept her right hand gripped to the Nissan's armrest, and her left pressed against the ceiling to keep from getting bounced out of her chair as Boxers pushed the vehicle well beyond its limits. His eyes had a fire the likes of which she'd never seen, a homicidal combination of anger and fear. He said nothing as he kept the accelerator pressed to the floor, steering toward the glow of the burning vehicle.

Over the noise of the engine and the pounding of the suspension, she heard an extended ripple of gunshots.

She didn't think it was possible, but somehow, the truck started moving even faster.

"Open the glove compartment," Boxers commanded.

"Why?" It would mean letting go of her death grip, and without a seat belt on, that risked getting thrown through the roof.

"Just open it!"

It was as she'd feared. The instant her hands were free, she felt as if she were riding a horse without reins. She braced herself against the dash with her left hand, and pulled open the glove box with her right. Instantly, a .357 Magnum revolver tumbled out onto the tray. She looked at the driver. "How did you know?"

"In this part of the world, nine out of ten pickup trucks have weapons in the glove box," he growled.

In Indiana, too, Gail thought. Only out there, you need a warrant to find them.

The pain didn't matter; he didn't even feel it anymore. The slide on the Glock locked open when he was halfway across the road, and he tossed it away. But he never slowed. He closed the gap with speed that he never thought he could have mustered with a bullet through his innards, and his stride never faltered as he scaled the opposite bank and entered the woods.

Ivan Patrick—clearly recognizable in the flickering light because of that hideous scar on his eye—sat propped at the base of a tree, his legs splayed, and his shooting hand still outstretched as he continued to try and squeeze more rounds out of an empty gun. Dark wetness spilled from his chest and his head.

Jonathan slowed to a fast walk as he approached and

slapped the pistol out of the man's hand before he kicked him full-force in the groin. Ivan made a miserable retching sound as the boot found its mark, and Jonathan felt a distant satisfaction that his nemesis could still feel pain. It was important that he could still feel pain.

He slapped the man hard across his face, launching a splash of blood, and then he slapped the other side, this time with the back of his hand. When he raised his had for a third blow, Ivan raised his arms. "Please stop," he begged.

Jonathan laughed. There was the fear he wanted to see. Only he couldn't sec it clearly enough. Grabbing the collar of Ivan's shirt just under his chin with his fist, Jonathan half-lifted, half-dragged the man back toward the road.

"Stop!" Ivan begged again. "I'm shot, for Christ's sake."

"Yeah, well so am I." He deliberately passed to close to a tree and knocked Ivan's head into it before dragging the length of his body along the rough bark. The man screamed in agony. "Jeeze, I bet that hurt," Jonathan said.

The SUV was a roiling fireball now, distinguishable as a vehicle only by skeletal frame members silhouetted against the flames. As they cleared the woods and entered the road cut, Ivan writhed in Jonathan's grasp, kicking his legs to get away and screaming out against the agony it ignited. "I don't want to burn!" he yelled. "Jesus God, I don't want to burn!"

"You're going to have one shitty eternity, then," Jonathan laughed. "I'm told that hell is all about fire and a daily ass-fuck with a straight razor." The image amused him.

As the adrenaline drained from his system, though,

the white-hot icepick returned. As he dragged his prisoner into the center of the road cut, the load got progressively heavier, every step adding another fifty pounds. A hundred pounds. A thousand. When they reached the center of the road cut, the world pitched sideways, and Jonathan fell.

He caught himself with his free hand, his nose just inches away from Ivan's.

His prey knew an opportunity when he saw it. Ivan snapped like a dog, trying to sink his teeth into Jonathan's face.

Jonathan recoiled. The teeth missed by millimeters, so close that he could feel the man's oniony breath and hear the click of his jaws. He tried to push away with a one-arm push-up from Ivan's chest, but his gut muscles spasmed and the effort aborted halfway through. He fell again. This time, as he came down he remained conscious of Ivan's mouth, and he caught himself with a forearm across the torturer's eyes.

Ivan moved with lightning speed. His head jerked to the side and he snapped again, this time catching the meat of Jonathan's left forearm with his incisors. With his teeth sunk in to the gum line, he started whip his head back and forth, exactly the way JoeDog would tear into the rope pull toys that lay strewn around the firehouse. The pain was exquisite, sharper, more intense even than the bullet wound. With his elbow bent, and his arm immobilized, there was no getting away. The whipping action of Ivan's head pulled him off balance. He pounded at the man's face with the heel of his fist, wide arcing hammer blows, but they had little behind them, and he was unable to do much more than bloody the torturer's nose.

In the dancing yellow light of the burning truck, Jonathan saw the blood—his blood—pouring from the corners of Ivan's mouth. The ugliness of that—the savagery of it—angered him more. Issuing a guttural yell that rallied his remaining inner resources, Jonathan rose up on the damaged arm and leaned on it, as if to stuff it down Ivan's throat. As the jaws closed tighter, he pressed even harder.

"There you go, asshole," Jonathan growled. "Swallow it. Choke on it, you son of a bitch." From this higher angle, he could finally get enough leverage to throw a solid punch to the man's nose. Blood fountained, and now his face was wet with it, slick with it. But the pressure from Ivan's jaws never slackened. If anything, his grip closed tighter.

Through the gleaming red-black mask, Ivan's eyes glared malignantly at Jonathan. He had this one chance at survival, and as long as he was still breathing, he wasn't going to squander it.

The eyes. One mangled and the other evil. Were those eyes the last thing that Angela Caldwell had seen when he'd killed her after he'd made her endure her children's suffering? Had Ellen witnessed the same defiant glare as Ivan raped her and broke her bones?

The eyes.

Jonathan stared at the mangled one as he jammed his thumb into the good one. It was a calculated move—one he'd learned and taught at the Operator Training Course at Fort Bragg. The body instinctively reacts to threatened eye injury by squinting the lids tightly shut, so you aim for the lower lid first. That way you can easily pry your way under the upper lid to the eyeball itself.

Ivan screamed even before the pad on Jonathan's thumb found the slick wet surface of the orb. The jaws relaxed, freeing his forearm.

"No!" Ivan yelled. "No! No! No!" Biting wasn't important to him anymore. Fighting wasn't all that important to him either. Hell, he'd have been Jonathan's best friend just to save the sight in one eye.

Jonathan pressed harder. He felt the eyeball deforming under the pressure. Now that he had the use of his left hand, too, he went for the mangled mess that was all the torturer had to help him navigate through hell. He straddled the bucking man's chest and—

"Scorpion!"

The sound of Gail's voice startled him, but he didn't turn. He knew what they'd done. Boxers had somehow found them a vehicle, and they'd come back up the fire road to rescue him.

Only he didn't need rescuing. He had a job to do.

"Jonathan Grave, stop it!" Gail's tone was that of a scolding mother. She'd moved from behind him to in front where he could see her. "Stop it," she said again.

"Fuck off," he replied.

"Let him go, Jonathan," she said. "This isn't what you're about. It's over. We've got him."

"She's right, Dig," Boxers said, putting a hand on his shoulder. "You're not an assassin, remember? You're not a murderer. You've said it a thousand times."

Those were the words that got through to him. The words and the big man's beefy hand on his shoulder.

Jonathan pulled his hands away from Ivan's face and rolled to the side onto the ground to let the man clutch at himself.

The reality of his wounds hit him. He felt old and he felt cold. He felt sick. He'd crossed a line with Ivan tonight. As he looked at the blood streaming from his arm, and the color started to fade from his surroundings, he wondered if the legend of the vampire somehow applied to bites from ordinary mortals. As he stared up to the smoke-blackened sky, he knew that he would soon be unconscious, and the thing that he dreaded most was the possibility of waking up with Ivan's blood in his veins, commingled with his own.

A gunshot startled him.

A lady's voice screamed, "What did you do?"

And then Boxers said, "I got no problem bein' an assassin."

Jonathan smiled as he drifted away.

LATE MAY

CHAPTER FORTY-NINE

Mount Comfort Cemetery in Alexandria had been the interment place for Tibor Rothman's family for at least three generations. As Dom piloted his Chevy around the circle, he glanced at his passenger, assessing emotional stability, Jonathan supposed.

"Is that your priestly concern or your psychologist's concern?" Jonathan asked, staring straight ahead.

"Let's call it a friend's concern," Dom replied.

Touché. "Then thank you. But relax. I'm fine."

"Sure you are," Dom said. Though his jaw was mostly healed, there was still a certain tightness to his words. "If you don't mind, we'll let your psychologist make that call."

Fair enough, Jonathan thought. After all, the priest had already heard his confession.

Over a month had passed since the shoot-out in the woods, and this was Jonathan's first real foray away from home. No doubt about it: he just didn't heal as quickly as he used to. It would be another two weeks before he'd be allowed to drive himself, and it had only been one week since he'd been allowed to be in a car at all. Doctors were annoying fussbudgets, he thought, but by all accounts, what the doctors had been able to accomplish by the time he'd gotten to the hospital was nothing short of heroic, so the least he could do was listen to their postoperative instructions.

During his convalescence, Jonathan had missed a lot. In the initial two weeks following the incident, everyone who'd been present had missed a lot, thanks to emergency quarantine. Further tests—and the fact that no one contracted a head cold, let alone a case of smallpox—led investigators to determine that the virus is best killed by intense heat. But man, oh man, was the public pissed. Even today, the newspapers and airwaves were still filled with fallout from the story that Will Joyce had managed to file from the isolation ward. The international community was shocked—*shocked*—that the United States was still manufacturing bioweps despite existing treaties. The Department of Defense in particular—as if they needed any additional strife—was being hammered about the shoddy accounting that could have allowed an unstoppable strain of smallpox to be released into the hands of terrorists. It wasn't a story that would go away anytime soon, especially since Charlie Warren, former security chief for Carlyle Industries, had made a deal with prosecutors to throw under the bus as many former colleagues as he could, in return for a jail sentence that might allow him to see freedom again in his old age.

If it was possible for an incident like this to actually be a boon to anyone, that person would be Irene Rivers along with her FBI. Will Joyce made it clear in his reporting that the Bureau's quick response to the emergency in the hills of Pennsylvania had prevented the Green Brigadiers from succeeding. It was her quick thinking, the story reported, that mandated the use of a robot to open the door of the truck and initiate the explosion in the barn, thereby saving the lives of every potential rescuer. The fact that robots had been standard operating procedure for years did not lessen the heroics of the evening.

At a time when the people needed a hero, Irene was the anointed one. After all, when was the last time anyone heard of an FBI director being so actively involved in a case? Jonathan was happy for her. As far as any official record was concerned, the final incident on the fire road never happened. Some local attention was paid to an emergency landing made by an FBI Blackhawk helicopter, but the rest of the evening's events wiped it from the news cycle.

The Hughes family, Jonathan had learned while passing time in medical isolation, had returned home, with Thomas being the proud owner of a titanium rod in his femur that was, as Boxers had predicted, very much like the one the Big Guy himself walked around with every day. Julie's head injury had never amounted to much more than a few stitches and a scar that was well concealed by her hair. The new management team at Carlyle Industries offered Stephenson a cash settlement to ward off any future lawsuits, and he accepted.

Dom stopped the car at the curb at the end of a row labeled with the number 600, and threw the transmission into Park. "This is it," he said.

Jonathan hesitated. His stomach fluttered and he felt as if his hands might shake if he extended them.

"How big a funeral was it?" he asked.

"Pretty huge," Dom answered.

"Was it all about Tibor?"

The priest sniffed. "Well, he was a pretty famous guy. He's the one the news folks were here to pay tribute to."

"Or just to make sure that the son of a bitch was really dead," Jonathan quipped.

"I won't let you get away with that, Dig. For ninety-nine percent of his life, maybe he was a complete ass, but he checked out in service to others. You above all people should—"

"I know, Dom. It's just such a hard notion to wrap my head around."

"You're stalling," Dom said.

Jonathan gave a wry chuckle. When he looked at Dom, he hoped that his eyes were nowhere near as red as they felt. "Would you believe I'm scared?"

"It's tough to say good-bye. I'm not sure there's any harder thing in the world." Dom reached out and rested a hand on Jonathan's forearm. "Want me to come with you?"

Jonathan didn't answer. He didn't trust his voice. Instead, he opened his door, rose with no small effort to his feet, and then hobbled down the row of plaques to be alone with Ellen.

He ended up spending only a half hour with her. Seeing the two graves side by side—Tibor on the left and Ellen on the right—Jonathan realized, perhaps for the first time, that she'd truly let him go years ago. She'd moved on, and as impossible as it was to believe, she'd loved Tibor Rothman. It was fitting, he realized, that they should spend eternity so close together.

It was time for Jonathan to move on, as well. That's what he and Dom discussed, in fact, during the two-hour ride back to Fisherman's Cove. As the Chevy pulled up to the front of the firehouse to drop Jonathan at the door, they were surprised to see a familiar figure sitting on the bench in the veteran's garden.

Dom chuckled. "Seek and ye shall find, eh, Dig?"

Jonathan laughed in spite of himself. There was certainly no denying the irony.

Gail Bonneville rose to meet him as he climbed out of the car. "You look a hell of a lot better than the last time I saw you," she said.

He smiled, and gestured with his head to follow him to his front door. "It helps to have blood in your veins," he said, fishing for his keys. "You know, instead of spilling it all over the ground."

"So how are you doing?"

He pushed open the door, and let her go in first. He braced for an assault from JoeDog, but remembered that Doug Kramer had taken more or less full-time custody, at least until Jonathan was strong enough to deflect an attack.

"I'm doing well," Jonathan said. "Turns out that God gives us way more intestine than we really need. Hack out a foot or two, and you don't even notice. Can I get you anything?"

"No, I'm fine."

"Beer? Wine? Soda?" His eyes narrowed. "Handcuffs?" He led the way deeper into the living room and lowered himself into a chair.

"No thanks to all," Gail said. "As luck would have it, I'm not even in the law enforcement business anymore."

Jonathan's eyebrows arched high. "You quit?"

She shrugged. "I couldn't stay. I broke my promise to the voters. I let you go, and I got my best deputy killed in the process. Bottom line, enforcement's just not my thing."

Jonathan thought he sensed where this was going, and he cocked his head. "Just what is your thing?" he asked.

Gail set herself into the sofa and crossed her legs. She was wearing a skirt today, and Jonathan enjoyed the confirmation that his assumptions about those legs were correct. "I've always considered myself to be a good investigator. You know, finding people who don't want to be found."

Jonathan's smirk became a smile. "God knows I'm the last one to argue."

She uncrossed her legs and leaned closer. "Do you know anyone who might be looking for someone with those skills?"

"I just might," he said. "What do you say we discuss it over dinner tonight?"

A stunning smile bloomed. "I've already made the reservations," she said.

ACKNOWLEDGMENTS

My wife, Joy, is the constant in my life. For reasons known only to her, she continues to love me, as I have adored her, for twenty-seven years. No man could be luckier.

Anne Hawkins, my literary agent and dear friend, is a force of nature. I treasure her ongoing counsel. One of her great favors was to introduce me to Michaela Hamilton, my editor at Kensington Publishing. With people like Michaela and Kensington CEO Steve Zacharias in your corner, it's hard to make a mistake.

The Jonathan Grave series would likely never have happened if my good friend and former collaborator Kurt Muse had not put in a good word for me. Through him, I gained access to people and places that lifelong civilians never get to meet. Kurt vouched for me, and I was in. I hope that Jonathan Grave exhibits even one-tenth of the honor and integrity of those who inspired his creation.

Life would be boring, and fictional characters horribly dull, were it not for the likes of Jeffery Deaver, John and Susan Miller, Pat Barney and Sam Shockley, Bob and Bert Garino, Cyndi and Duane Ellis, Charlie and Trisha White, Chuck Carr, David Taylor, Jack and Sharon Kennedy, Sandy and Richard Berthelsen, Dave and Judy Jackson, Anne Marie Horvath, Kent Kiser, Ed Szrom, Cap Grossman, Doug Kramer, Tom Herod,

Joe Bateman, and the dozens of friends that I have made through my day job at the Institute of Scrap Recycling Industries.

Then there's my son, Chris. When I first started writing acknowledgments in books, he was a little boy. Now he's twenty-three years old and a head taller than his old man. He's smart, he's handsome, he's funny, and he's one of the kindest souls I've ever met. I'm proud to call him my son and even prouder to call him my friend.

Don't miss the next exciting thriller by John Gilstrap

AGAINST ALL ENEMIES

A JONATHAN GRAVE NOVEL

Winner of the international Thriller Writers' Award for Best Paperback of 2015

Available in print and electronic editions from Kensington Publishing Corp.

Keep reading for an exciting excerpt . . .

I do solemnly swear that I will support and defend the Constitution of the United States against all enemies, foreign and domestic; that I will bear true faith and allegiance to the same; and that I will obey the orders of the President of the United States and the orders of the officers appointed over me, according to regulations and the Uniform Code of Military Justice. So help me God.

—US ARMY OATH OF ENLISTMENT

Chapter One

Behrang Hotaki smiled at everyone who made eye contact with him. He knew some of them but many more were strangers, and if he was friendly, the merchants at the bazaar were more likely to take pity on him and share a plum or a tomato. Maybe some rice or some bread. For lamb or chicken, he would have to do something in return, and all too often that meant doing things he did not want to do. These people, villagers and merchants alike, would show him pity, but they dared not show him kindness, dared not show him friendship.

They knew him as an orphan, a waif, a boy whose family name may never be spoken. With the Americans gone, the old ways had reemerged, and the Taliban knew everything. Behrang understood that anyone who wished to see old age needed to assume that the monsters' knowledge was perfect.

He smiled, and they mostly smiled in return. To smile was to be polite, and to be polite was to be invisible. If a boy were shy enough—invisible enough—he could be forgiven the sins of his family. By demonstrating that he knew his place, the gifts bestowed on him might be more generous. Even Satan and the others understood that a boy his age needed some tiny bit of pity.

Behrang intended to hurt them all, to kill them if he could. Not with a gun or with a suicide vest, but with a betrayal of his own. He dreamed of the day when he might see all of these animals dead, their brains blasted from their heads. The slower they died, the happier he'd be. He wished he could watch as they had watched, but without that false expression of concern. He would not pretend to mourn for them as they had pretended to mourn for his family. If he were able, he would spit on their corpses, piss on their faces.

But that would not be possible. When justice finally came, he could not afford to be nearby. After Charlie—the last remaining American, who was even more invisible than Behrang—killed Satan and his leaders, the rest of the Taliban monsters would murder everyone in the village. Behrang would be far, far away when that happened.

And it would happen soon.

Among Behrang's greatest blessings was the gift of patience. Six years had passed since people in this crowd had betrayed his father—six years since his sisters and mother were raped while Behrang was forced to watch. Six years since the Taliban slipped the thin rope around his father's neck and hoisted him into the air, his feet mere inches above the ground. The jackals had laughed as Father had kicked and stretched to reach the gravel street that remained barely out of reach.

It had been six endless years since Behrang himself had become a toy of the Taliban monsters. They thought they owned him, that they could do whatever they wanted without consequence.

So many people here in the bazaar knew everything.

They knew what his father had tried to accomplish—the education he'd tried to provide for everyone, girls as well as boys—and they all knew who, among them, had once been vocal supporters of his efforts. But to a person, they were cowards, unwilling to risk one one-hundredth of what Father had risked. Every one of them valued profit and their own safety above any point of principle. In the end, none of them rose to help, and now that it was all over and his family was dead, they dared to show pity to Behrang. In their minds, they were *better* than him because they had been too smart to be honest.

They all thought so little of Behrang that they would say things in his presence that should never be said in front of anyone. Because he was invisible, they assumed he was harmless. Perhaps they assumed he was deaf and blind. Either way, they talked in ways they shouldn't.

As a result, Behrang knew the secret of secrets. He knew where Satan would be tomorrow afternoon.

Behrang wondered sometimes if the man who called himself Satan—a blasphemy in itself—had a given name that was something different. He had to, didn't he? What parents could think so little of their son at birth that they would name him after the ultimate evil? Perhaps they could foresee the future. Or perhaps by giving him such a name they had shaped the man he would become.

Behrang had seen much cruelty in his thirteen years, but he had never seen anyone else who so enjoyed inflicting it. Satan showed no more emotion when he set a man ablaze than a merchant would show in selling a pomegranate.

Satan and the Taliban killed innocents for sport, for the sole purpose of turning children into orphans. The terror they inflicted was their greatest weapon, far larger and more effective than any cannon or bomb. Fearful people would stand and watch as girls—and boys—were raped, and they would do nothing as their fathers were lifted off the ground to be strangled to death.

Father would have told Behrang that he should not feel anger toward people who felt such fear, but rather that he should feel pity for them. *Men who live in fear cannot live a full life,* his father had told him. *Fear is a slaveholder that turns good people into obedient pets. It is far better to live a shortened life in freedom than it is to die an old man as a slave to others.*

Behrang knew that the anger in his soul was wrong, that it would disappoint his father, but Father had found his relief from slavery so long ago. He had seen the world as a professor sees the world, through the smeared and foggy windows of a classroom, where lofty philosophy stirred the intellect of men and women living in comfort. As an orphan on the street, living off the pity of your family's murderers, the realities of life were gritty and painful and foul-smelling. Behrang had no room for theories and philosophy in his life. He had room only for living or dying, and the space between those two options was so small as to be unmeasurable.

He scanned the flood of people at the bazaar for the single face he needed to see. Somewhere among the dozens of farmers' and craftsmen's stalls, Charlie would appear, and when he did, the American would wink at him, and then they would wander off to somewhere safe. That's when Behrang would pass along his news.

Few people knew that Americans remained in this part of the province, and of those who did remain, Charlie said that all of them were looking for Satan. "If you see him," Charlie had told him, "if you even *hear* of him, I need you to tell me."

From the very first day they'd met, Behrang had suspected that Charlie was a soldier, but the man had never told him that. In fact, Charlie avoided saying anything about himself. He asked all kinds of questions, from who knew whom to how things used to be back when life was normal. Charlie was nice. Behrang liked the fact that he never pretended to be something he was not. While he spoke Pashto very well, he needed to be careful of his accent. On good days, Charlie's dialect was good enough to pass as a native, but there were certain phrases, particularly when Charlie was amused or angry, where his American roots would show.

Charlie's other problem was his blue eyes. They weren't unheard of in Afghanistan, but they raised questions. Behrang had pointed that out on their first meeting, and the next time they saw each other the American's eyes were brown and red and watery. Charlie explained to him that he wasn't crying, but rather that his . . . *contract windows* . . . hurt his eyes. Behrang could only imagine. If contract windows could change the color of your eyes, how could they not hurt?

Charlie knew things—the kinds of things that he couldn't possibly know. On the very first day they'd met—what was that, two years ago?—after Charlie had bought him a beautiful plum from the vendor's cart, he'd said to him, "I'm very sorry to hear about your parents and your sisters." Behrang had heard the foreign accent in his words.

Behrang's head swiveled to see who might have overheard. "Are you American?" he'd whispered.

"I'd like to speak with you," Charlie had said. He kept his voice low. "Away from these other people."

Behrang considered running away. The Americans

had ruined his country, after all. They had killed so many people. But they had saved many, too.

"I want to hurt the people who killed your family," the stranger said. "My name is Charlie and I am your friend. You can trust me."

Behrang remembered smiling at those words.

And Charlie had smiled back at him. "I guess everyone you cannot trust tells you that you can trust them," he said, speaking Behrang's thoughts exactly.

Charlie's massive beard separated to show a happy display of white teeth. "The day comes when you have to trust someone," he said. "Why not start with the man who wants to make people pay for killing your family?"

From that very first meeting—the first of dozens—Behrang had trusted the big man with the thick neck and blue eyes. Charlie told him to meet in the fig grove north of the village. He said that Behrang should show up at eleven o'clock the next morning and wait. "If I do not arrive by eleven-thirty, that means it's not safe, and you should go on about your day."

Behrang remembered feeling his cheeks go hot with embarrassment. "How will I know when it is eleven o'clock?" he'd asked.

Charlie's eyes softened at the question. "Do you know how to read a watch?" he asked.

"Of course." Behrang could read Shakespeare. Of course he could read a watch. There had been a time when he'd actually owned one. He'd had to trade it for a blanket last winter.

Glancing over his shoulder to make sure no one was watching, Charlie slid his own watch off his wrist and handed it to the boy. "Here," he said. "Take this one, courtesy of Uncle Sam."

Behrang also looked around for witnesses. "Your uncle will be upset that you gave away such a gift."

Something in those words made Charlie laugh. "Not this uncle," he said. "My Uncle Sam is a very generous man."

The way Charlie laughed made Behrang wonder if he was being mocked.

"It's fine," Charlie assured him. "I am not laughing at you. One day, you will realize why that is funny. Please take it."

"Then how will *you* know when it is eleven o'clock?"

"I will know. I have many watches."

Behrang nearly didn't go to that first meeting. All through the night before, he'd asked himself why he would want to expose himself to even the smallest risk in order to help one of the men who'd invaded his country. To be caught was to be killed in the most horrific way.

In the end, though, he remembered his father's impassioned speeches about principle. *Principle and convenience are nearly always enemies,* his father had told him. *As are principle and safety. One cannot be without principle and call oneself a man.*

Those words had so angered Behrang's mother. She'd called them arrogant. Could she possibly have known when she'd said, "Ideas like that will get us all killed one day," that she had foreseen the future? Father had insisted that Behrang's sisters, Afrooz and Taherah, go to the secret school in the basement of the old doctor's building so that they could learn and one day become doctors themselves. Such things were just not done. Not anymore, anyway.

Behrang had been only seven years old when Satan crashed through their door and tortured and killed his family, yet the sounds of the screams still echoed in his head every night. The image of the blood spray from their severed throats occupied the darkness when he closed his eyes.

If Charlie could avenge that—if there was even a tiny, remote chance that Charlie could kill the men who'd ravaged his family—then any risk was worth it.

Now, all these meetings later, as Behrang leaned against the Coca-Cola signpost among the sea of merchants and customers, he worried what might happen after this meeting with Charlie. Once they had their prize, what would become of his American friend? After Satan was dead, would they need Behrang anymore? Charlie had promised to make sure that Behrang would be sent to a safe place, but Americans were famous for making promises that they never kept. Father had been a lover of history, and he had told his family how the Americans had abandoned their friends in Korea and Vietnam and he had heard stories of the people they'd abandoned in Iraq and more recently in Kabul. They promised to be trustworthy, and then they just walked away.

Surely, Charlie was the exception. They'd shared too many laughs—too many meetings that had less to do with the information Behrang brought than with just sharing time together—for Charlie to turn his back.

Surely.

Dylan Nasbe adjusted the *shemagh* at his neck and straightened his *kameez* so that he would look *just so* as he waded into the crowded bazaar. His heart raced as it always did when he mingled so close to the enemy. Because of the pressing crowd, he did his business without comm gear because even the smallest earbud could be seen in a crowd that was pressed this tightly.

He was also unarmed, at least by any reasonable measure of such things in a war zone. Again because of the tightness of the crowd and the resultant ease of casual notice, his only weapon was a hand-sized Smith & Wesson Bodyguard pistol, which he wore strapped tightly to his chest, virtually inaccessible through the shirt of his *kameez*. To draw it would require lifting his shirt and exposing his belly to expose the gun. Not a stealthy action in this part of the world.

Conscious that his accent was not always spot-on, and unable to tell the difference when he slipped out of dialect, he tried to say nothing, and as a rule, that was easy. In a crowd, a smile was usually enough. With his blue eyes camouflaged—he still blushed when he remembered the day Behrang had pointed out to him that he had forgotten his contact lenses—he felt most self-conscious about his size. This was a part of the world where people barely subsisted, where heavily muscled chests and necks were the kinds of anomalies that brought suspicion. Suspicion, in turn, brought death—preferably to the suspector rather that the suspectee, thus the S&W .380. As a hedge, he wore clothes that were too big, hoping that the extra fabric would make him look fat.

Afghanistan was a beautiful country when it wasn't on fire or cluttered with corpses. While the roads sucked beyond all comprehension, the landscape could be beautiful. On days like this—market day—the village became a stunning display of colors and aromas as vendors displayed their wares and hawked customers. The air seemed fat with the perfumes of fresh cardamom, cilantro, mint, and coriander, which combined with fresh flowers and cooking lamb and chicken to form a kind of atmospheric flavor that Dylan considered unique to this part of the world.

He prided himself in not understanding Afghan culture in too much depth—certainly not beyond the measure that was necessary for him to do his job. More than a few of his Unit buddies obsessed over the cultures into which they inserted themselves, but Dylan considered it a liability to become too deeply involved with anything that it was ultimately his job to destroy.

As far as Dylan was concerned, this entire mission was a waste of blood and treasure. The instant politicians declared their intent to surrender and walk away, every soldier left in harm's way became a pawn, and every drop of blood spilled became a crime. But he was a soldier, and his was not to reason why. His was but to accomplish the mission and get the hell out of there.

Fifty meters ahead, he saw the Coca-Cola sign that was his destination. Yesterday, a surveillance drone had picked up the image of the broken bicycle in the ditch on the eastern side of the roadway leading into the village—the sign from Behrang that he had new information—and thus here he was, a week earlier than their routine meeting.

Just as it was a mistake to become too attached to the country it was your job to destroy, so was it a mistake to become attached to people who lived there. Success in war required a unique brand of mental disengagement. Success at Dylan's level of the game—the United States' most elite warriors—it was that and more. Sources of information were not friends, even though you made them think they were. They were assets to be exploited until they were dry, and then they were to be cast aside in favor of newer, fresher sources of even more valuable information. Dylan had done the drill a hundred times, maybe a thousand.

But he'd never before worked with an asset who was a kid—much less a kid with huge eyes and a bright smile and an infectious laugh. There was a toughness about Behrang that Dylan found inspirational. Life had dealt him the worst possible hand, yet the kid adapted. He survived. He'd learned to be angry without being bitter.

And in a few weeks, if a thousand things went right with nothing going wrong, Behrang would be safely in the United States. If another *million* things went right with nothing going wrong, he would be the newest member of the Nasbe family. After nearly twenty years in the army, Dylan had racked up a lot of favor chits, and he was cashing them all in on this one. He'd gotten the endorsements he'd needed from the army, and another from the CIA, and now it all hung on a signature from some bureaucrat he'd never met from the Department of Homeland Security. Apparently, they knew more than the CI-freaking-A about terrorist threats.

It was a one-step-at-a-time process, and the idea had been in circulation for five months now. His wife, Christyne, was on board, and she assured him that Ryan was okay with it, too, though she discouraged Dylan from speaking to Ryan about it. That relationship was . . . complicated.

If Behrang bore the news that Boomer anticipated, the first step in the plan would launch immediately—getting the boy to safety. Once he'd been able to find out the location of the Taliban command structure, Behrang would disappear with the Unit's help to Pakistan, and from there, through a dizzying series of transfers, to foster care in North Carolina.

But first, Behrang needed to deliver. The Agency's endorsement made that as clear as crystal. As the chief of station had told Boomer to his face, "This isn't a charity case, my friend. This is a business relationship. The boy needs to earn his way to asylum."

Boomer believed that this would be the day when Behrang did just that.

Moving through this crowd was more an exercise in capillary action—human peristalsis, maybe—than it was of walking. He kept willing himself closer to the Coca-Cola sign, and he got steadily nearer. His approach was complicated by the fact that he didn't want to appear too focused. People noticed when others were trying to move to a particular location, and by noticing, that drew attention toward the target. Just try staring at the ceiling sometime and see how long it takes for others to wonder what's so interesting up there.

Afghanistan was a vigilant country. Constantly on the lookout for threats, residents had developed an instinct for sniffing out anything that was out of the ordinary, and once sniffed, that became the focus of attention and fear. Thus, Dylan pretended to shop. He kept his hands to himself and his mouth shut.

He'd closed to within fifty feet of the Coca-Cola sign when he caught his first glimpse of Behrang through spaces in the crowd. The boy leaned against the sign munching on a plum that dripped juice down his chin and onto the front of the rag that he called a shirt. He, too, kept a disinterested air about him, the posture of an orphan hoping not to be noticed.

Dylan was still thirty feet away when the commotion started behind him. The crowd surged toward him, nearly knocking him off his feet as people clogging the street hurried toward the sidewalk. To Dylan's left, a merchant's booth toppled over in the push of the crowd.

Not especially tall by American standards, Dylan was nonetheless taller than the average Afghan. As he stretched to his full height to see what the fuss was all about, his heart nearly stopped.

Satan was here. The highest of high-value targets was right friggin' *here.*

Behrang noticed the change in the rhythm of the day before he saw what caused it. The loud, vibrating sound of the assembled shoppers and merchants dipped suddenly, and then silence washed over everything. People parted from the street to move off to the sides. Someone might have screamed, but maybe it was just a loud gasp.

Instinctively, he wanted to run, but he stopped himself. To run was to get shot—if not by the Taliban or one of their sympathizers, then by a hidden American soldier or orbiting drone. As far as he could tell—and Charlie had confirmed it, though not in so many words—anyone who ran was automatically considered to be guilty, and therefore could be vaporized by a missile fired from so far away that no one knew it was coming until the shrapnel and body parts flew.

So he stayed where he was. What was the right move here? Should he gawk like all of the others, or should he pretend to be disinterested as he had been doing?

The best strategy was to blend in, so he pushed away from the Coca-Cola post and craned his neck to see—

Satan.

Fear twisted Behrang's insides as evil incarnate emerged from the crowd and walked right toward him, as if he knew exactly who he was looking for, and exactly where he could be found.

Blending no longer mattered. Running mattered. Survival mattered. He spun around to sprint into the countryside, but the path was blocked by another of the Taliban leaders. This was one whose name Behrang did not know, but he'd seen him in Satan's shadow many times. The man grabbed Behrang by his shirt and lifted him off his feet. The boy kicked to get away, but the man's grasp was too tight.

"Behrang Hotaki!" Satan yelled, silencing the crowd. "You stupid, stupid boy. Bring him here to me."

The arms that grasped Behrang around his middle clamped around him like an iron ring. The boy kicked and wriggled in an attempt to get away, but the grasp didn't weaken.

A wide circle formed around Satan as villagers and vendors alike watched with wide eyes. The man whose face Behrang could no longer see carried him into the center of the circle and dropped him onto the gravel road at Satan's feet. Pointy rocks ravaged his hands and his knees on impact.

"You are your father's son," Satan said in a voice so loud that it was clearly meant to be heard by everyone. "But you do not learn from your mistakes." From somewhere under his clothing, Satan produced a long, curved blade. Its razor-sharp edge gleamed in the bright sunshine. Behrang recognized it as the blade that had cut the throats of his mother and his sisters.

"This boy has betrayed me!" Satan said. "He has tried to kill me, and he has tried to kill you as well. I have shown mercy to him all these years, and this is what I receive in return."

The man who had carried him here now grabbed a fistful of his hair and pulled him erect, even as he stood on the backs of his knees to keep him from standing.

"No!" Behrang said. "No, it's not like that. I don't know what you're talking about."

Satan's eyes brightened as he stroked his thick black beard. He smiled. "Is this truly how you want to spend this moment?" he asked. He'd lowered his voice now. It was only the two of them talking. "Do you really want your last words to be a lie?"

Behrang's mind raced for something, *anything* that might save him. Ahead and to the left, he saw a man push himself through the crowd to the edge of the circle. The familiar face looked frightened. Angry.

Hope bloomed in Behrang's chest. "Charlie!" he yelled. "Help me!"

Three years later

CHAPTER TWO

Jonathan Grave concentrated on his sight picture, forcing himself to ignore the heat of the afternoon sun that threatened to strip the skin off the back of his neck. In Virginia in July, the tropical sun was part of the deal. He lay on his belly on the mulchy forest floor, the forestock of his 7.62 millimeter Heckler & Koch 417 supported on a stack of three beanbags. He pressed the extended collapsible stock against his shoulder and split his attention between what his naked left eye could see and the ten-times magnified circle from the Nightforce Optics sight that dominated the vision in his right eye. Somewhere out there in the woods, roughly a hundred yards away, a target would present itself.

Soon.

Jonathan told himself to watch his breathing and to relax his hand on the rifle's pistol grip. When the target showed itself, it would take only a slight press from the pad of his right forefinger to send the round downrange. After that, it was all physics. He watched the movement of the grass for wind speed, and the—

His naked eye caught movement left to right, and he brought his scope to bear in time to see the black silhouette of a man streak from one tree to another. The target was back behind cover before he could commit to a shot, but at least now he knew where the son of a bitch was. If he moved again—

There! The target darted back to the left, taunting him, but Jonathan was ready for it. He led by a couple of feet and released a round. Then a second. The woods echoed with the rolling sound of the gunshot.

"Did I get him?" Jonathan asked.

"You were behind him by five inches on the first shot and probably twelve on the second." The critique came from his spotter, a giant of a man named Brian Van de Muelebrocke—aka Boxers—who had saved Jonathan's ass more times than anyone could count.

"Are you sure?"

"Would you like me to show you the scars in the trees?" Boxers monitored the action from Jonathan's right, his eye pressed to a Leica spotting scope. "Would you like a warning for the next one?"

Jonathan felt his ears go hot. "No, I don't need—"

The target darted out again from behind a tree, and Jonathan fired two more times. He knew even as the trigger broke that he'd yanked the shots wide.

"If I'm ever a bad guy," Boxers said, "will you promise to be the sharpshooter who takes me out?"

"Bite me."

"No, seriously. I'm tempted to go ride the target," Boxers went on. "I can't think of a safer place to be." As he spoke he pushed the joystick in his hand to the right, sending the target out of hiding again.

This time, Jonathan didn't bother to press the trigger. He knew better.

"Hey, Digger," Boxers said. "How 'bout I give you a baseball bat and you can beat it to death."

Jonathan released his grip on the weapon and squatted up to a standing position, leaving the 417 on the ground. "Okay, Mouth," he said, cranking his head to look up under Big Guy's chin. "Let's switch places. I'll take a turn at the stressful work of pushing buttons. Let's see you hit Zippy." The target—Zippy—was a converted tackling dummy that Jonathan had mounted on rails that could be laid just about anywhere. Powered by a remote-controlled electric motor, Zippy was a great training tool.

Boxers grinned. "Look at you bein' all threatening and shit. Do you want me to shoot with my eyes open or closed?"

Jonathan held his hand out for the controller, and Boxers gave it to him. Big Guy settled on his belly behind the rifle. The back of his T-shirt read, *Never run from a sniper. You'll only die tired.*

"Let me know when you're ready," Jonathan said.

"That's your call, not mine—"

Jonathan jammed the joystick to the left, and the target took off while Boxers was still speaking. The 417 barked twice. Half a second after each blast, Jonathan heard the faint *pang!* of a solid hit.

Boxers didn't bother to look up as he said, "Hey, Boss, did I hit it?" He rumbled out a laugh.

Jonathan pulled away from the tripod-mounted spotting scope. "I hate you," he said. Boxers was the most natural shooter Jonathan had ever known, and he'd been that way since the beginning. It was as if bullets responded to Big Guy's whims.

Boxers stood, brushed off the front of his T-shirt and jeans, and held out his hand for the controller. "I push the buttons because you need the practice."

As Jonathan handed over the box, his phone buzzed in his pocket. The caller ID said *unknown*.

He pressed the connect button and brought the phone to his ear. "Yeah."

"Yes sir, Mr. Horgan," a man's voice said. "This is Cale Cook at the western guard shack. There's a visitor here to see you. He identifies himself as a Colonel Rollins, and he says it's important that he speak to you now."

Jonathan didn't know the security team out here at the compound very well, so Cale Cook could have called himself by any name, but he knew all too well who Colonel Rollins was. "Take a picture of him and send it to my phone. I'll call you back when I get it."

Boxers' face showed that he'd been eavesdropping. "What's up?"

"Roleplay Rollins is here."

Boxers recoiled at the words as anger settled in his eyes. There was a time not too long ago when Big Guy would have hurried to beat the man to death, and Jonathan would have let him. The three of them had a history that involved Jonathan and Boxers' last days with the Unit, and it had not ended well.

Jonathan extended his palm to settle his friend down. "Take it easy. Past is past. He saved our asses and we owe him a solid." His phone buzzed, and displayed a picture of the man the visitor claimed to be. Jonathan called the guard shack. "Send him up to the lodge and have him wait on the porch. We're on our way."

"Should we escort him?"

"Is he alone?"

"Alone and unarmed. I searched his vehicle."

"No," Jonathan said. "Let him go solo. It's hard to get lost when there's only one road." He clicked off and looked to Boxers. "This should be interesting," he said.

"Let's pick up the weapons and ammo. We'll break the target down later."

Boxers pointed through the Hummer's windshield toward the front porch of the stylishly rustic structure that had started life a hundred fifty years ago as a log cabin, but whose original owners would recognize nothing but a portion of the western wall. "There he is."

Colonel Stanley Rollins, US Army, stood from one of the porch's cane rockers as they approached. He wore jeans and a white polo shirt, and an expression that was impossible to read.

"Looks like Roleplay is a civilian today," Boxers said.

"He hates that name."

Big Guy chuckled. "I know. That's why I like it."

"Don't start anything," Jonathan said. "Not until we hear what he has to say."

"I'll call him Stanley, then."

"He hates that even worse."

Boxers looked across the console. "Yeah."

Jonathan opened the door and slid to the ground. "Hello, Colonel," he called as he approached the lodge. "This is a genuine surprise." He extended his hand as he closed the distance, and Rollins walked down the four steps to greet him.

"Hello, Digger," he said. His handshake wasn't the bone crusher that it used to be. "Nice to see you again."

"Stanley!" Boxers shouted, feigning delight. "Hasn't someone fragged your ass by now?"

Rollins didn't rise to the bait. "Big Guy," he said. "Pleasant as always." He pointed to the Hummer. "And still the environmental conscience that you've always been."

Dubbed the Batmobile by Boxers, the lavishly customized and heavily armored Hummer was one of Jonathan's favorite toys.

"Let's talk inside," Jonathan said. He led the way up the steps. He turned the key and pulled the heavy wooden door out toward them. He stepped aside to allow the colonel to pass.

As he did, Rollins rapped on the door with a knuckle. "Impressive. What is that, oak?"

"Something like that," Jonathan said. "I believe in living securely."

Inside, the foyer led directly to a living room, fifteen by fifteen feet, beyond which a dining area led to a closed door that hid the kitchen from view. A stone fireplace dominated the eastern wall—the wall to the right walking in. Stairs in the far northwest corner led up to the sleeping levels. In decorating the place, Jonathan had leaned heavily on his experience at Colorado ski lodges. Woodsy artwork hung from exposed pine walls across the way on the north wall, while a rack of eight long guns took up much of the front, southern, wall.

"Wow," Rollins said. "I guess I keep underestimating just how friggin' rich you really are. What is this place?"

"Pretty much what it looks like," Jonathan said as he nudged a switch on the wall to wake up two dangling chandeliers made of antlers. "This is a place to escape to, to unwind. Two hundred twenty-five acres of seclusion."

"And a guard patrol?"

"When did you become a reporter?" Boxers asked as he pulled the door closed.

"Who would see this and not be curious?" Rollins said.

"Which is a good reason to have a guard patrol," Jonathan said. He motioned to the leather sofas and chairs near the fireplace. "Have a seat, Colonel. Suffice to say that things happen out here that are best not witnessed by curiosity seekers. Think of it as my company's testing grounds." He let the words settle in. "Can I get you something to drink?"

Rollins waved the question away. "No, I'm fine, thanks."

Big Guy was already halfway to the wet bar in the back corner of the dining area. "I'm not," he said. "You want your usual, Boss?"

"Please." On his own, this would be the time of day for a martini, but since Boxers was tending the bar, that meant a couple fingers of Lagavulin scotch. Boxers didn't have the patience for the delicate chemistry that was a good martini.

Jonathan settled himself into a chair, crossed his legs, and locked in on Rollins's eyes. "You know, Colonel, I don't think either one of wants the charade of small talk. What say you get right to what you have on your mind?"

Rollins leaned forward in his chair and rested his elbows on his knees. "I presume you remember Dylan Nasbe."

"Boomer? Of course I do." Dylan had joined the Unit shortly before Jonathan was on his way out, but it was a small, tight community. Plus, Jonathan had had some recent dealings with Dylan's wife and son. "Is he okay?" The scotch floated over Jonathan's right shoulder, clamped in Boxers' fingers.

"No," Rollins said. "He's gone rogue."

"What does that mean?" Boxers asked as he took the sofa for himself.

"It means he's killing off Agency assets."

"Bullshit," Boxers said. "He was a good kid. No way would he do that."

"And yet he is."

"Why?" Jonathan asked.

Rollins shrugged. "Why does anyone do anything like that? Something went crosswise in his head, and he started wasting people."

Jonathan and Boxers exchanged looks. "I'm not buying it," Jonathan said. "I mean, I can imagine him whacking Agency guys—who among us hasn't considered that a time or two?—but I don't buy that he's crazy. He's got a reason."

"Lee Harvey Oswald had reasons, Dig," Rollins said. "So did John Wilkes Booth and Charles Manson. But so what? Murder is murder."

"The army is up to its nipples in shrinks these days," Boxers said. "*Somebody* has to have wondered the obvious."

"You already know some of it," Rollins said. "Those assholes who came at his family undoubtedly screwed him up at least a little."

"No," Jonathan said. "Well, of course it was traumatic, but I spoke with Boomer not long after that. He was okay."

"His deployments, then," Rollins said. With an acknowledging hand to Big Guy, he added, "Nipples-deep in shrinks as we are, there are no doubt hundreds of possible diagnoses, but none of them can be tested because we haven't been able to talk to Boomer because we don't know where he is."

"Why does it have to be Boomer?" Jonathan pressed. "You've got a couple of dead Agency guys—"

"Three," Rollins interrupted. "*Three* dead Agency guys, and they were all in the same AO as Boomer during his last deployment."

Jonathan recognized the acronym for area of operation. "So? After we punted on Iraq, Afghanistan was the only AO we had left. There have to be thousands of cross-links between the Agency dead and soldiers in country."

"And what makes you think they weren't killed by the Taliban?" Boxers asked.

"You're both getting defensive," Rollins said.

"Of course we're defensive!" Boxers yelled. Jonathan could tell he was spinning up to a bad place. "And why aren't you? Haven't you turned you back on enough of your brothers over the years?"

Jonathan extended a hand to calm his friend down. "Not now, Box."

"Screw you," he snapped, and his face instantly showed horror. "Not you. Him. Not only do you lay this on your own army, you have to lay it on our Unit brother."

"If you'll calm down, I'll explain it all to you!" Rollins shouted. He could get spun up, too.

Jonathan knew it was time to play peacekeeper. "Quit shouting, both of you. Colonel, I encourage you to make your case quickly, and with minimal bullshit, and as you do, keep in mind that you're talking about a friend who's given a hell of a lot for his country."

Some of the red left Rollins's face. None of it left Boxers'.

"Some bad things happened on Boomer's last tour," Rollins said. "I can't go into details, but he'd been working a source for quite some time, and then the source was killed. We think he blamed his CIA counterparts."

"Why would he do that?" Jonathan asked.

"Because we blame the Agency for everything," Rollins replied. "Some things never change."

"There's a giant step between blaming and killing," Boxers said. "What proof do you have?"

Rollins looked to the ceiling and scowled, as if to divine his next words. "There's proof, and then there's *proof.* We don't have any of the latter. What we do know is he came home, walked away from his marriage, and disappeared." His eyes bored into Jonathan. "And I mean *disappeared.* Off the grid."

"You know, we're trained to do that, right?" Jonathan said. "In fact, we're *paid* to do that when we're in hostile territory."

"But domestically? Who would do that?"

Jonathan waited for him to get the absurdity of his own question.

Rollins acknowledged with a nod. "Okay, other than you, who would do that?" He didn't wait for an answer. "Within a few days of his disappearance, the first of the Agency guys was killed, shot with a five-five-six round from a long ways away. Over two hundred yards, as I recall. He was on his way to his car in the driveway, and it was a perfect head shot."

Jonathan felt tension in his chest. That wasn't the kind of a shot most amateurs could make.

"Three days later, the second agent was taken out as he exited a coffee shop outside of Fredericksburg, Virginia, not far from your stomping grounds. Five-five-six again, center of mass, hollow-point round. Perfect shot and no one heard it."

Boxers' ire had transformed to concern. "Was this a coffee shop he went to regularly?"

Rollins nodded. "Every day. How did you know?"

"Was the first guy—the head shot—a hollow point?"

"No." Rollins smiled. He saw that Boxers got it.

"He was worried about collateral damage," Big Guy said. He looked to Jonathan. "He'd studied the guy's routine and used HPs as a safety."

"What about the third?" Jonathan asked.

"Another head shot," Rollins said, "again from long distance. The interesting thing there was that the shooter showed great patience. The agent had been standing for ten minutes with his kid at the end of the driveway, waiting for the school bus." He looked to Boxers. "Like before, this was a daily routine. He waited till the little girl was on the bus, and the bus was on its way before he shot. No one heard or saw anything. By the time his wife woke up and noticed he was missing—and then found the body—he was already stiff."

Jonathan took a pull on his scotch as he pushed the pieces into place. "That still doesn't mean Boomer did it," he said. Even he heard the weakness of his words.

"Doesn't matter," Rollins said. "The Agency thinks he did, and they'll move heaven and earth to find him and take him out."

"What about due process?" Boxers asked.

"Where have you been the past few years?" Rollins countered. "The alphabet agencies stopped caring about due process when the regime changed. That was about the same time when beat cops started riding around in tanks. This isn't your childhood America anymore."

"So, we've got a lot of conjecture and assumptions," Jonathan summarized. "Cut to the chase, Colonel. Why are you here?"

Rollins cast a nervous glance to Boxers as he said, "We want you to find Boomer and bring him home."

"Well, that's not gonna happen," Boxers said. "I don't hunt down my friends."

Jonathan said, "By 'bring him home,' do you mean alive or dead?"

"Preferably alive."

"But dead would be okay, too." Boxers growled.

Rollins worked his jaw muscles. "No, dead would not be *okay,* Box. But don't forget that every Agency wet work contractor is out looking for this guy. If they get him, he's toast."

"Then why not just leave it to them?" Jonathan asked.

Rollins recoiled. "You said it yourself, Dig. He's family. Boomer deserves better than a bullet. I don't care what he did, he deserves better than that. If you can get to him first, maybe you can talk him down. If he hears that you're the one hunting for him, maybe he'll take the time to at least tell his side of the story. This is serious stuff."

Jonathan leaned back into his seat and crossed his legs. The math here wasn't working for him. "You said bad things happened to him over there on his last tour. I won't even ask you for those details—at least not yet—but if the bad stuff is traceable to specific interactions with specific Agency assets, then I presume the remaining assets have become much harder targets."

"All the targets have been eliminated." Rollins said.

Jonathan exchanged a confused look with Boxers. "Then what's done is done," he said. "Good reasons, bad reasons, that's for others to decide. I'm not a cop. I'm not going to traipse all over hell's half acre to bring a colleague into custody."

"It's more than that," Rollins said. "The killings are real—they really happened—but that's not the punch line."

"Good Christ, Stanley," Boxers said with a derisive

laugh. “Can’t you just for once in your life deal from the top of the deck? Why does everything—”

“He’s a traitor, guys,” Rollins said. “He’s selling secrets to the world.”

Jonathan’s heart skipped. “What kind of secrets?”

“The most damaging kind you can think of,” Rollins said.